City in the Sky

CITY
IN THE
SKY

Luke Yesbeck

BELLE ISLE BOOKS
www.belleislebooks.com

ISBN: 978-1-951565-11-4
LCCN: 2021916586

Printed in the United States of America

Published by
Belle Isle Books (an imprint of Brandylane Publishers, Inc.)
5 S. 1st Street
Richmond, Virginia 23219

BELLE ISLE BOOKS
www.belleislebooks.com

belleislebooks.com | brandylanepublishers.com

To my family and friends:
Thank you for all your love and support—
and for occasionally reminding me
to get some sleep

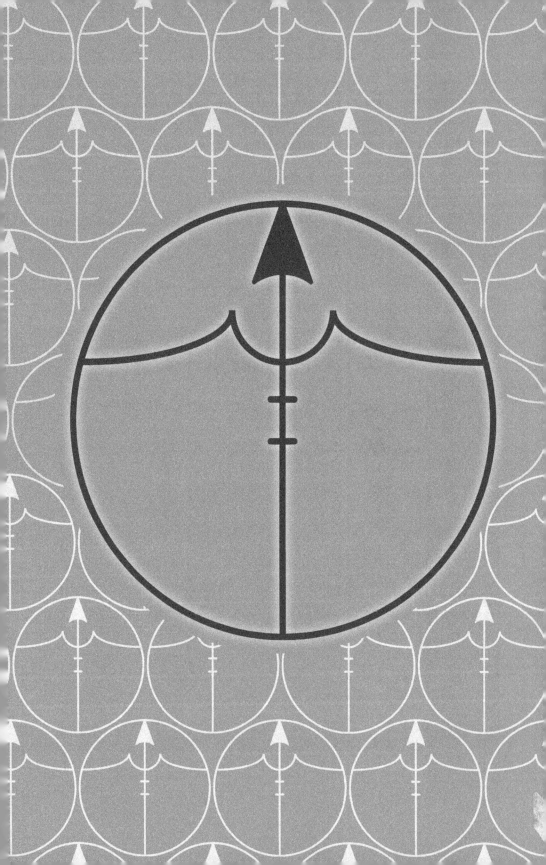

CHAPTER ONE
THE SINKING CITY

The violent, churning sea heaved all around him. Keeping his head above the surface was a constant challenge, yet still the young man fought desperately for air, even as the water dragged at his heavy robes. He could not breathe without swallowing huge gulps of saltwater, thickened by hot ash.

At last, the tip of his sandal brushed against a rock. Between high-crested waves, a small island of limestone boulders stood out against the burning orange sky. The man frantically kicked his way toward it—the first relief he had seen since disaster struck. He clambered onto the slick rocks and coughed up gouts of seawater, his throat burning from the combination of salt and bile.

As his breathing evened out, the man lifted a hand to wipe his mouth, only to find his palm smeared with soot. His soaked robes, once white, were in similar shape, stained black where they had dragged across the rocks. Despair choked him. He dreaded turning around, dreaded seeing the damage behind him, but he knew that he needed to look. Delaying it would change nothing.

He turned slowly, and felt his heart drop into his stomach.

The sea was on fire. Massive columns of flame danced against the darkening sky and roiling water. He was alone on an island barely larger than a chariot, adrift in the chaos. He searched the distant shoreline, trying to find some remnant of his home; but it was completely engulfed in flames that not even the Mediterranean Sea could douse.

A sharp cry for help broke the man out of his trance. He searched the raging waters and saw a panicked hand break the surface some thirty paces out. Putting his own safety aside, the man shed his waterlogged robes and dove back into the sea. Having regained his composure, and his bearings, he was able to cut through the churning waves with purpose. In no time, he reached the struggling survivor and scooped him into a rough rescue stroke. After what felt like ages kicking against the violent water, the two of them finally made it back to the small island.

"Marc? Is that you?" the first man asked, once his partner stopped coughing up seawater.

"Yes," Marc said, his voice hoarse. He took several deep breaths before he spoke again. "Tellaren . . . wha—what happened? Did anyone else make it? Is there anything left?"

Peter Tellaren shook his head.

"I only had a chance to look around for a second before I saw you in the water," Peter said. "But it . . . it doesn't look good."

"The Elder?" Marc asked.

"Katerina? Haven't seen her," Peter said.

"Who could have done this?"

Peter turned to look at his friend.

"You know who did this," he said darkly.

"The Order," Marc said, nodding slightly. He turned to survey the damage.

Neither of them spoke for a few minutes. Only the breaking waves and the distant crackling of the fires broke the silence. Between the acrid smell and the raining ash, it was hard for the two of them to breathe.

"The fire's going down," Marc said flatly, after a while.

"There's not much left to burn," Peter said.

He was right. Their city was disappearing into the sea. Soon there would be nothing left. Soon, their wonderful home would be nothing more than a memory, a legend.

"Everything we worked for is gone," Marc said slowly. "All my research . . . gone." He dropped heavily to his knees. "Peter, I left my family to come here. It was all for nothing. . . ."

"Hey! Hey there. None of that," Peter said, crouching down near his friend. "We're going to be fine. You're going to be alrigh—"

"We have no home!" Marc interjected with a note of hysteria in his voice.

"Remember why we chose this life," Peter said. His friend was breaking down, and they both needed to focus if they were going to survive. "We have a mission."

Marc looked up at Peter. It was becoming more difficult to make out the details on his face. The fire was dying rapidly. Soon there would be no light left—only the ash-choked sky.

"You're right," Marc said after a few seconds. He took a steadying breath and let it out. "We need to keep going. We need to look for other survivors. We can't be the only ones."

Peter nodded.

"Some of the city guards ran to the armory when the attack started," Peter said, thinking out loud. "Maybe they'll try to reconvene at the fort just west of here?"

"Good idea," Marc said. "We can head there. Maybe the Elder . . . Is that a boat?"

Peter turned on his heel to look behind him. A small bulb of light bobbed across the water—unmistakably a lantern on a ship being rocked back and forth by the sea.

"Marc . . ." Peter said as the boat turned broadside to them, and was suddenly illuminated by the dull glow of the distant fire. "It has a black sail."

"What?! Are you sure?"

"Yes! Yes, it's a black sail!" Peter said, crouching low against the rocks. "It's the Order!"

"To the crows!" Marc swore as he ducked down next to Peter.

Peter could feel his heart beating against the inside of his chest. He quickly ran his hand over the sooty rocks and wiped black ash over his skin and clothes. Mark copied him, until he too blended in against the dark rocks.

The two of them stayed low, covered in the remains of their home, for the better part of an hour while they waited for their enemy to pass, praying the entire time to whatever gods would listen that they would not be spotted. Neither of them moved. Peter's knees felt like they were on fire by the time the ship finally sailed out of sight.

"We should be safe," Peter said. His knees popped audibly as he stood.

"Do you think they were searching for us?"

"Or any other survivors," Peter guessed. "We need to be careful."

"How are we supposed to avoid all of Rome?" Marc asked, his tone hopeless.

"We can do it," Peter said bracingly, though in truth he was not sure if he was trying to convince Marc or himself. "We have to. We cannot let the Order win."

At his words, the last bit of light from the fire was extinguished. Peter turned just in time to see the iconic steeple, the highest point of their city, sink below the surface of the Mediterranean Sea.

The city was lost, completely underwater. Peter clenched one trembling hand into a fist.

"The Order can't win."

CHAPTER TWO
ANGEL FROM ABOVE

"**D**id you know that approximately eighty-seven percent of scientists agree that the sun is actually a planet full of dragons constantly fighting each other for the ultimate Throne of Fire?"

"Mhm."

"Yeah. The current dragon king is over four hundred years old. Unlike the other dragons, the king dragon breathes lightning, not fire. In fact, his lightning breath is largely responsible for what we call the 'solar flares' that disrupt the Earth's electromagne—"

"Wait, *what?*" Ryan Kendrick asked, as he finally peeled his blue eyes away from his microscope to stare uncomprehendingly at his lab partner.

Tasha Albinott burst out laughing at his flabbergasted expression, and Ryan could only chuckle at his own gullibility as he waited for her to regain her composure. He vaguely remembered that she had been asking him something a little while ago, but for the past quarter of an hour, all his attention had been dedicated to the sample on his microscope slide. "Sorry," he apologized sincerely once Tasha stopped giggling. "I got distracted. What were you trying to ask me?"

"It's okay," Tasha chuckled, her bright smile contrasting brilliantly with her dark skin. "I didn't know how much longer I could keep going anyway. I was asking if you could help me find the results file from your gene therapy trials. The ones from March? I've been going through all our folders, and I can't find it."

"Oh, yeah, sure!"

Ryan unfolded his lean frame from his aluminum laboratory stool and made his way to the computer where Tasha was working. Tasha leaned out of the way and handed Ryan the mouse as he bent forward to better see her screen. After a couple of seconds, Ryan navigated through a complex maze of folders and pulled up the correct file.

"Thanks!" Tasha said, grinning as she glanced over the final numbers. "Dr. Noret wants me to run significance tests on both of our projects, even though I told him that I have no idea what you're working on. Want to explain your results to me so that I can actually interpret these tests?"

"Yeah! They're actually fascinating," Ryan said as he sat down and cleared off a space to record his own findings in a notebook. "We altered a bunch of cells from mice to give them cancer, and then inserted a new gene to see what would happen. Most of the time, nothing special happened, and the cancer progressed as expected. But one of the mice actually got better, and its cancer disappeared! That gene could actually be the cure for cancer!"

Tasha chuckled as she watched Ryan become more and more animated.

"That's amazing," she said. "You really love this stuff, don't you?"

"Well," said Ryan, "I mean, you're right. It *is* amazing! I think we're really onto something here. Something huge. And it could potentially help thousands—millions—of people."

"Imagine casually bringing it up to your family on Mother's Day," Tasha said. "You're having a nice dinner, and you just casually drop into the conversation that you may have found the cure for cancer. You'd be the favorite child for sure!"

"Already am," Ryan said with a smile. "I'm an only child. Anyway, we haven't found anything conclusive yet. It's just a lead."

"Okay, sure; but it's still really impressive! And you're lucky. I love my sister to death, but I swear, we fought nonstop when we were kids."

"Older or younger?" Ryan said, returning to his microscope.

"She's a year younger."

Ryan nodded and bent over his slide again.

"Hey, I've never asked—how did you end up here?" Tasha said, after suffering through a whole twenty seconds of silence. "I mean, I enjoy this job, but I doubt someone like you grew up hoping to become a lab assistant."

Ryan couldn't help but smile again. He had started at the lab after graduating from college two years ago, and even though the job was pretty mundane—especially when he was just entering data into spreadsheets—Tasha almost made it bearable. Before she had started working at the lab three months ago, Ryan's options for entertainment at work had been limited to listening to music, searching for new podcasts, or—when he was craving human interaction—chatting with the building's cleaning crew. Having a fun lab partner was a definite improvement. Despite being assigned to work on completely different projects, Tasha had actually made an effort to get to know Ryan as a friend.

"You're right—this wasn't exactly part of the plan, but I like it here. It's a good job."

"What was the plan?" Tasha asked.

Ryan sat back on his stool and turned back to face her. Tasha fiddled absentmindedly with one of her light brown curls as she waited politely for him to respond.

"Well, the plan was to go to graduate school to get a PhD in genetics," Ryan said. "But at this point, that seems unlikely."

"How come?"

Ryan paused for a moment. It was never fun explaining what had happened.

"It's actually my own fault," he began. "I missed a test that counted for thirty-two percent of my final grade. It was during my final semester at Tufts, and my professor wouldn't let me make it up. I had already missed a test that semester, and his syllabus said, 'Students may make up one test per semester—NO EXCEPTIONS!'"

"And you missed a second test?"

Ryan nodded.

"For my cousin's funeral—Jack. He was only two years older than me. He was kind of like an older brother. We were always playing together when we were little." Ryan paused. "He was killed by a drunk driver while on a work trip in Canada. My aunt and uncle said they really needed me in San Diego, where we both grew up, so I emailed all my professors with an explanation and flew back home. I didn't know it then, but that professor was in a conference in Florida for the weekend and didn't get my email until it was too late. All my other professors were really understanding, but he wouldn't budge."

"Seriously?" Tasha said. "He wouldn't even let you make up the test for a funeral?"

"Nope," Ryan said quietly. Even two years later, talking about the funeral still made him feel empty. "'No exceptions,' like he said."

"I hope you told the jerk to go to hell."

"Nah. The syllabus was crystal clear," Ryan said with a shrug. The incident was in the past, and he had accepted the outcome a while ago.

"So why did you miss the first test?" Tasha asked, clearly hoping to steer the conversation toward something a little brighter.

"I was in the hospital. Severe dehydration from a case of food poisoning that gave me a week of nonstop diarr—I mean . . . uh . . . bowel issues," Ryan explained, his tone picking back up. "Anyway, missing the second test dropped my average to a D, and my lab grade to a D+. Between the hit to my GPA, student loans, and the cost of a last-minute flight across the country, applying to a bunch of graduate programs seemed like a bad idea." He looked up at Tasha, who seemed to be struggling to find a more sympathetic sentiment than "I'm sorry."

"On the bright side," he continued cheerfully, "I get to work in a genetics lab, do some research, and hang out with an awesome friend like you! You're kinda like the sister I never had."

Tasha didn't respond for a moment, a half-smile playing around her mouth as she made a small clicking noise with her tongue. But before she could say anything, their conversation was interrupted by Ryan's phone ringing.

Ryan looked at the caller ID and let out a small groan. Tasha laughed at his expression. She didn't have to look to know who was on the other end.

"Do I have to answer it?" Ryan asked.

"Come on," Tasha said encouragingly. "Maybe it's good news?"

Ryan shook his head and answered his phone.

"Yes, sir?"

"I need to speak with you ASAP," a gruff, self-important voice said. "Come to my office. We have things to discuss."

The caller hung up without waiting for a response. Ryan set down the receiver and looked up at Tasha, who was waiting curiously.

"I've been summoned. We have 'things to discuss. . . .'"

Tasha grimaced sympathetically. "Good luck?"

After taking as long as possible to shrug off his white lab coat,

Ryan grudgingly said good-bye and started toward his boss's office. As he walked down the depressing, windowless hallway, he wondered what Noret could possibly want from him now.

While Ryan honestly didn't mind working on gene research with Massachusetts Biomedical Research Corporation, he did have some issues with working under Dr. Thomas Noret. Historically, whenever Dr. Noret called someone to his office, it was to share disappointing news—most recently, that the company's promised holiday bonuses were being "reallocated" to upper management only. Or—memorably, after he had invited Ryan to accompany him to a weekend conference in Miami—news that the plans had changed, and the doctor's wife would be attending in Ryan's place.

There was also the minor issue of Dr. Noret's inability to remember Ryan's surname. He seemed to think it was "Kennic."

Ryan knocked twice on Dr. Noret's office door, and promptly entered when he heard a brusque voice say, "Come in!" He stepped into the lush office and waited for the middle-aged man to acknowledge him.

Noret was in the middle of a phone call. He impatiently waved to the brown leather chair across from his massive desk. Ryan sat down and waited a full three minutes for Noret to conclude his conversation—which Ryan sincerely hoped was with his wife, based on the doctor's flirtatious tone.

"Kennic," Dr. Noret began once he'd finally hung up, without looking at Ryan. "We have a problem."

We? Ryan thought to himself.

"The board of directors is asking for a full grant proposal to continue our research on the KC gene. You *do* know what that is, right? The Kill Cancer gene? Come on, Kennic. I need you to keep up with me here. At least nod or something. There you go—good. Anyway, the original email got caught in my spam filter, so it needs to be completed quickly, or you'll miss the due date. I need a rough draft in . . . let's say two days—that should give you enough time to review the final version before you submit it. The proposal needs to include an up-to-date project history, full literary analysis, proposed variables, expected results, project relevance . . . the usual. Oh, also, I forgot to tell you about a conference presentation I need to submit by the end of the week."

The end of the week?! Ryan thought. *It's already 3:45 p.m. on Tuesday!*

"A slideshow presentation should be good enough," Dr. Noret continued.

"Yes, sir," Ryan responded dutifully.

"Also, I need a copy of the conference proposal, the one we discussed last week, on my desk by Monday instead of next Friday. I'm surprising my wife and sons with a trip to England. My kids have been dying to see a British Premier League game. Anyway, I would like to review the proposal before our trip. That way you'll have plenty of time to make any changes I dictate before I get back."

"I'll do my best, Dr. Noret."

"Good. Also, I hate to tell you this, but we don't have the funds for overtime compensation in the budget. Management says finances are particularly tight this quarter. Just keep a record of your hours—I'll put in for reimbursement if we have the funds next quarter."

Ryan nodded. "Anything specific I need to include in any of the reports?" he asked, struggling to maintain his composure as his brain cycled over the same thought:

Typical.

◊◊◊

After his meeting with Dr. Noret, Ryan started working

feverishly in the laboratory, typing madly away and trying to finish as much work as humanly possible before he left for the day. Tasha had gone home hours ago, at Ryan's insistence. There was no reason for her to stay and suffer too. She'd kindly offered—multiple times—to bring him some takeout, but Ryan had politely declined, explaining that there was simply too much to be done for him to be able to eat now. After wishing Ryan the best of luck, she'd told him to call her at any time if he needed help—or just some friendly company—and left, seeming slightly crestfallen.

It wasn't until 9:32 p.m., when Ryan's clawing hunger finally got the best of him, that he decided it was time to leave. He'd only had time for a small protein bar at lunch, and was beginning to feel nauseated; but he was pretty sure he could still get a couple more hours of work done at home if he ate quickly.

Ryan stretched his aching back and straightened his workstation as much as he could before locking up the laboratory. As he left the building, he zipped up his light jacket, as if it was his own personal armor against the cool late-April air that followed an afternoon rain.

Ryan took his time navigating the familiar labyrinth of downtown Boston to the nearest T station, occasionally taking a few extra seconds to kick a loose rock and listen to the satisfying clatter as it skipped against the damp sidewalk. Despite taking his time, he still arrived at the station a couple minutes early to catch his train to Ashmont. Settling down on a relatively clean (save for a large glob of something he desperately hoped was mayonnaise) bench in the subway terminal, he pulled out his headphones and scrolled through his extensive library of songs, hoping to kill some time.

After scrolling past the second Spanish rap song he couldn't remember downloading, Ryan started to feel exasperated. He finally settled on an old classic rock hit that his father often played on repeat, and closed his eyes to block out the harsh light on the subway station tiles. He did his best to focus on the beat, allowing it to drown out thoughts of all the work he still had to do, and refused to open his eyes again until he felt the vibration of the arriving train under his feet.

Ryan hopped up as the train screeched to a halt in front of him, and jumped on board just before the dented doors closed. The train took off again before he could find a seat, nearly throwing him to the floor, but he managed to climb into an empty seat despite the jerking motion. Settling in, Ryan allowed his head to rest against the back of his chair and once again tried to focus on his music.

Once the train finally arrived at Ashmont, Ryan climbed out and put his headphones away before stepping out of the station. Even though he had called south Boston home for two years now, Ryan was always careful on the street at night. Violent crime was so common in his neighborhood that it rarely made the news. At least once a week, on his way home, he would hear a sharp bang that made adrenaline shoot through his body. Ryan always told himself the noise was from fireworks, even if he never saw anything light up the night sky. Last week, when he'd been taking out the trash, a loud crash in the alley behind his house had actually made him jump before he saw a stray cat dart past the still-rolling trash can. Maybe he was a little paranoid, but he knew one day it might just save his life.

Ryan turned left out of the station, careful to avoid the eyes of two scrawny men his own age who scuttled past wearing army jackets, clearly looking for a safe place to get high. As he walked farther away from the T, the surrounding buildings became more decrepit. He seemed to pass fewer people by the minute. The old streetlights, which offered some illusion of safety, were replaced by small, stunted trees that protruded haphazardly from the sidewalk. Soon, only the dim light from the quarter moon and the infrequent front porch light guided Ryan on his path. It was then that he first noticed the footsteps behind him, slapping against the wet concrete.

Ryan waited until he was just a few blocks away from his apartment to look over his shoulder at the person behind him. To his surprise, he found two men keeping pace with him only a few yards back.

It was odd. People in this neighborhood typically kept their distance from strangers—but these two men seemed to be getting closer. Walking side by side. Without talking.

It's nothing. They just walk fast.

Telling himself he was worried about nothing, Ryan crossed the street to give the two men space. But why were the footsteps getting louder?

Ryan turned to peer over his shoulder once more.

They were behind him. Again. They had followed him across his street. And it was not his imagination: they were definitely getting closer.

An icy certainty washed over Ryan, and he picked up the pace. He could hear the footsteps getting louder and louder behind him.

Ryan knew he had to come up with a plan quickly. He started looking around more desperately, and his heart soared when he looked ahead and saw two more people strolling toward them.

Okay, you can do this. When those guys are about ten feet ahead of you, start talking to them like they are old friends. Maybe "Hey! How have you been? It's been so lo—"

But before he could finish formulating his plan, Ryan realized with a sinking feeling that the two men in front were looking right at him from under their drawn hoods. Their eyes were locked on him, completely focused. They weren't talking to each other either. Could they be with the two men behind him? Were all four of them working together?

Trying to fight down the rising panic in his chest, Ryan moved to cross the street one more time and hoped that it was all just one big coincidence. He stepped off the curb.

All four men mirrored him.

Ryan broke into a jog as he crossed the street, and heard the footsteps behind him quicken to match his pace. The panic in chest transformed into a deadening weight in his stomach. Abandoning all pretense, Ryan turned his head to look at the pair behind him, and the taller of the two grinned menacingly as he saw the worried look on Ryan's face.

Ryan took off in a dead sprint toward his apartment building, less than four blocks away. He blew by the two men in front of him and looked over his shoulder as he ran. He was putting distance between himself and the four men. All he had to do was lose them in the alleys and duck into his building, and he would be safe.

Ignoring the growing stitch in his side, Ryan turned down the first alley he passed—and immediately had the wind knocked out of him.

Dazed, Ryan dropped to his knees on the sidewalk, trying desperately to circulate air back into his empty lungs. He looked up to see yet another man, this one in a Red Sox cap, standing over him and grinning. He'd clearly been waiting around the corner.

Ryan snapped his head around as the other four men turned down the alley. His way out was blocked, and he could barely breathe. Their trap had worked.

Ryan stayed silent. Saying that he didn't want any trouble seemed ridiculous. Besides, he doubted he could do anything more than wheeze at the moment.

"Stand up!" barked one of the guys from behind him.

Ryan shakily stood as the five men surrounded him. Clearly, they were enjoying the moment.

"Listen carefully: wallet. Phone. Keys. Address. Now," ordered the same man.

"Ad—address?" Ryan gasped, against his better judgment.

The speaker, who was clearly the leader, produced a revolver from his jacket, as did the man in the baseball cap who'd clothes-lined Ryan. The other three immediately conjured knives.

"Yes—address," said the leader, looking as though he was en-joying himself tremendously. An emerald-green snake tattoo was inked across his jawline. The tail twitched as he broke into a sadis-tic smile.

Ryan looked around desperately. There had to be a way out. He looked at each knife and gun in turn. Despite his best efforts to stay calm, he felt his hands shaking. There was nothing he could use to defend himself. Even the dumpster across the alley was empty. He tried to think fast, but his mind was blank.

Apparently, he took too long to respond.

"Look. I have a gun. I aim good," the leader said impatiently. Ryan had to make a conscious effort not to stare at the serpent tattoo. "You can't get away. We'll kill you dead before you take three steps. Then my boys will have fun with their knives. I'll tell you the truth: you're dead no matter what. Do as I say, and I'll make it quick. Keep stalling, and I promise you I'll make it painful. Now stop screwing around and give me your da—"

"Excuse me," a new voice chimed in from behind the leader.

All six men turned to see a new man standing at the entrance to the alley. The stranger appeared to be in his late twenties, and even through the shadows, it was easy to see his bright blond hair. He was looking at the thugs with mild interest, seemingly at ease and completely oblivious to what was unfolding in front of him.

"Do any of you have a light?" the blond man asked.

"You need to get outta here," said one of the men who had chased Ryan. He had two lower lip piercings that glinted in the dim light when he spoke. A second flash of light caught Ryan's eye. The man was brandishing his knife so that the stranger could see it.

But the stranger was not looking at the weapon. In fact, he wasn't looking at any of the five men who were threatening him. He was looking directly at Ryan.

Ryan caught the stranger's eyes, closed his own, and nodded somberly—giving the stranger permission to leave him, guilt-free. There was no reason for both of them to get murdered.

The stranger stared at him for a second longer before addressing the gang's leader.

"Kindly let my friend go."

Friend? Ryan was confident he had never met this man before in his life.

"Enough," growled the man with lip piercings. He motioned to his partner, a redhead who was also carrying a knife, to join him, and together they advanced on the blond man.

The stranger moved as if to take a step back. He looked between his two assailants and quickly glanced around. Before the stranger could say anything, the two men lashed out.

Ryan didn't even have time to shout "No!" before the stranger took a step toward his attackers and, with amazing speed, grabbed the redhead's wrist. With a quick maneuver that Ryan couldn't follow, he threw the man against the dumpster with a resounding crash. Before the man with the lip piercings could retaliate, the stranger swept his feet out from under him and knocked him out with a single blow to the head.

Ryan stood in complete shock, and he wasn't alone. It took

a few seconds for the other three attackers to respond. The last man with a knife, who for some reason apparently felt it was warm enough to wear nothing but a sleeveless vest, charged, while the tattooed leader and the other gunman took aim.

The stranger sidestepped the knife before turning his attention to the man in the Sox cap. He quickly flipped the gunman over his shoulder, sending his cap flying before he hit the ground with a satisfying full-body *smack*. Before the man with the tattoo could fire, the stranger lashed out with one hand and sent him flying against the alley wall. The movement was so quick that Ryan was not sure if the stranger had even touched the tattooed man. He had been thrown backward, as if hit by an invisible truck.

The stranger turned without saying a word and quickly dropped the last attacker—the one in the vest—with a few well-placed jabs. Just as the attacker collapsed, the flipped gunman found his hat and started to climb to his feet. The blond man turned back toward the struggling attacker with the Sox cap, who was still a yard away from him, and pushed his right hand down toward the ground as if he were trying to push off an annoying dog. This time, Ryan was sure that the stranger hadn't touched the gunman—but the man hit the ground chin-first and lay there, facedown and still.

For a moment, all was silent, aside from the groans of the injured men lying at the stranger's feet. The blond man turned at last to Ryan and looked as if he was about to say something; but before he could, the redhead who had been thrown against the dumpster found his footing and charged the stranger again.

Seeing the danger before his rescuer did, Ryan reacted instinctively. He kneed the criminal in the gut and punched him once on the temple, knocking him unconscious.

For a second, Ryan just stared at the man. He couldn't believe he had just done that. He'd never been in a fight his entire life, and here he was, responsible for one of the five unresponsive men on the ground. He finally looked up at the blond man, who was looking quite pleased with himself.

"Thanks," said the stranger. With a smug smile on his face, he glanced down at the man Ryan had just hit.

Ryan's head was spinning. Time seemed to slow down. He looked around once again at his five would-be murderers, who were all now too incapacitated to form an intelligent sentence, if not out cold. He had a million questions about what just happened—and about his "friend," who had come to his rescue seemingly out of nowhere—but he decided to start with the first question that came to mind.

"How did you do that?"

He was still looking at the five men on the ground when he realized nobody was answering. Ryan looked up, only to find that the stranger had vanished without a word.

Deciding he would rather not be present when everybody woke up, Ryan started for the mouth of the alley, but stopped before he hit the main street. Although they were horrible people, Ryan could not in good conscience leave the battered criminals like this, especially if one actually had an injury that required medical attention.

Ryan crouched to pat down the nearest victim, the leader with the snake tattoo, assuming any of the resulting groans were from pain and absolutely nothing else. He finally felt a small bulge in the man's pants pocket, and gingerly reached in to pull out his phone. He dialed 911 and briefly told the operator his location and that there were five men there who needed medical attention, then hung up without giving any identifiable information. Ryan quickly wiped the cell phone clean and moved to set it on the ground next to the man when something caught his eye.

Half of a small portrait photograph was hanging out of the

leader's pocket. It must have slid out as Ryan pulled out the phone. He carefully grabbed the tip of the picture to confirm what he already knew.

Staring up at him was a photograph of himself. It was clearly a candid shot, perfectly focused on his face. Even though the background of the image was blurry, he could see an obnoxious orange advertisement behind his head—one that he recognized from the T station near his laboratory.

Ryan suppressed a shudder. This hadn't been a random attack—he was being followed. Targeted. These men had been waiting for him to come home so that they could hurt him. Kill him? The leader had said he was "dead no matter what," but why did they want him dead? Why would anyone?

Unfortunately, Ryan didn't have the time to really think it over. He could hear distant sirens, and he didn't want to explain to the police why he was standing there surrounded by unconscious men.

Ryan looked at his picture one more time. Somehow, he was sure that nothing good would come if he left it at the scene. He crumpled the photo in his hands and left the alley in a hurry, checking over his shoulder every ten steps for the next block and a half until he reached his apartment, pulled himself inside, and quickly bolted the door shut.

Once inside, Ryan immediately drank a glass of water, double-checked to make sure the front door was locked, and finally collapsed onto the couch. He lay still for about five seconds, glanced at the door for a third time to make sure it was locked, and then absentmindedly turned on the television, without even looking to see what was playing. His mind was racing, trying to figure out what had just happened.

The first thing he noticed as he lay there taking stock was that his hand stung. Ryan looked down at the hand he'd used to hit the man in the alley. Despite the obvious inflammation around his knuckles, the skin was intact, and he doubted anything was broken. He was confident that his ribs would bother him in the morning, but overall, his injuries were not too concerning.

The next thought that hit him was that he'd just almost been mugged. No, that wasn't right. He'd almost been murdered. And the attack hadn't been random—his picture in the leader's pocket confirmed that. But why him? Maybe someone had hired those thugs to kill him? It could explain why they had gone through the trouble of setting up a trap for him in the alley. The leader didn't strike Ryan as much of a planner, but if someone had paid them enough, perhaps they would have been motivated to make sure the job was done, and done right.

Still, that didn't explain why someone would want him dead in the first place. Ryan couldn't fathom anything he could have done that would warrant a hit against him; though, to be fair, he also couldn't imagine being callous enough to even consider taking another man's life, so maybe he was out of his depth here.

Even as he tried to figure out why anyone would want him dead, a third realization began to take form. A random stranger, who had called Ryan his "friend," had risked his life to help him. Ryan racked his brain, trying to think of where he might have met the blond man before, but he found nothing.

It was sad, Ryan reflected, that he was honestly less confused by his attackers than he was by a passing stranger helping someone in need. But then again, in the middle of the night in an alley in south Boston, up against five armed men, even the most dedicated good Samaritan would have just called the cops.

Regardless, the blond man had stepped in and come to his rescue. Ryan could only hope that he would one day get the opportunity to learn the stranger's name and thank him.

But there was still one thing Ryan found more disturbing than everything else combined: the invisible force that had taken out two of his attackers in the alley. Ryan was absolutely sure that he had seen the criminals move through the air as if something were pushing them. Scarier still, the stranger had seemed completely unconcerned. In fact, the unseen force had almost seemed to work *with* the stranger, lashing out against his attackers as he fought.

Ryan shook his head. *It must have been the adrenaline,* he concluded. The same endorphin that had blocked the pain in his hand until just now must have played tricks on his mind, causing him to imagine an invisible force. Anyway, the blond man obviously had some kind of martial arts training.

Ryan sat back and tried to clear his head, knowing he still had work to do. He pulled out his laptop and turned off the television just as the news camera panned to an obese man being arrested in Washington, DC, as he shouted something about Three Mile Island and a government cover-up.

After listening to music—maybe that Spanish rap album wasn't so bad after all—and staring at his screen for a solid twenty minutes with absolutely no desire to get any work done, Ryan finally admitted defeat. No matter how hard he tried, the ambush continued to replay in his mind, and a deep feeling of panic was bubbling in his chest, threatening to boil over.

Grudgingly, Ryan closed his laptop and tried to plug it into the charger at his desk, but his hand suddenly started shaking so badly that he couldn't get the connector into the port. He stood there, hunched over his desk, and forced himself to take deep breaths.

It was all hitting him at once. Nothing could truly distract him from obsessing over every detail of what had happened. It was too much. He desperately wished he had someone to call—someone he could vent to.

These were the moments he missed Jack the most. His cousin had been on Ryan's mind ever since his conversation with Tasha that afternoon. Jack had always been the one person he could confide in, and no matter how crazy life got, he'd always been able to count on Jack to help ground him and get him through the chaos.

Still shaking, Ryan reached into his desk drawer and pulled out a small navy-blue flash drive. Jack had given it to Ryan only a month or two before he was killed. It was the last time they had seen each other.

The flash drive made Ryan feel better and worse at the same time. He always thought about Jack when he saw it, but he also remembered how squirrely Jack had seemed when he'd handed Ryan the drive. Admittedly, Jack had seemed a little off for about a year before then, but that day it was like he was a completely different person. He'd told Ryan over and over how much Ryan meant to him, before asking him to keep the flash drive safe. Ryan had agreed, and Jack had instructed him not to open it unless something happened to him.

And that was why the flash drive made Ryan feel worse: no matter how hard he tried, he couldn't open the file on the drive. He'd tried multiple times over the months since Jack's death, but without success. It required some type of password that he did not know. He'd asked his cousin's parents if they had any idea what the code could be, but they were no help. Every month or so Ryan would try to open the file again, but each attempt ended in failure.

He knew that he needed to try to open the flash drive again—but not tonight. It was too late, he had too much to get done at work tomorrow, and he was in no state to try to figure out the password now.

Ryan reluctantly slid the flash drive back into his desk drawer, making a silent promise to try to open the file tomorrow. Ready for this day to end, he checked two more times to make sure the door was locked, then crawled into bed and stared at the ceiling, dreading the next morning.

Ryan lay in bed, tossing for what seemed like forever, trying to shut out everything that had just happened and everything he still had to do. He knew he had an insane week of work ahead of him, but still his last thought before finally drifting off to sleep was about the blond stranger who had come to his rescue.

CHAPTER THREE
THE INTERVIEW

Ryan's alarm clock went off far too early the next morning, and he woke with a start. He lay in bed for several minutes, summoning the willpower to drag his feet slowly across the room and turn it off.

As the morning fog cleared from his mind, the events of the night before started to come back to him. As much as Ryan would have liked to believe it had all been just a vivid dream, his aching hand and bruised chest proved otherwise.

Making gentle movements to avoid aggravating his sore ribs, Ryan slowly made his way through his morning routine while trying to piece together the details of the previous night. To his surprise, his memories weren't just a jumbled mess. Everything was clear.

In the end, Ryan decided that nothing out of the ordinary had happened after all, other than his almost being killed. All the invisible forces he'd thought he had seen, every odd thing he'd thought had happened—it was just his mind's way of processing a traumatic event. As for the photograph—well, professional criminals chose their targets carefully, didn't they?

Ryan wasn't sure what he had that the men last night could possibly have wanted, but they were probably all in jail by now, if not the hospital, so he likely had nothing to worry about. Still, he decided to start looking at new apartment listings that afternoon. He'd been thinking about moving to a safer neighborhood anyway.

Ryan's journey to the subway station that morning was unremarkable, all things considered. He swept his head from side to side as he hurried through his neighborhood, trying to remain vigilant even as he fought down paranoia whenever he heard someone behind him. At one point, he was absolutely certain that an elderly woman in a bright yellow jacket and skirt had been following him for two blocks. It wasn't until she turned left into the nearest Dunkin' Donuts that he breathed a sigh of relief.

Immediately, Ryan began to feel absolutely ridiculous. Nothing about his commute was abnormal at all. Everyone was keeping their head down and minding their own business.

Ryan boarded the graffiti-covered train heading into the city and collapsed onto one of the unforgiving subway seats. He recognized several of the strangers on the train with him, many of whom he saw every day, and smiled as he watched the forty-something-year-old attorney with the receding hairline try and fail to brush a spot of powdered sugar off his jacket. There was the older gentleman who was constantly talking on his flip phone, using speaker mode so that he—and everyone else on the train—could hear the poor person on the other line. And there was Ryan's personal favorite: the young professional woman who wore the same hat with a distractingly large ink stain on it every day, who chewed her nails when she thought no one was looking.

Ryan smiled and leaned back in the hard chair, finally able to relax. To pass some time, he started creating a mental to-do list for the upcoming day.

Suddenly, a bright flash in his peripheral vision caught his eye. The fluorescent lights of the train car were bouncing off the cell phone screen of a man just a few aisles ahead of him. Ryan was about to look away when something made him stop.

With his green quarter-zip sweater and black cap, the phone's owner looked like any other Boston native. He appeared completely at ease, listening to music and leaning against the wall. Normally, Ryan wouldn't have given the stranger a second thought; but in just the few short seconds Ryan spent watching him, the man checked his phone half a dozen times—without ever going past the lock screen. In fact, he kept his phone at such an odd angle that Ryan could actually see one of the man's eyes reflected on the blank screen.

Before he could ponder the strange man any further, the train pulled in at Ryan's station. Ryan hopped off the subway—and saw the man in green do the same, one door down.

Ryan shook his head. At least a dozen other people got off at this stop every day. Firmly telling himself to stop being paranoid, he set off down the familiar path to the laboratory, trying his absolute best to not think of the man in the green sweater. But he was finding the task increasingly difficult. Every time he turned a corner, Ryan was sure he saw the man in green out of the corner of his eye.

Becoming more and more certain that he was being followed for the second time in just two days, Ryan opted to duck inside the next office building he passed. He wasn't quite sure why he thought this was a good idea. He just knew that he did not want the man in the green sweater following him to work.

Ryan crossed the lobby, heading toward the main elevator bank as quickly as he could, and glanced over his shoulder. Sure enough, the man was there, fighting his way through the crowd. His eyes locked onto Ryan.

Ryan broke into a jog, weaving between mindless office drones as he tried to come up with a plan. Luckily, an elevator opened up just ahead, and he slid inside between two disgruntled men with identical briefcases. He let out a sigh of relief just a few moments before he heard someone call out, "Hold the door!"

The man in green calmly stepped into the elevator, muttered a word of thanks to no one in particular, and took a place in front of the closing doors.

Ryan was completely on edge. He no longer had any doubt: the man was here for him, and he had to find a way to get away.

As the other passengers departed one by one, Ryan's mind started to fill with escape plans, each more complicated and daring than the last. Even as the elevator emptied, the stranger did not once move from his position in front of the doors, barely shifting to the side to let the listless office workers squeeze past. Before long, it was just the two of them left in elevator, apart from a woman in a pencil skirt on her way to the twenty-third floor.

Ryan watched, desperately trying to come up with a viable plan, as the numbers ticked by with each floor. Thus far, his best option involved jumping the man by using his keys as a weapon, and the elevator walls for momentum.

Twentieth floor . . . twenty-first . . . twenty-second . . . twenty—*ding*.

The elevator shuddered to a halt, and the doors opened as the woman moved to leave the confined space. Ryan looked uneasily at the man in the green sweater. In a few seconds, once the doors closed, they would be alone.

Ryan sized the stranger up, wondering if he could overpower him. The man was about the same height as Ryan—around six feet, and lean, like a soccer player. The previous night had marked the first "fight" Ryan had ever been in, and he'd barely participated. He didn't like his odds. Maybe he could pin Green Sweater to the wall before the man had time to defend himself? Ryan saw no other solution.

The elevator doors slid closed. This was it.

Ryan sprang at the stranger—and found himself pinned to the elevator wall. The back of his head stung, and the elevator rattled from the impact. The man had used Ryan's momentum against him and slung him around. There was nothing Ryan could do. He was completely at the man's mercy.

"Not bad," the man said with a laugh.

That voice was familiar. Ryan looked up, and finally got a good look at the face underneath the ball cap. The man had bright green eyes and very pale blond hair, almost white.

A sudden realization washed over Ryan like a bucket of cold water. This was the man who had saved him in the alley the night before.

The stranger smiled as recognition dawned on Ryan's face.

"You're quick," he said. He let go of Ryan and took a step back. "Nice to officially meet you, Ryan. I'm Drew."

Thoroughly confused as to why "Drew" knew his name, Ryan tried to form about ten different questions at once, and ended up stuttering. "Um . . . it's . . . was . . . nice . . . nice to meet you too," he finally managed. He was unsure how to continue, considering he had just tried and failed to tackle the stranger. "Thank you," he added after a moment. "I mean, you know, for last night."

"You're welcome," Drew said cheerfully. "I'm happy to help. You did pretty well yourself."

Ryan was about to respond when the elevator doors opened again and more nine-to-five workers trudged in, forcing Ryan and Drew to squeeze together in the back. Drew's eyes darted to the incoming crowd, and he spoke to Ryan in an undertone.

"Look, I can already tell that you have hundreds of questions.

How about we get some coffee, and I'll explain everything?" he offered.

Ryan nodded immediately, before he fully realized what he'd agreed to. The man was right: Ryan had more questions than he could count.

Drew smiled at him. He seemed nice enough.

"I don't have a light," Ryan said, remembering how Drew had originally announced his presence the night before.

"That's fine. I don't smoke."

◊◊◊

"Look, I always appreciate a good cup of coffee, but I really can't stay very long. I have a lot of work I need to get done today."

They had just sat down at a small café with outdoor seating a block away from the office building. Drew was sipping a cup of tea, while Ryan couldn't bring himself to touch his coffee and bagel.

"Well, the grant, presentation, and proposal are all done," Drew said. "They're waiting on your computer for you to proofread, but I think you're going to be pretty happy."

Ryan stared at Drew in disbelief. They sat in silence for what felt like an hour but was probably no longer than two minutes. Ryan started to feel awkward. He wasn't trying to be rude, but he had no idea where to start. Thankfully, Drew seemed to be accustomed to steering a conversation.

"So," Drew began, "like I said, my name is Andrew Tellaren, but I go by Drew. I'm sure you have a ton of questions, and I'm going to do my best to answer all of them.

"To start, I represent a discreet tech development company that has evolved over the years into a multicultural conglomerate with a simple goal: to help better the world through technology. Every year around this time, we scout for young people who we believe have the potential to truly make a difference. More specifically, we're looking for intelligent individuals who are underappreciated in their own fields of interest."

Ryan stared back, stunned. Clearly this was a well-rehearsed speech that Drew had given many times. Drew took a sip of his tea before continuing.

"We frequently look for people whose circumstances—poverty; or say, a death in the family, for instance—somehow limited their chances for future success," he said with a nod to Ryan. "To make a long story short, I'm here to offer you a job. I typically have this conversation with potential initiates a couple of times every year, but . . . I don't know . . . there's something different about you. I really think you would excel with us, and I hope you consider it. I sincerely believe this is your chance to really make a difference in the world. I know this is a lot to take in all at once. Unfortunately, I'm not allowed to divulge too much information unless you're interested in the new position."

"A job offer?" said Ryan. Of all the things he had expected when he'd noticed Drew following him that morning, this was the absolute last thing he would have guessed. "Why me? How did you find me? I didn't apply for anything, and I never met you before last night. I mean, you can't know but so much about me." Ryan felt the words falling out of his mouth, uninhibited. He wasn't sure why he was arguing with someone who was trying to give him a job, but his curiosity overpowered his sense of courtesy.

Thankfully, Drew didn't seem at all offended by Ryan's reaction.

"We monitor postgraduation college surveys where you put your job title. From there, we look at academic records, and if you meet our criteria, we run a thorough background check. For example, I know that you, Ryan Kendrick, are twenty-four years old and grew up as an only child in San Diego. You played club soccer throughout your childhood. You generally prefer to maintain a small group of close friends rather than a large number of acquaintances. ISTP Myers Briggs. You've had two . . . no, wait . . . three serious girlfriends. Father is a marine biologist; mom an anthropology professor. Parents divorced in your first year of high school. Your father remarried two years later, to a much younger woman, and your mother crashed—and practically ruined—the reception. The video on YouTube is actually hysterical—sorry. Mother remarried two years after that. Because of the associated drama, you generally avoid family gatherings. You've stayed in Boston since your second year at Tufts, and when you do go home, you spend most of your time at Sunset Cliffs.

"Academically, you were placed in an accelerated program during grade school. You took an impressive number of Advanced Placement classes, with only one B in your public high school career. And your college records were outstanding until that last semester. After that, you started working for Dr. Noret at Massachusetts Biomedical Research Corporation, where you work grueling hours and receive no recognition for your assistance researching the KC gene—which is an amazing discovery, by the way—despite being the one who sets up the experiments and annotates the results. And that brings us to today." Drew paused to take a breath. "You are what we're looking for. I have no doubt."

"Um . . . I mean . . . thanks," Ryan said lamely. "So . . . you've been watching me. Obviously."

"For a while. Like I said, the job requires a lot of discretion, so we're very careful whom we scout."

Ryan examined Drew carefully. He did not seem abashed at having just been called out for spying.

"Well . . . what else do I need to know about the job?" Ryan asked.

Drew kept his face impassive, but a slight crinkle at the corner of his eyes gave away his excitement.

"It would require you to relocate," Drew said. "Do you have strong ties in Boston that would make that difficult? We cover all your expenses—food, lodging, utilities—and we'll even pay your rent here for the next six months and help you find a new job if you change your mind and want to come back."

Ryan considered his answer carefully before responding.

"You've . . . been monitoring me for a while now, right?" Ryan questioned.

Drew shrugged, nonchalant. Ryan decided to take this as confirmation and continued.

"Then you know that other than my job, I really don't have any ties here. My friends from college are all in other cities. It's awful, but we've kinda been drifting apart since we haven't been able to get together a lot. And because my work hours are so intense, I really don't have time for much else. I volunteer when I can, but it's sporadic. Do you consider strong social ties before handing out job offers?"

"We do."

"Because the job is top secret?"

"Exactly."

Ryan considered everything Drew had told him. The chance to do something meaningful—and get away from Dr. Noret at the same time—was undeniably attractive, but Drew was giving him practically no information about the actual job. Ryan wondered vaguely if it was too early to ask about salary.

"It sounds amazing so far," Ryan said. "But what else can you tell me about the job? It sounds almost too good to be true."

"Well, it's a sales pitch!" Drew chuckled. "What else can I tell you? We try to help the general population through technological and advanced sciences research. We have people working on computers, medicine, energy, and other . . . more classified areas with great potential. We also have a branch focused on military advancements. Before you ask," Drew said quickly, seeing the look on Ryan's face, "we don't create bombs, firearms, drones, or anything like that. We recognize that a military is an unfortunate necessity, so we focus primarily on defensive measures, intelligence, and strategy."

Still vague, but the military part is definitely interesting. "What's the name of the company?" Ryan asked, realizing Drew hadn't mentioned it yet.

"Atlantis Technologies, Incorporated," Drew said.

"Never heard of it."

"Well, it wouldn't be a really good secret if everyone knew about it," Drew said playfully.

"What else can you tell me about the company?" Ryan asked. "Or about what I'd be doing there?"

"Unfortunately, not a whole lot," Drew said, leaning back in his chair. "This is where working for a secretive organization gets tough. Like I said, I can't divulge too much information unless I know you're interested."

Ryan paused for a minute and swirled his rapidly cooling coffee. How was he supposed to make an informed decision with essentially no information?

"Showing interest isn't binding, right?" Ryan asked carefully.

Drew smiled, as if he could tell Ryan was close to giving in.

"Of course not," he said. "But I will say, I've never had anyone say no after they've shown interest."

Ryan looked at Drew for a few seconds before asking his next, obvious question.

"What about you? Do you regret it?"

"Never," Drew replied immediately. "It's been amazing. I can't imagine doing anything else."

Ryan nodded.

"When did you start?"

"When I was twenty-four. Same as you. It's about the standard age."

"Did you start recruiting right away, or did you do research for a year or two first?" Ryan asked. He was surprised; Drew only looked a few years older than him, and Ryan couldn't imagine such a secretive company letting an inexperienced person recruit new hires. Maybe the turnover rate was really high.

"No. They require at least twenty-five years of service before you become a scouter, but it's normally more like thirty-five or forty years on average," Drew said. "I look good for my age," he added, at Ryan's confounded look.

Ryan made a mental note to come back to that point later. For now, he was keen on wheedling as much information as he possibly could out of Drew.

"Have there been any notable individuals who have worked for you all?"

Drew's face twisted thoughtfully, as if he was debating whether or not he was allowed to answer that question. Ryan wasn't sure if it was part of the act, or if he was really trying to make a decision.

"Well, a couple," Drew finally said, with a sly smile. "Steve Jobs. Einstein. Newton. There were others we looked at, but they were doing fine on their own, like Gates. He was already on track to revolutionize technology without our help."

Ryan smirked. *Newton? I guess that was a question he couldn't answer without giving too much away.*

Ryan studied Drew, and Drew waited patiently in return, happily people-watching as he sipped his tea.

Thankful that Drew wasn't staring at him as he tried to think, Ryan looked down at his hand, still bruised from the night before. The bruise—or more specifically, the pain throbbing dully under it—made him feel more anchored to the real world.

Ryan looked back at the man who had saved him the night before. Other than some odd white patches of keratin in his nailbeds (*Weird manicure?* he wondered.), Drew's hands looked normal and unscathed, despite his having done the bulk of the fighting. Ryan looked up and saw a confident expression on Drew's face—but not, he decided, an arrogant one. Drew simply knew that his offer was enticing. He caught Ryan's eyes and smiled kindly.

Ryan was on the verge of asking Drew about the night before— about the men who'd attacked him, and whether Drew knew anything about why they'd been after him in the first place—when Drew finished his tea and spoke up.

"Listen," Drew said, "I hate to end this, but I really can't say anything else unless you're interested. Here's the deal: you don't need to make a decision right now, but it does need to be soon. Go to work. Go home. Sleep on it. Do whatever you need to do, but I need to know by this time tomorrow."

"Tomorrow?"

"Yes, in twenty-four hours," Drew said. "Unfortunately, we are under a bit of a deadline. You see . . ." he trailed off.

"Yes?"

"Well . . ." Drew continued hesitantly, "like I said, you've been on our radar for a while now. In fact, we've been following your progress in the lab, and we were originally considering waiting another year to contact you to see how your research on cancer goes. But . . . last night kinda changes things."

"How does last night affect a job offer?" Ryan asked.

"We believe," Drew said slowly, "that the people who attacked you last night were sent to kill you because of the progress you've been making with your research. And . . ." he paused again. Now it looked like he was genuinely debating whether to go on, frowning down at his empty cup. After a moment, he sighed and continued: "We believe the people who ordered the hit on you . . . are the same ones who were responsible for your cousin's death."

Ryan felt his stomach drop like he was on a roller coaster. "*What?*"

"Your cousin, Jack Kendrick, he . . . well, he worked for us," Drew said. "He worked with Atlantis Technologies at our California campus. He believed in us—in what we do. He was working on a covert project, and we believe he was killed because of it."

"He was killed by a drunk driver," Ryan said. "He was up in the mountains in Canada for work and was hit head-on by a truck."

"He was in Canada," said Drew, nodding. "He was there on an assignment from Atlantis, and his car was hit by a truck. But it wasn't an accident, and the other driver wasn't drunk. We believe he was killed over a piece of sensitive information that could have really helped us, and people all over the world."

Ryan stared at Drew, finding the man's confident gaze now full of empathy. Ryan didn't know what to say. Part of him wanted to yell at Drew, tell him that he was a liar. But what if Drew was actually telling the truth? Jack had been acting strange for the last year or two before he died.

"Why would I want to join an organization that got my cousin killed?" Ryan asked, working under the assumption that Drew wasn't lying.

"Because at the end of the day, Atlantis Technologies really wants to make the world a better place," Drew said simply. "All we want to do is help people. I haven't met a single person who regrets joining us."

"What about Jack?"

"Jack believed in our cause," Drew said. "He knew his assignment was dangerous, but he honestly believed in our mission. He wanted to help people, just like I know you do. He was a good man. His death was hard on all of us."

Ryan said nothing. It was all too much to take in at once.

"Ryan," Drew began, "you don't need to say anything right now. Just think about it for a bit and let me know. I'm going to give you my number. If you are really interested in joining our organization, give me a call. We would love to have you."

Drew took out a business card and passed it across the table to Ryan. Save for a single telephone number, it was blank. Ryan slid the card into his wallet and tried to pull out a few bills to pay for his breakfast, but Drew waved him down. After a polite back-and-forth over who would pay for the meal, Ryan caved, thanked Drew, and stood to leave. He was already late for work, and he was not looking forward to having Dr. Noret shout at him.

Ryan looked back at the table as he was walking away. Drew hadn't moved from his spot. He was politely watching Ryan, as if Ryan were a curious present he couldn't wait to open.

Ryan slowly made his way the last few blocks to the lab. He kept trying to rehearse what he would say to Dr. Noret when he got there, but his mind kept pulling him back to his conversation with Drew.

Jack had been murdered. That was what Drew seemed to think, anyway. And apparently the same people who'd murdered him wanted Ryan dead too. Frankly, Ryan was more annoyed that Drew wouldn't tell him who these mysterious people were than he was by the idea that Jack had been secretly working for some covert corporation. Jack was always looking for a way to help people. If somebody dropped something, Jack would be the first person bending down to pick it up. It was one reason Ryan had admired his cousin so much.

But his cousin was dead, apparently because of his work for this secret company. Did Ryan really want to sign up for something so dangerous? He knew that he didn't want to work with Dr. Noret forever. The man was undeniably horrible, amazing though his research was. Yet supposedly, that research was why these mysterious enemies wanted Ryan dead. But who would want to kill someone for researching cancer treatments? That should be a good thing!

Ryan was so distracted by his own thoughts that he didn't even realize he'd made it to the lab until his hand was on the front door. He pulled the door open and slowly made his way to his workstation, trying further to delay the inevitable. He was already almost two hours late. Another five minutes wouldn't make much of a difference.

"Good morning, Ryan!" Tasha said in an overly cheery voice.

"Morning," he said back, attempting a smile. No reason to bother her with everything that had happened since he'd left work the night before. "Sorry I'm a little late."

"Don't worry about it!" Tasha said, again a little too enthusiastically. "It's no big deal at all!"

Ryan glanced at his coworker and found a forced smile on her face.

"What happened?"

Her grin immediately faded.

"Dr. Noret came by this morning," Tasha said in a defeated tone. "He wants to see you in his office."

"Of course he does," Ryan sighed as he turned on his desktop. "Do you know when he wants to see me?"

"I believe he said, 'As soon as he decides to grace us with his presence,'" Tasha said with a grimace.

Ryan sighed, slowly took off the lab coat that he'd just pulled on, and made for the door.

"Want me to call your cell in about ten minutes with some type of family emergency?" Tasha asked sincerely, making Ryan laugh.

"No," he said reluctantly. "I better just take what's coming to me. Thank you, though."

Ryan trudged out of the lab and down the hall to Dr. Noret's office with Tasha's well wishes behind him. He knocked twice on his boss's door, and heard a curt "Enter," before he even finished the second knock.

"Well, look who finally showed up to work," Dr. Noret said as soon as Ryan opened the door. "Can I offer you something to drink? Scotch? Bourbon?"

"No, sir," Ryan said immediately, knowing the offer was insincere. "I'm sorry I'm late, Dr. Noret. There was an . . . incident on the T this morning." It wasn't a complete lie.

"Well, next time, leave your house a little earlier," Dr. Noret said dismissively. "Anyway, that's not my problem. Listen, I need you to attend some ridiculous HR retreat this weekend for me. It's all day Saturday. I have plans with the family this weekend, so I can't do it. Sounds like something you'd be good at, right?"

"Right," Ryan said, although he wasn't sure what there was to be "good at" in an HR meeting. "But sir, there's something you should probably know. I may not be able to attend the retreat. I actually met someone who offered me a jo—"

"Look," Dr. Noret said impatiently, shaking his hand pointedly at Ryan as he spoke, "someone on our team needs to go to the retreat. I can't. So if you don't go, then I have to send Tasha. Frankly, I'm not too sure about her, so I'd rather send you. So, are you going to be a team player or not?"

"Yes, sir," Ryan said, trying not to grit his teeth as he spoke.

"Good!" Dr. Noret said. "Now, you've got a lot of work to do from yesterday, so I'd get on it if I were you."

"Yes, sir." Ryan turned to leave.

"And Kennic?"

"Yes?"

"If you're late again, you're fired."

Ryan nodded and left the office without saying a word.

"How bad was it?" Tasha asked as soon as he returned to the lab.

"Pretty bad," Ryan said, wiggling his computer mouse back and forth to leave the screensaver. They were always honest with each other about how Dr. Noret treated them. Solidarity was the only thing that kept them both sane. "I need to attend an HR retreat for him this Saturday, apparently."

"Seriously? That's ridiculous."

Ryan was about to answer Tasha when he froze. On his typically organized computer desktop were three new files he had never seen before, each title starting with the word "COMPLETED."

"What the—" Ryan muttered.

"What?" Tasha asked.

"Nothing," Ryan said quickly. "I just . . . I forgot how much work I actually got done last night."

Ryan opened each file. The grant proposal was perfect. He couldn't find a single mistake. He quickly scanned both conference documents, and couldn't help but be impressed. Drew had told him that someone at Atlantis Technologies had taken care of all of his work, but he still hadn't been expecting this. How did they know everything about his research? Did they have access to his computer?

No sooner did he finish scanning the documents than an email from an address at Atlantis Technologies, Inc. popped up on Ryan's screen

Hey Ryan!

It was a pleasure speaking with you this morning. I hope everything looks good on your end! Let me know if you aren't satisfied with our work. We can make any changes you need from our office. We want to make sure it's perfect. Have a great day! I'm looking forward to hearing from you.

Best,

Drew Tellaren

P.S.—Light3xposes5hadow

Ryan shook his head in disbelief. This company was good. He had no idea how they were able to access his computer, but he wasn't complaining.

Determined to learn more about this company, Ryan pulled up a search engine and typed in "Atlantis Technologies, Inc." He was not at all surprised to find the results underwhelming. Other than a tropical resort, an engineering company, and an extreme sports outfitter that all shared the mythological name, there was very little online about Drew's company. Although he did stumble across one particularly entertaining blog run by someone with the username BigJosh202 who kept rambling about how the government was covering up the "undeniable" fact that the Lost City of Atlantis was real and interfering in global politics.

"What are you looking at over there?" Tasha asked as Ryan chuckled at one of BigJosh's posts ("Atlantis: What's Really in the Depths of Loch Ness?").

"Just a random blog," Ryan said. Despite the laugh he'd gotten out of it, his research hadn't been very helpful. He still wasn't sure what to do. "Can I ask you a question?"

"Of course."

"If someone you barely knew walked up to you and offered you a . . . a mission, one that would help a lot of people but would also turn your life completely upside down, would you do it?" Ryan asked. He didn't want to tell Tasha about the job offer just yet. That would be a conversation for another time.

"Is this, like, for some type of fantasy role-playing game, or are we talking about real life?" Tasha asked, looking slightly confused.

"Real life."

"Well," Tasha said, taking a moment to think, "I feel like I would have to take the mission. I mean, that's what we're doing here, right? Researching cancer so that one day, it'll no longer be a problem? If someone told me there was a way I could really make a difference in the world, I think I'd jump on board."

Ryan nodded in agreement but said nothing. He could see Tasha watching him out of the corner of his eye. She looked like she wanted to say something, but after a moment, she turned her attention back to her computer without speaking. Ryan was grateful. He needed time to think, but not here. Not at work.

Compared to the previous sixteen hours, the rest of the workday was absolutely mundane. Considering Drew or one of his colleagues had completed all of his pressing assignments, Ryan desperately searched for some way to keep himself entertained for the rest of the day. After scrolling through the news and winning at solitaire three times in a row, he finally resorted to flicking little balls of wadded-up paper at Tasha, until she caved and joined him in slacking off for the rest of the day.

For a brief second, Ryan almost felt guilty about wasting the day, and considered asking Dr. Noret whether there was something he could help with. But at the thought of talking to his boss again, Ryan quickly got over the guilt and challenged Tasha to a game of paper football.

During his commute home, Ryan couldn't help but think about how often he and Tasha had fun messing around at work. Now that he thought about it, Tasha was the closest friend he had in Boston. Even though they had never hung out after work, he would still hate to say goodbye, and would feel even worse about leaving her to deal with Dr. Noret's wrath all alone. Still, he didn't know how much more of Dr. Noret he could take, and Tasha had even encouraged him to take the new position, whether she knew it or not.

She was too good for that place anyway, Ryan thought. He hoped that if he did take the job, Tasha would get sick of Noret all the faster, and move on to a job in which she was actually appreciated.

After taking a horrifically long way home from the T (though at least no one tried to kill him this time), Ryan finally made it back to his apartment. As he walked through the door, he threw his keys onto the kitchen table.

Most days after work, Ryan crashed on the couch for an hour before eventually slapping together something to eat—but not today. Today, Ryan went straight to his desk and took out the flash drive Jack had left him. He *had* to unlock the file today. If Jack had really worked for this company, the drive would prove it. Ryan was positive.

He plugged the flash drive into his laptop and waited for the security window to pop up. The text cursor blinked endlessly in the empty field, waiting for him to enter the right password.

He typed "Atlantis" and waited; but almost instantly, a familiar window popped up: "Password Incorrect."

Ryan frowned. He'd thought for sure that would work. He tried "Atlantis Technologies Inc" ("Password Incorrect"), and even tried spelling out "Incorporated," to no avail.

Ryan pulled out Drew's business card, and tried the phone number without much hope. "Password Incorrect."

After holding the card up to the light to ensure it had no hidden watermarks, Ryan felt the familiar feeling of frustration that he associated with the flash drive start to settle in. Perhaps Drew had given him some kind of clue earlier that morning? But after nearly twenty minutes of further failures, Ryan concluded that Drew hadn't really told him much at all.

As a last effort, Ryan pulled up his work email, hoping against all odds that Drew's email address might be the password. He opened Drew's email, glanced at the message for any clues, and swore loudly. There it was, at the bottom of the email, not even remotely hidden:

Light3xposes5hadow

Ryan typed in the password and jumped out of his chair with an excited shout when the security window disappeared. He was finally in. A new window popped up on his screen, with the heading "SURFACE VIEW."

Ryan furrowed his brow. Apparently, the flash drive contained only two items: a pixelated folder icon with a name in complete gibberish (Ryan was certain some of those letters were Greek), and a video file simply titled "Ryan."

Ryan clicked on the video icon without hesitation. The screen went black for a brief moment until it was suddenly filled with his cousin's face.

Ryan's heart leapt at the sight. For a moment, it was like he was in college again, opening a video chat with his best friend in the world. But of course, it was just a recording.

Ryan felt his eyes sting as Jack sat back in his chair and began to speak.

"Ryan," Jack said with his familiar soft smile. "Man, I wish we were able to hang out more. I'm sorry I've been acting so weird the past year or two. Life's been a little crazy on my end, and I haven't been able to tell anyone about it. But if you're watching this, then you know about Atlantis! I had to make sure you couldn't access my files unless you were already aware of them, but I'm so proud of you, cous. I knew they'd contact you before too long. What we're doing here in Atlantis is huge—it's amazing. I know you'd do great there, and we'd be lucky to have you!"

Jack took a deep, shivery breath.

"Unfortunately, if you're watching this, it also probably means I'm . . . no longer around. Ryan, if that's the case, I just want you to know how much you mean to me. You have no idea how many times I wanted to tell you everything that has been going on, and how much it killed me to have to lie to you. I hope you can forgive me.

"Make me proud, Ryan," Jack said. Ryan saw his lower lip twitch for a fraction of a second. "I know you will. And remember: light exposes shadow."

Jack turned away for a second as if done, then looked back at the camera for one last statement: "Oh yeah! If you're still in the Boston area, watch out for Hillner. Dude's insane."

And with that, the video closed itself.

Ryan took a deep breath. A mix of elation and grief fought within him. Seeing Jack and hearing his voice again had made Ryan's heart soar, but it also hurt.

Hoping to find another video, Ryan tried to open the folder in the flash drive, only to be greeted by an automated alert: "FILE CORRUPTED." Instead, Ryan opened Jack's video again and watched it a second time. This time he was less mesmerized by seeing Jack on the screen, and was able to really listen to what his cousin had to say. Drew hadn't been lying; Atlantis Technologies was clearly something Jack really had believed in.

Ryan closed his laptop, picked up his phone, and dialed the

number on Drew's card. Maybe it was impulsive; maybe he was letting his emotions get the better of him; but it felt right. The phone rang once before Drew picked up.

"Hey, Ryan," Drew said. "What's up?"

"I'm in," Ryan said. He was suddenly exhilarated. He was following in Jack's footsteps, doing something good.

"Fantastic!" Drew said. Even over the phone, Ryan could tell he was thrilled.

"So . . . can you tell me more about the company now?"

"Absolutely! But how about I show you instead? Meet me by the Boston Waterboat Marina at ten a.m. tomorrow. I'll explain everything then!"

◊◊◊

"Morning, Ryan!" Drew said with a big smile. Ryan had found him sitting on a small retaining wall just outside the marina, looking quite pleased. "You ready?"

"All set," Ryan said, pulling slightly on the straps of his backpack. Drew had told him last night to bring a small day pack, but had mentioned no specifics. Other than Jack's flash drive, a water bottle, and a notepad, the pack was essentially empty. Ryan had asked Drew if he should dress for an interview or bring a change of clothes, but Drew assured him there was no need.

"However," he'd said over the phone, "cell service where we're going isn't great, so you might want to notify anyone who'd start worrying about you that you'll be out of touch for a while. You could say you've decided to take a road trip to do some soul-searching. Or that you're thinking of hiking the Appalachian Trail—that usually works."

Ryan had finally settled on sending a vaguely worded to email to each of his parents, telling them he would be taking some "time away" to "figure some stuff out" and not to worry. It should be enough; they were both pretty busy anyway. For a brief moment, he almost sent the same email to Tasha, but he was pretty sure she wouldn't buy the excuse. He didn't really know what to say to her—after all, it wasn't as if he knew a lot about this mysterious company. In the end, he decided to send her a simple message: *I'm taking the mission.* It wasn't much, but he hoped she would understand.

"Were you able to let your friends and family know you'd be away for a while?" Drew asked, hopping to his feet.

Ryan nodded. "I didn't email my boss, though," he admitted. "To be fair, he won't exactly miss me, but he'll probably notice when I don't show up to work—especially since he threatened to fire me yesterday if I was late again."

"Sounds charming," Drew said. "Don't worry—I can take care of that from one of our computers once we get there."

"Is Atlantis Technologies all the way out here?" Ryan asked as Drew started to make his way down to the marina.

"Kinda," Drew said as he spun around, walking backward so he could face Ryan as they talked. "You'll see. Oh, and that reminds me. The whole 'Atlantis Technologies, Inc.' thing is just a cover. Sorry about that. We just have to be careful. Our real name is just Atlantis."

"Yeah, I noticed Jack just called it 'Atlantis,'" Ryan said, remembering his cousin's video.

"Oh, good! You got into the flash drive," Drew said. "We knew Jack had left it for you, but he never mentioned what exactly was in there. I was wondering if that had anything to do with your decision. But let's talk about it more once we get where we're going. We are in a bit of a hurry." Without waiting for a response, Drew turned back around and started walking a little quicker. Ryan had to resist the temptation to pull out his phone and look up the company again, but he was confident that searching for "Atlantis" wouldn't yield anything more useful than what he had found in his search the day before.

Ryan was dying to ask more about the company—and, for that matter, about Drew. He still knew next to nothing about this man, and was a little surprised by his own willingness to blindly follow him. "Um, Drew?"

"Hm?"

"Where are we going?" Ryan asked. He'd been under the impression that he was about to embark on a job interview, but he was growing increasingly dubious. Drew was leading him down a wooden dock, and they were now approaching a small sporting boat at the end of the row. "You're not taking me out to sea to kill me and dump my body, right?" he added, not entirely joking.

"Nah. If I wanted to kill you, I would've done it after you saw me the other night," Drew said. He laughed at the look on Ryan's face. "We're headed to Atlantis. More specifically, the Northeast American City of Atlantis. There's a ship a couple miles east of the harbor, waiting to take us there."

"You guys really like playing up the whole 'Lost City of Atlantis' thing, huh?"

"It's hard to resist," Drew admitted.

They climbed aboard the small boat, and Drew gunned the engine before expertly piloting the craft out into the harbor. As they exited the bay and picked up speed, Ryan looked out over the horizon. With the boat bouncing rhythmically over the rough water and the wind blowing through his hair, he couldn't help but feel elated. He had no idea where he was going, or, really, who he was with; but there was something liberating about being on the sea. And there was something else to appreciate: he never had to see Dr. Noret again.

CITY IN THE SKY

Completely at ease, Ryan leaned against the bow and turned to face Drew, who was also obviously enjoying himself behind the wheel. Maybe it was being outside the crowded city and on the open water, but Ryan already felt much more comfortable with Drew.

"How old is the company?" Ryan asked. He practically had to shout to be heard over the wind.

"No one knows for sure!" Drew called back. "Best estimate— about four thousand years."

Ryan laughed. "Fine, don't tell me." Drew simply shrugged.

"So what type of research did you do before you became a scouter?" Ryan asked.

"I originally started off researching different types of medical technology," shouted Drew. "I worked with medical imaging de- vices for a while, trying to make a quicker, more compact and more accurate MRI. After a couple of years, I switched to improving medical tech for the military. I actually did a lot of work with body armor. After that, I became a practicing physician. I did some re- search on bone growth during that time, too. I'll help out if they need a provider on short notice, but now I pretty much just focus on recruiting."

"You can switch fields like that?" Ryan asked.

"Oh, sure! Most people end up switching once or twice."

"That's awesome!" said Ryan. He liked how flexible the com- pany sounded. "What made you go into medicine?"

"I broke my femur playing Toss when I was eleven, and I've been interested in the human body ever since! Toss was still pretty new at the time, so the game was a lot rougher back then. They've introduced more fouls now, to protect the players."

"What's Toss?"

"It's a game," said Drew. "I'll show you when we get there.

There's our ship!"

Ryan turned around, expecting to see some impressive company yacht. Instead, squinting against the wind, he saw what appeared to be a fighter jet sitting on the surface of the water. As they slowed for the approach, Ryan leaned as far as he dared over the edge of the boat to get a better look.

It was like no jet he had ever seen before. The craft's sleek, aerodynamic design was enhanced by its dark, seamless metal exterior. Two rectangular engines were stacked vertically on each side of the fuselage. The cockpit looked just large enough to fit two people.

Drew pulled their boat up broadside to the ship and hit a switch near the boat's throttle. Ryan heard a hissing noise and turned in time to see the back half of the jet's top open like a set of barn doors.

"This is us!" Drew said as he swung his legs over the side of the boat and hopped onto the floating jet. Ryan's eyes widened as he watched the jet tilt back and forth to stabilize under the extra weight. "Come on," Drew said with a smile, apparently not at all bothered by the rocking motion.

Ryan looked skeptically at the slick, wet surface of the jet. He really didn't feel like slipping and falling into the ocean right before a job interview.

"You won't slip—trust me!" Drew called.

Well, I've trusted him this far. . . .

Ryan hopped down—and felt his shoes stick where they landed. As he regained his balance, he looked up at Drew, impressed.

"Nanotech," explained Drew. "When the doors are open, it makes tiny grooves along the surface of the ship to allow for better traction. We'll take this straight to Atlantis. Let's go!"

He ducked into the jet. With one last look at the open ocean, Ryan followed.

Ryan lifted his head—and froze as soon as he cleared the threshold. The interior of the ship was like something straight out of a science fiction movie. As Drew started the engines, heads-up displays sprang to life over the windshield, and red and blue LED lights blinked on all around him. Looking from screen to screen, Ryan tried to discern the function of each blinking light and switch. Most appeared to be various kinds of sensors, though he could only guess what they sensed.

Ryan glanced down—and instantly regretted it. The floor of the ship was transparent. Between the rocking of the ship and the water visibly roiling beneath his feet, Ryan found the effect extremely disorienting.

"Easy," coached Drew. "Come sit in the copilot seat, and buckle up."

Despite the relatively short distance, Ryan made his way slowly to the front of the ship. With every step, he spotted some new piece of stupefying technology.

The ship was actually made to seat four people, with two passenger seats facing the rear. Ryan sank into the seat next to Drew and navigated the confusing restraints while Drew continued to flip switches and adjust settings. After a moment, he turned to Ryan.

"Ready?"

Ryan nodded.

"Fantastic! By the way, do you like roller coasters?"

"Of course. Why?"

"No reason," Drew said with a sly smile. "Just hang on."

Ryan felt the ship gently rise straight up into the air. Astonished, he looked around, trying in vain to figure out how the jet could move vertically.

"Look straight ahead," Drew directed. Ryan shot Drew a

confused look, but the other man was already facing forward, eyes fixed on the horizon. Ryan quickly followed suit.

As soon as the back of his head touched the seat, the craft shot forward faster than Ryan could have thought possible. A steady pressure settled in the center of his chest as Drew continued to accelerate. Just as the pressure became worrying, the ship turned sharply skyward and continued at a constant speed.

Ryan looked over at Drew in shock. A manic grin was stretched across the man's face. Between the street fighter from the alleyway, the businessman he'd had coffee with the day before, and now this adrenaline junkie flying like a madman, Ryan couldn't pin him down.

"What do you think?" Drew asked a few minutes later as the ship gradually leveled out. They were still climbing, but no longer quite so vertically.

"This is amazing!" Ryan said. "The engines are really quiet."

"Everything is solar powered. The entire outer surface is covered with panels."

Ryan was astonished. He'd had no idea solar energy had come so far.

"How can it move straight up and down?"

"The stacked engines rotate three hundred and sixty degrees. They're able to steer the ship in any direction."

Ryan looked around in amazement. They were already well above the lower clouds. Squinting through the bright sunlight, he thought he saw something shimmering in front of them, but his view was interrupted as Drew banked to the right.

"We're going to go just a bit higher," Drew said, in the same tone that a comfortable tour guide might use. "I want to get you a great first view."

Ryan was extremely impressed by the power of this little ship.

They had been traveling for a while. He was confident they were already higher than most domestic flights went—and they were still climbing. Surely they were almost at the company by now.

Just as Ryan was about to ask how much farther they had to go, Drew leveled out the ship.

"Alright," he said. "We're just about there! You're gonna get your first look at Atlantis in a second!"

Ryan was skeptical that he would be able to see anything from this altitude, but he was excited nonetheless. The technology on the ship was amazing, and he was dying to see what else the company had to offer.

Drew started their descent, and Ryan straightened up to get a better look, peering out over the nose of the ship. What he saw made his whole body go rigid.

He was looking at something impossible. His gut instinct was to write it all off as a hallucination, but his brain told him otherwise—he knew it was real. He had no doubt. It was just as real as the ship. Just as real as Drew. As real as the insane way they had met. What he saw, nestled in the clouds miles and miles above the surface of the ocean, was a city.

A floating city.

"Welcome to Atlantis, Ryan!"

CHAPTER FOUR
CITY IN THE SKY

Ryan leaned forward in his seat, straining to get a better view. The pain in the back of his neck told him he wasn't dreaming. Above the clouds, laid out in almost perfect quadrants, was a small city bustling with movement.

There was far too much for him to take in at once, and Drew was descending rapidly. Ryan had just enough time to discern a beautiful, vibrant park surrounded by gleaming buildings before the ship dropped below the city's surface. Around the base of the city, lush green vines grew horizontally along rows of what looked like hydroponic gardens strung between long cables anchored into a series of girders. As they came closer, Ryan saw people in harnesses gliding across the cables to pick fruit and vegetables, with nothing but open sky beneath them.

The ship continued its descent, and before he knew it, they were soaring under the city itself. Ryan gaped at the shimmering blue underside, which appeared to be covered by a mosaic of small mirrors that reflected the sea and clouds below, so that the giant city almost disappeared into the sky above.

Ryan was about to ask Drew about the reflective panels when he felt his jaw drop in surprise. Just ahead of them, the blue surface was splitting in two, the crack widening into a bay door. The opening reminded Ryan of a mouth, barely large enough to swallow the jet as it passed through.

"Just a minute now," Drew said as he released the controls. He flipped a switch on the console in front of him and leaned back as the ship continued to move on its own. Normally, Ryan would have been amazed to watch as the ship steered itself perfectly into the open doors ahead of them, but compared to the giant slab of earth above him and the open sky below, the autopilot function seemed downright normal.

"We are . . . underneath a city . . . in the air," Ryan said, working through the concept slowly.

"I'll answer all your questions once we're up top," Drew promised.

"That may take a while," Ryan said honestly. His head was spinning. He watched as the ship piloted itself through what appeared to be a landing bay and touched down with only the lightest bump, the hatch in the back opening with a pressurized hiss.

Drew immediately undid his restraints and climbed out. Ryan dutifully followed him out into the bay, his footsteps echoing in the cavernous space as he tried to take in every detail. Imposing ships lined their path to a wide marble staircase at the far end of the bay. Drew led Ryan up the stairs quickly, as if worried Ryan might formulate more questions than he could answer at once if they lingered.

As they hiked up the wide stairs, they passed several groups of people on their way up and down. While most of them were dressed casually in light sweaters and comfortable pants, one small group of men and women, who were practically running down the staircase, wore odd metallic blue suits that loosely resembled full-body motocross pads—if the gear had been designed to protect the wearer from ray guns instead of a crash. Every single person either greeted them or politely nodded as they passed, and most of them addressed Drew by name.

The stairs eventually reached a small landing. Across from him, Ryan saw a narrow tunnel leading back down into the bowels of the city, and another, larger set of stairs ascending off to the right. The tunnel was illuminated by small, evenly spaced blue-white orbs resting on small rings along the walls. He had never seen any lamp like them. Distracted by the odd lights, Ryan failed to notice that Drew hadn't stopped with him, until his new friend called out.

"That tunnel leads to the Monorail," Drew said over his shoulder as he started up the staircase. "Come on. We're going up."

Ryan hurried after Drew. Thankfully, the second staircase was much shorter than the first, and the two of them soon emerged into open air.

Ryan blinked rapidly as he waited for his eyes to adjust to the blinding sunlight. He looked around, trying to get his bearings, and found himself in the middle of a park.

Drew led him along a winding, unpolished granite walkway to a small stand of trees on the edge of a strikingly green field, where he proceeded to plop down on a patch of grass under a tree. Ryan took his cue from Drew and sat down next to him, looking around in astonishment.

They were miles above the Earth's surface, yet it all seemed so . . . normal. He should be freezing, yet his light jacket was more than enough to keep him warm. The slight breeze, the warm sun— it was eerie.

Ryan looked at Drew, hoping the man would be able to explain everything.

"I think you're the first person to actually wait until we sat down before asking any questions," Drew said, seemingly impressed.

"Well, I'm not quite sure where to begin."

"That's okay," Drew said dismissively. "I can start if you'd like." After waiting for Ryan to nod, he continued: "This is Atlantis. Or more accurately, the Northeast American City of Atlantis. There are actually twenty-five cities around the world that make up Atlantis as a whole. Like I told you yesterday, we're an organization that recruits individuals who we believe have the potential to make a positive difference in the world and apply their talents in different fields of interest. Specifically, we tend to focus on technological and military advancements. Having cities dispersed across the globe allows us to tailor our research to an area's specific needs and accommodate different languages and cultures."

Drew finished and remained quiet, graciously waiting for the next question.

"We—this pl—how are we floating in the middle of the air?" Ryan stammered.

"Quick version? We developed static propulsion a long time ago. We were trying to make a hover board, ended up making a flying city. It happens. Anyway, we use a mix of solar and thermal power to generate electricity for the entire city. That's also what we use to power the propulsion engines, which are organized in a ring along the underside of the city and provide constant propulsion. Each one is equipped with a sensor to balance the weight distribution of the city and make sure we stay level."

"Has a city ever fallen?" Ryan asked as he ran his hand through the grass.

"Never. Engines are inspected daily, and we have a near-constant supply of energy. All the sidewalks and buildings have solar capabilities, and the turf we're sitting on can capture thermal energy from the sun and even the excess heat from the engines. We also have massive batteries that store excess charge. You'll learn more about it if you accept the position here."

Ryan nodded. It was all a little fantastical, but considering they were sitting in the sky, he could hardly argue the point.

Around them, people were wandering along the winding paths through the park, enjoying the nice day. Two runners jogged by them, neither seeming unusually out of breath.

"How is there enough oxygen up here for us to function?" Ryan asked. "Shouldn't we all be gasping for air? And why aren't we freezing?"

"Ah, that one's a little more complicated," Drew said. "We were able to manufacture a pseudoatmosphere around the city using charge particles. Like the Earth's atmosphere, it keeps the oxygen here concentrated. It also produces a greenhouse effect that helps us stay warm. Plus, the buildings are strategically designed and positioned to act as windbreaks."

For the first time since they had sat down, Ryan took a good look at the city beyond the park. Behind them, he saw the awning over the underground stairs from which they had just emerged. Through the trees, he could see a variety of marble buildings, all in shades of dark green, blue, and gray. Each one was a beautifully crafted blend of modern and classical architecture, adorned with high domes and majestic columns. But Ryan noticed that, unlike the tall buildings of downtown Boston, none of the buildings on Atlantis stood more than two or three stories high.

Despite its relatively short structures, however, the city was clearly quite large, which led to another, more obvious question. "So, there are twenty-four other cities scattered across the world, right?" Ryan asked.

"Yep."

"How come I've never heard of a single flying city? How can you hide twenty-five cities around the globe?"

"Well, it helps that we're well above the clouds and away from large, populated areas," Drew began. "Plus, we use a system of small screens along the underside of the city that mimic the color of the sky. It's almost like a mirage, so people on the Surface don't notice us. We also use deterring radar and strategically placed agents in the FAA to avoid being compromised by any flights. It took a while to set up, but nowadays it's a well-oiled system. We even have people monitoring and altering any satellite images that may catch one of our cities. We rarely have any problems."

"Rarely?"

"Nothing's perfect," Drew said with a shrug.

Ryan was impressed. The place was simply amazing.

"So . . . this is Atlantis? Like, *the* Atlantis?" Ryan asked. Drew nodded. "It never sank?"

"Actually, it did sink," Drew said. "You see, four thousand years ago, Atlantis was a man-made island utopia in the middle of the Mediterranean Sea. It was a place where people of all cultures lived harmoniously, where the world's greatest minds would gather to work without distraction to advance technology, philosophy, government policies, and even moral codes. Since its inception, Atlantis has always been about helping others and improving society.

"As Atlantis grew, we started using different techniques to help people," Drew continued. "While some of its citizens continued to work on new innovations, others were researching different strategies that included some . . . unorthodox techniques."

"Like what?" Ryan asked. He had a feeling they were converging on an important topic.

A burst of laughter caught his attention. He looked over to see a group of people his own age playing in a glistening ornate fountain about thirty yards away. It occurred to him that these were probably some of the world's greatest minds, shrieking and splashing each other in the shallow pool.

"Like war," Drew said simply. "Nothing serious, just a skirmish," he added quickly at Ryan's horrified look. "It was a long time ago. We don't engage with nations on the Surface these days. We still have a military and use it like any other country, but we no longer use our military to 'help' any society. Although, the results were hard to argue with."

"What results?"

"It's actually in the only documented account of Atlantis," Drew explained, leaning back against a tree. "Around 350 BCE, Plato wrote about how Atlantis attacked Athens and how Athens successfully repelled the naval attack. Granted, there are some in-accuracies; but the battle was twelve hundred years before his time, and overall, he did a pretty good job."

"What did he get wrong?" Ryan asked.

"Well, for one, we didn't start the war. It was Athens's own fault," Drew said. "Athens liked to think of itself as the center of the world, especially when it came to knowledge and learning. And they got upset whenever Atlantis tried to recruit their citizens. For a while, we even stopped reaching out to people in Athens, to try to appease the city; but then they decided they didn't like the fact that other great minds from around the world would rather study in Atlantis over Athens. So they started to raid our ships and take our scholars captive. They were acting like pirates, and then of course they'd get mad when we defended our ships and won. So, in the end, they declared war against Atlantis to save face.

"Trouble is, their military at the time was awful. This was well before they became a major city-state. They were so focused on cultivating their philosophical schools that their military suffered, whereas even though Atlantis didn't have a really large army at the time, our navy was unbeatable. It came with the territory of being a man-made island. Athens would never admit it—they were way too proud—but they essentially started a war they couldn't win. So, before they had the chance to build up their military, we attacked."

"And . . . you were defeated?" So far, Ryan was not overly impressed with this military.

"No, it was a strategic retreat. No, seriously!" Drew added at Ryan's skeptical look. "We retreated of our own accord. The sole purpose of the attack was to put pressure on Athens, to make them call off their hopeless war. Don't forget, some people on Atlantis were from Athens. We didn't want to destroy the city; we just wanted them to leave us alone. And in the end, the attack actually helped Athens."

"How on earth did attacking the city help them?" Ryan asked, registering the irony of using the phrase "on earth" while sitting on a floating city.

"Think back to even modern history. Look at Germany after World War I and the United States right after the Great Depression. Both economies flourished at the start of World War II. Depressed economies tend to soar under the threat of war due to a boom in industry."

"Germany's economy was crushed after World War I, and the Confederacy was decimated after the Civil War," Ryan countered.

"True; but remember, this was only a small skirmish. Athens quickly made peace after the naval battle in order to avoid a full-blown war," Drew said with a small smile. "We wanted to light a fire under Athens—and it worked! They called off the war, and emerged stronger for it. Studies show that students perform best on tests when under moderate pressure—not too much and not too little—and the same thing happened to Athens. After the battle, they spent a lot of resources improving their navy, and because of this, they were able to engage in more overseas trade. Within a decade or so, they were a major economic hub. And then, before too long, they became the powerful city-state."

"And since then . . . if Atlantis felt like a city needed help . . . you all would attack them?" Ryan started.

"Not necessarily," Drew said quickly. "It's true, we tried it a few times here and there, and unfortunately, it worked. But that was thousands of years ago. We've evolved a lot since we first attacked Athens, and our methods have evolved too. At the end of the day, we were still killing people, and that never sat right with us. So we changed tactics. We haven't attacked anyone to 'help them' in a long time. But the war with Athens is still a significant moment in Atlantean history. It was the first time we used military forces, and we've maintained a military ever since."

Ryan nodded. "Still, keeping a military has to take up a lot of resources that could be used to help others, right?" Ryan winced, hoping he wasn't sounding too accusatory toward the people who were offering him a job.

"Yes and no," Drew said. Ryan was relieved to see that he didn't look the least bit offended. In fact, he acted as if he had to answer these questions all the time. "A lot of amazing technologies come from military research. Most of our advances in medicine were originally procedures we developed to heal our soldiers efficiently. Even personalized computers came from the military! Our units couldn't carry huge processors into combat, so we made a compact version early on. We still use a similar design today."

"Makes sense. But why do you still have a military? You said you don't use it to spur societies on anymore, so why not disband it altogether if there's no more war?"

Drew didn't answer right away. In fact, he looked slightly uncomfortable. "This . . . this isn't something we normally discuss at this point. We normally wait until initiation starts. . . ." Drew's voice trailed off. He paused for a few seconds, looked at Ryan, and finally shrugged before asking, "I assume you've heard of the Trojan War?"

Ryan was taken aback. "From *The Iliad?*" he said.

"Yes, but the history . . . differs somewhat from Homer's account," Drew said. He hesitated again. "Around 1190 BCE, there was a huge war between Greece and Troy. Most of the Atlantean troops sided with the Greeks, and the war ended up showcasing some new Atlantean technology, like a primitive flamethrower, ballistae, and even basic grenades. Some of the weapons were so advanced that some people actually thought the Atlanteans were their ancient gods. In retrospect, that ego boost was the worst thing that could have happened to us. You see, some of the Atlanteans started acting like they *were* gods, and they developed their own ideas about how Atlantis should operate. There was this one guy, Aeneas, who really thought we were going about things the wrong way.

"Once the Greeks won the Trojan War, there was some civil unrest within Atlantis," Drew continued. "Aeneas, who was one of the few Atlanteans who favored Troy and their more . . . domineering philosophies, believed it was time for Atlantis to be more involved in the wider world. Until then, Atlantis had been working as an independent society, and was growing into a powerful source of ingenuity. But Aeneas said we needed to be doing more."

"I thought you *were* helping people," Ryan said.

"We were!" Drew exclaimed. "People who studied in Atlantis often returned to their home countries with their newfound knowledge, and used all they'd learned to promote learning, improve infrastructure, and generally help those in need. But that wasn't enough for Aeneas. After Atlanteans were called gods, Aeneas believed Atlantis had a calling, a duty even, to govern other societies, ruling over the people. He argued that we represented the best and brightest of the known world, studying math, science, and philosophy. Who better to be in charge, he would ask. Aeneas claimed that we could prevent wars and drive out the corruption that naturally comes with the democratic society Greece had adopted.

"Of course, we tried to fight back. Atlanteans argued that it wasn't our place to control others. That wasn't why Atlantis had been founded. We were meant to help others—but only to guide them when asked. Not to be their leaders." Drew paused for a second before continuing.

"The debate lasted for centuries. The more he preached, the more supporters Aeneas gained, and his descendants continued to spread his ideology long after he passed. They legitimately believed they were better than everyone else, and that it was their duty to rule others. So, after arguing with the Atlantean elders for four hundred years, they left, along with all of their followers, and traveled for a while before finally settling in central Italy."

"Wait . . . they founded Rome?" Ryan asked.

"In a way, yes," Drew said. "There were others already in the area. The Etruscan people already had a strong hold in western Italy. The deserters, who started to call themselves the Order, joined a southern Etruscan settlement. They never attacked the Etruscans—they didn't need to. Instead, the Order came pleading asylum from Atlantis and gained the Etruscans' sympathy, and even more followers. By the time the Etruscans started expanding south, thousands of people, both former Atlanteans and Etruscans, were loyal to the Order. In the end, they essentially led the Etruscan expansion south, until ranking members of the Order started families on the Palatine Hill.

"There, Aeneas' great-great—however many 'greats'—grandson Romulus became the first King of Rome. The Order was smart, though. Atlantis had an eye on them at this point, so after Romulus died, they stuck to the shadows, mostly serving as advisors in the Roman Kingdom and, later, the Republic. They stayed out of the public eye and kept their numbers small to avoid backlash, but the Order was always in some ruler's ear, guiding him toward making the decisions they wanted. The Order continued to spread Aeneas' ideals as they gained power. They wanted a more direct say in the lives of individual citizens. While it would take years until Rome was officially recognized in Greece, Atlantis always knew about the city, and was constantly worried about what the Order would do."

Ryan sat, staring at Drew with fascination. He couldn't believe how much Atlantis was intertwined with ancient history as he knew it—and yet, in a weird way that could only be explained by a city floating in midair, he had no doubt that it was all true. He looked around again and realized that all the roofs and domes of the Grecian architecture surrounding them seemed to be made of colored solar panels. The glimmering of the panels, with their strange mix of blues and whites, almost gave the structures the appearance of being underwater.

"But . . . how did Atlantis sink?" Ryan asked. He could barely believe he was seriously having this conversation.

"Well, as you can imagine, there was a ton of animosity between Atlantis and the Order," said Drew. "With Atlantis working tightly with the Greek city-states and the Order well established in Rome, they argued and fought just as often as the two civilizations that hosted them did. Armed conflicts were common, but eventually it turned really ugly. The Order was small, but it grew in power as Rome did. It took a while, but eventually the Order realized that they had the numbers and the resources to finally finish off Atlantis, allowing the Order to take full control of the Mediterranean and beyond without any opposition.

"It was extremely well planned," Drew admitted. "They chose a night when most of Atlantis would be attending an open-forum debate at the city's center, and came right as the sun was setting.

While everyone was at the debate, their small strike force infiltrated the city and quietly killed the few guards stationed at the city's arsenal. Then they set off the Atlanteans' own explosives and flamethrowers at key points throughout the entire city. You have to remember that at that time, Atlantis was a man-made city in the middle of the sea. Its entire foundation was made of wood. The destruction took only a few minutes. What didn't burn up just broke apart and sank. The floor was gone. People burned to death, were crushed under falling buildings, or drowned amid the explosions. Many who tried to escape were slaughtered by the Order. Although the Order lost a few of their own, Atlantis was utterly destroyed." Drew spoke so matter-of-factly. He didn't sound bitter at all.

The pair sat in silence after Drew finished, while Ryan tried to absorb all that he'd been told.

"So if Atlantis really was destroyed, then how . . . ?" Ryan asked, trailing off.

"The city was gone, but some of us still survived," Drew explained. "A bunch of survivors washed up on a few small islands not too far from the city. They watched the whole thing—their life's work—sink. But the Elder survived, and they started over. They fled north to get away from the Order, and finally found sanctuary by the North Sea. At the time, that area was generally unexplored by the Greeks and the Romans, and hostile Germanic tribes acted as a barrier between the survivors and the Order in Rome.

"The descendants of Atlantis stayed up north for centuries. We slowly grew, and eventually became a distinct ethnic group. Even today, you'll notice a lot of native Atlanteans with blond hair and green eyes."

"Like you," Ryan said. Drew nodded.

"You can actually trace my family back to the sinking. Around here, a lot of the native Atlanteans with similar backgrounds have the same features, but that's not true everywhere. Since we expanded to recruit all over the world, many Atlanteans are starting to look more and more like their counterparts on the Surface."

"So there's no way to tell if someone is a native Atlantean?" Ryan asked. "You know, besides them actually having a clue what's going on around here?"

"There is one way," Drew said, holding up his hand. At first, Ryan was unsure what he was supposed to see, but once he noticed it, he couldn't stop staring: Drew's hand was indeed sporting the strange discoloration Ryan had noticed at the café. Now that he could actually make it out, Ryan saw that there were diamond-shaped patches of white on every one of Drew's nail beds.

"Do you have that on your toes, too?" Ryan asked, before he could stop himself. He was relieved when Drew started laughing.

"You know what?" Drew began through his laughter. "No one has ever asked me that. Yeah, my toes have them too. We're not quite sure how or when it happened—could've been an experiment or just a random mutation—but at some point, the Atlantean people developed this diamond pattern on their nails. It's a pretty recessive gene, though. Sort of like red hair—you need to get it from both parents for it to manifest, and even then, it doesn't always show up. Not that it really matters, but if you ever want to know for sure whether someone is a native Atlantean, look at their nails."

It took Ryan a few seconds to realize he was staring at Drew's hands. He quickly looked away and asked, "So are we still there? In the North Sea?"

Drew raised an eyebrow at the word "we," but didn't comment.

"No," he responded. "There's a long, complicated history involved, but we left the North Sea after a while."

"What about the Order? Are they still around?"

"They are, but they're no longer in Rome. Like us—" Ryan registered the use of the word "us," but did not comment. "—their power has risen and fallen throughout the years. They're still trying to undermine us constantly, and we're trying to do the same to them. It's a constant back-and-forth. Most of the time it's pretty minor stuff, but sometimes it can get . . . deadly."

"The Order . . . were they the ones who hired those thugs to kill me the other night?" Ryan asked slowly as he started putting the pieces together. Then something else occurred to him. "Did they kill Jack?"

Drew sighed.

"We believe so," Drew said. "Whether you knew it or not, you and your research were a threat to them. One they couldn't risk. So was Jack. He risked his life trying to gain intel on the Order for us in Canada. Unfortunately, they found out and staged a car accident to make it look like a drunk driver hit him. I met Jack once. He seemed like a great guy. I'm really sorry he's not here to see you join Atlantis."

Ryan stayed silent. What was there to say? He could tell Drew's sentiment was sincere, and he appreciated it. Part of him wanted to know more about how researching a cure for cancer could be a threat to anyone, but he definitely wanted to get off the subject of him and Jack.

"Has there ever been a full-on war between Atlantis and the Order?" Ryan asked.

"Unfortunately, yes," Drew said. "There have actually been multiple wars. The most significant one occurred during the Third Reich."

Ryan's eyes widened in surprise. Not because there had been a war—he should have figured there would be some tension lingering between the two organizations, considering Atlantis had a standing military. But . . .

"Hitler was part of the Order?"

"No, no. He was just a typical man. Well, maybe not typical; but he wasn't in the Order. There *were* one or two high-ranking officials in the Nazi party who were members of the Order—but the same has gone for almost every world government for the past century. At the end of the day, the Third Reich was formed by nothing more than a powerful group of individuals with deep-seated xenophobia. But the Order *was* heavily involved in a few influential groups that supported the Nazi party. That's how they prefer to operate. Advisory positions, indirect influence—funneling money into small cells they can form and dissolve at a moment's notice. Almost everything they do is from the shadows, and that's exactly how they supported the Third Reich. The details aren't really important. The point is, things got bad enough that we felt the need to intervene. At the time, we still had a foothold in England, especially since Churchill was a citizen of Atlantis."

Ryan nodded, as if a famous historical figure being part of a secret organization was trivial. "Are most Atlantean wars mirrored on the surface?"

"Only some of them. Most often with civil wars, actually."

"Really?" Ryan was surprised that Atlantis would involve itself in a single country's internal matters.

"Well, it depends on why the war was star—"

"What about the American Civil War?" Ryan interrupted. He wasn't trying to be rude, but the Civil War had always been fascinating to him.

"Yes and no," Drew said, seeming completely undisturbed by the interruption. If anything, he looked mildly amused. "Atlantis and the Order both agreed that slavery was horrific and completely wrong. Nobody was arguing that point. Instead, while the United States and the Confederacy were fighting about slavery, the conflict rekindled the major debate between Atlantis and the Order: freedom versus control. The Order's agenda was more in line with that of the controlling, wealthy plantation owners in the South, who promoted an almost feudal economic system based on slavery. We, on the other hand, argued for freedom against an overbearing, wealthy ruling class like the one that the Order supported in the South. And a fight ensued. It wasn't a full-blown war like the one between the Union and the Confederacy, but there were some similarities. Neither Atlantis nor the Order declared any major alliance with either side. Both of us wanted to stay under the radar."

"So, was there ever a battle?"

"Not really," Drew said. "We used basic blockade techniques to essentially starve the Order out of the United States."

"So no troops were deployed?"

"Nope. We avoid that whenever possible."

Drew looked down at a wide black band that spanned half his forearm, and tapped the device a few times. His eyes widened in surprise. "We should probably get moving," he said to Ryan as he stood up. "Normally we would have a little more time for Q and A, but we're cutting it a little close for comfort—I prefer to be early. Come on; we can walk and talk."

Not quite sure where they were headed, Ryan slowly got to his feet and brushed off his pants. Together, they set off down a sidewalk of solar panels, heading deeper into the park. As they walked together, Ryan kept expecting to feel the ground beneath him tilt or shake, but it was just like walking in downtown Boston—if significantly cleaner. Drew even allowed Ryan to indulge himself jumping up and down a few times, just to be completely sure that the ground was stable.

"When did Atlantis move to the sky?" Ryan asked as they

resumed walking. "And what's going on with the Order now?"

"It all started changing around 1720. We needed a safe place where the Order would have trouble finding us. But it took a good sixty years or so before we were permanently airborne, and we stayed near the Surface for a while, until we worked out most of the, uh . . . kinks."

"Kinks?"

"Well, the first prototype we put in the sky was located much farther out in the Atlantic Ocean, for safety reasons. It experienced some . . . turbulence, and a couple of sudden drops. But we worked out those issues in the end."

One thing Drew said stuck out to Ryan in particular. "So, are we in hiding from the Order then?"

"Sort of," Drew responded. "We're fairly certain they have a good idea where our cities are located at this point, but we're not going to make it too easy for them. That's only part of the reason we're up here. Being in the sky allows us to act as an independent, international organization. We get to avoid Surface politics and offer aid to those who really need it without worrying about red tape. It even minimizes corruption. The fewer people who know of our existence, the more people we can help.

"As for the Order, they did the exact opposite of us. They went underground," Drew added at Ryan's puzzled look. "They have major bunkers all over the world. We have a good idea where some of them are, but others are still pretty well hidden."

The two of them continued making their way through the park. They passed several grassy sporting fields as they followed the solar pathway. Some contained familiar soccer nets or other equipment that Ryan recognized immediately, but others were completely foreign. Ryan could not help but stare at one pitch that housed two large funnels at either end until he was practically walking backward. Despite his curiosity about the odd field, he had a more pressing question on his mind.

"So with Atlantis hidden in the air and the Order below, has either society ever been discovered by . . . well, anyone else?" Ryan asked. "I know Atlantis takes secrecy seriously, but it seems impossible that no one has ever noticed it. Especially if there have been wars."

"There have been some sightings," Drew admitted, "but nothing we haven't been able to take care of."

"'Take care of'?" Ryan echoed nervously, thinking of the Order taking out a hit on him.

"Not like that," Drew laughed. "We either induct those who spot us into Atlantis, or arrange to have their accounts dismissed as UFO sightings. Although, some people tend to come up with more mythological explanations. Those are always pretty entertaining."

"How so?"

"Well, there's a history of people mistaking our troops for angels, and the Order for demons."

Ryan laughed. "Why's that?"

"Mostly because of our wings," Drew said simply.

Wings? thought Ryan.

"And with Atlantis' use of light technology and the Order's utilization of fission, well, you can see how angels and demons would seem like a plausible explanation to someone not in the know," Drew continued. He chuckled. "Plus the Demons shooting directly out of the ground with their jetpacks certainly encouraged the analogy."

Ryan stopped and stared at Drew. A lot of what the other man had just said had gone straight over his head.

"It'll all make sense later," Drew promised. Ryan decided to let it go for the time being. "Just know for now that if you hear someone talk about Demons, they're referring to the Order."

"I take it Atlantis tries to keep those sightings quiet?"

"We would," Drew began with a mischievous smile, "but we tend to like the angel and demon comparisons." He laughed. "How can you pass up being called an angel?"

Ryan laughed with him. "It must be weird staying separate from the world below," he said.

"It's actually not too bad. We've developed our own culture here, like any other city, and we love it. But we still interact with the Surface. There are scouters like me all over the world who go down looking for new initiates. Some of our citizens even choose to go back and live on the Surface after a while."

"Like Newton?" Ryan asked, suddenly realizing that Drew had actually answered his question honestly back on the boat.

"Exactly. It's tricky, though. People who return to the Surface need to be good actors. They have to explain where they've been for years and years, and abandon the advanced technology they've grown accustomed to on Atlantis. We typically try to introduce new concepts and technological advances gradually, in academia, before announcing them to the public. Otherwise people would be insanely suspicious. Take gravity, for example! The whole apple falling from the tree thing was Newton's not-so-subtle way of introducing the concept to modern science."

"I don't understand how Atlantis could be so much more advanced than any other country, though," Ryan said.

"We devote nearly all of our resources to technological development. We may have a military, but even they are engaged in research during peacetime. Not only that, but our government is all but superfluous. Crime, unemployment, resource allocation—none of these are issues on Atlantis. All citizens vote on social and ethical matters. And unlike the Order, we aren't worried about trying to control people on the Surface. When you don't have to govern people constantly, it frees up a lot of resources for advancement."

They continued along the serpentine path as it led them to the edge of the park. As they passed another gleaming entrance to the monorail system below them, they stepped into the cool shade of a stand of trees. Ryan vaguely wondered whether the nearby entrance connected to another landing bay.

"Being here isn't a lifelong commitment, then? I mean, Newton returned to Earth," Ryan said, turning back to Drew.

"Not at all! Eventually, most people return to the Surface when they retire, but some choose to live out their whole lives in Atlantis. I know I will."

Ryan suddenly remembered one of the many odd points in their conversation. "You said you need to put in at least twenty-five years of active service before working as a scouter, right?" he asked.

"Correct."

"How long have you been scouting?"

"Since 1995," Drew said. "I actually started scouting right after finishing my twenty-five years, which is pretty unusual. Most people need to complete a couple more years of service before they become a scouter."

"After twenty-five years of being on Atlantis? You were born here, right?"

"I was, but it's actually twenty-five years after I became a full citizen at twenty-four years old."

Ryan stopped walking and stared at Drew. If what he was saying was true, he would have to be over seventy years old.

"I was born in 1945," Drew said, as if reading Ryan's thoughts.

"No you weren't," Ryan said.

"Yep."

"There's no way!"

"Promise!"

"You don't look a day over thirty!"

"Well, that makes sense," Drew said.

"No, it d—what?" Ryan asked weakly.

"Come on," Drew said bracingly, gently prodding Ryan to get him walking again. "I'll explain, but we should keep moving."

Ryan fell in step beside him as Drew said, "Recently, we figured out a way to stop the aging process. You've heard about telomeres, right? The cap at the end of chromosomes?" Ryan nodded. "Well, it's an oversimplification, but we basically figured out over a century ago that telomeres are responsible for aging. The details are a little technical. You'll go over them in class."

Class?

"The whole process isn't perfect, though. If you try to stop a seventy-year-old from aging further, it's less effective. Only delays the inevitable. But for someone in the prime of their physical development, it virtually stops them from aging, so we usually start the process around twenty-eight years. Maximizes physical and mental maturity."

"How long have you been able to stop people from aging?"

"We did some test runs in the late 1800s that successfully slowed aging, but never stopped it. We really figured it all out in the 1910s and '20s. We still have some Atlanteans kicking around who were born in the 1840s. They look like they're in their late sixties."

Before Ryan could think any further about the implications of eternal youth, he and Drew finally reached the end of the walkway. The path had led them to a magnificent cobblestone plaza with a beautiful decorative fountain of white marble at its center, topped with a fierce angel that reminded Ryan of Renaissance paintings of the archangel Michael. At the end of the plaza opposite them was a massive ornate building that practically demanded attention. Its domed roof was held aloft by a double row of intricate columns, evenly spaced on either side of an enormous set of double doors that must have weighed a few hundred pounds each. Smaller, simpler buildings flanked the two adjacent sides of the plaza, with the last remaining side opening into the park behind them. Ryan supposed that the smaller buildings were beautiful as well, but they paled in comparison to the marble behemoth looming over them.

Drew led Ryan toward the water feature, and the two of them sat down on one of the steps leading up to its small pool.

"Are you okay?" Drew asked. "You're awfully quiet."

Ryan nodded. "Sorry. It's just the whole not-aging thing is . . . weird," he finished lamely.

"Weirder than being in an ancient city miles above the Atlantic Ocean?" Drew asked, raising an eyebrow. Ryan chuckled.

"Fair point," he said. "I guess I'm not really handling all this very well."

"You're doing fine. Better than most, in fact," Drew said encouragingly. "Most people have trouble accepting any of this. It normally involves a lot more consoling."

Ryan wasn't sure if Drew was just saying this to make him feel better, but he appreciated it nonetheless.

The sound of laughter pulled Ryan's attention away from their conversation, as the plaza slowly started to fill with people. Ryan smiled as a family with two boys and a little girl, all with white-blond hair, passed him and Drew on their way up the steps, enjoying the pleasant day. The two brothers started wrestling dangerously close to the fountain's edge, while their little sister egged them on. The parents sprang forward as the two kids rolled toward the water, and quickly snatched them away from the edge before they could fall in. As soon as they were released, the two boys immediately resumed play-fighting, despite their parents' warnings.

As Ryan watched, one of the brothers charged the other, and Ryan had a sudden flashback to the fight in the alley. He turned away from the children and looked at Drew.

"I have another question . . . one that I may regret," Ryan started.

Drew followed his line of sight and nodded, as if he'd been expecting this.

"This is about the other night, I take it?" he asked.

Ryan nodded, still watching the kids, as the parents resigned themselves to guarding the edge of the fountain.

"The other night," Ryan began, "I watched you . . . or, I thought I saw you do something impossible—but then again, a few hours ago, a flying city was also impossible. Maybe it was just the adrenaline, but it kind of looked like you pushed those men without . . . actually touching them." Ryan's voice trailed off shyly. It seemed ridiculous to admit it out loud. He looked up at Drew, unsure how the other man would respond.

To his surprise, Drew smiled at him, then reached out toward the fountain and made a curling motion with his fingers. Immediately, a sphere of water no bigger than a tennis ball rose from the pooling water and hovered just over Drew's outstretched hand.

"It wasn't adrenaline," Drew said. He continued to undulate his fingers in small movements, up and down, and the ball of water spun in wobbly somersaults. Finally, he flicked his fingers, and the water shot back into the fountain with a splash. Ryan stared blankly at the rippling surface.

"How . . ."

"It's hard to explain," said Drew. "Basically, we found a way to stimulate brain waves to allow us to manipulate matter. I wish I could do the theory justice; I really do," he added, checking the band on his wrist again, "but we're running short on time. You'll learn all about it during the initiation, and we have a couple other things we need to discuss. See the huge building on the other side of the fountain? We call it the Temple. It's the center of everything that happens here. The initiation will begin in a couple of minutes, and I need to make sure you're completely on board before we head in."

Ryan looked at the ornate domed building that, despite being only a few stories high, dwarfed everything around them. People were starting to make their way toward it from across the plaza, and Ryan saw that some of them—particularly those dressed in crisp, blindingly white shirts—appeared to be at ease, laughing and joking with friends. Others were more like Ryan, dressed in casual wear, craning their necks and gazing nervously up at the Temple as they passed through the heavy doors. Ryan sympathized—he felt as anxious as they looked.

Drew was obviously asking for some type of commitment. Ryan took a deep breath, feeling the air fill his lungs. He was being asked to leave his life behind. To start over completely. He found it overwhelming, nerve-wracking—but also exhilarating. Atlantis was incredible. He had only been in the city for an hour, but Ryan knew he could never go back to Boston after seeing this place.

"I am," he finally said with a small smile, which Drew returned.

"Awesome," Drew said. "Before we head in, there's one thing I need to make sure you understand."

"Like, a catch?"

"No, not a catch," Drew said. "But it's something we need to be clear about. Your initiation will be kind of a trial run. Think of it like a tryout. We use this time to evaluate our initiates, and their performance during initiation helps us decide which role in Atlantis would best suit them. At the end of your initiation, you'll be assigned to one of two groups."

"What if neither group wants a specific initiate?" Ryan interrupted, suddenly nervous.

"That would never happen," Drew reassured him.

"Hey, Drew! Y'all coming?" called a voice.

Ryan and Drew turned and saw two men walking across the plaza toward the Temple. Both looked to be from the Surface, with their dark hair and street clothes. One of them seemed around Drew's age, though Ryan quickly reminded himself this was a meaningless observation on Atlantis. The other seemed slightly younger, about Ryan's own age, and had the distinct expression of someone who was trying to look calm. The facade would have been convincing, had he not been rapidly tapping his fingers against his jeans. Ryan suspected that this man was also seeing Atlantis for the first time.

"Yep! See you in bit, Colt," Drew called back, before turning back to Ryan. "Anyway, what was I saying? Right—so you'll be assigned to one of two sects: Technology or Military."

"I could be drafted?" Ryan said, shocked.

"No, no, not a draft," Drew said quickly. "But you may not be devoting one hundred percent of your time to technological development. Military is obviously important during wartime, but they're still very busy in times of peace. Right now, for instance, we have some soldiers scouting, addressing security breaches, acting as diplomats, and working on long-term strategies against the Order; but most of our troops are currently working alongside Tech to create and test new innovations. In times of peace, soldiers normally spend two-and-a-half days per week on fitness and maneuvering exercises, and two days working with one of the Tech departments or other nonmilitary positions, depending on their individual strengths. You may not develop a true specialty like those in Tech—or at least, not in the same way—but you would still get to work on new developments that could really do a lot of good!"

Ryan looked at Drew skeptically. "Are there any real benefits to being Military?" he asked. He'd never considered himself a soldier.

"Absolutely," Drew said, looking slightly relieved that Ryan hadn't left on the spot. "It's less monotonous than working in a lab, and you get a lot more variety in your opportunities outside of your sect. You get to spend more time outside. And there's generally less stress—in peacetime, at least. Soldiers get to let off steam through physical activity. There's also flying."

"Flying?"

Drew waved his hand, dismissing the question. "It's nothing like boot camp on the Surface. Our leaders are professional, and they demand a high standard, but they're never cruel or harsh. Look," he said in a lower voice, "you see that family over there? With the wrestling kids? Both of the parents are Military. Colt? The guy who said 'Hi' just a second ago? He used to be Military, and now he's a scouter, like me."

"Were you Military?" Ryan asked hopefully. Drew smiled.

"No, I was Tech. And I loved it. But I do know that Jack was a soldier for our Californian city before he started working with Intel, and he loved being there too," he said bracingly. "But between you and me, I think you'll be Tech too. I've seen your work in the genetics lab—you'll be fine."

Ryan nodded. For some reason, he had no doubt that Drew was being honest. Drew really believed he would be Tech. Still, the threat of being in a military was daunting.

"If . . . I am chosen for Military," Ryan started slowly, "am I obligated to stay?"

"Not at all!" Drew said quickly. "You can leave Atlantis anytime you want. If you want to stay here though, you'd be expected to put in twelve and a half years as a soldier. After that, you can transition to Tech if you want, and you'd have already fulfilled half the required time to be a scouter. But you'd be surprised how many people choose to stay Military forever. It's a good life, and there are a lot of opportunities for advancement."

Ryan stared at Drew for a minute, trying to process everything he'd been told.

"There's no way to know which group I'll be in?" he finally asked.

"Sorry, no. Both sects have some upsides and downsides. Some people get really freaked out by the prospect of being Military, but we haven't been at war since World War II. I know it's a lot to take in, Ryan. I just want to make sure you know exactly what you're signing up for. No surprises. We're not trying to trick you. But like I said," Drew lowered his voice again, "I'm confident you'll be Tech. After scouting for a while, you can kinda tell who's going to end up where."

For a long moment, neither of them spoke.

"Can I ask one other thing?" Ryan asked.

Drew nodded with a smile.

"Is it worth it?"

Drew smiled even wider.

"Ryan, I have never, *never* met anyone who hasn't fallen in love with Atlantis, regardless of which sect they end up in. Every single person here would say the same thing. This is our home. Well," Drew added in an undertone after thinking for a second, "okay, there was this one guy in Tech. . . but there were some underlying issues there anyway. Definitely an outlier. Not the point!" His voice picked up again. "Atlantis has persisted for thousands of years, and it's full of Atlanteans who proudly call it their home."

Ryan raised an eyebrow.

"Very inspirational," he said, fighting back a laugh at the speech's tacky ending. Fortunately, Drew laughed.

"Sorry. Like I said yesterday, I may be a scouter, but I'm also in sales. What do you say?"

Ryan didn't have to think for very long. "Let's do it," he said.

Drew smiled and leapt to his feet, holding out his hand to help Ryan up. Then he led Ryan across the plaza and into the shadow of the Temple's massive domed roof. Above the huge doors was a short phrase engraved in what looked like ancient Greek. Ryan was about to ask Drew for a translation, but before he could, Drew started talking rapidly.

"We only have a couple of minutes, so I'm gonna make this quick. In just a bit, you and the rest of the initiates will hear some boring speeches about Atlantis—most of it will be stuff I've already told you. Then they'll split you up into groups. From there, your initiation leader will take over, your initiation will start, and then you'll be on your way to becoming a functioning citizen of Atlantis. You're going to do great. No doubt in my mind. Ready?"

It took Ryan a few seconds to realize Drew had asked him a question. He found the Temple much more daunting while standing before its doors. He looked at Drew and tried to say "Yes," but only succeeded in making an odd, high-pitched squawk.

Drew looked at Ryan, clearly unsure how to interpret the noise. Ryan cleared his throat and nodded.

"Then let's go!" Drew said, and he gently pushed Ryan through the doorway and into the Temple.

CHAPTER FIVE
THE ELDER

T he cool air inside the Temple hit Ryan as his eyes slowly adjusted to the dark interior. He was standing in the vestibule of what appeared to be an odd mix between a theater and a basilica. Positioned along the edges of the curved walls was a half-ring of elevated seats, all facing a raised platform that was nestled in its own alcove at the far end of the Temple. In the center of the smoothly descending floor was a flood of yet more seats, most of them full, also facing the stage. The indoor amphitheater was constructed from pale blue marble with large columns rising to the ceiling. Looking around, Ryan saw light filtering through long, thin windows, as well as from a large oculus at the pinnacle of the domed roof.

"Go ahead and take a seat with the others in the center," Drew whispered to Ryan. "I have to go sit with the other scouters. I'll try to check in regularly. Good luck! You'll do great."

Without waiting for a response, Drew climbed up the ring of seats on the left, walked all the way around to a group of about fifteen people waiting beside the stage, and sat down next to Colt, whose feet were propped up against the backs of the seats in the row in front of him.

Feeling suddenly naked, Ryan made his way down the nearest rows, looking for an open seat. Most of the people around him appeared to be around his age, in their early and mid-twenties. Ryan noticed that about a third of the assembled group was dressed similarly, in navy pants and bright white collared shirts that seemed to emit a faint, nearly imperceptible glow. On closer inspection, Ryan saw that a soft pattern that resembled chain mail was stenciled onto the fabric, giving it a shimmering effect. Were these people native Atlanteans? Some of them had pale hair and features similar to Drew's, but others were dark-haired like Ryan, and several dozen had darker complexions that suggested they could be from anywhere in the world. Maybe they were from other cities. If so, Ryan was amazed there weren't more of them. He wondered if the others had all come from the Surface. Certainly, many more of the people in street clothes were staring nervously around the Temple or apprehensively at the stage in front of them.

Most of the people were sitting down already. Suddenly feeling self-conscious, Ryan quickly took a seat in the row nearest to him, just a few rows from the back.

"Please tell me I'm not the only one who thinks this is insane," came a voice to his left.

Ryan turned and saw a familiar guy leaning over to talk to him from a few chairs down the mostly empty row. Given his black hair, brown eyes, and expression of awe, Ryan guessed that he too was from the Surface.

"I'm not quite sure what's happening either," Ryan responded, grateful to have someone else to talk with.

"Good, it's not just me. I'm Zach Lauder," said the man, holding out his hand.

"Ryan Kendrick. Nice to meet you," Ryan said, reaching over to accept the handshake.

"You came in with Drew, right? Colt pointed him out to me," Zach said as he slid down to take the seat next to Ryan. Ryan quickly realized where he recognized Zach from: he had been with

Colt when they'd passed the fountain outside.

"Yeah, Drew's the one that ... found me ... I guess," Ryan said.

"That's awesome!" Zach said excitedly. "Colt told me Drew's really big here. Everybody admires him. What's he like?"

"He's ... nice," Ryan said, knowing he was not describing Drew well. "He seems like he'd be fun to hang out with. I had no idea he was important here, though." Ryan looked up at where Drew was sitting. He was leaning back and laughing with Colt. It looked like they were sizing up some of the initiates. "What's Colt like?" he asked Zach.

"He's really positive. Kinda down-to-earth. I was ready to strangle him when he started playing country music in the ship, though," Zach joked.

Ryan laughed, but before he had a chance to respond, the background chatter died rapidly. He and Zach turned toward the stage, where three imposing figures had just emerged from an oak door in the very back and were taking their places at the front. All three were dressed in dazzling white collared shirts and perfectly ironed navy slacks. Each of them had something like an insignia embroidered on both sleeves, in bright gold thread that flashed in the light, though Ryan was not able to discern the exact design from his seat. Ryan was unsurprised to find that two of them, a dark-skinned man and a blonde woman (Was she Atlantean? He never had such a strong desire to look at someone's nails), appeared to be exactly twenty-eight years old, though they both walked with such a defined air of purpose that Ryan had no doubt they were in fact much older.

The man and the woman stood to either side of a white granite podium in the middle of the stage. The man glanced over the sea of initiates, his face impassive, while the woman's eyes rapidly darted from person to person, as if analyzing each of them in turn.

Ryan was so busy watching the man and woman to either side of the podium that it took him a moment to realize that the man behind it appeared much older, in his mid-sixties. Despite his graying hair and weathered face, he obviously took fastidious care of himself. Ryan was quite sure the older man could beat him in a race.

Unlike the two individuals flanking him, the older gentleman was not looking critically at the crowd. Instead, his relaxed shoulders and good-natured smile spelled welcome. In fact, Ryan thought, his smile actually smoothed away some of his wrinkles, making him look younger. Ryan was relieved when he was the first to speak.

"Welcome!" he began. Even with just one word, his passion and charisma were palpable. "My name is Michael Stamaris. I am the Elder for this city, and I must insist you address me by my first name only," he said. "Whether this is your first time setting foot in the Northeast American City of Atlantis, or you grew up on one of our esteemed sister cities, I wish to welcome each and every one of you to what will undoubtedly be an adventure of many, many lifetimes. You are here because we believe that each of you, as an individual, has the potential to better Atlantis and to help those in need.

"During your time here, and once you leave, I invite you to think of this city as your home. As an organization, we pride ourselves on our sense of community and unity in purpose. So, from all of us to you, welcome home," Michael said with a beaming smile.

Ryan looked at the two figures on either side of the Elder. The woman abandoned her inquisitive stare for a gentle smile. The man, too, was smiling, although his smile appeared slightly forced.

"For those of you who are unfamiliar with the structure of our cities," Michael continued, "the citizens of each Atlantean city are split into two sects: Technology and Military. With me are Anna Valloris, Head of Technology"—Michael indicated the woman to his right, who held up a hand in a friendly gesture—"and Daniel Amerrest, Head of Military." Amerrest gave a slight nod in acknowledgement.

There was an awkward pause, during which one or two initiates began to clap hesitantly. Realizing that it was the polite thing to do, the others soon joined in. Michael's expression indicated that this was par for the course, and he waited for the applause to die down before he continued.

"While you will learn more in orientation, I need you all to know that both Tech and Military play a vital role in . . ."

Michael carried on speaking, but Ryan quickly became distracted when the ground beneath him started vibrating. For a heart-stopping second, he was sure that one of the engines holding up the city had failed. Ryan looked wildly over at Zach, mouth open to ask whether he felt the shaking too—only for him to see that the other man was bouncing his leg rapidly. Ryan huffed a quiet laugh, relaxing, and wondered whether Zach was vibrating from boredom, excitement, or nervousness.

Zach must have seen him staring, because he looked up at Ryan, mouthed "Sorry," and immediately stopped bouncing. Ryan whispered, "You're fine," and Zach resumed tapping his foot with a smile.

"So," Michael continued, "over the next seventeen weeks, your evaluators will judge your performances and determine your placement in either Technology or Military. From that point on, you will be a highly valued citizen of Atlantis. I am very excited to see what all of you will accomplish.

"At this point, I will turn the podium over to Ms. Valloris, who will give you all instructions on how to proceed. I wish you all the best of luck in all your endeavors. Please, come up and say hi when you have the chance! I look forward to getting to know each of you. Thank you!"

The Elder stepped down to an enthusiastic round of applause that lasted until the Head of Technology stepped up and raised a hand for silence.

Even without an obvious microphone or speaker system, Ryan realized he'd had no issues hearing the Elder's speech from the back of the Temple. He vaguely wondered what amplification technology these Atlanteans used as the Head of Technology started speaking in a crisp yet kind voice that carried throughout the entire Temple. Looking up at the dome, Ryan wondered if it was technology at all. Maybe the Temple's architecture was designed to improve the acoustics.

"In just a few minutes," Valloris began, "I will be calling names to split all of you into four groups. From there, you will follow your evaluators to the dorms, where they will explain the initiation process. The groups have been carefully selected so that nobody's scouter—the person who introduced them to Atlantis—will act as their primary evaluator. That being said, all the scouters are involved in the evaluation process in some manner. Also, we have ensured that each group has the same number of native Atlanteans from our sister cities to make each group as equal as possible. Now, when I read your name, please stand so we may separate you.

"Alexander, Janet . . . Anders, Kimberly . . . Chen, Nicholas . . ."

One by one, each person stood as his or her name was called. Valloris continued to read off names until about thirty people were standing.

"If I have called your name, please follow Colt Ponner, your main evaluator, to the side of the Temple."

Ryan looked over at Colt, who was holding up a hand and

smiling, as those whose names had been called headed over to where he was standing. Valloris resumed calling out names for the next group.

"...Garnett, Margret...Kendrick, Ryan...Lauder, Zachary..."

Ryan stood at his name, relieved when Zach followed suit moments later. Together, they waited until the Head of Technology called the last individual in the group (Williams, Benjamin). Even when he was standing, Zach's foot was a blur.

"Please see Sam Dennings, to your right," finished Valloris.

With her dismissal, Ryan shuffled to the right side of the Temple, along with thirty other people.

"Can you see our guy?" whispered Zach from behind him. Standing, Zach was a couple inches shorter than Ryan, and he was craning his neck, trying to peer around everyone in front of them.

"Nope," Ryan muttered back. All he could see was the back of the head of the white-clad Atlantean in front of him.

The mob of initiates stopped in front of a large vertical window. Ryan stood on his toes to try to get a better look. With the extra few inches, he could just barely see the top of a close-cropped head of blond hair at the center of his group.

Valloris continued reading off the final two groups and directed them to their corresponding evaluators. Ryan tried to hear whether Drew was leading one of the groups, but Valloris never mentioned him. Just as Ryan was peering around to see where Drew had gone, his thoughts were interrupted by a curt male voice.

"Alright, listen up!"

Ryan turned in time to see a short man with close-cropped hair climbing onto a small ledge along the wall so that he overlooked the group of initiates. He crossed his arms and glowered down at them, as if already disappointed with his group, and Ryan spotted the characteristic diamond pattern on his nailbeds.

"I'm Sam Dennings. I'll be your primary evaluator. For the next seventeen weeks, you will be known as Initiation Group Beta. Can anybody tell me why your group is Beta?"

Ryan looked around as several hands went up to answer the question. Before anyone was called upon, a man in one of the bright white shirts spoke up.

"Because we're the second group to be named," he said in a lazy voice. For a second, Ryan thought that the man was wearing an odd brown earring in his right ear, but then he realized there was simply a mole, perfectly placed, on the man's earlobe.

"Correct," Sam responded gruffly. The man who had answered grinned smugly, his dark, overly styled hair unnaturally still as he looked around at his competition. Craning his neck to look at the man's nails, Ryan was unsurprised to see the diamond pattern there, too.

"Throughout the initiation process," Sam continued, "we encourage you to answer as many questions as possible . . . assuming your answers are correct, that is. Don't bother answering if you're wrong. It'll make you look idiotic." He paused. "I got off topic. So, for the next seventeen weeks, you all will be known as Betas. These next few weeks are critical, and you should take them seriously. The other evaluators and I will be judging your performances to determine whether you would do better in Tech or Military. At the end of these seventeen weeks, you will be selected for one of the two sects in the Final Choosing Ceremony. But we have almost four months until then, so for now, relax, and do your best.

"Now, if you'll all follow me, I'll show you to the dorms."

Sam hopped down from the ledge and led the Betas out through the main entrance of the Temple. Feeling a bit like a kid on a school field trip, Ryan brought up the rear with Zach. As Sam led the group to the back of the large building, away from the plaza with the fountain, they skirted an amphitheater carved from snow-white stone. Ryan peered into it and saw that another group of initiates had already settled into the theater's tiered seats and were listening to their evaluator.

A row of trees to either side of the theater shaded Ryan's group from the otherwise unobstructed sunlight as they marched onward. Ryan peered between the rows of perfectly spaced trees to inspect some of the buildings surrounding them, which all appeared to be constructed from the same dark stone. In fact, Ryan realized that many of the buildings, despite being made of what appeared to be very expensive materials, would not have looked out of place on a college campus. One of the buildings closest to the group appeared to be under construction, and Ryan could see a group of men and women using a manual lift to transport huge slabs of stone to the roof, while another group cautiously leaned over the edge to grab it.

As they made their way onward, leaving the amphitheater and Temple behind, Ryan and the rest of the Betas came to an artfully carved pavilion of pure black stone. The structure was open on all four sides, and Ryan was confident that it could easily seat a few hundred people.

Sam led the Betas into the pavilion, hopped onto one of the tables, and waited for the group to catch up. Ryan couldn't help but notice that even standing on a table, Sam wasn't much taller than anyone in the group.

"Before I show you the dorms, I thought we'd go over some of the basic details of initiation. Like I said before, we'll be evaluating you over the next seventeen weeks. About forty percent of you will be chosen to be in Tech, while the rest will likely be chosen for Military. Even though your initiation class was split into four groups, you'll be judged as a whole. The small groups just allow us to evaluate you all a little more easily.

"Next week will be the calm before the storm: orientation," Sam continued. "We'll show you the four main districts of the city, and review different ways you can volunteer once your initiation is complete. After orientation week, you will alternate every two weeks between Tech and Military rotations for the remainder of your initiation. As Betas, your first rotation will be Tech with the Deltas."

"What will we be doing during the rotations, Sam?" asked a girl with shoulder-length blonde hair. She was also wearing a white shirt. Her hand shot in the air as she spoke.

"Yep, she has them too," Zach whispered to Ryan as he leaned to catch a glimpse of her raised hand. Colt must have told him about the nail pattern.

Sam smirked before responding.

"Your family never told you, huh?" he said roughly, with a hint of satisfaction. "Good! They weren't supposed to say anything. You don't find out any specifics until the beginning of each rotation. But I will say this: it's nothing bad. So try to relax a little bit, okay?

"Now, let's head to the dorms. There are four buildings behind me. Which one will you all be staying in?"

Ryan was ready this time. "The second!" he shouted along with another half-dozen Betas, including the Atlantean girl who had just spoken. Ryan glanced over at Zach, who hadn't joined in, and saw that he was distractedly watching the construction workers, who were now precariously placing an ornate keystone to complete a decorative arch.

"There ya go! You guys are getting the hang of this," Sam said. "Now let's go."

Sam hopped off the table and promptly led the way out of the pavilion and straight toward four identical single-story buildings made of sea-green stone.

"What do you think?" Ryan asked Zach as they approached the second building.

"This place is incredible," Zach said. "Sam seems . . . interesting."

"Yeah, he's kinda . . . short."

Zach snorted, as if trying to not to laugh too loudly. Ryan suddenly realized his mistake.

"I meant his personality!" Ryan said, also stifling a laugh.

"I mean . . . regardless, you're not wrong."

The two of them chuckled as they crossed the threshold of the building and found themselves in a large common room, complete with couches, tables, and even a small, fully stocked kitchen nook. Ryan and Zach made their way over to the rest of the Betas, who were congregating around the countertop where Sam was waiting for them.

"Welcome to your dorm, Betas," he said. "This is the common area. Feel free to relax here. The bunks are through the door on your left. Bathroom's on the right. During your initiation, you're free to use any of the public areas in Atlantis. Scheduled meals will be held in the pavilion outside. The meal schedule is posted on the notification board by the front door"— Ryan turned and saw a computerized screen full of alerts and graphics next to the door—"as is the time you are to meet me in the amphitheater each morning. Don't be late."

On that note, Sam gave a small nod and strode through the crowd of Betas toward the door. As he reached out to turn the handle, he paused and turned to face them.

"On a personal note: do me a favor," Sam said. "I need you guys to destroy the Deltas. Their primary evaluator is my sister—I need to beat her. I mean, they're your competition anyway, so you'll want to do well regardless. But make sure you bring your A game."

Sam turned again and left the dorm without saying farewell. For a few seconds, all the Betas stood in silence. Ryan had the distinct impression that everyone was slightly taken aback by their evaluator's sudden departure. After a second, the whole group broke into conversation.

"Look at this kitchen!" Zach said as he slowly examined each of the appliances. While Ryan was able to recognize some of them immediately, others were totally foreign to him. "I wonder how much we'll be able to cook during initiation."

"You like to cook?" Ryan asked.

"Love it! I'm not quite sure what this thing is, but I'm going to use it!" Zach was leaning over an odd, cube-shaped appliance. He straightened with an excited grin. "It looks like a food processor, blast chiller, vacuum sealer, and smoker, all in one."

"You'll have to teach me—I'm an awful cook. Want to check out the bedroom?" Ryan asked as the rest of the Betas began to leave the common room.

Zach cast one last longing look at the kitchen before following Ryan and the rest of the group into the bunk room. Twenty pairs of aluminum bunk beds lined the room, each with a dresser on either side. The other Betas were slowly spreading out, claiming beds and dressers. With a jolt, Ryan realized that in his haste to make it to what he assumed would be an interview, he had brought nothing but the clothes he was wearing, his cell phone, his wallet, and a nearly empty backpack. Drew had warned him that he would have to relocate, but Ryan had expected he would be able to pack after he saw the place.

Remembering Drew's advice from the night before, Ryan pulled out his phone and was unsurprised to see that he had no service. He had no idea how far they were from the New England coast, but he was confident that Atlantis was miles from any cell towers. No wonder Drew had suggested he tell his parents that he'd be out of touch for a while. Still, he wished he had brought at least one change of clothes. Judging by the look on his face, Zach seemed to be having similar thoughts.

"I didn't pack anything. Did you?" Zach asked Ryan tentatively.

"Nope, but it looks like we're not alone," Ryan said. None of the Betas, including the ones from Atlantis, seemed to have brought many personal belongings. However, while most of the people from the Surface seemed mildly disturbed by this realization, the Atlantean initiates appeared completely unbothered. After a minute, it was obvious why—all the dressers were stocked with outfits, toiletries, and other basic needs.

Following the Atlanteans' examples, Ryan and Zach claimed the nearest bunk. Zach jumped up and pulled himself onto the top bunk.

"I've never slept in a bunk bed before. This is great! Mind if I take the top?" Zach asked Ryan, leaning over the edge.

"Go for it," Ryan said with a laugh, tossing his useless phone onto the lower bunk to claim it before opening one of the drawers in the dresser to his right. Inside, he found a mix of soft shirts and thin sweaters in a wide variety of solid, muted colors. It reminded him of a new box of crayons.

The next drawer contained different jeans and slacks, all of which looked new but felt worn and comfortable. Looking around the room, Ryan got the impression that these clothes were standard for Atlantis. Thankfully, not all of the shirts seem to glow like the ones the Atlanteans were currently wearing. With almost all the Betas packed into one bunk room, the soft light from the shirts was much more noticeable.

One of the Atlanteans—the one with the mole on his ear—was having a rather loud conversation across the room.

". . . not worried at all," he said in a carrying voice. "I've had the chance to personally speak to Valloris multiple times. I got to spend a year doing research under her assistant right after college. We've talked a ton. She knows me by name. I'm guaranteed to be Tech. Not that I need the extra help, mind you. I still don't understand why Atlantis keeps trying to recruit people from the Surface. It's not like they *really* have any chance of being Tech anyway. They probably just keep bringing them up here as cannon fodder."

"Ignore him—he's an idiot," said a female voice.

Ryan looked up and saw the Atlantean girl who had asked about rotations leaning against the bunk bed next to him, shaking her head with her arms crossed in disdain. She turned to Ryan.

"It doesn't work that way. Everything here is merit based. Who you know doesn't matter at all," she said.

"Good," Ryan said. "That would suck. People from Atlantis would have a huge advantage otherwise."

"Nah, they're pretty good about being fair here. We have safeguards in place to make sure there's no favoritism. Besides, he's not even from Atlantis—he just acts like it. His parents were born here, but they moved to the Surface to do work there before they had any children. He may have Atlantean blood, for all that's worth, but I know for a fact he grew up on the Surface." She spoke so rapidly that it took Ryan a second to register everything that rolled off her tongue.

"Huh. Good to know," Ryan said as he watched the man show off to a small crowd at the other end of the room. "I'm Ryan Kendrick, by the way," he said, holding out his hand. She took it quickly.

"Carrie Mancerus, and that's Roy Graylor," Carrie said, indicating the loud Atlantean. "Please don't judge all of us based on him. Most Atlanteans are chill."

"Glad to hear it! I'm Zach. Lauder," Zach said as he hopped off the top bunk and landed next to Carrie.

"Carrie. Nice to meet you. You guys excited?" she asked them.

"Definitely, and kinda confused," Ryan said, Zach nodding vehemently next to him. Carrie laughed good naturedly.

"You'll get use to this place real quick. You wouldn't have been selected otherwise. Your computers can help too," she said.

"We . . . we don't have any computers," Zach said uncertainly.

"Sure you do. They're part of the beds. Look." Carrie sat down on the end of Ryan's mattress, tossed his phone toward the pillow, and faced the open frame at the foot of the bed. She ran an index finger across the bed frame, and at once, a dull-blue image appeared in front of her, suspended in midair. She tapped the image, and a holographic keyboard appeared, on which she typed Ryan's name.

"There you go!" Carrie said as she stood up from his bed. "It should be configured to your credentials. You can browse the web, or"—She touched the image again, and a list of options appeared in front of them—"you can read up on Atlantis. Basic history and culture stuff to help you guys from the Surface acclimate yourselves. Here, Zach, let me help you. . . ."

As she climbed onto Zach's bed, again without waiting for an invitation, Ryan familiarized himself with his new computer. The interface was remarkably intuitive, and Ryan was able to navigate with surprising ease. It only took him a minute to find all sorts of settings for the bed, including a white-noise generator and privacy blinds. Even though they were only images, the computer responded as soon as he touched the hologram. He was examining a map of the city when Carrie hopped down from above him.

"Are all the beds in Atlantis like this?" Ryan asked as Carrie flopped down on the next bed over. He was unable to tear his eyes away from the complex image in front of him.

"Oh, no! The beds outside the dorm are much nicer," she responded happily.

By dinnertime, Ryan and Zach had learned much more about Carrie.

"I'm actually from the Canadian City of Atlantis," she said quickly between mouthfuls of food. The three of them were sitting at a table along the edge of the pavilion, enjoying the cool breeze and setting sun. "My parents are back home, but my older brother and sister live here! I'll have to introduce you guys to them. My whole family is in Tech, so I better be in Tech too. . . ."

"Is Military really that bad?" Zach asked Carrie tentatively. "That Roy guy kept going on about how he 'knew' he was going to be in Tech, like it's a bad thing to be in Military."

"It's not bad," Carrie explained. "In fact, it's a good life, but Tech is just . . . better. Everyone wants to be in Tech. I mean, that's why we're all here, right? To help people. You can explore whatever field you want, and you get to really make a difference. Oh, oh, Will! Sit over here!"

Carrie hopped up and practically dragged a male Atlantean over to sit next to them. He had the same blond hair and green eyes as Carrie. He took a seat next to Zach, looked up at him and Ryan, then turned his eyes bashfully back to his plate.

"Will, this is . . . wait a minute . . . Richard? No. Ryan? Yes? Okay, Ryan and . . . Zach. They're both great. Guys, this is Will Natares," Carrie said quickly. "He grew up down the street from me."

Ryan and Zach both said hello and shook hands with Will. Will offered a friendly greeting, but seemed unsure what to say. He sat hunched in on himself, his furtive expression that of a man who felt like he was intruding.

"So you're from the Canadian city too?" Zach asked kindly.

"Yep. We both flew in yesterday," Will said.

"How many of the Atlantean initiates here are from the Canadian city?" Zach asked.

"About half of us," Will answered. "The other half are from the Caribbean City of Atlantis. They pull initiates from the southeastern United States, central America, and the Caribbean islands."

"Wait, so none of the Atlantean initiates here are from this city?" Ryan asked.

"Nope," Will said. "We're not allowed to complete our initiations in our home city. It's one of the ways they keep the process fair to the Surface initiates."

"So you've never been here before?" Ryan asked.

"No," Will said.

"I have!" said Carrie at the same time.

Ryan and Zach looked at Carrie in confusion.

"My parents are both in the engineering branch, specifically the infrastructure subdivision," she said, as if that explained everything.

"And?" Zach pushed.

"Well, they did a lot of collaboration with the infrastructure subdivision in this city," Carrie explained. "So we used to travel here a lot when I was little, for their research. I mean, we didn't spend a ton of time here or anything, but I got to know the city pretty well. I think the last trip they brought me on was four or five years ago. But other than quick day trips here to celebrate my brother and sister finishing their initiations, I haven't been back since then!"

"And you said both of your siblings are still here, right?" Ryan asked.

"Yep!" Carrie said. "You're required to work in your initiation city for three years once you're assigned a sect. My brother's finishing up his last mandatory year here, but my sister has been done for almost two years. They both just really love it here. Apparently this city's Tech District is amazing. I'm telling you: Tech's the way to go."

Zach nodded. He seemed convinced. Ryan looked at Will and noticed that the quiet Atlantean seemed overly interested in his food. "What about you, Will?" Ryan asked. "Which do you want? Tech or Military?"

"Tech," Will answered immediately. "Although either would honestly be fine. My mom's Military, Dad's in Tech. Both of them are happy, but . . . I'd rather be in Tech. I just don't know if I'll actually get it or not."

"Don't sell yourself short!" Carrie said. "I've known you all my life. You totally have a shot at Tech! And like I said, everyone wants Tech. Just watch; everyone will be talking about it tonight."

True enough, different aspects of the Technology sect were all any of the Atlanteans would discuss that night. Some of the Atlanteans even came over from other initiation groups to talk to friends about the new technologies they hoped to develop and implement after initiation. Many of them seemed completely unconcerned that the majority of the initiates would be selected for Military.

Ryan was relieved to find that most of the Atlantean initiates were more than welcoming of the confused initiates from the Surface. Almost all of them made a conscious effort to include their new Surface friends in conversations, and everyone seemed genuinely interested in the Surface initiates' first impressions of the city. Soon enough, people were huddled together in small groups, comparing notes on their respective home cities. Carrie in particular seemed to have no qualms about striking up a conversation with anyone. Unfortunately, she also seemed to have an awful time remembering people's names. She had to ask one girl from the Surface who wore her hair in a loose ponytail for her name about five times. Thankfully, the girl, who introduced herself—repeatedly—as Rebecca Wallace, was so eager to ask questions about Atlantis that she hardly seemed to mind.

On the other hand, Roy appeared averse to talking to people from the Surface. Instead, he seemed determined to talk to as many Atlanteans as possible and remind them all that he had pure Atlantean blood—which, if he was being honest with himself, suited Ryan just fine.

Knowing they had a big day ahead of them, all the Betas resigned themselves to an early night and went to get some sleep. As he was preparing for bed, Ryan realized for the first time that the bunkroom and bathrooms were coed. It didn't make him uncomfortable, exactly; he had just never lived with a woman before. His last real relationship had ended in his senior year of college, and it had been an ugly separation.

The first thing he couldn't help but notice when he was in the bathroom that night was how much space all of the women's hygiene products took up on bathroom counters. He knew he wasn't the only one noticing this, based on how Zach, who he'd learned was also an only child, was eyeing all the toiletries in amazement. Regardless, the counters were spacious enough that everyone's things fit easily, and in no time at all, the bunkroom was full of the soft white noise of quiet conversation as, one by one, the Betas started dropping off to sleep.

Ryan found himself unexpectedly exhausted. Just two days ago, he'd been at his job, worrying about all the work he still had to do—and now it was like he was on another planet. Drew had told him so much about this foreign city and promised that Ryan would learn much more during initiation. Now, Ryan tried to recall everything he'd learned so far that day—but the list of revelations was just too long. Before he knew it, his eyes were closed, and instead of mentally prepping himself for everything coming up in the next seventeen weeks, as he'd intended, he drifted off to sleep.

CHAPTER SIX
A NEW LIFE

Over the next few days, Ryan grew so accustomed to feeling like his head was spinning that he seriously wondered whether he was developing vertigo. He wasn't quite sure what he'd been expecting of his first week of initiation, but if he'd been betting on the people of Atlantis to ease the Betas into their new environment, he soon learned he was sadly mistaken.

Sam wasted no time in showing the Betas around the Northeast American City of Atlantis, and he seem to expect them to remember everything after just one demonstration. Ryan struggled to remember the layout of the streets, which he'd seen when he'd arrived with Drew, and could only vaguely recall that Atlantis had four distinct districts. He wasn't alone, either—Ryan could tell that most of the initiates struggled to catch every detail, regardless which city they called home.

Sam spent the entire first day of the Betas' initiation walking them around the northern district, which was apparently the main residential area. It was nearly impossible to differentiate between the various buildings, since they all sported a mix of modern and ancient Greek architecture. Often, Sam would just walk though and skip entire blocks of the city at a time as if they were unimportant, dismissively telling them to explore those areas on their own time— they would have plenty of time to learn the layout once they were full citizens of Atlantis.

Carrie, on the other hand, proved to be a much more useful tour guide than Sam. She frequently pointed out her favorite parks, shops, and restaurants she had visited to Zach and Ryan—even when Sam breezed by the areas and insisted the Betas keep moving.

Ryan quickly gave up on attempting to create a mental map of the walkways and buildings around the northern quadrant. Luckily, the Temple, which was visible from almost anywhere, acted as a constant reference point as the center of the Residential District. Ryan was also pleased to see that although the buildings seemed to have been arranged in a tightly packed labyrinth; every available foot of space was covered with grass, solar-paneled sidewalks, quaint cobblestone plazas, and attractive small trees, giving the whole area the feel of a refined research park.

Sam only marginally slowed down the next day, when he showed the Betas the Military District in the western part of the city. In his typically brusque manner, he led the Betas to a set of incongruously normal-looking metal bleachers overlooking a jogging track before addressing the group.

"This track behind me is the center of the Military District," he said as the Betas took a seat on the bleachers. "Surrounding it are training facilities, along with some public gyms that are open to civilians. The farther away from the track you get, the more specialized the buildings become. You have your armory, for weapons and body armor; labs and military R and D facilities; and conference centers where the top brass discuss strategies. You don't have to be Military to come over here and use the facilities, but you won't have access to some buildings without specialized clearance."

Ryan could tell that a lot more planning had gone into the organization of the Military District than Sam was letting on. It seemed much more organized than the Residential District. The buildings closest to the track were much shorter than the buildings farther away, as if the more specialized the buildings became, the taller—and presumably more important—they were.

Before he could give the matter any more thought, Sam walked down the metal steps and called over the clanging of his feet for the Betas to follow him.

As Sam led them in a large, ever-growing spiral away from the track and through the Military District, Ryan had the deep suspicion that Sam was just trying to mess with the new initiates. He also noted that there was significantly less grass around the Military buildings than there had been around the structures in the Residential District. Instead, these buildings were connected by paths the width of small roads, which Ryan was confident also contained solar technology. To his disappointment, the group didn't go inside any of the buildings, although Sam assured them that they would get to explore many of them later.

As they toured the Military District, they passed several Atlanteans going about their days. While many of them seemed to be wearing normal Atlantean clothes, others appeared completely battle-ready, dressed in form-fitting full-body armor. Ryan noticed that a good portion of the armored Atlanteans were jogging around the track or the buildings, clearly building their endurance. They frequently stopped to talk to Sam for a moment, or to congratulate the Betas on beginning their initiation.

Ryan's spirits lifted slightly as he walked through the Military District. All the Atlanteans he saw were friendly and upbeat. They didn't seem at all put out about being in Military. He wasn't the only one who noticed either. Some of the native Atlanteans initiates whispered excitedly to each other as they passed military simulation buildings. He even saw Roy raise an eyebrow once or twice, as if he was trying to hide that he was impressed with anything that even remotely dealt with Military.

Even though Carrie was familiar with the Residential District thanks to her previous visits to the city, Ryan and Zach realized that she wasn't at all familiar with this part of the city. Moreover, she appeared to have a difficult time identifying any of the Atlanteans they met.

"He was my neighbor in the Canadian city for about five years when I was younger," she told them, pointing out an Atlantean who was waving to her. "I feel so bad! I know exactly who he is, but I couldn't tell you his name for the life of me."

"How long have you known him?" Zach asked.

"At this point, about nine years," Carrie said, shaking her head sadly. "Even after he moved to this city, he kept in touch with my dad. He's always been so nice."

Even if Carrie occasionally struggled to remember names, Ryan and Zach were still grateful to have a native Atlantean friend who could answer their questions. Sometimes, the more Sam tried to explain a concept, the more confused Ryan became; but Carrie was always more than happy to clarify.

Even though he was impressed with the Military District's facilities, Ryan couldn't help but be excited when Sam told them they would be touring the Technology District along the eastern edge of the city the following day. Ryan, Zach, and Carrie agreed to wake up early to ensure they weren't late for the outing, and none of them were surprised to find that every single Beta had had the same idea.

The next morning, all the Betas were up at dawn, and they spent breakfast speculating excitedly about what they would see. The other initiation groups were no help: the Alphas and the Gammas, both of which had toured Technology earlier that week, weren't telling the other groups anything, though they could easily be seen talking in hushed voices at meals and during free time.

"Betas!" Sam called before they departed for the Technology District. "Are you guys ready? Let's get going!"

Zach shot Ryan an eager look. The fact that Sam had asked whether the group was ready rather than just summoning them like he usually did showed that even their evaluator was enthusiastic for the day ahead.

The Betas chatted excitedly the entire way to the Technology District, until they found themselves crossing what resembled a massive college campus. They followed a winding sidewalk through a lush quad. Every few hundred feet, the sidewalk branched off, leading to impressive, sprawling academic buildings and shady pavilions. People milled about as they passed, strolling along the paths or lounging in the grass, enjoying the day outside. Some sat talking in lively groups with thin, translucent tablets in hand, while others typed in midair, watching their words appear before them on projected, floating screens. Even though they were busy, all of them—with the exception of one man who was softly banging his head against his table with a truly grueling looking report open in front of him—wore satisfied smiles, clearly pleased with the progress of their work.

"Ryan, look!" Zach said, pointing to a building up ahead. Ryan saw that he was looking at the second floor of a large green building, where someone was writing complex chemical equations across a plate glass window.

"My sister's lab is in there," Carrie said absentmindedly, looking at the building with awe.

"Have you been inside?" Zach asked.

"No, but she sent us some pictures of her coworkers and her new lab when she changed her focus," Carrie said. "She started working on a collaborative project in there about a year and a half ago. They have about five different departments working together.

I think it may have something to do with space, but my sister just said it's confidential until I become an official citizen of Atlantis."

"Aren't you already an Atlantean?" Ryan asked, confused.

"By blood, yes," Carrie said. "I'm one hundred percent Atlantean; but you don't become a citizen until you complete your initiation."

As they wove their way deeper and deeper into the district, Ryan noticed that the buildings gradually changed from futuristic designs with sharp, odd angles of steel and glass to steady structures with ancient Roman, Greek, and even Egyptian elements. Sam led the group of Betas toward the center of the Technology District until they reached an open courtyard filled with picnic benches. In the center of the courtyard was a large black pillar that stood about eight feet high. Ryan had seen similar pillars throughout the entire city, but he had not yet had the opportunity to ask anyone about them. He opened his mouth to ask Carrie what they might be—only to be cut short by Sam.

"Alright, Betas," Sam said happily. "We're in the heart of the Technology District. All of the buildings surrounding us are dedicated to new technological innovations. Throughout the district are multiple courtyards like this where we share ideas and work together on projects. The Gothic building right over there"—Sam pointed to a building behind the initiates—"is where I worked for the last five years before I became a scouter."

"What's that large building?" asked Rebecca, pointing.

"That's the city's main hospital," Sam said, looking over his shoulder to the building in question. "It's the center for patient care and medical research. We also have a few small clinics in the Residential District, as well as a smaller military hospital in the Military District."

Ryan looked around and saw some of the other initiates staring eagerly up at the hospital. One man, an Atlantean from the

Caribbean city, who had an unusually long neck, broad shoulders, and a deep tan, took a few extra seconds to gaze at the building as the Betas started walking out of the courtyard.

Sam took some time to show the Betas different buildings specializing in medicine, energy, and other things Ryan did not fully understand. For some reason, a great many buildings seemed to be dedicated solely to studying light. Ryan noticed that most of the Betas from the Surface appeared to find this fact as interesting as he did, but the Atlanteans seemed unperturbed.

If Sam said anything else of import, by the end of the day, none of the Betas heard a word of it. They were all talking excitedly amongst themselves about what they would do if they were chosen for Tech.

◊◊◊

The rest of orientation week, it turned out, was dedicated to the Industrial District.

The day after they toured the Technology District, Sam gathered the Betas along the southern rim of the park through which Ryan had walked when he'd first come to Atlantis. Behind Sam, Ryan saw an expansion of buildings that looked completely different from those in any of the other districts. Sam began explaining that the majority of the Betas' future volunteer work would take place in this southern district: the Industrial District. Of course, it didn't take him long to contradict himself.

"Once you're a citizen of Atlantis, you will be expected to volunteer regularly," Sam told them all. "Everyone here pitches in, and everyone helps out. As Military or Tech, you'll work four-and-a-half days a week, and spend the other half of that fifth day volunteering in some manner. You'll have the other two days of the week off to do whatever you like. Some people like to volunteer even more of their time, and others simply like to rest. You can pick any days of the week to rest or volunteer, which can allow you to meet up with any friends in the opposite sect.

"Atlantis has three main categories in which you can volunteer: infrastructure, agriculture, and water," Sam continued. "The centers that support agriculture and water are both located in the Industrial District, but you can work in infrastructure anywhere—it's responsible for building and maintaining all the structures in the city."

"Why would anybody choose that?" Roy asked no one in particular.

"Because it's important, that's why!" Sam barked, making Roy jump a little. "Think you're too good for some manual labor, huh? Well, we need people to help keep Atlantis running smoothly. And most of the infrastructure volunteers are Techs! They go stir-crazy working indoors all day, so they tend to appreciate the fresh air."

Sam spent the rest of the day showing the initiates construction sites all over the city. Ryan was amazed that such an advanced civilization still used simple hand-operated pulley lifts to move giant slabs of granite and marble up the sides of buildings. After they'd toured what had to be every construction site across all four districts, Sam finally let them adjourn for the day.

Exhausted after spending the day circling the entire city, Ryan, Zach, and Carrie opted to cut through the park in the center of the city to get back to their dorms rather than follow most of the Betas, who took the Monorail. The three of them were discussing some of the construction sites they had seen, including one building that they all agreed was so ugly it didn't even merit maintenance, when Zach stopped abruptly, causing Carrie to bump into him.

"What's that?" he asked. He was staring at the same field Ryan had spotted on his first day in Atlantis. That day it had been empty, but this time it was being used. Two Atlanteans were throwing a ball back and forth as they made their way down the field toward a twelve-foot-high funnel, while another two Atlanteans tried to stop them. They watched as one of the defenders crossed a large circle painted on the ground around the funnel and swore loudly, making her opponent laugh as he threw the ball perfectly into the funnel.

"It's Toss," Carrie said, also laughing at the defender. "She just fouled," she added, at Ryan's and Zach's puzzled looks.

"Wait, I've heard of this!" Ryan said. "Drew said he broke his leg playing it once."

"You know Drew?" Carrie asked, turning so fast to look at Ryan that he was sure she had whiplash.

"Uh-huh . . ." Ryan said, taken aback at her sudden interest. "You know him?"

"Drew? Yeah. A little. He's nice. I mean, he's pretty cool," Carrie said, turning pink. "Come on—I'm hungry. Let's get some food."

Ryan and Zach shared a look as Carrie took off without waiting for affirmation, and once they finally caught up to her, they allowed her to believe she had successfully switched the topic to the weather without them noticing.

Other than casually asking Ryan how he knew Drew the next day at breakfast, Carrie did not bring up Ryan's scouter again—which was good, since Sam was being annoyingly technical while showing them the water collection facility that day. He led the Betas into a long, squat building in the Industrial District that reminded Ryan oddly of the Parthenon, and the group descended a steep staircase and poured out into a large, underground chamber filled with a vast tangle of winding, transparent pipes. The space was illuminated by more of the white-blue light spheres, which caused the deep blue marble walls to shimmer as if the entire room were underwater.

"This is our main source of water on Atlantis," Sam said as he led them through the snaking pipes. "The original design was created by one of the descendants of Poseidon. No," Sam said, cutting off Rebecca, who had been asking questions every eight minutes on the dot, "not the god. Poseidon was the name of an Athenian man who made groundbreaking discoveries about water while studying in Atlantis. As homage—and as something of a joke—we call this place the Temple to the Ocean God; but in all seriousness, this place is vital to the existence of Atlantis.

"These pipes are made of pure quartz, and extend throughout the entire city. They collect all the waste and gray water used on Atlantis, and run it through a filtration system. The new, clean water is redistributed throughout the city, and it's approximately nine times cleaner than any drinking water you'll find on the Surface."

Sam walked away as soon as he finished the sentence, before any of the initiates could ask questions. Used to his behavior at this point, the Betas all followed him, ducking to avoid hitting their heads on low pipes.

Sam paused again outside a set of ornate sea-green doors, looked at one of the light spheres for a second, and then turned to the initiates.

"We're about to go into a poorly lit area—low light helps the volunteers see their screens better," Sam said. "If you ever need extra light on Atlantis, you can use one of the light spheres." Sam tapped the bottom of a sphere, and it popped up into the air like a bubble. He caught it and faced the group. "You can take the spheres with you anywhere you go. If you're near a computer, you can even adjust their brightness. The spheres' batteries will last for about six hours before they start to dim. To recharge the light spheres, just place them back on any empty holder you can find along the walls." Sam pointed to the ring that had originally housed the light sphere. It reminded Ryan of a cupholder.

Without further explanation, Sam turned on his heel and led the group through the doors and into a dimly lit room. Along the walls were a dozen or so volunteers, all hard at work. Each volunteer sat in front of a screen, completely ignoring the incoming initiates.

The Betas followed Sam's bouncing light sphere to the back of the room and formed a circle around their evaluator, who looked eerie in the sphere's white-blue glow.

"This is the main way we collect fresh water on Atlantis," Sam said in an odd, almost mystical voice. He held the light sphere just under his chin, as if he was telling a spooky story. Ryan was sure the effect was intentional. "We send out drones and pilot them remotely through clouds to collect water. All the drones are solar powered, so they can fly great distances to find large clouds. Once sensors indicate the drones have reached capacity, they fly back to the city on autopilot, and the volunteers here immediately send out new drones."

The Betas spent the rest of the day learning to pilot the drones, while Sam explained how the filtration systems were maintained. Even though the system appeared complicated at first, Ryan was amazed at the elegant, sustainable way Atlantis ensured the city always had water.

But as impressed as he was with the Temple to the Ocean God, what he saw the next day was staggering. To show them how they could volunteer with agriculture, Sam led the Betas to the far end of the Industrial District until they stood on the actual edge of the floating city. In front of them was nothing but the seven-foot-high fence that surrounded the entire perimeter of the city, and beyond it, the empty blue sky. Just ahead of where they were gathered was a small opening in the fence. Strands of wire anchored into the sides of the outermost buildings were strung overhead, passing through the gap in the fence only to disappear beneath the city. Sam practically had to shout to be heard over the wind that howled past the ledge, trying to push them backward.

"This is where you can volunteer for agriculture," he called out to the group. "Each of you needs to grab a vest and stand over here to my right so I can clip you into the wire system using these magnetic carabiners. It's the only way to really see what's going on here."

Once all of the Betas were sporting harnesses, Sam used an odd, open-ended carabiner to clip each of them to an industrial cable. Ryan inspected the device uncertainly. The "clip" looked more like a large "C" than a true clamp. He didn't know how the magnets worked, but Ryan hoped they were strong.

Sam smiled and turned to face the group.

"For this next part . . . I need you all to trust me," he said slowly.

As they watched, Sam tugged on his own tethered harness in what seemed to Ryan to be a rather unthorough safety check, before calling out again: "Follow me!"

Before any of the Betas could react, Sam turned around, sprinted toward the edge of the flying city, and threw himself into the air. He almost seemed to levitate for a second before he plummeted out of sight.

Ryan heard many of the initiates cry out in shock, and he felt his own stomach do a small flip. He had no idea what had just happened. Zach looked at him, gaping in horror. Nobody moved. Even Carrie seemed too stunned to speak. All of the initiates looked at each other uncertainly until they heard a faint but familiar voice call from below.

"What are you all waiting for? Let's go!" Sam shouted from somewhere out of sight.

Carrie and several of the native Atlantean initiates smiled. As some of them started running toward the edge, Carrie leaned over to Zach and Ryan and spoke in a hushed voice.

"Come on, guys," she said. "Be the first ones from the Surface to go. It would look really good!"

Before Ryan could say anything, she took off running and followed Sam over the edge.

Ryan couldn't believe what he was seeing. Was he really expected to jump off a flying city? Surely his harness would keep him safe, but this was insane!

The sounds of giddy laughter filtered up over the edge. Ryan took a tentative step forward and stopped. There was a throbbing, achy knot in his throat, one that he couldn't swallow.

Ryan felt a gentle pat on his back and looked over to see Zach give him a small nod. Ryan wondered whether he looked as nauseated as Zach did. He shakily returned Zach's nod and steeled himself, clenching his fists so that no one would see his hands shake.

"Come on," Ryan heard himself say.

Together, he and Zach took a few steps toward the ledge. Before Ryan knew what was happening, they were jogging, and then running.

Ryan looked out past the city's horizon and tried to run faster. He couldn't think. If he started to think, he wouldn't be able to go through with it.

He was getting close. He was at the edge. No thinking.

Ryan jumped.

He felt a moment of sheer elation and fear before he started to fall. Then, just as he dropped below the surface of the city, Ryan felt an upward jerk as his harness's clamp abruptly caught the cable.

His wire seamlessly converged with the other lines into one large cable, and Ryan laughed with relief as the wire guided him back toward a small ledge built into the side of city's foundation, where Sam and Carrie stood waiting.

The carabiner must have had an automatic braking system, because the zipline slowed to a steady pace as he approached, and Ryan was able land surprisingly gracefully next to Carrie. He looked up as Zach landed next to him with a shaky laugh.

They were about fifteen feet below the surface, in a large open greenhouse that was built into the city's foundation. A complex of wires and lush plants surrounded them, sprouting horizontally from the edge of the city and supported by the wires. The ground, if he could call it that, was made of a mesh weave that kept the roots firmly supported.

As his fellow initiates arrived one by one, emboldened by the others' success and lack of screaming, Ryan looked around to see Atlantean volunteers working all across the vast vertical garden, either standing on platforms similar to the one the Betas now occupied, or dangling in midair, supported only by their harnesses.

"Now that all of you have finally joined us," Sam said, glaring at Carrie's friend Will, who it turned out was deathly afraid of heights and had just arrived, still hyperventilating, "this is where Atlantis grows all its food. We have crops growing along the entire southern perimeter of the city to allow for maximum exposure to sunlight. Integrated pipes carry nutrient-rich water just below this mesh scaffolding, allowing all our crops to grow well without soil. If you volunteer in agriculture, you will travel along the wires, maintain the crops, and harvest as needed. *You* should avoid this option," he added to Will, who nodded weakly in agreement.

"Is it safe?" asked Rebecca.

"See anybody falling?" Sam asked her. "Each clip has four

high-powered magnets that ensure they stay on the wires, and each cable is equipped with sensors that immediately detect any instability. The harnesses are also inspected at the start and end of each day. It's normal to be nervous at first, but we've never had any accidents. Now follow me! I'm going to show you guys where we store the food."

Without looking behind him, Sam leaned backward and let gravity pull him off the platform toward a small inlet where volunteers could be seen working busily to sift through bins of grains and vegetables. Will groaned loudly. Carrie turned around and gave Ryan an excited grin, and Ryan felt himself return the smile. Jumping off a flying city was insane, but now that he'd done it, Ryan knew the rest of the day was going to be fun.

◊◊◊

"Deltas, Betas, over here! Let's go!"

"Well, that's definitely Sam's sister," Zach whispered to Ryan as they approached a native Atlantean woman who they were delighted to see was a few inches taller than Sam.

The group wasted no time forming a large semicircle around the Sam and his sister, all the while muttering excitedly between themselves. This was the first time that the Betas and Deltas had been brought together, and all of them were clearly eager to prove themselves—especially since this was their first day in the Technology District. They were gathered in a small room in the basement of a building near the main courtyard, and their whispering carried throughout the enclosed space.

"For the Betas who don't know me, my name is Jen Dennings," Sam's sister announced. "Deltas, this is my brother Sam. The first Tech session is primarily about bringing you all up to speed. There's a lot of technology on Atlantis that's advanced well beyond the Surface standard, and it's important that you understand how and why all of this came about. And yes, there will be a test! The last three Tech sessions will be more hands-on. That's when you'll prove your worth. For now, let's have some fun. Follow me!"

Jen and Sam led the initiates down a narrow passage into a large chamber that looked like a mix between a gym and a shooting range. The floor was covered with soft mats and haphazardly placed free weights, which Will managed to trip over twice in a row. Looking past the mob of initiates, Ryan saw an array of targets of various sizes painted along the walls, many of them scarred with large scorch marks. Judging by the damage, none of those who had shot at them previously had had particularly good aim.

"Alright guys," Sam said, "go ahead and line up along this wall right here. Jen and I are going to demonstrate some of the technology you'll have to be familiar with once you become a citizen of Atlantis. First, you ha—"

"Don't spoil it, Sammy!" Jen said with an evil smile as her brother shot her a reproachful look. "We'll show them. I take the left target, you take right?"

Sam nodded. He and Jen each picked up an odd, metallic glove from a rack against the wall, and faced the wall of targets side by side. As they slid the gloves on all the way up to their elbows, Jen looked over at her brother and muttered something Ryan couldn't hear. Apparently it meant something to Sam, who promptly retorted with a nasty face, making Jen laugh.

"Ready?" Sam asked.

Jen nodded. They each held out their gloved hands toward the wall of targets.

All the initiates were silent, listening as Jen slowly counted down from five. As soon as she said, "Zero," short beams of blinding light shot from their open palms and exploded against the walls one after another, filling the room with an unrelenting, near deafening roar. Ryan could barely see the silhouettes of the two instructors as he squinted against the searing light.

Between the blinding flashes and deafening explosions, the demonstration seemed to take much longer than the twenty seconds it actually lasted. Sam and Jen continued to shoot light out of their gloves until the targets could no longer be seen through the dust. As they lowered their arms, Sam shot his sister a smug look.

"Computer: Results," he said to no one in particular. His voice sounded strangely soft, though that may have had something to do with the dull ringing in Ryan's ears.

"Identifying," a cool, computerized female voice said as Ryan's hearing gradually returned. "Accuracy for Jennifer Dennings: seventy-one percent. Accuracy for Samuel Dennings: sixty-nine percent."

"Yes!" Jen shouted before the computer had even finished relaying Sam's score. Sam glared sullenly at Jen as she turned to face the initiates with a broad smile.

"This is one of the many technological advances you will become familiar with while you're staying on Atlantis," she said, a little more loudly than necessary. Apparently her hearing had not yet returned. Ryan wondered whether Atlantis had any earplugs. "Not only do we harness solar energy to power most of the city, but we've developed special lenses to concentrate that light. It can be used both industrially and as a weapon."

"Enough of that," Sam said. "Let's show them the next thing."

"You're only saying that because you know you can beat me!" Jen pouted as she and Sam peeled off their gloves.

"It's not even a competition," Sam said in a lofty tone.

There was now a definite air of excitement among the Deltas and Betas. Sam looked around for a second and smiled as his gaze fell on a fifty-pound weight lying on the floor. He reached out and slowly lifted his hand. As if guided by invisible wires, the weight rose slowly off the ground and started turning cartwheels as Sam made a twisting motion with his hand. Shocked whispers broke out among the initiates. Clearly, many of the other initiates' scouters had not demonstrated the Atlantean telekinetic ability.

"Once you become a full citizen of Atlantis," Sam started loudly so he could be heard over the chatter, "each of you will be given a small computerized chip called a beacon, which will be safely inserted in the back of your neck. We all have one." Jen turned around and lifted her hair so that the initiates could see a scar the size of a pea on the back of her neck. "Simply put, the beacons stimulate your brain. We can communicate between the beacons with just our thoughts, and the chips allow our minds to produce artificial brainwaves that we call omega waves—high-energy, fast-moving waves that have the ability to move objects. It's not easy to control them, but once mastered, they can be tremendously powerful."

Sam made the large weight revolve around him at a dizzying pace before, with a sudden shoving motion, he sent it rocketing out of orbit and toward the target wall. Unfortunately, the weight was still spinning, and Sam's aim was off. The weight slammed into the wall between two targets and fell with a loud clunk.

"I think you damaged the soundproof insulation," Jen said.

"No, it was like that when we got here," Sam said hastily. "That's enough demonstration for now, anyway. Time to get to the hard stuff. Let's go, guys!"

Sam wasn't joking. He and Jen led the initiates to an amphitheater-style classroom full of desks—which was where the initiates ended up spending the rest of their first two weeks learning about Atlantean technology. Jen and Sam took turns going over the basics while the Betas and Deltas furiously took notes on the computers that were built into their workstations.

Ryan quickly realized that Atlantean technology was decades, if not centuries, ahead of the Surface. He had trouble keeping up with all the futuristic applications of physics and chemistry, and he could tell that he wasn't alone. Carrie kept glancing over with slight scorn at another Atlantean Beta with blond hair and green eyes. Her name was Sarah Gall, and Carrie had confided in Ryan and Zach that the two of them had developed a sort of rivalry while growing up together in the Canadian city. Sarah kept shooting covert looks at Carrie as well, obviously trying to make sure she wasn't falling behind her nemesis. Zach, meanwhile, had moments when he seemed to keep up just fine, followed by ten-minute periods when he completely zoned out to the point that Ryan sometimes thought he was sleeping with his eyes open—until he noticed that Zach was still tapping his foot.

Unfortunately, the initiates soon learned that they needed to be alert the entire time they were in the classroom, because at any moment, Sam or Jen could randomly announce a pop quiz. Ryan strongly suspected that they waited to drop tests when everybody was having difficulty focusing. Some questions were fairly basic, such as explaining why Atlantis focused more on developing technologies that improved quality of life than, for example, space exploration. Others, to Ryan's disappointment, were much more specific, and tended to involve certain areas of expertise such as medicine, military advancement, entertainment, or quite frankly, anything else they wanted.

Ryan was pleased to find that for the most part, he seemed to follow discussions on genetics and human health without major issues. Luckily, they had a fantastic teacher.

"Aging was one of the first issues we tackled on Atlantis," Drew told them on perhaps their fourth day in the classroom. Sam and Jen had decided they needed a break from the initiates and had asked him to come in to teach a few lessons. In fact, Ryan was confident that he heard Sam mutter something nasty about the Betas under his breath as he left the room. The environment was laughably more relaxed with Drew teaching: everyone seemed much more attuned than normal, especially the Atlantean initiates, and Ryan noticed that Carrie actually blushed slightly when Drew called on her by name to answer a question.

"It took us a while to truly understand gene therapy," Drew said, pulling up a large display in front of the whole class. "We spent so much time trying to understand aging and DNA that some other areas of medical technology were ignored for a while. It was actually our current Elder, Michael Stamaris, who discovered how to halt the aging process. He first found a way to slow aging in 1901, and finally perfected agelessness in 1917."

Drew flicked his wrist, and a complicated diagram appeared onscreen. Some of the initiates stared at the screen in obvious despair, knowing they would never be able to copy all of it down. Ryan watched as the broad-shouldered Atlantean initiate with the long neck—who he'd since learned was named Jonathan Fowler—frantically tried to draw the diagram on his tablet. The day before, Jonathan had been telling Ryan and Zach that both of his parents were doctors in the Technology District back on the Caribbean city, and that he hoped to follow in their footsteps. Ryan had noticed that he'd sat up a little straighter when Drew walked into the classroom, though Ryan wasn't sure whether it was because he was concentrating, or simply trying to make a good impression.

"As an overview," Drew said, "the Elder altered bacteriophages to target human cells. These viruses insert genes that allow the targeted cells to produce new telomeres, in a manner similar to the lysogenic cycle in bacteria. This essentially stops the cells from aging. Starting in 1919, we began to administer the altered bacteriophages to Atlanteans over the age of twenty-eight who consented to agelessness.

"It took us about thirty years to realize we still had to address another aspect of aging: arthritis. We quickly found that cartilage was comprised of three main elements: collagen, proteoglycans, and chondrocytes. To prevent cartilage loss, we . . ."

Ryan stared at Drew, unable to comprehend anything else he was saying. Zach looked over at him and raised a hopeless eyebrow, apparently also completely lost. They tried to take notes on anything they could, but, frankly, they were lucky to catch every third word Drew said. Even Jonathan was sweating profusely, though he was still at least trying to keep up.

After another twenty minutes, Drew paused midway through his own lecture, which had reached a complicated portion on oxidative stress, and told the overwhelmed initiates that there was a full copy of his notes on agelessness in the city database, accessible at any time.

"Once we finished tackling aging," Drew explained to the class, who had collectively given up on taking notes, "we turned our focus toward illness. Looking at cancer, we found ways to protect and, if necessary, repair tumor suppressor genes p16 and p53. We then used similar gene therapy and repair techniques to address issues in pancreatic beta cells that resulted in Type 1 diabetes and similar life-altering diseases—"

"So there's a cure for everything that's killing people on the Surface?" Rebecca asked incredulously. "Why isn't Atlantis doing anything to help?"

"What makes you so certain we aren't doing anything?" Drew said with a smile. "Our cures and vaccines are gradually being introduced into society as we speak. It's a challenge, because in order for Atlantis to remain a secret, the introduction must be a gradual process. We have purposely stationed Atlanteans in companies that are known not to patent new drugs—which is a challenge in itself—so that we can be sure the drugs will be made available to the general population at a reasonable price. The biggest roadblocks we face are government restrictions."

"Why would the government try to ban a cure for cancer?" Rebecca asked.

"Because they're being told to," Drew said simply. "For those of you who don't know, there is a group of individuals called the Order who are constantly trying to undermine our work on the Surface. You'll learn more about them in your first Military rotation, but for now, all you need to know is that the Order is largely responsible for delaying many of our advances from reaching mass production and distribution, including medical innovations. They've infiltrated powerful lobbying firms that not only help fund their operations, but also allow them to manipulate governments and legislative groups around the world from the shadows, in ways that help further their agenda. Sometimes the Order tries to hamper technological advancement on the Surface until it is advantageous for them to reveal it themselves. Other times, they try to block our work altogether. Because of this, we're having a lot of trouble getting our lifesaving treatments approved—but we're always trying. Most of our research on cancer was accepted in academic institutions about a year ago. We hope that by working with both private and public universities, our work will have a better chance of being recognized by the government.

"Also, while we've made amazing strides in medicine, we still have major shortcomings in the field of neurology. For example, we haven't yet found a way to regenerate damaged brain cells and help people predictably recover from serious strokes—although we can prevent the vast majority of strokes nowadays! And memory has also proven to be really tricky. We're looking at different gene therapy techniques, but so far, none have been promising."

"What about some of the controversial issues surrounding genetics and gene therapy, like designer babies?" Ryan asked.

"We separate the idea of 'designer babies' into two different categories," Drew said, with a nod to Ryan. "First, we looked into treatment options involving gene therapy for children who would have been born with illnesses that would drastically shorten their expected life spans. I'm not talking about things like heart disease, but predictors that correlate to cystic fibrosis or other similar issues. Our studies have shown no adverse long-term effects in individuals who are treated for these diseases in utero. Within the parameters of this category, we allow the parents to decide whether they want any type of medical intervention.

"The other category involves altering a fetus to affect how the person would look or act. Even though the technology is available, altering a person's genetic code for this purpose is forbidden. We have no way of testing what type of person the original fetus would become or what they would accomplish, so Atlantis refuses to take the risk. That being said, both of these categories are still debated regularly. Twice a year, we hold debates that are open to all citizens of Atlantis to discuss how we will address any major issues, including ethical ones. Anyway, returning to our discussion on medical advances . . ."

◊◊◊

"How the hell did they do all this?" Zach said desperately to no one in particular a few days later.

It was lunchtime on the last day of the Betas' and Deltas' first

Technology session, and all of the tables in the pavilion were covered with papers and tablets. They had a test in two hours that would cover all the technological achievements unique to Atlantis, and the two groups had been frantically studying for the last three days. Ryan was trying to review his notes on his tablet, but whenever he wanted to go to the next page, he kept accidentally swiping the screen too hard and sending the document to another person's computer.

"No idea," Ryan said as he sat down after retrieving the document and apologizing for the fourth time to an annoyed-looking Delta at the other end of the table. "Who was it again that pioneered concentrated light for industrial use before it was used in the military?"

"Kristen Gallenes," Carrie answered without looking up from her notes.

"Did you guys learn any of this in school as kids?" Zach asked Carrie desperately.

"We brushed over it briefly, but not nearly in this much detail," Carrie answered in a flat tone, clearly trying to memorize something important. "Didn't Sam say the average for this test is around fifty percent?"

"After explicitly telling us that we aren't supposed to do well, yes," Ryan said with a weak smile. "I guess that's a little less pressure."

"True," Carrie said, "but I still want to do well."

"Me too," Ryan and Zach said at the same time. After listening to everything Atlantis had accomplished with all their new technology, Ryan was swept away like everyone else in the feverish desire to join the Technology sect. Every class over the past two weeks had ended in excited chatter as everyone marveled at what they had learned. Now the initiates were all studying intensely, determined to make a good impression for their evaluators.

Two hours later, Jennifer called both groups into the classroom. As they filed in, Ryan noticed Jennifer and Sam lounging in a couple of chairs at the front, watching the initiates literally squirm. He couldn't help but smile as the desk he was logging into shook slightly from Zach's nervous fidgeting. He looked over and saw Carrie on Zach's other side, muttering facts under her breath.

"Alright, Betas," Sam started as he stood up. "Now that you've all logged into your stations—" Jennifer made a small coughing noise behind Sam's back. "—Er, and Deltas," he added awkwardly. "Now that you've logged into your stations, you may begin your exams. Just try to relax. Do your best. It's supposed to be hard. Good luck!" He walked back to his seat, and Ryan could have sworn he saw Jen mouthing something at him about being a "big softie."

Ryan looked down at the screen on his desk and smiled. The first question was about genetics. Maybe this wouldn't be too bad.

◊◊◊

"Okay, okay," Jennifer nearly shouted over the cheering and applause. "I know all of you are excited, but the last classroom session is important, so please *try* to pay attention. Just try. Today is the only day of the Military portion of your initiation that you will spend completely in the classroom. Everything else is very hands-on. For our native Atlantean initiates, today may be a little boring; but everyone from the Surface should pay close attention, because we're going to be discussing an abbreviated history of Atlantis."

Almost all of the native Atlantean Betas and Deltas groaned, but Ryan heard Zach whisper an emphatic "Finally," and he agreed. He sat up a little straighter in his chair, and noticed that most of the Surface initiates were doing the same. Hopefully they would be getting some answers about Atlantis.

But as it turned out, the lesson wasn't all that interesting for the Surface initiates either. The first part of the class consisted of the siblings largely reiterating everything Drew had already told Ryan about the rise of the Order and the sinking of the original city—although Ryan noticed that unlike Drew, both Sam and Jennifer preferred to refer to the Order as "Demons" more than anything else.

"The Demons were careful not to sink Atlantis until they had a strong base in Rome," Sam said as Ryan started doodling absent-mindedly in the corner of his screen. "This allowed the Demons to flourish while we desperately tried to regroup and avoid further conflict in our weakened state. In fact, while we were in hiding, the Demons ruled Rome for a time. Both Julius and Augustus Caesar were part of the Order. It was rare for Order members to be such public figures, but because they advertised their empire as an oligarchy, the Demons were able to completely control both the first and second triumvirates without too much civil unrest—until Caesar's assassination, of course. He got a little too cocky. If you need further proof that Demon ideology leads to bloodlust, trag-edy, and corruption, just take a look at Rome's history."

"It wasn't until about 100 CE that we finally escaped Rome's area of influence and settled near the North Sea, with a decent barrier between us and the Demons," Jennifer continued as her brother took a seat. "From there, we mounted our counterattack. This is where it starts getting a little technical, so try to keep up," she added, without a lot of hope in her voice.

Ryan would have liked to say that he really tried to pay atten-tion, but that would have been a lie. He still felt exhausted from the Technology test the day before, and the Military classroom session was dragging. His mind felt heavy and thick. It was hopeless. He would never remember all the names and dates that fell out of the

Dennings' mouths. Soon, Ryan found that he was catching only small flashes of what Sam and Jennifer were saying.

". . . the damn Demons fled east to another major hub after Rome fell . . ."

"The Demons used the Church to stay in control . . ."

". . . never Pope, but their evil influences spread throughout the Holy Roman Empire."

"We were well established over all six populated continents, so Atlantis was finally able to take control . . ."

"We promoted the Protestant Reformation to gnaw away at the Demons' power as the Catholic Church started to weaken, especially in England, given the establishment of the Anglican Church. Being a large island, Britain's natural defenses allowed us to house a military stronghold in London."

". . . Demons again fled the Holy Roman Empire in 1672, after trying without success to promote the acceptance of Calvinism within the Catholic Church, in an effort to prevent the complete collapse . . ."

"Then, sensing the pivotal shift of Western civilization," Sam drawled on with a note of finality that brought Ryan back to the conversation, "both Atlantis and the Demons turned their attention to the American colonies. Atlantis, of course, promoted freedom and subtly aided the colonies however they could—"

"James!" Jennifer snapped at one of her own Surface initiates, who looked half asleep. "Pay attention! We're almost done."

Sam stared at his sister for a second, clearly unsure whether he appreciated her support or resented the interruption. Ryan was just thankful they had failed to notice his own daydreaming.

"Um . . . right, so . . ." Sam said, trying to get back on track. He sighed and shrugged. "Screw it. That's all the important stuff anyway. Atlantis is still here. The Demons are still here. While they keep trying to control how and when technological advancements are made available for their own ends, we continue to counter their efforts, serve those on the Surface through technological innovation, and protect society from the Demons. You know the spiel by now. Get out of here," he finished lazily.

"Well, at least we're finally done with that awful classroom! Now on to the fun stuff," Zach said bracingly as he, Ryan, and Carrie crossed the main plaza outside the Temple a few minutes later. Despite their exhaustion from constant studying, there was definitely a sense of shared satisfaction among the initiates. In fact, James and Rebecca were running around the fountain, singing some odd song they had made up with a chorus comprised only of the words "I'm free!"

"It's gonna be great!" Carrie said enthusiastically. "That last classroom session was pretty brutal. I never actually realized how boring Atlantean history is, despite the whole, you know, on-again-off-again secret war."

"Aw, come on," Will said to Carrie as he caught up to the three of them. "There are some interesting parts."

"Ahhh, I know what you're referring to," Carrie sang playfully, making Will turn slightly red from embarrassment. "Do you actually still believe in *him*?"

"Well, I mean . . . look, there's a ton of evidence he was real— no, seriously!" Will said at Carrie's friendly but exasperated look. "I mean, I don't think everything they say is true, but—"

"It's just a story!" Carrie said. "It's supposed to teach us not to take work too seriously, and show us why we need to be responsible!"

"What are you two talking about?" Ryan asked as Will opened his mouth to respond.

"The Atlantean Psycho," Carrie said mysteriously, with a devious grin.

"The what?" Zach asked immediately.

"It's this story about an Atlantean from the Surface who went completely insane while working one day. He just snapped under the pressure. Started causing a bunch of chaos. The story goes he even made it to the Surface and had a little fun there. In the end, he ended up killing a bunch of people . . . that is, if you believe he actually existed."

"He *did*," Will insisted. "I don't know if everything we've been told is true, but he existed! I've heard theories that he may have been from this city, too!"

"Every Atlantean across the world knows that story, Will," Carrie said as they reached the dining pavilion and sat down for dinner. "That's because it's supposed to be a *lesson*. I'm sure every city has some version of the story that makes it sound like the Psycho is from their city."

"*Or*," Will countered, "every Atlantean knows the story because it's true."

"You guys talking about the Psycho?" Jonathan asked as he sat down next to Ryan. "Dude was crazy! I heard he set an entire park on fire!"

"I like the one when he made all the water in a fountain turn blood red," Carrie said between bites of food.

"What, like Moses?" Zach said, making Ryan laugh and sending water up his nose.

Hearing different Atlantean initiates tell and retell the story of the Atlantean Psycho, Ryan understood Carrie's skepticism. Every Atlantean had a different tale about the Psycho, each one featuring more grandiose acts of chaos than the last. The Atlantean initiates were clearly enjoying themselves, with every one making sure his or her version of the story was told—especially to Rebecca, who was unabashedly eager to know everything about the maniac.

After staying up far too late exchanging urban legends from both Atlantis and the Surface, none of the Betas were alert enough to handle the Dennings siblings the next morning. Possibly sensing that his group was not fully up to snuff, Sam seemed unusually cheerful, and was definitely speaking even more quickly than normal as he went through all the different weapons stored in the Military District.

"Even though the Atlantean military utilizes our light technology," Sam said, standing in front of a wall gleaming with racks upon racks of different weapons, "we still have more conventional weapons, which we store in emergency armories like this one. As you can see, we've stockpiled thousands of swords, spears, bows, and shields for our soldiers. If you're chosen for the Military sect, you will have access to custom-made weapons that—"

"Why aren't there any guns?" Rebecca interrupted.

"To avoid mutual destruction. We signed the Great Arms Agreement of . . . of . . ." Sam looked at his sister for help.

"1192," supplied Jennifer.

"Great Arms Agreement of 1192," Sam said. "The agreement banned the use of all firearms in war. Both sides, the Order and Atlantis, have remained fully compliant. About three hundred and fifty years later, the agreement was ratified to include missiles, atomic bombs, and nuclear weapons. Despite all our differences, Atlantis and the Demons agreed that the decision was for the betterment of all humanity. In the end, it made sense for both groups: we wanted to minimize casualties, and the Demons wanted to make sure there will still be a world to rule after all the fighting is over."

◊◊◊

"You know, for just one city, you all sure have a lot of weapons," Zach said to Carrie a few days later.

They had just returned to the dorms after their last day on their Military rotation, which had been spent touring the armories strategically placed around the city. Ryan was amazed at the sheer number of stockpiles Atlantis possessed. During their tour, Sam and Jen even pointed out several artificial trees throughout the park that housed hidden weapon vaults, and Ryan made a mental note to be suspicious of all foliage and decorative rocks on Atlantis.

"We like to be prepared!" Carrie said as the three of them sat down on a pair of couches in the common room. "You can't trust those—"

"—damn Demons," Zach and Ryan finished for her, making all three of them laugh. Sam muttered the phrase so often that all the Surface initiates were confident it was a common saying on Atlantis.

Before Carrie could continue, they were interrupted by a voice that carried across the dorm too well for its volume to be accidental.

"Obviously, they'll keep it impartial," Roy said loudly as he walked into the room with a small group of native Atlanteans, "but at the end of the day, there *will* be more initiates from Atlantis chosen for Tech than those from the Surface. There may be more initiates from the Surface overall, but as native Atlanteans, we are simply better prepared for the critical thinking necessary to work in Tech. It's like my parents always said: if they keep allowing people from the Surface to come in . . ."

"He makes me want to puke," Zach said under his breath. Ryan nodded in agreement. Carrie looked downright disgusted.

"Come on," she said to them as she got up and headed to the bedroom. "I can't stand to listen to him."

"*Do* more native Atlanteans get chosen for Tech?" Ryan asked as he and Zach sat down on Ryan's bunk. Carrie flopped onto her own bed and paused for a second before answering.

"Maybe a few more?" Carrie admitted as she sat up. "I mean, we grew up with Atlantean technology, so it's possible . . . but they really try to keep it fair overall," she finished confidently. "That's why we're not allowed to complete our initiations in our own cities—to make sure no one gets special treatment. They know you guys may not be as familiar with some of the technology on Atlantis as we are; I'm sure they take that into consideration."

Ryan and Zach must still have looked apprehensive, because Carrie smiled and continued, "The next few weeks are the important ones, anyway. That's when they really evaluate you and see what you're made of. You guys are gonna be fine."

Despite her confidence, Ryan still had a slightly uneasy feeling. He'd always had a keen sense of right and wrong, and the idea that such an advanced society could still be vulnerable to bias was worrisome.

As he continued to think on the matter that afternoon, Ryan eventually settled on a simple solution: if the system was broken, he would just have to beat the system. He'd done it before, in college, taking way too many advanced classes and been involved in far too many clubs, all while working a part-time job. Multiple people had told him there was no way he would be able to do everything he'd signed up for, but he had. Sometimes his stubbornness was a blessing. Even if Atlantis had some type of hidden prejudice, he would beat it.

After everyone else in the bunk room had gone to bed, Ryan pulled up his tablet, opened his notes, and reviewed them so he would be ready for the next Technology and Military sessions as the other Betas snored.

CHAPTER SEVEN
TANTUS AND TOSS

"**K**endrick! Where's the damn meter?"

"Sorry, Dr. Tantus. Here it is," Ryan said, handing over a strange device that looked like a cross between a Tesla coil and a video-game controller.

Ryan's second Technology session was coming to a close—and the end couldn't come soon enough. At the start of the session, all of the Betas and Deltas had been paired with an Atlantean citizen in the Technology sect for two weeks. Even though the Technology Atlanteans were working on projects that were generally far too advanced for the initiates to contribute much, they were still supposed to try to help their mentors in whatever way possible.

"Remember," Jennifer had told both groups as Sam was passing out their assignments almost two weeks ago, "you're not just there to help them with their research. You will also be evaluated constantly. Sam and I, as well as some of your scouters, will stop in from time to time to see how well you work with other Technology Atlanteans."

"And the Atlanteans you're assigned to will be grading your performances, too," Sam said as he finished passing out the assignments. "So actually *try* to do well. Since you'll be with them for two weeks, their markings carry a lot of weight in the final decision."

"That said, if it doesn't go perfectly, don't stress too much," Jennifer added bracingly. "This is only the second of four Tech sessions, and you'll get another chance to impress someone in the Technology sect. You'll be paired with a different Atlantean for the third session to ensure a fair evaluation. Generally, we try to take your preferences into consideration. That being said, we want each of you to spend one session in the health branch and one session in the engineering branch, so you may not get exactly what you want. We also try to make sure one session is more technical in nature and the other is more theoretical. Good luck, guys!"

"Who'd ya get?" Carrie asked Ryan and Zach excitedly once the initiates started going their separate ways.

"Bane Tantus, in the Energy Lab," Ryan said. "I ranked the energy subdivision as my first choice on that survey we had to fill out, so that's g—what? Is he okay?" Carrie's face had twitched slightly when he mentioned Tantus' name.

"Yeah!" she said, a little too quickly. "He's really smart. Native Atlantean. I'm pretty sure he's from this city. My sister has mentioned him once or twice. He's just . . . a little grumpy sometimes. Who did you get, Zach?" she asked without skipping a beat.

"Lauren Mellow, in Coding and Defense. It's part of the military subdivision of the . . . engineering branch, I think. Do you know her?"

"Only by name—I think she's from the Surface. Never heard anything bad, though! I'm actually a little worried about my assignment. . . ."

"How come?" Ryan asked.

"I got Kylee," Carrie said uncertainly. "She's nice, but she my brother's ex. I mean, I know there are some safeguards in place that prevent native initiates from rotating in the same department as close relatives, especially since Atlantean families can end up spread across a couple different cities, but apparently that doesn't extend to past relationships. . . ."

Ryan tried to keep a straight face as Zach started laughing, making even Carrie smile reluctantly. Together, they tried to reassure her that her brother's ex surely wouldn't hold anything against her, and the three of them wished each other good luck before heading off to their assignments.

Now, two weeks into the session, Ryan wished Carrie had given him a little more warning about Dr. Tantus before they started—like mentioning how Dr. Tantus insisted on being addressed as "Dr." despite all degrees on Atlantis being purely honorary. Frankly, Ryan thought Carrie's description of the man as "a little grumpy" was generous. No matter what he did or how hard he tried, Dr. Tantus never seemed satisfied. Even when Ryan arrived early and tried to anticipate his needs in the lab, Dr. Tantus always found something to bark at him about.

"Took you long enough," Tantus grumbled as he took the meter from Ryan. Ryan stayed silent and watched Dr. Tantus take measurements as he hunched over a microscope. The native Atlantean grumbled so much that Ryan was certain he was really an old man, but of course he didn't look a day over twenty-eight, so there was no way of knowing for sure. Despite his unpleasant demeanor, the man's laboratory was completely pristine, with sterile white walls, spotless tables—the chairs didn't even squeak. Ryan tried to move as little as possible to avoid contaminating anything, even though there was no reason for the lab to be sterile at all.

"You *do* remember what I'm doing here, right?" Dr. Tantus scowled at Ryan with thinly veiled contempt.

"You're researching a way to produce antimatter with low-energy, everyday reactions so that Atlantis can one day be powered completely by the energy produced by annihilation reactions," Ryan recited immediately. Every day, Dr. Tantus asked the same question, and every day he criticized Ryan's paraphrased answers.

Today, knowing this would be his last chance to impress the man, Ryan had come prepared: yesterday, when Dr. Tantus had (predictably) corrected him, Ryan had recorded the doctor's response with a portable microphone taken from the Betas' dorms. Ryan had spent half of the following evening reviewing the recording, and he was certain he'd recited the doctor's words perfectly.

"Just say that I'm working on making sustainable energy," Dr. Tantus said disapprovingly. "No need to be so technical. It's unbecoming."

Ryan gaped at Dr. Tantus, his heart sinking. The first time Dr. Tantus had tried to tell Ryan what he was working on, he'd used horrible particle physics and thermodynamics jargon.

Apparently Dr. Tantus took Ryan's look of disbelief for confusion. "Look," he began, "it's all very complicated. Let's start at the beginning . . ."

Oh, no, Ryan thought. *Not again!*

". . . when I perfected cogeneration for Atlantis . . ."

Shit. Every. Single. Day.

Every day since Ryan had started working with him, Dr. Tantus invariably told the story of how he'd "perfected cogeneration" for Atlantis. Not only could he now recite the monologue from memory, but it constantly reminded Ryan of a withered undergraduate professor he'd had in sophomore year, who loved reminding everyone that he had tenure.

"I felt I had a personal responsibility—no, a *duty*—to solve the problem of cogeneration for Atlantis. While other so-called 'energy experts' on this city tried, and *failed*—miserably, too, if I do say so myself—I *knew* I could do it," Dr. Tantus stated loftily. "Now, just so you know, boy, cogeneration is the process of recycling waste energy, like the heat created from a light bulb, so that it can be used as electricity, too. No waste energy equals one hundred percent efficiency. That may seem like an impossible task for *some* people, but to me . . . well, I knew all I had to do was . . ."

Ryan nodded absentmindedly as Dr. Tantus continued to lecture him. Thankfully, over the course of the last two days, Ryan had realized how much easier it was to tolerate the condescending spiels if he imagined Dr. Tantus as Daffy Duck. Considering Dr. Tantus wore a black lab coat most days, the transformation didn't take too much imagination.

Ryan had to hide his smile as Dr. Tantus' voice shifted in his head into a lisping, squawky croak. Still trying to get on the evaluator's good side, Ryan started cleaning equipment from the latest experiment to make sure everything was in perfect condition for the man who would help determine whether or not he worked in the Technology sect.

". . . and once that was done, I had to convince the genius Elder that my solution would actually work. Honestly can't believe I actually had to explain my work to him, but—Kendrick, what are you doing? I don't need you cleaning that! Start entering these values into the computer! I don't want to have to do that myself."

Ryan set down the lab equipment and grabbed a list of over two hundred small energy values so that he could start the painstaking task of logging every data point. "Thought by now you would know what I need around here! Where was I? You made me lose my train of thought. Anyway, I spoke to the Elder about my research . . ."

Ryan continued to nod, entering nanojoule energy values into the computer as the Daffy Duck voice in his head finished the doctor's story. He wasn't quite sure why he was expected to predict that he needed to enter numbers into the computer, especially considering Dr. Tantus had never asked him to do it before, but Ryan knew he just had to play the game. It was all politics, and after working with Dr. Noret, Ryan knew how to carry on with his work, no matter how unreasonable the supervisor. Thankfully, Ryan knew Dr. Tantus' story would take almost a full hour, and he was ready.

"And now, absolutely no energy on Atlantis is wasted. Next step, using antimatter and annihilation to produce energy. Are you done with the data yet?" Dr. Tantus quacked at Ryan.

"Yessir," Ryan said at once. "I also analyzed the data you previously entered, and I constructed a graph so you can easily compare data sets."

"Not bad, Kendrick," Dr. Tantus quacked. The Atlantean hit a button on the computer and a hologram of the graph appeared above the desk. Ryan tried to hide his surprise. That was the most praise he had received in the past few weeks. He hoped it was a good sign.

◊◊◊

"Well, it sounds like it ended on a high note," Zach said encouragingly.

It was the day after their second Technology sessions had ended, and Zach and Ryan were swapping stories in the amphitheater behind the Temple. Considering that Lauren Mellow had told Zach to contact her if he needed anything, and Dr. Tantus had ended their final session with a curt nod, Ryan was pretty confident that Zach's experience had been much more positive. Thankfully, Zach took his good fortune graciously, and Ryan was happy for his friend.

"I think so," Ryan said, enjoying the sun. Even by a flying city's standards, it was a beautiful day. "On the last day, he only quacked at me once, so I definitely improved over the two weeks."

"Quacked?" Zach said, confused.

"Uh . . . snapped . . . my bad," Ryan said quickly as he spotted Carrie heading down the amphitheater steps to join them. "Hopefully he still gives me a good review."

"I'm sure you did fine," Carrie said as she sat down. "At least you didn't knock over three flasks filled with hazardous chemicals on your first day."

"Oh, sorry, Carrie," Ryan said as he and Zach tried not to laugh.

"It's fine," she said, waving down the apology. "Kylee was actually really nice about the whole thing. She could tell I was weirded out by working with her, and she promised that it wouldn't be awkward at all. But enough dwelling on the last few weeks. You guys want to go see Toss?"

"The game?" Zach asked, sitting up straight. "Absolutely! Where's it at?"

"The central park," Carrie said. "We passed the field when we were coming back from the Industrial District, remember?"

As Carrie led the two of them to the park, she tried to give them a crash course on the rules of Toss.

"The game's simple," she said quickly as they hurried down a path crowded with people all heading toward the center of the city, laughing and talking as they went. "It's kind of like basketball, but each team has six players: four ground players and two aerial players. The teams pass four balls back and forth, and try to score by getting the balls into the large funnels at the ends of the field. If a ground player scores, the team gets two points. If an aerial player scores, the team gets one point."

"What do you mean by 'aerial'?" Ryan asked as they continued to weave through the crowd.

"You'll see," Carrie said simply before continuing. "Anyway, each team tries to defend its own funnel. Obviously, the ground players aren't much help when it comes to defending against aerial players; but aerial players do have a weakness. It's kinda like their Achilles heel . . ."

"Let me guess," Zach said. "Achilles was an Atlantean."

Carrie stopped abruptly, causing Ryan to run into her.

"I think so," she said slowly, before resuming her fast pace. "Anyway, each aerial player wears two pegs—one on each calf—that are magnetically attached. The opposing team tries to knock off the pegs, either by grabbing them or by hitting them with a ball. When an aerial player loses both pegs, they're out of the game. The game ends when one team loses both aerial players. The score of the team that still has an aerial player at the end is multiplied by 1.5. So, if a team originally had fifty points and the other team loses all their aerial players, the first team ends with seventy-five points."

The three of them finally arrived at the Toss field and found it packed with people. Ryan had been on Atlantis for over a month and a half, but he'd had no idea there were so many people in the city. The same field that had been nearly empty a few weeks ago was now surrounded by a mob of children and adults. Even though he had grown used to the idea that people on Atlantis didn't age, it was still odd seeing virtually no one over the age of thirty. As Carrie weaved through the crowd toward the bleachers, Ryan had to do a few double-takes whenever he heard native Atlanteans around his age refer to people in their late twenties as "Mom" and "Dad."

"Who's playing?" Ryan asked Carrie as they found seats at the top of the bleachers.

"The top two teams in the city: the Blizzards and the Tornadoes. All the teams in this city are named after natural disasters," Carrie explained. "The winning team will go on to the intercity tournament next year. They hold the tournament every two . . . look! Here they come!"

Carrie had to shout at the end, because the bleachers around them suddenly erupted into cheers. Ryan watched as two teams of six—one team in dark blue uniforms and the other in heather gray—entered the field near the midline. Four players from each team were wearing typical moisture-wicking athletic shirts and shorts, but the other players were wearing something on their backs that Ryan had never seen before.

For the first time, Ryan understood why people from the Surface would refer to the Atlanteans as "angels." In addition to helmets, gloves, and boots, two players on each team stepped onto the field wearing what could only be described as a set of metallic wings. Even though it was hard to tell from the bleachers, each set of wings appeared to be made of layered metal feathers that shimmered faintly as they moved. Ryan watched as one of the aerial players on the blue team looked over his shoulder to watch his wing contract and expand, almost as if he was warming up.

"Can those things actually fly?" Zach asked Carrie in amazement.

"Yup!" she said, not taking her eyes off the aerial players from the blue team.

"I take it we're rooting for the Blizzards?" Ryan asked, looking sideways at Carrie. She nodded, and her cheeks turned slightly pink.

Before Ryan could ask Carrie what was wrong, the entire crowd went eerily quiet. Ryan turned back just in time to see the Elder walk onto the field and set down a bulging bag before spreading his arms welcomingly.

"Good afternoon, everyone!" Michael Stamaris said. He spun

around as he talked, so that he could address all the spectators. Ryan couldn't help but smile at the Elder as the crowd cheered. He had seen Michael a few times since that first day in the Temple, and each time, he had found himself more and more impressed by the graying leader's mild manner and good nature. "I know none of you came here to listen to this old man speak, so I won't waste any more of your time! Captains, please step forward."

Both of the aerial players from each of the two teams walked up to the Elder and shook his hand, and in turn, the Elder gave each of them a solid white ball about the size of a volleyball. He said something to the captains that Ryan couldn't hear from the stands, and all four winged players nodded in agreement. The Elder then raised his hand in farewell and strode off the field to a roar of approval as the players took their positions and put on their gloves.

On either end of the field, the sides of each of the funnels displayed a large zero for the entire audience to see. Despite the hundreds of spectators, the stands were completely silent as the players stood ready. All Ryan could hear was a light breeze rustling through the trees.

Beep! The funnels at each end of the field flashed yellow for a second.

Beep! They flashed yellow again.

BEEP! Both funnels turned green.

The field exploded into motion.

All four aerial players threw their balls and shot up into the air. The balls, never still for more than a fraction of a second, were passed between the players with dizzying speed.

Ryan watched in amazement as the aerial players flew around the field, seamlessly swooping in and out of the excitement to help their field-bound teammates. Their wings extended and curved to complete complicated maneuvers, but Ryan noticed they never flapped. He tried to keep up with the excitement of the game, but there was simply too much happening at once. It seemed that on every other pass, the balls changed color to either red or green. Between four different balls being passed around and the aerial players swarming, Ryan found himself overwhelmed. He looked over at Zach, whose head was turning in every direction as he also tried to take in everything at once.

"This game is insane," Ryan said, grinning.

"It's awesome!" Carrie said, cheering when the blue team scored twice, back to back. The large number projected on the funnel changed to keep track of the score. "It gets a little easier to follow once they start taking away the balls."

"When does that happen?" Ryan shouted over the crowd.

"Every time an aerial player leaves the game, they take away a ball!"

A loud gasp and a cheer snapped Ryan's attention back to the field. One of the Tornadoes' fliers had lost a peg, and Ryan could see it spinning back to the ground. The gray flier, clearly frustrated, dove and intercepted a ball that two Blizzards field players were passing back and forth. As soon as his gloves touched the ball, it turned from green to red. The two aerial players for the Tornadoes quickly passed the ball back and forth before dropping it into the funnel for another point. The Blizzards' field defender picked up the ball as it exited the funnel, and the ball turned green as it touched her glove, before she passed the ball to a teammate.

Ryan could hear Zach asking Carrie a question, but the crowd was so loud that he couldn't make out what Zach had said. Thankfully, Carrie responded loudly enough for all of them to hear.

"The ball's color changes based on who touched it last. Green for a field player, red for an aerial player. So the funnel can keep track of the score automatically."

"Why don't the fliers just hold onto the ball?" Ryan asked Carrie, cheering when a Blizzards flier blocked a shot from one of the Tornadoes' field players, allowing the Blizzards to keep their lead with a score of twenty-five to twenty-one.

"They can only hold onto the ball for four seconds before passing or shooting!" Carrie yelled back. "And nobody on either team is allowed inside the foul circle around the funnel for more than three seconds unless they're getting the ball after the other team scor—*No!*"

Ryan looked up just in time to see both of the Tornadoes' aerial players descend on one of the blue fliers. At first, Ryan thought they were going to fight in midair, but after a few seconds, the gray players broke away and left the Blizzards player flying alone. The entire crowd was screaming. Ryan wasn't sure what had happened at first, but after a few seconds, he realized that each of the Tornadoes players was holding a blue peg. The two Tornadoes fliers had removed both of the Blizzards player's pegs at the same time. Ryan watched as the defeated blue flier landed outside the field and tore off her helmet, swearing loudly.

Ryan found that Carrie was correct—the game was a lot easier to follow with even one less ball on the field. He watched as both teams executed more and more complex plays. Probably the most impressive play was one during which all four ground players for the Blizzards finally gained control of all three remaining balls and ran down the field in a box formation, passing the balls back and forth so perfectly that it looked as if they were juggling. The crowd cheered as the Tornadoes tried desperately to predict the next pass and intercept a ball—without success—until the Blizzards perfectly shot all three balls into the Tornadoes' funnel, for an extra six points.

Clearly frustrated with her team's lack of progress, one of the Tornadoes' fielders grabbed all three balls out of the funnel and passed each of them to a teammate. She and the gray flier who still had both pegs passed the ball back and forth, steadily making their way down the field to score. Just as the flier passed the ball to his teammate to set up a shot, a blue missile shot across the field and grabbed the ball before it reached the gray field player.

Ryan watched as the remaining blue flier spun in midair and hummed the ball directly at the gray flier. The Tornadoes' player realized what was happening a moment too late, and was unable to dodge the ball, which squarely struck one of the flier's pegs, knocking it clean off. Before the Tornadoes' player could retaliate, the blue flier soared away in triumph.

Sensing the end of the game was close, the ground players started moving with a new ferocity. The remaining Blizzards flier still had both pegs, the two Tornadoes fliers had one peg each, and the game wasn't slowing down at all. But the score was still too close to predict which team was going to win: thirty-eight to thirty-seven, Blizzards.

Ryan watched as the blue field players again gathered all three balls and began to run their box play down the field. For a second, he was certain that the Blizzards players would score with all three balls again. One of the Tornadoes' fliers must have thought the same thing, because as soon as the Blizzards started passing the balls between themselves, he dove into the middle of the play to intercept one. The crowd shouted in warning, but the blue players must not have heard: they weren't able to stop the interception.

The Tornadoes' aerial player caught a ball, completely disrupting the play. As soon as the ball turned from green to red, however, all of the blue field players lunged toward the flier. It took the flier too long to realize the entire play had been a trap. Before he could free himself from the Blizzards players, one of the blue fielders yanked off his last peg and held it in the air in triumph.

The entire crowd erupted into a roar, knowing that both teams only had one remaining flier. At first, Ryan wasn't sure why all the Tornadoes supporters were also cheering—until Carrie pointed to what was happening thirty feet above the ground.

The two remaining fliers were caught in an out-and-out dog-fight, with the Tornadoes' player relentlessly chasing the Blizzards'. The Blizzards' player dodged and weaved, trying desperately to lose the gray flier on his tail. After a minute of furious aerial maneuvers, the Tornadoes' flier reached out and tore off one of the blue player's pegs. The Tornadoes supporters cheered wildly as the blue peg fell to the ground. Both fliers had only one peg left.

Despite the game still being neck-and-neck, Ryan was almost certain the Tornadoes were going to win. Even though he only had one peg remaining, the gray flier was still chasing the Blizzards' with uncompromised focus. The blue flier could not escape his pursuer. As Ryan watched, the Blizzards' player became so desperate that he began to circle the base of one of the large funnels at dizzying speeds. The Tornadoes' flier copied him, obviously hoping to get a hand on the last peg. Ryan watched as the player extended his hand . . .

A loud horn blared on each side of the field, making Ryan jump, and both of the funnels started rapidly blinking red. All of the players immediately stopped. The gray flier swore loudly and glared at the Blizzards flier. Without saying anything, each flier drifted over to the funnel their team was defending and sat down just outside the field of play.

Once both aerial players were off the field, the funnels beeped, flashed yellow, and then turned green again. The ground players immediately resumed playing with the two remaining balls, while the fliers sat on the sidelines.

"They fouled!" Carrie explained to Ryan. "It was a trap! He tricked the Tornadoes flier by staying inside the foul circle for too long. They both fouled, and it broke up the chase. Now both of them have to sit out for two minutes."

Ryan watched all the ground players fight to keep their team in the game until the fliers returned. The two teams were practically trading points. After a few short plays, there was a loud *BEEP*, and both fliers shot back onto the field, aiming straight for each other. For a second, Ryan thought they were going to collide; but right before impact, the two fliers changed trajectories and flew straight up, soaring higher and higher.

Just as Ryan was wondering how high they would go, the Blizzards player accelerated upward, putting a few yards between him and the other player, and suddenly tucked his wings in. The crowd screamed as the blue player hovered for a moment in midair, then started to free fall. The Tornadoes flier tried to dodge, but the move was so unexpected, he wasn't able to get out of the way fast enough.

The Blizzards player collided with the Tornadoes player's legs as he fell toward the pitch. The blue player fell another ten feet before his wings sprang open again. He hovered in midair and faced the audience, raising his arm in triumph. In his hand was the last gray peg.

The Blizzards fans erupted into cheers. The ground players had kept the score almost tied the entire game, and the score was now seventy-two to seventy, with the Blizzards in the lead. At that play, however, Ryan watched as the Blizzards' score jumped from seventy-two to one hundred and eight. The game had ended, and all the Blizzards players began celebrating their victory.

The blue flier glided down to land on the field as his teammates rushed up to meet him. Through the celebrating crowd and the elated players, Ryan saw the aerial player remove his helmet—to reveal Drew's beaming face, grinning wildly.

CHAPTER EIGHT
BEAM

They were going to die. There was nothing Ryan could do. It was his job to protect them, but he was going to fail, and they were all going to die.

Ryan inspected the massive hologram in front of him, which covered the entire surface of a large conference table. He circled the table, trying to take in every detail of the simulation.

The hologram showed a mock battle taking place on a large, open field with a narrow tree line along the southern edge. The goal was to outsmart the computer's AI and win the battle with as few casualties as possible.

Ryan looked hopelessly at the scene before him. His own troops were greatly outnumbered, and the enemy had formed two large square formations, with only a small passage in between. If he tried to charge, their formations would easily allow them to overpower Ryan's troops from the front while flanking his units simultaneously on both sides.

Ryan swore under his breath as he tried to come up with a quick plan. He had done well on the previous levels, but each time the computer was beaten, the next simulation was harder. Each new iteration came with more enemy troops, fewer reinforcements, and more surprises that inevitably led to greater casualties.

Ryan was now reaching levels that seemed to be inspiring Sam and Jennifer to watch him a little more carefully. In fact, he had seen the siblings talking in undertones after he completed the last level, and Jennifer had even given him a small nod.

Ryan looked around the practice hall to see whether any of the other initiates were struggling as much as he was. The Betas and the Deltas had spent the past few days in a large building in the Military District. Each initiate had been given their own table with a hologram shimmering over it, casting an eerie glow throughout the entire space and giving the impression that the whole exercise was taking place underwater.

Even now, a little more than half the initiates were stuck on easier levels. Two tables down, Zach was sweating profusely, struggling with an earlier scenario that took place on a forested mountainside. He had told Ryan the day before that he had lost the same round about fifteen times, and his tactics were growing steadily more desperate. Last round, he'd sent all his troops charging into enemy territory in a single unbroken line, and had lost horrifically. Ryan was happy to see he wasn't repeating that mistake now.

On Ryan's other side, Carrie's hands were a blur as she maneuvered her holographic troops seamlessly around her opponents. She was doing noticeably better than almost all the initiates, including Ryan, and the evaluators were definitely taking an interest in her.

In addition to the initiates, Sam, and Jennifer, several other evaluators—presumably ranking military officials—slowly circled the room to see how everyone was managing. Sometimes they would pose a question about someone's strategy or offer friendly advice, but for the most part, they simply studied the Betas and Deltas in silence.

A few hours ago, Ryan had noticed a couple evaluators watching him and taking notes on a tablet. While he thought it was a good sign, it definitely added to the pressure.

Now, Ryan turned his attention back to the hologram in front of him. His opponent had been relentless in this simulation. Sometimes the enemy was less bold, but this level gave the computer so many troops that the AI was able to chase down Ryan's forces almost carelessly. He hated to admit it, but Ryan thought the computer's strategy was working pretty well. Every decision he made seemed to result in huge losses. No matter what he did next, the computer would chase his troops across the open plain, and it would be over. Unless . . .

Ryan straightened and leaned over the edge of the table so far that his chest interfered with the holographic display. He flicked his wrist so that a holographic menu full of command options appeared in front of him, selected all his troops, and gave the order before he had a chance to second-guess himself. He needed to be confident.

As one, all of Ryan's holographic troops turned their backs toward the enemy and sprinted to the south. Their formation broke, but Ryan cared much more about speed than appearances at this point.

It took the AI a second to process what was happening, but it quickly forced its own troops to give chase, just as Ryan had known it would. As soon as his troops reached the tree line, Ryan brought up the menu again to see whether there were any new strategies available now that the terrain had changed. A new option popped up, and he selected it without hesitation.

Ryan's troops stopped running and took their positions inside the wooded area. By the time the opponent's forces reached the tree line, Ryan's troops were ready. Using a guerilla strategy that was never an option on an open field, Ryan's meager army weaved through the trees to hack at the AI's troops. Whenever he saw an opening in the computer's formation, Ryan highlighted new areas on which to focus his own troops' attacks. It only took a few minutes, but in the end, the enemy's forces had been almost completely destroyed, and those that remained turned to retreat. Despite taking heavy losses, Ryan's forces were victorious.

"Well done, Kendrick," said a flat voice behind him.

Ryan spun around to see the Head of Military watching him. Daniel Amerrest had turned away from Carrie's hologram, which he had been watching for a while, and faced him.

"You were in a tough spot, and you came through," Amerrest said tonelessly. If not for the compliment, Ryan wouldn't have been able to tell whether the man was pleased with his work or not. "Next time, try to read your opponent a little earlier—it can save lives."

"Yes, sir," Ryan said. "Thanks for the . . . tip," he trailed off. Amerrest had already turned his attention away from Ryan and back to Carrie, as her troops dismantled a shockingly large army.

◊◊◊

"That was awful," Zach said.

Ryan and Carrie had walked out of the simulation facility a few hours later to find Zach waiting for them. He'd been one of the first initiates to leave after Sam had dismissed the Betas. He obviously had no desire to spend any more time with the simulations than necessary.

"Some of the scenarios were hard," Ryan agreed. "Carrie, you were incredible! I think you got further than anyone."

"Thanks," she said, obviously trying and failing to hide how happy she was. "Don't stress about it, Zach. You killed in the Tech session!"

"True," Zach said, although he didn't look any less dismayed. "The first aid part wasn't too bad either. At least I didn't pass out like that Delta guy!"

Carrie and Ryan both laughed. They had started the second

Military session by learning how to treat common combat injuries. Sam had been demonstrating how to dress a stab wound on his sister when a large pouch of fake blood on her chest had burst open violently. A small pump in the pouch caused the "blood" to spurt realistically, and Sam later told Ryan—with an evil grin— that he'd personally added a benign iron-based compound to the liquid to make it smell like actual blood. Together, the effects made the scene rather disturbing, and one poor Delta initiate had fainted when some of the fake blood had sprayed into his mouth.

"I kinda felt bad for him," Ryan said. "But the look on his face before he dropped was hysterical!"

"Yeah, and Rebecca looked like she was going to puke," Zach said.

"Well, Sam got all of us the first day we used the holograms," Carrie said, smiling.

Ryan and Zach both half groaned and half chuckled. The first day the initiates had set foot in the simulation facility, Jen hadn't been feeling well, so Sam was in charge. He spent the entire day demonstrating how to use the hologram tables; but apparently he was bored without Jennifer around, so he decided to prank the initiates by convincing all of them that the simulations responded to voice commands. Jennifer, still rather pale, came back halfway through the next day to a large room of initiates hopelessly shouting at the holograms, trying desperately to move their holographic armies around. It wasn't until she found her brother by the evaluator's station, in tears from laughing, that she fully understood what had happened to the otherwise intelligent group of initiates.

Zach, Ryan, and Carrie slowly made their way to the pavilion for dinner, talking about some of the battle strategies they had tried. Ryan was halfway through a retelling of how half his army had drowned when he ordered them to cross a river when they spotted a large crowd of initiates gathered by the pavilion.

"What's going on?" Carrie asked Will, who was standing near the back of the crowd.

"They're preparing a banquet for us," Will said, "to celebrate our being halfway done with initiation. I think I heard Sam call it the 'Initiation Social.'"

Even by Atlantean standards, the dinner was extravagant. The volunteer cooks went all-out, preparing five courses for all four groups of initiates, plus several visitors. Ryan and his friends couldn't have been seated for more than a few seconds before a server rushed up to greet them, practically tossed each of them a bowl of soup, and disappeared into the crowd. Each course was more decadent than the last, and by the time dessert was served, Ryan had to muster every last bit of determination to finish his pastry before pushing the empty plate away with a slight huff. All the other initiates looked equally stuffed, but all of them seemed to be enjoying themselves. After stressing for almost two months about how well they were doing and which sect they would be placed in, the Initiation Social was a welcome break.

Even the evaluators seemed to be having a good time at the event. Instead of studying the initiates, they went from table to table and sat down with people, getting to know the future citizens of Atlantis.

A handful of people Ryan had never seen before were also circling around the pavilion, engaging initiates in conversation. He watched as a woman sat next to Rebecca and made grand gestures toward one of the buildings lining the amphitheater, as if she was trying to show Rebecca something hidden in the marble. The two talked excitedly for over an hour.

A few seats down from Rebecca, Will wasn't so lucky. He looked rather uncomfortable, talking to a man who drank coffee from a still-hot mug with no regard for the hour as he scrolled through seemingly endless diagrams—complete with large images of tightropes and aerial hoops—on three different tablets. Ryan thought he heard the man saying something about an Acrobatics Guild—which, given his fellow initiate's last experience with ziplines, might have explained why Will was looking slightly green.

By the time everyone finished dessert, the sun had set well below the surface of the city, and people were finally starting to clear out. None of them had realized how late it had gotten, and the Betas knew they had to make a good impression the next day for their third technology sessions. Carrie had already left to get ready for bed, and Zach was just saying something about heading back to the dorm when Ryan felt someone sit down on his other side.

"Hey, Ryan. How have you been?" Drew asked with a smile. "Sam treating you guys okay?"

"Mostly," Ryan said. At the same time, Zach gave a noncommittal "Eh . . ."

"That sounds about right," Drew said, chuckling. Zach gave Ryan a friendly pat on the shoulder before nodding to Drew and heading off toward the dorms. "You like it here?" asked Drew, as he returned Zach's parting wave.

"Atlantis? This place is unbelievable," Ryan said immediately. "Still trying to get my bearings, but Carrie's been really helpful—she's teaching us about the city."

"That's right," Drew said. "She's spent some time on this city before, right? I worked with her parents when she was really little. Extremely nice family. They had me over for dinner a few times. They love to feed people."

"Well, there's no way it was as good as this dinner," Ryan said.

"Glad you enjoyed it! Has anyone told you about the guilds yet?"

"Guilds?"

"They're the ones who put on this dinner," Drew said, nodding at the man sipping coffee, who still had poor Will cornered. "Each Atlantean city has a dozen or so guilds in which people can pursue their creative hobbies. We have the Painters' Guild, the Musicians' Guild, the Writers' Guild . . . I think there's an Acting Guild here, too. I know I'm forgetting some . . . oh, yeah, the Sculpting Guild. They're the ones petitioning the city to be allowed to carve statues directly on our buildings."

"Are they that good?" Ryan asked, impressed.

"No—not at all. Well, I guess a couple are," Drew said, "but they're the exceptions. Most of the guildmembers are just hardworking citizens looking for a way to express themselves. The guilds are another way for the cities to stay connected, too. Every year, each guild holds a major event at one of the Atlantean cities where everyone can come and admire their work. It's actually a lot of fun. If I remember correctly, the Guinean City hosted last year's Musicians' Guild Convention. But anyway, all the guilds work together to prepare this dinner for you guys. It gives the initiates a break and allows the guild members to introduce themselves and get the word out . . . though apparently they're slacking a bit."

"I had no idea," Ryan said. "Are you in a guild?"

"I'm a member of the Painters' Guild, but I'm not really active with them," Drew said. "They tend to meet up every other Tuesday, and since Toss practice is held on most Tuesdays and Thursdays . . ."

"We saw you play Toss!" Ryan said. "You won the game for the Blizzards. It was amazing!"

"Thanks, man," Drew said. "You enjoyed watching?"

"I did! That was my first time seeing wings. Have you always been one of the aerial players?"

Drew nodded. "I've always loved flying," he said, with the same smile he'd worn right before he'd launched the ship to reach Atlantis. "But enough about me. How are you doing with your initiation? Is it going well?"

"It's been . . . good," Ryan said slowly. It was mostly true, but he was actually really nervous about his session with Dr. Tantus. His stomach twisted in knots whenever he thought about it. He wanted to talk to Drew about the session, but Ryan could see Roy over Drew's shoulder a few tables away, throwing not-so-subtle looks over at them and clearly wondering why Ryan was talking to such a highly esteemed evaluator.

Drew followed Ryan's gaze, and nodded in understanding.

"Come on," he said suddenly, standing and jerking his head to indicate Ryan should follow.

Ryan followed Drew out of the pavilion and past the amphitheater, making for the Temple and central plaza. At first he thought they were going to talk by the fountain again, but Drew surprised him by opening the massive Temple doors and heading inside.

The interior of the Temple looked completely different in the dark. Without sunlight beaming through the tall, narrow windows, the only source of illumination came from the light spheres positioned around the columns, giving the space a shadowy, haunted look.

Drew led Ryan across the Temple and onto the elevated platform where the Elder had first addressed the new initiates a couple months ago. Then, proceeding to the left wing of the stage, he opened a small door that Ryan hadn't noticed before. Before them was a shockingly steep spiral staircase, which Drew began to climb without a word.

Ryan followed dutifully, his thighs burning as he tried to keep up. After a few minutes of climbing, he felt a cool breeze on the back of his neck, and looked up just in time to see Drew exit the stairwell through a door a few feet above. Grateful for the prospect of getting off the staircase, Ryan climbed the last few steps—and froze.

The doorway led to the roof of the Temple. Around them, the amphitheater and dorms all looked surprisingly small. About forty feet below, Ryan could see the pavilion, where dozens of Atlanteans were still finishing dinner.

Ryan looked over at Drew, who was standing precariously close to the edge of the building, and to what would almost certainly be a lethal fall without a set of wings.

"Come on!" he said to Ryan. "The view from the other side is better."

Drew was right. After a slightly shaky walk around the edge of the Temple's dome, Drew and Ryan stopped at the front of the Temple. From where he stood, Ryan had an amazing view of the main plaza, the fountain, and the park, all of which were lit by blue-white light spheres.

Drew took a seat on the roof, using the natural curve of the dome to stretch his back with a satisfied groan. Ryan sat down next to him and gazed out at the city he had come to know over the past two months.

"This is where I go when I want some peace," Drew said after a few seconds, admiring the view. "When I was a kid, I would sneak out onto the roof of our house all the time. It took my parents forever to realize where I kept disappearing to." He laughed to himself. "Now—really, this time—how has your initiation been?"

"It really has been okay," Ryan said earnestly. "Just . . . the second Tech session didn't go as smoothly as I wanted."

"Really?" Drew said in evident surprise. "Who were you with?"

"Dr. Tantus."

"Oh." Drew's face fell slightly. "Look, I wouldn't worry about it. He's a jerk. All the evaluators look at how your matches rate you guys, and we curve the scores according to their . . . er . . . grumpiness." Ryan laughed. "We all know he grades harshly, and we take that into consideration."

"Good," Ryan said, feeling a little better. "Other than that, I think it's gone pretty well. The tests were tough, but I think everyone thought that. And I did well on the military simulations!" Something suddenly occurred to Ryan, and he frowned. "Will that count against me if I want to be in Tech?"

"Absolutely not," Drew said without hesitation. "Strategic thinking has a lot of applications. Besides, we can tell when someone is trying to do poorly in the Military sessions just to better their odds of being Tech. It doesn't work—at all. Of course, some people truly just aren't great at strategy, and that's fine. But it's important that you try—and it's obvious that you do."

"I just really want to do well," Ryan said. "It would be awesome to be Tech. What about being from the Surface?"

"What do you mean?"

"Well, that guy you saw, Roy—he's been saying that more native Atlanteans than people from the Surface get picked for Tech. He's been going on about the people he knows, and how he has all these advantages, and—"

"I'm gonna stop you right there," Drew said gently. "He's wrong. I mean . . . sure; maybe there was some bias decades ago. But it's not an issue anymore. Are there some . . . purists out there? Absolutely, and they tend to have a long Atlantean lineage. His parents are definitely some of them. Both of them were in my initiation class, and his father was a complete a—I'm getting off topic. The point is, most of us know better. We fight to make the choosing process as fair as possible. That's why initiates swap cities for initiation, and that's also why they aren't allowed to complete any Tech rotations in the same department as a direct relative. I'm not worried about you at all. You're going to do fine."

"Thanks," Ryan said, and he really meant it. He definitely felt better after talking with Drew, and it was nice to have someone apart from the other initiates to talk to about his nerves.

For a long moment, they sat in companionable silence, watching the stars and spotting the occasional person strolling through the park.

"Are all the Demons really that bad?" Ryan asked suddenly.

Ever since he had arrived on Atlantis, something about the Atlanteans' disdain for the Order had made Ryan uncomfortable. He could understand the existence of some bitterness between the two groups, considering the fact that the Order had sunk the original city; but a lot of the comments Ryan had heard the Atlanteans make about the Order had sounded downright hateful. He'd been hoping to ask someone about the Order for a while now, but he worried that even his simple question could come across as treasonous. "I mean, I'm sure some of them still want to help people on the Surface, right? They were originally part of Atlantis, after all."

"Maybe," Drew said slowly. "I mean . . . I understand where you're coming from. There probably were some people in the Order who used to want to do good, but . . . not anymore. Their leader brainwashes them. He trains them to think that the Order is meant to rule people on the Surface. Not that they *can* rule people . . . that they're *supposed* to. That it's their 'right.'" Ryan nodded in understanding.

"Besides, Atlantis has gone to war with the Order so many

times. There's definitely some bad blood there," Drew said.

"You're right," Ryan said. "Sorry for asking."

"Don't apologize!" Drew said with a smile. "It's good that you don't just accept things blindly. You seek out new information and actually think things through. No need to apologize for that."

Ryan smiled back appreciatively.

They talked for a little while longer before Drew reminded him that he really needed a good night's sleep before the next Technology session started tomorrow, and they got up to descend the stairs.

"Do you know who you're with yet?" Drew asked as they stepped through the Temple's main doors and out into the plaza.

"No, Sam refuses to give us our assignments in advance," Ryan said.

"Of course," Drew said as he shut the Temple door. "Sometimes I think he has a real stick shoved up his aAAAAH!"

Ryan and Drew spun around to find themselves face-to-face with a man dressed completely in black. He was so silent that neither of them had heard him approach. It took Drew a moment to find his voice again.

"Jeez, Gray!" Drew said weakly. "Don't do that!"

"Scared the stick out of you?" the man said slyly, the corner of his mouth twitching with the start of a smile. He had dark hair and extremely pale skin that instantly reminded Ryan of traditional depictions of a vampire.

Drew laughed good-naturedly and turned to Ryan. "Ryan, this is Gray . . . um . . . Gray . . . sorry, man, I can never remember your last name," Drew said to the man, with a small wince.

"It's fine, Drew. It's Morte. Grayson Morte. Most people just call me Gray. And you must be Ryan Kendrick. It's nice to meet you." Grayson stuck out his hand.

"Nice to meet you, too," Ryan said carefully.

"Didn't mean to scare you guys. My bad," Grayson said with a smile. He seemed friendly enough, but something about him made Ryan slightly uneasy. Was it his smile? Did he have fangs? No. Was he blinking? Ryan wanted to peer at the man's face, to watch his eyes; but he couldn't think of a way to do it without being creepy.

"All good," Drew said. "What are you doing over here?"

"Just helping out the Elder with some stuff," Grayson said vaguely. "Actually, he's expecting me, so I have to run. But it was good seeing you, Drew. And nice to finally meet you, Ryan."

Both Drew and Ryan said goodbye, and the two of them watched Grayson disappear down a small alley that extended off the side of the plaza.

"So ... who was that?" Ryan asked Drew as they started walking back to the dorms.

"That's Grayson. He's a little odd, but he's nice," Drew said. He took a breath, as if he wanted to say more about Gray, but then seemed to think better of it and remained silent.

"Is he Tech or Military?"

"Uh, he's ... Military ... I think," Drew answered uncertainly. "Honestly, I don't know too much about him. He really keeps to himself."

"I guess he's close to the Elder," Ryan said. "Must be doing something big."

"Yeah ... well, who knows. I'm sure he'll keep whatever he's doing with the Elder private," Drew said. "Even if they're just jogging buddies."

"Yeah, but one thing was kinda weird," Ryan said. "He knew my last name."

◇◇◇

"So in other words, you're crazy enough to try to solve three big problems at the same time," Ryan joked.

Ryan's third Technology session was already going remarkably better than his time with Dr. Tantus had. He'd been matched with a native Atlantean named Olivia Freeman, who had returned to the Northeast American City after completing her requisite service period in the Californian City, and she was possibly the kindest person he had ever met. Ryan was only four days into his rotation, but the two of them had worked together seamlessly from the beginning. Even though most of their work was theoretical and research-based, Ryan found that he was easily able to predict and find the information Olivia needed for her tests. He found the work enjoyable, not only because he was working with someone pleasant, but also because he felt like they were doing real work that could help a ton of people.

"Not really!" Olivia said with a laugh. "I'm trying to find a way to revitalize destroyed brain cells, restore memory after the cells have been damaged, and recreate neural pathways to improve motor control. Okay, yes, I know that's three problems!" she chuckled, as Ryan tried to hide his laughter. "But I have to figure out how to revitalize the cells before tackling the other two. So, for now it's just one problem."

"That reminds me," Ryan said. "I noticed you always say 'damaged' or 'destroyed' brain cells—never 'dead.'"

"Between you and me, 'dead cells' would probably be more accurate," Olivia said. "But there are some serious ethical issues if we start talking about bringing dead cells back to life. It's all going to come up sooner or later, and eventually there'll be an ethics meeting where the entire city will discuss whether we have the right to bring anything 'dead' back to life. But I'd rather that discussion happen after I figure this out. For now, we're rolling with 'revitalizing damaged brain cells.'"

"Makes sense," Ryan said. He turned his attention back to the stack of neurology and biology textbooks spread across the table in front of them. "When I started a few days ago, you said you were focusing specifically on stroke patients, right?"

"Yes," Olivia said, not taking her eyes off the page she was reading. "Many stroke patients have difficulty with simple tasks when their brain cells die . . . I mean, are damaged. If we can find a way to revitalize the *damaged* cells, hopefully the patients who are really struggling will be able walk and talk normally again, even years after the stroke. In the long run, we may even be able to reverse memory loss."

"How?" Ryan asked, amazed at the idea.

". . . I don't know," Olivia admitted. "I'm working on it. Like I said: we need to figure out how to revitalize the cells in the first place."

◊◊◊

"I think she's going to do it!" Ryan said excitedly to Zach a few days later.

The two of them were relaxing by the amphitheater near the end of the third Technology session. Carrie was putting in extra hours at her lab. She was getting along so well with her Atlantean evaluator that she frequently missed dinner because they were busy brainstorming together.

"That's awesome, man!" Zach said. "Sounds like this session is going better than the one with Dr. Tantus."

"A lot better!" Ryan said. "Olivia's really cool, and I think she'll give me a good review. How was your session?"

"It went well," Zach said. "It was a lot more hands-on this time. We were building different prototypes to help improve the city's propulsion system—it reminded me of being back in the shop. I made extra money as a mechanic after I dropped out of college," he added at Ryan's puzzled look.

"You dropped out?"

"Yeah, midway through my sophomore year," Zach said. "Never really felt like I was getting anywhere. I liked coding, especially programming automated cars; but everything else was just boring. To be fair, I was never really great at school to begin with. I got straight Cs in high school. But this is totally different. Everything on Atlantis is amazing. I'm never bored here! Sometimes I miss working with my hands, though."

"I get it," Ryan said. "I take it you like to be constantly moving? Is that why you're shaking your leg again?"

Zach looked down at his tapping foot and laughed.

"Probably," he admitted. "Most of the time, I don't really notice it."

"Guys! Guys! Guys!"

Ryan looked up at the entrance of the amphitheater to see James—one of the Delta initiates—running down the steps toward the two of them, followed closely by Carrie and Will. All three of them were wearing devious grins.

"What's up?" Zach said.

"We gotta move quick!" James said rapidly, out of breath. "The Alphas and the Gammas. They're busy. It's gotta be—" He took a deep breath. "—gotta be now!"

Ryan and Zach both looked at Carrie for an explanation.

"We're pranking the other two groups," she said slyly. "The evaluators have them in a meeting and their dorms are empty. We're going to tie their mattresses to their bed frames and then flip all their bunks. A bunch of Betas are headed there now! James and Will found me as I was headed over here. You guys in?"

Zach looked over at Ryan with a gleeful expression.

"Let's go!"

◊◊◊

"GOOOOOOD MORNING, BETAS!"

Ryan jerked awake—and slammed his head against the under-side of Zach's bunk, as Sam's overly cheery voice burst through the dorm room. Judging by the other loud bangs and the colorful mix of swear words echoing through the dorm, most of his fellow Betas were equally startled.

A few of the initiates managed to turn on their bunk lamps, groaning and rubbing their eyes. Ryan blinked and peered around, but he was unable to find Sam anywhere.

"What the actual hell?" Ryan heard Zach mumble above him.

Ryan swayed slightly, trying to keep upright. His eyes felt as if they were receding into his skull, and his mind was fuzzy. He doubted he had gotten more than a couple hours of sleep.

"BETAS!" Sam's voice boomed again. "Get up and meet me by the track in the Military District. You have twenty minutes—don't be late!"

There was a slight buzz after Sam finished speaking, followed by a small click. Ryan realized groggily that there must be speakers embedded in the bunks. Another delightful Atlantean innovation.

"Isn't it a fifteen-minute walk just to get to the track?" Ryan asked Carrie weakly. She nodded sleepily, clearly not in the mood to talk.

Ryan flicked his wrist to bring up his bunk computer's clock display, which read 3:01 a.m. He groaned. He had a feeling Sam would be absolutely unbearable this early in the morning.

He was right.

"Welcome to your third Military session!" Sam said when the Betas arrived. Even in the dark, it was obvious that Sam was happy to see his initiates shivering and blinking groggily in the chilly pre-dawn. Jennifer stood next to him, looking noticeably grumpier than her brother in the moonlight. Clearly, Sam was the morning person out of the two of them.

Sam turned to the group of disheveled Betas and Deltas and continued: "This session is pure training: physical training, combat training, weapons training. We're going to see how well you all do over the next two weeks. If any of you drop out of initiation, it's going to be during this week—but I hope that isn't the case for any of our initiates."

"Remember," Jennifer spoke up groggily, "each of you was chosen to be a part of Atlantis for a reason. You can do it. It's not fun, but you're supposed to be here."

Sam looked at his sister for a second, eyebrows raised, before resuming.

"Anyway, we're going to start with a three-mile run. Go ahead and change in the locker rooms on the other side of the track and meet me back here in ten minutes. We have workout clothes for all of you. Oh," he added as the initiates started to shuffle toward the buildings he had indicated, "and I heard some of you mumbling when you got here." He gave Zach a pointed look before continuing with a sly smile. "I loved the stunt you all pulled against the Alphas and Gammas. Especially flipping their beds. It was awesome! This isn't a punishment at all—we were gonna do this anyway. But seriously, good job!

"So, get this: when I was an initiate," he continued, cackling to himself, "we were awful. We mixed up some cement and snuck into the other groups' dorms while they were asleep, and—"

Jennifer elbowed Sam in the ribs. Definitely not the morning person.

"—and . . . uh . . . I'll tell you guys later. Now go get changed."

As it turned out, the three-mile run would prove to be the easiest of the day's tasks. Not having run much since graduating from college, Ryan was thoroughly out of breath by the end of the jog; but Sam wasted no time giving the initiates their next assignments.

After a few days full of long runs, push-ups, squats, and a bizarre Atlantean exercise that somehow combined the most strenuous components of Zumba and yoga, Ryan was barely able to move—and he wasn't alone. Everyone in the Beta dorm groaned and moved as if they were ninety years old—even if that didn't mean much on Atlantis. It wasn't until halfway through the first week in their third Military session that they finally had a small break.

"Today we're going to begin combat training," Jennifer announced. A small groan went up among the initiates. They had just finished a five-mile run with Sam, and most of them were still sore. "You will be broken into pairs and take turns attacking and defending on your assigned mats. You'll find basic tutorial holograms at each of your stations. Please remember that this is *training*—we don't want any of you to actually get hurt. Good luck. Don't kill each other."

"Come on, man! Let's go!" Zach said excitedly to Ryan after Jennifer paired them together. He threw his arm around Ryan's shoulder as they made their way to one of the mats near the back of the building. On the way, they passed Carrie. She was already scowling at her partner, Sarah, who appeared equally displeased at the match.

Once at their station, Ryan and Zach watched a few projections to learn some basic techniques before squaring off to face each other.

Ryan had never noticed—or at least, had never truly appreciated—just how strong Zach was. The first time Ryan tried to attack him, it felt like running into a solid wall. He quickly realized that despite being thin, Zach was made mostly of muscle—a fact that Zach quickly proved when it was Ryan's turn to defend himself.

Ryan stood facing Zach with his feet apart and arms up as Zach charged. Just as Ryan tensed to absorb the collision, Zach dropped to one knee, positioned his other knee between Ryan's legs, grabbed Ryan around the waist, and used his momentum to spring upward. Ryan felt his feet leave the ground a second before Zach slammed him down onto the mat.

Stunned, Ryan lay still for a moment and tried to regain his bearings. Behind them, he heard Sam snort in amusement.

"Ryan, I'm so sorry!" Zach said quickly as he hopped up. "Dude, I have no idea what happened. I wrestled for a couple years in high school, and I guess it all came rushing back to me. Did I hurt you?"

"No, you're fine, man," Ryan said with a wheeze as he slowly sat up. "I just wasn't ready for that. It wasn't one of the moves on the hologram. Will you teach me that one?"

After being knocked down a few more times, Ryan finally started making some progress. It soon started taking Zach a few seconds to pin Ryan, and once or twice, Ryan was actually able to beat Zach. Zach never showed him specific counters, but Ryan kept trying to predict how Zach was about to strike, where his body would be, and how to best counter him. He found he was right more often than not, but Zach was still able to slam him down onto the mat every few bouts.

After one particularly painful takedown, Ryan took a moment to look around at the other initiates as he got slowly to his feet.

Most of the Betas and Deltas were simply exchanging minor jabs back forth, and blocking almost lazily. Watching them, Ryan doubted the utility of merely learning the simple moves recorded on the holograms. Surely the Demons would put up a real fight on a battlefield.

Ryan was suddenly extremely grateful for Zach's improvised lessons. Zach was an excellent teacher, and although Ryan had no real experience with hand-to-hand combat apart from the incident in the alley, he felt he was improving much faster than he'd initially thought he would.

The next day, Ryan was paired with Will, who looked both nervous and determined. Ryan stood ready, waiting for Will to attack. When Will took a step forward on his rear foot, Ryan was immediately able to visualize the next four steps straight from the training hologram.

Will took another step and lunged, but Ryan was ready. He feinted as if he was going to fall for Will's move, then quickly ducked below his punch. Before Will could respond, Ryan used his body weight to throw Will off-balance, struck him once in the ribs, and swept his feet out from underneath him.

Will landed on the mat with a satisfying *fumph,* and blinked up at Ryan in shock.

"You okay, Will?" Ryan asked immediately.

"I think so. How . . . how did you do that?"

"Zach did something similar to me yesterday. Twice. I have the bruises to prove it."

"Can you . . . I mean . . . would you . . . show me?" Will asked hesitantly.

Ryan smiled and promised to try. As he held out a hand to help Will stand, Ryan caught a glimpse out of the corner of his eye of Sam and Jennifer, watching him. In fact, for the remainder of the training session, Ryan kept catching the siblings studying him and Will with unusual interest.

After a few days of hand-to-hand combat training, Ryan realized that most of the initiates had adopted a hybrid style of fighting that was a mix of the standard Atlantean training regimen and total improvisation. Even though it improved the other initiates' technique, Ryan savored the new challenge. With all their studying and cerebral work, the chance to do something physical and aggressive was a welcome change, and he was getting better and better at taking down opponents, even ones much bigger than him. Every day, other initiates approached Ryan or Zach to ask for help, and Ryan was happy to see Will helping some of the others as well near the end of combat training.

On the last day of the third Military session, the initiates entered the training facility to find the mats cleared out and targets projected along the walls. Ryan was talking to Carrie about the Delta girl he'd been paired with yesterday, and how she'd accidentally slipped and fallen during one of the rounds, when the Dennings called for order.

"Alright, guys, listen up!" Sam called over the dull chatter. "Today's gonna be a little different. Instead of fighting each other—which was hysterical to watch, by the way—we'll be doing some target practice."

"We're going to start with some basics," Jennifer said, taking over. "For now, each of you pick a station and await further instructions." There was a mad dash as all the initiates tried to grab stations with their friends. Zach, Carrie, and Ryan skittered off toward the edge of the building and found a free area, each taking a place next to a separate small gray podium. Each podium housed a worn bow, a quiver full of ruffled arrows, and a small black pouch.

"Quiet down," Jennifer said as the initiates found their spots.

"When we say 'go'—*not* now, James—" She glared at the Delta for a second, and he sheepishly put down the bow he'd been inspecting. "—you all can pick up your bows and begin firing at your targets. Do not retrieve your arrows until everyone is done firing and we give you the all clear."

Jennifer stepped back, and as she did, a buzz rose around the room. One or two of the initiates reached for their bows before quickly pulling their hands back as if they'd been shocked. Everyone looked at Jennifer uncertainly.

"What?" she said. Sam whispered something to her with a smirk on his face. Jennifer blinked. "Oh. Right," she said. "*Go!*"

Ryan reached for his bow and grabbed an arrow. He vaguely remembered trying archery at summer camp when he was ten years old, and he was fairly certain he'd done poorly. He nocked an arrow, drew the bow, and tried to aim. As he looked down the length of the arrow, the target seemed to dance in front of him. It took him a second to realize his nerves were affecting his aim.

Without releasing the tension on the string, Ryan took a deep breath and focused on feeling his chest rise and fall when he exhaled. He cleared his mind, looked down the arrow's shaft, and released.

To his great surprise, his arrow found its mark. It wasn't a perfect shot, but it was within the target. Ryan was also pleased that he'd managed not to hurt himself: he heard several initiates gasp in pain as they released their own arrows, and the tense bowstrings rapped their forearms.

After a few hours, Ryan's arm and back felt like they were on fire from repeatedly pulling the taut bowstring, but he was pleased to see that his aim was steadily improving. He was regularly hitting the bullseye, and almost never missed completely anymore. To his right, Carrie was proving an equally good shot. The two of them made a game out of it, both determined to beat the other in every round. On Ryan's other side, Zach, who now had a nice, multicolored bruise on his forearm, lagged behind; but Ryan was always quick to celebrate with Zach whenever he hit the occasional bullseye.

"The bow was the easy part," Sam said to the gathered Betas and Deltas after they returned from lunch. "Each of you should have a small black bag by your podium. Inside you'll find a metallic sleeve. It should look familiar—you've already seen Jen and me use them. These are Bright Electromagnetic Aggregation Mechanisms, or BEAMs. For the record, I didn't come up with the name. Go ahead and put them on now, and do *not* mess with them."

Ryan reached into the bag and pulled out his BEAM. Sam may have called it a sleeve, but Ryan thought it looked more like a gauntlet as he pulled it on. It consisted of small metallic plates that overlapped like a set of reptilian scales, and extended all the way up to his elbow. Other than two small gray panels on either side of the wrist, the plates had the classic dark-blue color that Ryan had grown to associate with solar panels.

Ryan looked down curiously at his armored hand. If not for the golf ball-sized ring on his palm, he wouldn't have known he was wearing anything. The entire mechanism was so light and flexible that he was able to move his wrist without any restrictions.

"Usually, BEAMs are operated via beacon-link," Jennifer explained to the group. "Since none of you have your beacons yet, these BEAMs have been altered a bit. Excuse me, Ryan." Jennifer stepped up to Ryan's station and faced his target. "To fire your BEAMs, you need to extend your arm and open your hand so your palm is facing the target. Once you're ready to shoot, use your other hand to press both gray panels over the wrist at the same time, and your BEAM will fire."

Jennifer pointed her hand at Ryan's target and pressed both sides of the gauntlet at her wrist. There was a blinding flash of light, a frizzle of ozone, and a deafening explosion. Ryan instinctively covered his ears and squinted. When he opened his eyes again, blinking away the green-black afterimage of the flash smeared across his field of vision, he saw a smoldering black mark in the center of his target.

Jen lowered her hand, looking satisfied. "Do ten shots, wait for everyone to finish, and then check your accuracy on your podium's computer. We'll do this for a few hours to give you some practice. And don't forget your hearing protection. Begin!"

Ryan replaced Jennifer at his station as the sound of explosions filled the chamber. He quickly put in his ear plugs and faced his target, then held out his hand, palm up. It wasn't a natural position at all.

Ryan reached up with his other hand, braced himself for the recoil, and pressed his wrist. A searing light burst from his hand and connected with the target. There was absolutely no kickback from the BEAM. He fired again, and again. It was actually pretty fun, and he was hitting the target!

Ryan smiled, and fired again.

CHAPTER NINE
FINAL EXAM

Ryan tapped his foot nervously. His heart was racing. He felt like a kid again, being called into the principal's office—although admittedly, he'd only ever gone to the principal's office once, in elementary school, when his mother had dropped off a sandwich for him after he'd accidentally left his lunch box on the bus.

Now, Ryan was sitting in a plush chair in Sam's corner office near the border of the Technology and Residential Districts. He knew he wasn't in trouble—Sam was meeting with all of the initiates individually, and because Sam was going through the list alphabetically, Ryan had been called before most of his friends. Jonathan, one of the few initiates to have already met with Sam, had told the rest of them that all the evaluators were meeting with their initiates before the final Technology and Military sessions to let them know how well they were doing. Of course, after his own meeting, Roy had loudly reported to the whole dorm that Sam had personally told him he was going to be chosen for Technology.

"Kendrick!" Sam shouted as he burst through the door.

Ryan jumped at the sudden noise, and could have sworn he saw Sam smile a bit as he took a seat across from Ryan. "I'm supposed to read from a script here—but I'm not going to do that. It's stupid. Ryan, you know that there's only one Military and one Tech session remaining before we make our final decisions. This meeting is normally when you and I would discuss your goals and your performance during the initiation thus far. I take it you want Tech, right?"

"Yes, sir," Ryan said immediately, trying to be as respectful as possible.

"Don't 'sir' me," Sam said. "I'm not that old."

"Well . . . it's kinda hard to tell around here."

Sam smirked in response.

"Well, you have a real shot, Ryan. You've been right at the Tech cutoff pretty much the entire time. Right now, you actually fall just short of the mark. That being said, it's still possible for you to get there during these next four weeks. From this point on, only the Elder, the two heads of sect, Jennifer, and I will be evaluating you, and we all treat these last two sessions a lot like finals. You can really make up a lot of points in the next month.

"Now, just so you know," Sam continued, "these next few weeks can suck. We test your ability to think and make decisions with little sleep and under a lot of stress. You need to make good decisions—not just academically, but in general."

"Do you have any advice?" Ryan asked.

"Nothing specific," Sam said with a slight shrug as he leaned back in his chair. "We'll be giving you guys about a week to prepare for finals, and there's a lot of downtime during these last sessions, too. It gives you all the opportunity to continue studying, or to recover as necessary. We tell everyone that one of the . . . tests is related to Atlantis itself, so not only do you need to review everything we've taught you so far, but you also need to know about the city in general. Try hard; do your best." He paused as if he was unsure what to say next. "Aside from that, just know that we really like you and we think you'll fit in great here, whether you end up in Tech or in Military. Good luck."

Ryan blinked at Sam for a second, surprised at his compassion. After exchanging a few more pleasantries, he thanked Sam and headed back to the dorm to tell Carrie and Zach about the meeting.

As he made his way through the Residential District, thinking about what Sam had said, Ryan found that he felt conflicted. On one hand, he was doing well, and he had a real shot at being chosen for Tech. On the other hand, the outcome was still far from certain. He could end up a soldier. Drew had assured him that it was still a good life, but he just knew it wasn't for him. Maybe he could find an Atlantean and ask. . . .

Ryan had almost made it back to the dorms and was passing the amphitheater when he spotted Drew relaxing at the very bottom of the pit with a couple other Atlanteans. He stopped abruptly in the middle of the walkway, wondering. Maybe . . .

Ryan started to make his way down the amphitheater stairs—but stopped on the second step. Drew wasn't Ryan's evaluator, and he was obviously enjoying his time laughing with friends. Ryan didn't need to interrupt him for something as minor as this. He could ask Drew for help another time.

Ryan turned around and started to walk back up the steps—only to hear Drew's voice calling out.

"Ryan!" Drew shouted from below. Ryan winced at being caught, but turned around and smiled as Drew climbed the steps toward him two at a time.

Drew clapped Ryan on the shoulder as he reached him. "What's up? Did you wanna talk?"

"Yeah," Ryan said, "but it can totally wait. It's not a big deal."

"Don't be ridiculous, man. What's up?"

Hesitantly, Ryan told Drew about his meeting with Sam and how near he was to the Tech cutoff. "Do you have any tips or anything that can help?" Ryan asked. "Or is there a gym or something I could use for practice?"

"I can definitely give you a code to let you use the gym after normal hours," Drew said. "There are some punching bags you can use along with the normal workout equipment. As for Tech stuff . . . well, I can't give you anything the rest of the initiates don't have access to—"

"Of course!"

"—but there are some study guides made by previous classes that you could check out," Drew said. "There's nothing new on them, but it's more concise than the official study materials, and it may help you review before your Tech final. You should be able to search for them on any computer here."

Sure enough, once he got back to the dorms, all Ryan had to do was search the term "initiation study guide" to find decades' worth of compiled information. He wasted no time in showing Zach and Carrie everything, and the three of them quickly hunkered down to study in one of the libraries a few blocks away from the dorms.

As the week progressed, Zach and Ryan made a habit of running to the Military District every evening so that they could train in one of the empty practice buildings. Ryan would help Zach with basic battle strategies in case something like the holograms came up on the final exams, and Zach continued to show him new moves and takedown techniques.

By the time their week of preparation was up, Ryan was ready for the exams to be over. Admittedly, he was aware that there was still a ton of information he didn't know. His head was swimming with facts and figures, and he was fairly confident that he wasn't going to be able to absorb any new information.

Ryan woke up on the first day of his Technology exam session with an odd mix of anxiety and peace fighting for dominance in the pit of his stomach. Breakfast that morning was unusually quiet. Not only were the Alphas and Gammas noticeably absent from the pavilion as they started their Military exam session, but many of the Betas and Deltas looked slightly pale. Carrie was silent, barely touching her food, and Zach's foot was tapping even faster than normal.

After the meager meal, Sam and Jennifer came to collect their initiates, leading them to a large research building in the Technology District before gathering them into a waiting room. Such a confined space would normally have been unbearably noisy with all the initiates filling it, but only the sound of nervous muttering could be heard. Sam had no issue getting everyone's attention.

"Alright, guys," Sam said. "You're about to start your final Tech exam. There will be two separate seventy-two-hour problems for each of you to solve individually. These problems have already been solved after years and years of work on Atlantis, and we don't expect any of you to complete them in such a short period of time, but try to finish as much as you can. Remember, you must complete a comprehensive write-up of your solutions.

"You will have a couple of days to rest between the two questions. Each of you has been assigned a suite complete with a kitchen, bathroom, and sleeping area, as well as a large workspace that contains everything you'll need to solve the exam problems, including a computer with limited internet access that you can use for research. You will not be allowed to leave your suite until you've finished. Know that we have video and audio recording equipment set up throughout the suites."

"Go ahead and enter your rooms. The computer will prompt you when it's time to begin. Good luck," Jennifer concluded, "and make good choices."

Carrie looked at Ryan and Zach, mirroring their expressions of alarm now that the exam was about to start. Ryan tried to offer her an encouraging smile, but he was sure it came across as more of a grimace. Other than slightly shaking his head back and forth as if in refusal, Zach stood shockingly still. For once, he wasn't tapping his foot.

The Betas and Deltas slowly funneled through a set of doors into a long hallway. Zach, Ryan, and Carrie found themselves assigned to adjacent rooms near the very end of the hall. Ryan stared at the industrial door for a second, took a deep breath, and opened it with a shaky hand.

The suite was exactly as Sam had described it. He first entered what must have been the work area, which resembled a lab complete with a computer and smartboard. At the opposite end was an open doorway, which he assumed led to the personal area.

Ryan walked over to the sleek computer, which showed a greeting:

WELCOME RYAN KENDRICK
THE TECHNOLOGICAL EXAM
WILL BEGIN SHORTLY.

The countdown displayed below the message showed only a little over a minute left to zero. Ryan tried to control his breathing. He knew the exam was going to be tough, and he tried to remind himself of what Jennifer had said, something all the evaluators had repeated over the last few hours: "Make good choices."

Ryan looked up as the computer made a small beep. The welcome message had changed:

TECHNOLOGICAL EXAM - PROBLEM 1
KEEPING IN MIND EVERY ASPECT OF THE
CITY OF ATLANTIS, SOLVE AND/OR DESCRIBE
ALL MATHEMATICAL AND SYSTEMATIC

EQUATIONS, COMPONENTS, AND CONSIDERATIONS NECESSARY FOR THE CITY'S PROPULSION SYSTEM IN THE GREATEST DETAIL POSSIBLE.

Ryan stared at the screen for a few seconds, his mind completely blank. Below the message, a countdown was already ticking away. He had seventy-two hours to essentially design or critique something Atlantis had already perfected—something people on the Surface could only dream about.

Ryan continued to gaze at the screen as he considered the overwhelming task, already making a mental checklist of every factor that needed to be considered. He knew he would need to know the weight of the city, but this was so much more complicated than merely knowing the weight of the ground he stood on. There were all the buildings to consider, all made of different materials; the people moving around; ships coming and going; hell, the entire subway system. . . . He could only hope that the computer would be able to provide him with some type of map, and maybe a materials list. For the first time since he'd arrived, Ryan truly appreciated how amazing the city in the sky was.

Ryan ran over to the smartboard on the wall and wrote down every factor he could think of. In no time, the entire board was filled with a list of all the aspects of the city's infrastructure that he would need to include in his answer, and an agenda he hoped to follow. And to top it all off, he had to present all his findings and calculations in a paper.

Ryan saved his notes, and swiped to clear the board so that he would have space to write out the complex physics equations he dreaded using. For a moment, he was fairly certain he would get only a couple hours of sleep each night—but the Dennings' warnings lingered in the back of his mind. Glancing up at the corner of the ceiling, he spotted three different cameras and microphones.

He was willing to bet that going without food or sleep would negatively affect his final score. He had to make good choices.

Still, Sam had warned him that he would likely be sleep-deprived at some point during the exam sessions. He had to find some type of balance.

With all of this rushing through his head at once, Ryan looked at the smartboard, took a deep breath, and started to write out an equation.

◊◊◊

"What. The. Hell."

Ryan could only shake his head in response. Carrie sat across from him in the pavilion, looking completely drained. They had just finished their second problem for the Technology final, and Ryan couldn't feel a thing. He collapsed onto the bench and stared blankly at Carrie.

"I mean, seriously—what was that?" she asked.

"That was awful," Ryan agreed.

"I mean, the first problem was rough, but that last one was insane! 'Solve the health problem referred to as autoimmunity.' We never talked about that!"

"I think I failed it," Ryan said. "They don't even do pass-fail here and I still think I flunked."

"Well, it's done," said a voice behind him.

Ryan didn't even have the energy to look up as Zach plopped down next to him. Although his fellow Beta had bags under his eyes and looked a little haggard, Zach somehow seemed to be sporting a slight smile.

"How did you do?" Ryan asked.

"I have no idea. I slept the first night, but I went for an all-nighter last night just so I could finish," Zach said.

"You . . . you finished?" Carrie asked incredulously. "Like, you were actually able to solve it?"

"I mean . . . I had a solution," Zach said modestly. "It probably has a ton of holes, though."

Ryan couldn't help but laugh at the look on Carrie's face. During the break between problems, Zach had downplayed how well he had done on the first part of the exam, too. Like the other initiates, he'd agreed that the test had been difficult; but it wasn't until he and Ryan were alone a little later that Zach had shared some of the ideas he'd put forth on improving the city's current propulsion system, and Ryan was sure the evaluators were going to love them.

"Do we have any kind of break before our Military exam session?" Zach asked.

"No idea," Ryan answered. "It officially starts tomorrow, but Sam said that initiates never know when they're gonna be tested. It could be tomorrow. It could be in a couple of days."

"Great," Zach said. "I'm gonna go get some sleep then, just in case."

"He actually finished. . . ." Carrie said softly as Zach walked away from them. "I'm kinda tempted to smother him while he naps."

◊◊◊

As it turned out, taking a nap would have been smart for all of them.

"Why do they always wake us before the sun's even up?" Zach yawned.

Ryan merely grunted in agreement as he tried to listen to Jennifer rattling off instructions. It was difficult to see her in the dark, especially with the new moon, but from what he could tell,

—187—

she didn't appear to be in a particularly good mood. Considering that it was a quarter to four in the morning and everything on the west side of the Residential District was covered in a chilly dew, however, perhaps that was to be expected.

"Alright," Jennifer grumbled, eyes half-open. "Right . . . so . . . it's early . . . and we're about to start the first battle. As you know, we've split the combined Betas and Deltas into two groups. Sam is talking to his group on the other side of the Residential District due east of here. The groups will change each battle, and even though you're all mixed up now, the last battle will be Betas versus Deltas. To win each battle, you must completely destroy the other team."

"'Destroy' how?" Rebecca Wallace asked hesitantly.

"Behind me is a case full of charged swords, shields, spears, and bows and arrows. All the weapons have been blunted, so they aren't lethal; but they'll deliver an electric shock that will stun your opponent for a good ten minutes. Each of you will select one weapon. You are to stay in this courtyard until the dome of the Temple—" Jennifer pointed off into the dark morning in the direction of the Temple. "—is lit a bright blue, signaling the start of the battle.

"I'm only allowed to give you one piece of advice: you'll absolutely need a battle strategy if you want to win, so develop one and stick to it. Good luck, and try not to get tased—it hurts like hell."

On that dark note, Ryan rushed forward with the rest of the group to grab a weapon, hoping he could grab a sword before all of them were taken. He tried to be civilized about it, but he found himself shoulder-checking some people who just wouldn't move, and once he actually had to stop himself from shoving Carrie, who had ducked in front of him. By the time he and Zach finally made it to the weapon pile, Ryan's only options were a spear or a bow.

Grudgingly, Ryan picked up a spear and a spare shield, and

tested the weight of the unfamiliar weapon in his hands. None of the initiates had trained with weapons yet, but somehow, carrying a long spear felt comfortable—at least, until he turned around and nearly knocked Zach over with the shaft.

After stumbling for a second and regaining his balance, Zach opted for a bow, and he and Ryan walked over to join the other initiates, who were all arguing with one another. Everyone was shouting, trying to convince one another that their own battle strategy was the best. Clearly, no one was listening.

"If we get to the roofs, we can pick them off one by one!"

"I say we charge them head-on. They'd never expect it!"

"Let's go around and attack them from behind."

"Oh, yeah? And how do you know where they're gonna be for sure?"

"This is chaos . . ." Carrie muttered to no one in particular, her head sweeping from side to side as she watched the initiates bicker. Zach nodded solemnly in agreement.

"Nobody's listening to each other," Carrie continued, speaking so softly that only Ryan and Zach could hear her. "The other team is going to slaughter us if we don't figure out what we're doing and work together. We need a leader. . . ."

"Good idea," Zach said. "You got this!"

Without waiting for Carrie to respond, Zach put his thumb and forefinger in his mouth and let out a shrill whistle that pierced through the arguing. "Alright, everyone," he said in a booming voice. "Listen up! Carrie has something to say."

Carrie, whose mouth was hanging open, blinked several times in stunned silence as all eyes settled on her. Clearly, she hadn't been expecting Zach (who gave her an encouraging thumbs-up) to elect her as leader, and she suddenly looked as if she would rather be anywhere else.

"We . . . we need to be smart," Carrie said to the group of now-silent initiates. "We need some type of advantage. The enemy is on the opposite side of the Residential District. There has to be something we can to do to give us the upper hand."

Ryan wracked his brain. The evaluators would never make the battles unfair. There had to be something in the city they could use to their advantage.

Conversation broke out among the initiates, but nobody came forward with an idea. Ryan found himself slowly pacing back and forth in front of Carrie.

"It's dark . . ." Carrie said softly.

"What?" Ryan asked.

"It's dark. . . . They can't see!" Carrie said excitedly.

"And neither can we . . ." Zach said slowly, as if he were talking to a confused child.

"Not now. But soon, the dome of the Temple will light up! If it's as bright as Jennifer said, it'll light up the amphitheater, the pavilion, and the area behind the Temple!" Carrie said.

"And if we position ourselves in the shadows . . ." Ryan said, catching on.

"They won't see us, but we'll be able to see them as soon as they step into the open," Carrie confirmed.

"And then we'll have the advantage," Ryan finished. "We can make that work." Grinning, he turned to address the others. "As soon as the Temple lights up, everyone sprint to the back side. Make sure you stay in the shadows. Once the enemy is exposed, archers fire first; then the rest of us will follow up and take out whoever is left. Even if we don't get all of them right away, we should be able to do enough damage to make it an easy win from there—especially if we stick together."

"What if they reach the Temple first?" a Delta asked. "What if they have the same idea?"

"They won't," Carrie said in a small voice. "Well, I don't think they will. I mean . . . they shouldn't."

"They'll play it safe," Ryan told the Delta confidently. "What we're doing—it's bold. Like, really bold. Bold enough to work. We got this!"

As soon as he finished, the Temple's lights turned on, and the entire area was lit up in bright blue.

"Go! Go! Go!"

◊◊◊

Ryan's arms shook as the vibration traveled through his spear and into his body. The weight of the attack he'd just blocked sent him to his knees.

James Green's eyes widened in surprise. He clearly hadn't been expecting Ryan to block his attack. He lifted his sword again and tried to jab at Ryan, but Ryan quickly sidestepped the jab and swung his spear in a low, broad arc.

The dulled blade made contact with the back of James's calf, the shock from the weapon forcing his leg to buckle. James collapsed, then leaned back in the dirt and waited for the final hit, knowing he couldn't get away with a dud leg.

Ryan couldn't help but laugh as the Delta stuck out his tongue in good fun. Then he gently tapped James's chest with the tip of his spear.

"Trying to make up for last time?" Zach asked from behind Ryan, as James started to twitch on the ground, overcome by the spear's electricity.

The originally awkward and bulky weapon now felt comfortable in Ryan's hands. Over the course of their final Military session, it had become his weapon of choice.

"Just trying to keep my teammate alive," Ryan said with a smile. He turned and looked down at Zach, who was still sprawled out awkwardly over the log he had tripped over a few moments ago. James would have finished Zach off if Ryan hadn't been there to save him. "Last time, you were an enemy. No regrets."

"Dude, you knocked me out!" Zach said.

"You were trying to stun me!"

Zach laughed. He had been assigned to the opposing team for the second battle, which had taken place in a warehouse. Ultimately, he and Ryan had faced off in the middle of the building, exchanging strikes and parries before Ryan had finally been able to sneak past Zach's guard and deliver a sharp strike to the back of his head by using his shield as a weapon.

"Does your head still hurt?" Ryan asked Zach sincerely.

"Nah," Zach answered. "The headache only lasted a day. I think I may have taught you a little too well. Besides, your team took control and won right after you zapped me. I like to think my team was just hopeless without me."

Ryan laughed.

"Come on! My team won the first two battles—let's see if we can make it three out of three," he said, picking up his shield and taking off with Zach in tow.

They ran through the woods toward the Betas' rendezvous point. After being on Atlantis for months, Ryan found the feel of the soft ground under his boots as they ran through the hazy forest a welcome change—one well worth the long trip in the packed personnel ship. The news that they would be heading on an excursion to the Surface for their mock battle had surprised Ryan, but Sam had explained to the initiates that the Elder was acquainted with the mayor of a small Vermont town just a few miles away from where they'd landed, and they had some type of standing agreement that allowed Atlantis to use this land whenever they needed. Apparently Atlantis had connections everywhere.

Ryan and Zach hopped over a small stream, ignoring the branches that swiped at their faces, before coming to a small clearing. Carrie was already there with a group of Betas. She was bent over, drawing something in the soft dirt with a stick. Ryan was pretty sure he would find a rough outline of the terrain around them if he took a closer look.

"How are we doing?" he asked her as they approached.

"Not well," she said without taking her eyes off her drawing. "The group that we sent north to flank the Deltas was completely destroyed. And the few who went ahead to scout the Deltas' position haven't come back yet. I'm sure they're out by now, too."

"So . . ." Zach started.

"We're screwed," Carrie finished for him. She turned to Ryan. "Do you have any ideas?"

Ryan moved to crouch next to her, careful not to step on her sword, which she had set down. Looking at the crudely drawn dirt map of the area, he grudgingly had to agree with Carrie's assessment: they were outnumbered. Badly.

"The group we sent north . . . they were wiped out?" Ryan asked Carrie.

"Uh-huh."

"And the Deltas started east of us?"

"Yes."

Nobody spoke. Ryan, Carrie, Zach, and Will all stared at Carrie's makeshift map. The remaining Betas formed a circle around them, anxiously waiting for directions.

"What if we flush them out?" Carrie asked finally. "The group of Deltas to the north?"

"We're outnumbered," Ryan reminded her. "And considering

the Deltas were able to take out all the troops we sent north, there's probably a ton of them up there."

"Right; but we might still be able to flank them without taking heavy losses," Carrie said, still looking at the map. "And we don't even have to venture into their territory. How many archers do we have?"

"Five," answered Will, who carried a bow.

"What if we take the five archers and have them ambush the group of Deltas to the north?" Carrie said, beginning to sketch out her idea with her stick. "They could draw the Deltas back into this clearing, and give the rest of us the element of surprise."

"How does that allow us to flank them?" Zach asked.

"We would need a spot that the rest of us could use as a hideout. Preferably one close by and in that direction," Carrie said as she scanned the woods west of the clearing hopefully. "Then, once the Deltas are out in the open, we could come out and hit them from behind."

"The nook where you tripped over the lo—sorry—where we took out James," Ryan said, glancing at Zach. "It was a little north and west of here. The trees were kinda thick. We could camp there. The Deltas would never see us."

"And," Carrie said, "if one of us stays hidden just on the north side of the stream, then we should be able to see the Deltas as they make their way south into the clearing!"

"And once the Deltas chase the archers into the clearing, the rest of us can attack from behind," Ryan finished. "Let's do it."

As the group began to break camp and pick up their weapons, Carrie ushered Ryan aside. "Do you really think it'll work?" she asked in a low voice. "What if they end up wiping all of us out?"

"Carrie, you did better than any of us in the strategy simulations," Ryan said. "If it's your idea, it's going to work."

Carrie grinned sheepishly. Ryan waited for her to give the other Betas orders, but she stayed silent, looking back at her map.

Ryan sighed and looked around at the other Betas. Will, who had been listening from the beginning, nodded at him in understanding, but remained quiet. Zach, on the other hand, looked as lost as the other Betas.

"Give us five minutes to get into position before you start shooting," Ryan said to Will, who was gathering the other archers. "If you can take some of the Deltas out, awesome, but the main goal is to get them back here."

Will nodded as the archers turned to make their way north through the forest. Once they had left, Ryan corralled the rest of the Betas and began to lead them back to the stream.

"Who's staying behind to watch for the Deltas?" Zach asked as the Betas began to jump over the brook and head toward the hideaway Ryan had suggested.

Carrie looked at Ryan uncertainly. She was clearly torn between wanting to stay and act as the lookout, and wanting to go with the group to make sure everything went according to plan.

"I'll stay," Ryan said confidently.

Carrie nodded in agreement, then ushered the remainder of the group on. Ryan watched his fellow Betas disappear into the woods over a small hill before looking around for a spot to camp. Finally settling on a patch of dirt between two ancient trees, he set down his weapons and crouched low. He had to part the leaves of the low-lying brush in front of him to get a clear view of the stream, but he was fairly certain none of the Deltas would see him, especially if they were busy chasing Will.

It only took about two minutes of silence for Ryan's mind to start wandering into idle fantasies of working alongside Carrie, Zach, and Drew in Tech. He didn't know how long he stayed there, crouched in the dirt, but he had to shake his foot awake a couple times. The gentle noise of the nearby stream and the warmth of the sun were almost enough to put him to sleep.

After what seemed like an eternity (he was all but sure by now that Will had been zapped), Ryan heard a rustling just east of his position. A few seconds later, he saw Will and the other archers retreating quickly across the stream toward the clearing, the Deltas hot on their heels.

Will quickly turned and fired a shot toward their thundering enemy. Will had really impressed Ryan in this battle. The way he fired off a shot while being pursued and leading the other archers conveyed a level of confidence Ryan had never seen in him before.

Ryan was about to signal the rest of Betas when he froze. They had never agreed on a signal.

Ryan's heart sank. He'd ruined what would have been a great plan. In the time it would take him to reach the Betas, the Deltas would easily overwhelm the archers. He made a mental note to compliment Will later—after profusely apologizing for screwing up so badly.

Still, Ryan had to try to alert the Betas. He turned—and smiled at what he saw. Crouched low, barely visible on the top of the hill, was Carrie. She must have realized their mistake before he had, and she did not disappoint.

Silently thanking her for her brilliance, Ryan waved her over. Carrie turned and motioned over her shoulder before running over and joining him. By the time she reached him, the rest of the Betas were en route.

Carrie and Ryan made their way to the clearing while the rest of the Betas caught up. Their timing had to be perfect. If they reached the clearing too soon, they risked being caught in the open; but if they waited too long, the Deltas would wipe out the archers.

Carrie and Ryan slowed as they approached the clearing, allowing the other Betas to catch up. Carrie threw out an arm to stop Ryan and signaled the other Betas to halt. Across the clearing, they saw the group of Deltas doing almost the exact same thing as Will and the other archers shot at them from about twenty yards away. Ryan smiled with satisfaction as he watched an arrow make contact with the hand of one of the Deltas, making him drop his weapon.

"Now?" Ryan whispered to Carrie.

"As soon as they enter the clea—NOW!" she responded as the Deltas rushed forward.

At her cry, the Betas charged. Ryan was one of the first ones out, and went straight for a Delta he didn't know. Before the Delta could turn around, Ryan struck her in the center of her back with the tip of his spear. He didn't wait to see if she went down, but he felt the current buzzing through his weapon.

Ryan turned his attention to the Delta who had just been hit by Will's arrow. The Delta held a spear uncertainly in his left hand, clearly uncomfortable with it. Ryan shoved the weapon away with his shield and jabbed. His spear made contact just below the Delta's heart, and he watched his opponent drop with a satisfying thump.

At the sound of loud footsteps behind him, Ryan instinctively ducked. He felt his hair stir as a sword went whistling over his head, and spun to face his attacker. The opposing Delta had somehow got hold of two swords, and was swinging them both ferociously. Ryan had to roll to the side as one sword swung downward—the Delta was relentless.

Ryan hopped from side to side, ducking, jumping, and occasionally blocking the oncoming attacks. The Delta was pushing him toward a tight cluster of trees, essentially cornering him. Ryan desperately used his shield and spear to deflect the mad swings, but one finally made contact with his shield hand.

Ryan gasped and dropped his shield as an intense, burning pain spread through his entire hand. He couldn't move his fingers. He looked up at the now-grinning Delta, who brought both swords to bear. Ryan started mentally preparing for the shock. His heart was racing, and his good hand shook as it clutched his spear.

The Delta started to lunge—and then froze, shock clear on his face. Almost in slow motion, he collapsed forward, revealing Will behind him, with his bow primed. Ryan looked at the fallen Delta, and found an arrow on the ground next to him.

"Nice shot," Ryan said with a smile.

"Thanks," Will said. "I think that's about it."

Ryan looked around and saw that Will was right. Two Betas had teamed up to take care of the last remaining Delta in the clearing, and after a short but intense bout, she collapsed on the ground with her teammates. Other than Jonathan, who had never shown much aptitude for combat, the vast majority of the bodies that littered the grassy clearing were Deltas.

Ryan smiled. Their strategy had worked.

Carrie jogged up to Ryan and clapped him on the shoulder.

"You killed it!" she said with a huge grin. "Your plan was amazing."

"The plan was all yours, not mine. You're the one who saved us," Ryan said. "Plus, if you hadn't realized we didn't have a signal, the whole thing would've been ruined."

"Not to interrupt the celebration," came a dry voice, "but aren't there still some Deltas out there?"

Ryan and Carrie turned to find Zach hopping toward them. Ryan tried not to laugh as his friend attempted unsuccessfully to control his limp foot.

"You're right," Carrie said shakily, as if she was having a difficult time controlling her own laughter. "After this, we should outnumber them about two to one. Now it's just cleanup."

Ryan hefted his spear in his good hand. He may have been without his shield, but it didn't bother him. At this point, he was confident that the Betas could clear the Deltas.

"Let's go."

CHAPTER TEN
THE CHOSEN

"**R**yan, get up!"

As Carrie shook him awake, Ryan became vaguely aware of the noise all around him. The dorm was bustling with so much movement that he could hardly believe he'd slept through all the noise, but he was still exhausted after the final battle that had occurred the day before.

Carrie's face glowed with excitement as she hovered over him. During the final exam, his friend had been noticeably more reserved than usual, but it only took one look at the gleam in her eyes for Ryan to know that she was back to her usual animated self.

"Today's the day!" Carrie said, so fast he almost missed it.

"What day?" Ryan asked.

"The day we find out if we're in Tech or Military!"

The entire bunk shook as Zach hopped off the bed above Ryan.

"We just finished initiation yesterday," Zach said as he pulled on a clean shirt. "They decide that quickly?"

"Yeah! It's August twenty-ninth," Carrie said, as if that explained everything. Ryan and Zach shared a look.

"Of course . . ." Zach said slowly.

"The Elder will explain it," Carrie said dismissively. "And you can't wear that," she added as Zach started pulling on a sweatshirt. "We gotta dress up. Check your top drawer."

Ryan made his way to his dresser and opened the top drawer. Inside he found a soft, collared cotton shirt dyed deep red, and navy slacks. The shirt shimmered like scales as he took it out of the drawer and threw it on. He was unsurprised to find that the clothes fit perfectly—nothing in Atlantis was left to chance. He *was* surprised, however, to see his shirt emitting a soft aura, like the ones around the white shirts he had seen the native Atlanteans wearing on his first day in the Temple. Based on everything he'd learned in initiation, Ryan suspected that his body heat activated a subtle lighting system woven into the fabric. He looked around at the rest of the Betas, and noticed that the girls were wearing almost the exact same clothes.

There was a definite buzz of energy in the dorm as the soon-to-be-former initiates began to file out. As they made their way toward the Temple, the Betas met up with the other three groups of similarly dressed initiates around the pavilion. In no time, Ryan lost track of the rest of the Betas as the initiates formed a cohesive mob. Everyone was laughing, joking, and jumping on one another. It was a celebration, and Ryan couldn't help but absorb the energy of the group. He hadn't felt this excited in a long time.

As they approached the Temple, the initiates were cheered on by passing Atlantean families. One family was hanging halfway out a window, radically trying to get the attention of an Alpha who grinned and waved back, and Ryan sincerely hoped they were using omega waves to telekinetically ensure they didn't fall.

Ryan was about to point out the precarious family to his friends when a pale-haired man weaved through the crowd, nearly tackled Carrie in a hug, and ran off again without a word.

"That's my brother!" Carrie shouted over the crowd as the Atlantean disappeared in the mob. "I'll introduce you guys after the ceremony."

"How come we haven't met him yet?" Zach asked.

"Atlanteans aren't allowed to see their families during the initiation process," she said as they approached the Temple's main doors. "It's stops them from giving us an unfair adva—whoa."

As they entered the Temple, Ryan felt himself sharing in Carrie's awe. Even though he had been inside the Temple a few times, Ryan felt as if he was stepping into a new building. The most obvious difference was the noise: the entire place was packed with people. Ryan saw thousands of Atlantean families, all dressed in white robes with gold trimming. Their dazzling clothes amplified the brightness of the massive domed space, which was lit with hundreds of glowing spheres. Bringing the entire ensemble together were striking white banners evenly draped between the many columns. The shining banners were also edged in gold, and each one was emblazoned with a large circular symbol.

Ryan, Carrie, and Zach found a seat among the initiates and joined the buzz of excited conversation. After a few minutes, the entire building shook as the massive front doors slammed shut.

A hush fell over the crowd as Sam, Jennifer, and two other native Atlanteans who must have been the Alphas' and Gammas' primary evaluators stepped onto the stage. The evaluators took a row of seats along the side of the stage, and Zach snickered as Sam squirmed uncomfortably in the chair beside Jennifer's. Ryan couldn't help but grin too: Sam looked completely out of place in his formal clothes. When he wasn't tugging on his collar, he was fidgeting constantly.

The door behind the platform opened again, and this time Anna Valloris and Daniel Amerrest stepped out. The heads of the Technology and Military sects strode forward to stand on either side of an ornate podium that faced the crowd. Again, Ryan was amazed at the confidence both Heads exuded as they took their spots, Valloris to the right and Amerrest on the left.

The two leaders stood tall, chins high as they looked down on the crowd. They wore the same clothes they had on the day Ryan had first seen them. This time, Ryan was finally able to discern the golden emblems emblazoned on their snow-white shirts. The symbol matched the insignia on the banners that lined the Temple.

The door in the back of the stage opened again, just as it had on Ryan's first day in the Temple; and the sound it made was immediately echoed by thousands of scraping chairs. Every Atlantean in the Temple jumped to their feet, and the initiates quickly followed suit, despite having no idea what was going on—until they saw Michael Stamaris beginning to make his way to the podium.

"Please, please," the Elder said with a large smile once he finally took his place. "Sit. I've always found the formality silly, but who am I to argue with the traditions that have carried Atlantis forward for millennia?"

There were chuckles all around as the crowd took their seats.

"My beloved Atlanteans," the Elder began after the crowd had settled again. "This is my favorite day of the year. Every year on August twenty-ninth, we celebrate the day that truly marks the beginning of Atlantis. It was on August twenty-ninth, thousands of years ago, that Atlantis sank into the Mediterranean Sea. It was on this day that all seemed lost; and it was on this day, thousands of years ago, that we rose from our watery grave to become the glorious civilization we are today. And make no mistake: we are a civilization. One that has risen like a phoenix from its own ashes with a simple, magnificent goal: to help those in need.

"Every year I say this, because every year, I want to remind everyone of one undeniable truth: we are all family. I consider myself blessed to know each of you; and to the initiates that I have not yet had the pleasure of meeting: I am confident that we will be steadfast brothers and sisters on this wonderful city in the sky. I am proud to call every one of you an Atlantean, whether you are in Military or Technology; whether you are from the Surface or from one of our wonderful sister cities. You are all Atlanteans. You are all equals. It is because of each and every one of you that we are able to continue in our mission. Atlantis will always be there to help those in need, to cure disease, and to guide others out of the darkness and into the light.

"And so, it is with great pleasure," the Elder continued, "that I welcome the newest citizens of Atlantis. They have successfully completed their initiation, and have proven their merits to their evaluators. They will make excellent additions to our family, and I know that they will all help us soar to new heights.

"And now for the moment you've all been anticipating," Stamaris said with a huge smile. "Some of our initiates have displayed an aptitude for technological innovation, while others have demonstrated courage and fortitude on the battlefield. With this in mind, it is time to reveal who will have the honor of serving in the Technology sect, and who will have the honor of serving in Military. At this time, I will call up the initiates one by one in alphabetical order and announce which sect they will be joining, and they will be presented with the Insignia of Atlantis, symbolizing their role here in our great city. When your name is called, please come up and join me onstage.

"Without further ado, let us begin. First up: Melissa Abraham—Technology!"

Applause erupted from every corner of the building. Melissa, a Delta from the Caribbean City, stood up, her smile taking up her entire face. Atlanteans whooped and cheered as she bounced her way up the stage toward the Elder.

Melissa embraced the Elder as he opened his arms for a hug,

and then walked over to her evaluator, Jennifer, who slipped something around Melissa's neck before shaking her hand. The crowd continued to cheer all the way until Melissa finally returned to her seat.

"Janet Alexander—Military!"

Again, the entire Temple broke into loud applause as the Alpha initiate made her way to the Elder. Ryan clapped and cheered with the rest of the crowd, but he couldn't help but wonder whether the audience seemed slightly less enthusiastic than it had been for Melissa. In the end, Ryan decided it was all in head; but a nagging voice in the back of mind continued to question.

Still, Ryan was determined to cheer as loud as possible as Janet walked across the stage. It had been a long initiation for all of them, and he wanted to show his support.

One by one, the Elder called out the names of the initiates, along with the name of the sect they would be joining. It was a surreal experience. Regardless of where they came from, each initiate was met with amazing, undeniable support from the Atlanteans as his or her name was called. Caught up in the moment, Ryan cheered along with the rest of the crowd. He didn't know it was possible to feel so happy for other people, and he could feel each initiate's excitement as he or she crossed the stage to hug the Elder.

But with each named called, Ryan's sense of euphoria became duller and duller. Ryan knew there were a limited number of spots for Technology, and every time the Elder called someone else's name for Tech, his odds worsened. He was starting to get really nervous. He knew he'd done well on the final exams, but the weight in his chest was steadily growing, weighing him down with each breath.

Jonathan Fowler claimed a spot in Tech, as did Sarah Gall. Ryan heard a small hissing noise when Sarah's name was called, and he turned to see Carrie clapping obligatorily, with little more enthusiasm than that of a bored high school student.

Much to Ryan's delight, Roy Graylor joined the Military sect, along with James Green. Roy's face was one of utter disbelief as he shook Sam's hand.

Ryan was frankly shocked at the number of initiates whose last name began with the letter G—but he didn't have to wait long for the Elder to move on to the next letter of the alphabet; and suddenly, Ryan wished they were back at G again. Surely there was some type of Atlantean technology that could slow time—or maybe even speed it up to allow him to skip the whole thing. He wasn't sure which would be better.

By the time the Elder called up Tyler Jackson, a Gamma initiate from the Canadian City who was selected for the Technology sect, Ryan was tapping his foot even faster than Zach. There couldn't be many people left before his name was called. He was going to be chosen for Tech. It was going to happen. It *had* to ha—

"Ryan Kendrick . . ."

Did the Elder pause after saying everybody's name, or just his?

". . . Military!"

Ryan heard Stamaris, but it took a second before understanding finally washed over him. He stood up, taking great care not to trip over Zach's legs, and walked down the center aisle toward the stage. The moment seemed unending, and he felt completely exposed, almost numb.

He hadn't made it.

Ryan looked up at all the cheering Atlanteans he had never met. He wondered how many of them were like him, in the Military sect. In the midst of the roaring crowd, Ryan saw Grayson, Drew's odd, pale friend, clapping encouragingly in the shadows. Maybe he was Military, too?

Ryan paused when he saw one Atlantean who was not cheering with the others. Drew was staring at him, mouth hanging slightly open. Ryan could see the disbelief etched on his face. Somehow, he found solace in Drew's expression: Ryan wasn't the only one shocked about his results.

Drew must have noticed Ryan was watching him, because his demeanor immediately changed to that of a proud parent. He started clapping and shouting, and even though Ryan knew it was impossible, he could have sworn he could actually hear Drew's cheer over the general ruckus.

Ryan mounted the stairs to the platform where the Elder stood. Michael Stamaris was absolutely beaming.

"Congratulations, Ryan," Stamaris said as if talking to a favorite grandson, his graying hair further solidifying the impression. "You're going to make a wonderful addition to Atlantis."

"Thank you, sir," Ryan said as he accepted the Elder's friendly hug. After they broke apart, Ryan made his way past the Elder and stepped toward Sam.

"You did well, Kendrick," Sam said. "You should be proud."

His evaluator took a dark brown cord out of a small pouch and slipped it around Ryan's neck. Ryan saw a brief flash of gold as the necklace slid past his eyes. Not wanting to inspect the necklace while he was onstage, Ryan thanked Sam and walked back to his seat. With every step, a small piece of metal bounced against his chest.

Ryan finally found his seat. Desperate to maintain composure—and to avoid his friends' concerned glances—he took a look at his necklace as the Elder called up the next initiate. A small gold emblem hung from the plain brown cord. Glancing up, Ryan realized that the symbol on the emblem matched the odd insignia on all the banners, and he was sure it was the same symbol emblazoned on the evaluators' clothes.

Ryan took a closer look at the emblem. The gold circle was split down the middle by a thin arrow, pointing upward, with two small notches along its shaft. Two curves extended from either side of the arrow, almost like a pair of wings, and arced up to meet the edge of the circle. Ryan wondered whether the symbol had some type of significant meani—

"Zachary Lauder—Technology!" the Elder boomed.

Ryan and Carrie turned to Zach and immediately began cheering. Zach didn't move, apparently too stunned even to tap his foot. Ryan clapped him on the back and gave him a light push, trying to stir him out of his shock.

Zach finally got to his feet and headed up the aisle. As they cheered, Ryan was sure that he and Carrie could be heard above everyone else, but he didn't care. Any thoughts of self-pity evaporated as he celebrated Zach's success.

His friend, still slightly dumbfounded, greeted the Elder with a huge grin, and started walking back to his chair after Sam placed the cord around his neck.

"You did it, man," Ryan said softly as the Elder resumed calling names.

"I . . . I honestly don't know how," Zach said, beaming. "I didn't think there was any way I'd get in. You should've been Tech, too."

Ryan shook his head and said nothing. He was genuinely thrilled for Zach, and for now, he just wanted to focus on celebrating with his friend. He cheered, striving to match Zach's enthusiasm, as three more initiates were called up—Military, Technology, Military—and then—

"Carrie Mancerus—Military!"

Carrie stood promptly as the Elder called her name, her face completely passive. Ryan and Zach cheered on their friend as she walked to the stage with her eyes forward and her head held high. But even though he had only known Carrie for a few months, Ryan could tell how much she was hurting as she accepted the necklace from Sam. Anyone else watching would have seen a strong, proud Atlantean accepting her necklace; but Carrie's normally expressive face showed no joy or excitement. Maybe she was just too stunned to know how to feel; but Ryan doubted it. She was putting on a brave face, a mask to hide her true feelings.

Once Carrie slid back into her seat, the Elder began calling names again—but Ryan was no longer listening. He absentmindedly started tracing the emblem that hung at his chest. His new life was about to begin, and it would be a dangerous one. He had willingly left his safe job on the Surface to come to Atlantis, to join the Technology sect; and he'd failed. Now he was part of the Atlantean military—a soldier.

The impact of that word started to weigh on Ryan. He leaned forward in his chair, resting his elbows on his knees. Even though he'd known this was a possibility, Ryan could honestly say he hadn't been expecting it. He was supposed to be in Tech—but he wasn't good enough.

Ryan let out a deep, shaky breath as an uncomfortable chill ran down his arms and legs. This couldn't be happening.

A comforting hand landed on his shoulder, and Ryan turned to see Zach watching him with a look of concern. Ryan tried to brave a smile for his friend, but he was sure he looked more sad than anything else. Zach gripped his shoulder in support, then leaned forward to look farther down the row. Ryan followed his gaze.

Carrie's head was in her hands. She looked distraught—all pretense abandoned. Ryan watched her mouth and chest to see if she was crying, but he saw no clues. Knowing better than to say anything, Ryan reached out and put his hand on her knee.

Carrie looked up and flashed him the same pitiful smile he'd just given Zach. Before Ryan could say anything, she reached over and hugged him.

Ryan returned the hug in silence, both of them conveying all their disappointments in the embrace. They were going to be in the Military sect, but at least they would be together.

"Once again," the Elder said, interrupting their hug, "please join me in welcoming the newest citizens of the Northeast American City of Atlantis!"

There was another robust round of applause before the Elder spoke again. "Every citizen of Atlantis wears a necklace identical to the one each of you has received. With it, you are no longer initiates—you are Atlanteans.

"For those of you who are not familiar with the Insignia of Atlantis, please allow me to explain," Stamaris continued. "Over the millennia we have existed, this symbol has evolved with us. Originally, the insignia was nothing more than a large wave, depicting the sinking of our beloved city. As Atlantis grew stronger, we added a spear to symbolize our military strength. More recently, we connected the two symbols, allowing the waves to become our angelic wings, sprouting from the spear. Twenty-five Atlantean cities around the world are united under this insignia. It symbolizes our strength and endurance as a society, as well as our technological prowess. Let the spear and wings act as a compass, forever pointing north.

"As new citizens, each and every one of you is charged with upholding the values of Atlantis that have been passed down through the millennia. We implore you to act as guides for those on the Surface, and to keep the best interests of all humanity at heart. It will not always be easy. The Order continues to try to stifle us at every turn; but don't be afraid. While the Order try to instill their dark oppression on the Surface, we will continue to be the shining light that protects those we have promised to serve. And that is why I am confident that we will be victorious—because, as you all know, light exposes shadow.

"But you don't want to hear an old man talking anymore, do you?" the Elder finished with a large smile. "Now, we celebrate!"

◊◊◊

"Ryan! Zach! Over here—you gotta meet my family."

Carrie grabbed Ryan by the wrist and led him and Zach through a mob of Atlanteans, most of whom had shed their glowing white robes and donned more casual attire. The entire city had congregated in the park to enjoy the festivities. As they squeezed through the crowds, Carrie explained that every year, after the new initiates received their assignments, the Atlantean cities celebrated August twenty-ninth with a massive outdoor festival. The city's guilds had gone all out in arranging the festivities—proving once again that Atlantis did nothing by halves.

Everywhere he looked, Ryan saw people laughing and eating—sometimes at the same time, making him wonder whether Atlantis had developed some kind of superior Heimlich maneuver. Throughout the park, a vast number of buffet tables loaded with finger foods, entrees, and desserts created a maze that was occasionally interrupted by odd carnival games. While some of the games were obviously geared toward children, Ryan was more interested in those that were undoubtedly unique to Atlantis. He saw a couple that involved levitating a ball through an obstacle course, and one that looked like an odd telekinetic tug-of-war, with three people on each team. There was also some type of costume contest, wherein both male and female Atlanteans dressed up in ancient unisex robes to resemble Katerina Geno, the Elder who had led the surviving Atlanteans to safety after the sinking of the original city thousands of years ago.

Unfortunately, there wasn't much time to take everything in as Carrie dragged Ryan and Zach recklessly through a massive, crowded tent adorned with a large banner that read "Join the Painters' Guild Now!" Inside the tent, Atlanteans were showing off their artwork. One waterfall landscape in particular had attracted a large crowd of people who seemed to be bidding for it

On the far side of the tent, one painting stood out from the rest. It was a magnificent representation of the original city of Atlantis floating in the Mediterranean Sea at sunset. A small plaque under the picture's frame announced that the painting would be representing the Northeast American City of Atlantis at that year's intercity Painters' Guild Convention.

Ryan was tempted to stop to admire the painting, but Carrie weaved through the crowd with a purpose, and in no time, the three of them left the tent and continued to make their way through the park. Finally, they reached the edge of the park closest to the main plaza.

"Mom! Dad!" Carrie said, getting the attention of a fair-haired couple sampling drinks from a side table. "These are my friends, Ryan and Zach. Guys, these are my parents, and my sister, Amanda."

"Mr. and Mrs. Mancerus! It's so nice to meet you," Ryan said. Even though he was used to everyone in Atlantis looking like they were in their late twenties, it was still odd to be introduced to his friend's parents when they only looked a few years older than himself. He started to extend his hand, but was interrupted when Carrie's mother wrapped him in a smothering hug.

"Sweetie, please, it's Sheryl," she said with a smile. "Mrs. Mancerus is my mother-in-law."

"And call me Kurt," Carrie's father said with a huge smile. He surprised Ryan with a second hug as soon as his wife let go of Ryan to move on to Zach. "It's so amazing to meet you both. I always love meeting Carrie's friends. Are you guys hungry?"

"Oh, yes!" Sheryl immediately said. "Do you boys want something to eat? With all the training, you must be starving. Amanda's place is only a few blocks away! We're staying with her for the weekend. We can run back there and make something real quick. Seriously, it's no trouble."

"Our family shows love by feeding you until you burst," Amanda said as she stepped forward and gave Ryan and Zach each a hug. "It's nice to meet you guys."

"It's nice to meet you all too!" said Ryan.

"We actually haven't met any Atlantean families yet," Zach said. "Or anyone other than the evaluators, really."

"Well, like I said, we're just here for the weekend, to celebrate Carrie finishing initiation," said Sheryl sincerely. "But if either of you are ever in the Canadian city, I want you to know that you're both welcome at our place anytime!"

"Yes! We must have you over!" Kurt said immediately. "Do you guys like steak? Tell you what: next time you're in the Canadian city, just let me know, and I'll go out and get us a couple of rib eyes. How does that sound?"

"Sounds amazing!" Ryan said, while Zach nodded ravenously.

"CARRIE!"

Ryan turned just in time to see a blur of blond hair run up to Carrie and hug her.

"Pat!" Carrie cried with a big laugh. "Guys, this is my brother, Patrick. Pat, these are the friends I was telling you about, Ryan and Zach."

The Atlantean smiled and shook their hands. He seemed to

twitch for a second before extending his hand, and Ryan suspected he was resisting the temptation to hug two people he had just met. After meeting Pat, Ryan could confirm that all of Carrie's family had the standard northern Atlantean blond hair and green eyes, along with the diamond pattern on their fingernails.

"Ryan, you're in Military with Carrie, right?" Pat asked kindly.

"Yep," Ryan said. "Normally I'd say 'I'll look out for her,' but something tells me I'm going to be needing her much more than she'll need me."

"Well . . ." Sheryl said, her smile fading slightly for the first time, "I know you guys will be there for each other."

"I have no doubt. And I wouldn't worry about a war," Kurt said, putting his arm around his wife. "We've been at peace with the Demons for a while. You two should enjoy your time with Military! Lots of people find it more enjoyable than Tech. You're less stressed, more active. Sounds a bit like our Carrie, huh?"

Ryan and Zach laughed. Carrie smiled sheepishly.

"Pat, would you be willing to show Zach around a bit? Let him see what you're working on in the lab, and maybe give him some tips?" Carrie asked.

"Yeah!" Pat said, and he turned to Zach. "Why don't you come by my office tomorrow? I'll show you around and introduce you to some people! If you see a project you like, I can get you in with the leader so you can work with them for a while before starting your own research."

"That would be awesome! Thanks, man," Zach said appreciatively.

"Happy to do it!" Pat said. "If you guys don't have any plans in an hour or so, you should totally come by the main plaza. I'm doing some improv with the Acting Guild—it should be great!"

After promising to attend Patrick's show, Ryan and Zach talked with Carrie's family for a little longer before excusing themselves for food. Carrie wanted to stay behind with her family, but promised to catch up with them in a few minutes.

After loading up on so much food that both of their plates sagged under the weight, Zach and Ryan walked to the fountain in the center of the main plaza. They stopped along the way to talk to Will, who had also been picked for Military, and to congratulate Jonathan, who was celebrating being assigned to the Technology sect with his family.

Ryan was about to sit down on the edge of the fountain when something caught his eye. For the first time, he took a minute to truly appreciate the fountain's beauty. The white marble protruding from the center of the water fixture stood tall, supporting the statue of the angelic warrior that stood at its apex. Taking a closer look, Ryan saw that the angel was not wearing traditional flowing robes, but rather a suit of fierce armor, and holding aloft a powerful spear that pointed straight up to the sky. His wings were free of any feather patterns, and instead mirrored the metallic wings used on Atlantis.

Ryan couldn't help but smile. Was that what he would look like once he started wearing armor? He really needed to try on a pair of wings.

Just below the angel, Ryan noticed a familiar engraving on the fountain's white marble centerpiece: the Insignia of Atlantis. Ryan subconsciously reached up to touch the necklace around his neck. Although he'd been on the city for just three months, seeing the matching insignia cemented the idea that he was truly a part of the amazing civilization that had built it.

"Would you look at that," Zach said.

Ryan nodded as he continued to stare at the symbol, but Zach was actually looking at something above the fountain. Ryan followed his gaze. Water was shooting from the tip of the angel's spear, producing a fine mist above the fountain; and in the mist, a hologram was being projected from somewhere in the plaza. The projection played with the mist from the spraying water to create an almost magical effect.

Above the fountain hovered a list of all the former initiates, which initiate group they had been in, where they were from, and whether they had been assigned to the Technology or Military sect. Ryan looked through the list and was pleased to see that Rebecca had been assigned to the Military sect, too. He hoped that he, Rebecca, Will, and James would be able to hang out some, since they were all Military. He didn't want to lose the friends he'd made during initiation.

Ryan read through the rest of the lists, trying to see whether he recognized anyone else. He saw Roy's name listed under the Military sect, and fervently hoped they wouldn't bump into each other too often as soldiers.

As he continued to read through the names, something arose in the back of Ryan's mind, prompting him to pause. He could have sworn he saw a pattern. At first, he thought it might just be his imagination, prompted by a trace of cynicism born from his disappointment over failing to make Tech—but a second look confirmed that, disappointingly, his initial, gut feeling was correct. The initiates had been warned that about two-thirds of them would be placed in Military, and they'd known that most of the initiates were from the Surface, but the vast majority of the initiates who had been chosen for Technology were definitely native Atlanteans.

Ryan looked at the list of names a third time. There should have been far more initiates from the Surface in Technology, just based on probability. Ryan couldn't help but wonder whether there was some frank prejudice involved, or simply an inherent bias against initiates from the Surface, like him. Either the evaluators naturally favored native Atlanteans over the Surface initiates, or the selection process for the Technology sect was more inclined to pick native Atlanteans, since they had been around the amazing Atlantean technology all their lives.

Ryan was about to ask Zach what he thought about all this—but he froze as soon as he looked at his friend. Zach was still looking at the list, his face shining with pride. Ryan couldn't help but feel slightly guilty. He was happy for his friend, and Zach had undoubtedly earned his spot. He'd done such an amazing job throughout initiation, and had aced all of his exams. And although Zach could have been much more boisterous about being chosen for Tech, he hadn't once boasted.

As he looked back at the list, Ryan only wished that he could be as good a friend in return. He was certain that there was some type of bias here, something to explain why there were so many Atlanteans and so few people from the Surface chosen for Technology, but today was not the day to fight those battles. Instead, he clapped Zach on the shoulder and offered him a huge smile.

"Congratulations, guys."

Ryan and Zach turned to see Drew approaching them. Zach and Drew shook hands, Zach grinning sheepishly as Drew imparted a further quiet but heartfelt congratulations. Ryan held out his hand too, but Drew surprised him with a hug. Maybe this was an Atlantean gesture?

Regardless, Ryan returned the hug. It was enough for him to know that he hadn't let Drew down, no matter how Ryan felt about his own performance.

"You good?" Drew asked in an undertone.

"Yeah, I am," Ryan said. "I've made some awesome friends who are gonna be with me in Military. Sucks that *we* won't be together, though," he said, turning to Zach.

"Doesn't matter," Zach said dismissively. "We'll still hang out."

Drew looked at the two boys and smiled.

"You guys are going to do great," Drew said. "Both of you. The Elder's speech may have been a little . . . over the top, but I really think you're both going to kill it here."

"Thanks, man," Ryan and Zach said at the same time.

"Well, I mean it," Drew said. "Come on. Let's go get something to drink."

Zach's face lit up. "Please tell me you guys have something strong?"

Drew laughed and opened his mouth to respond—but was interrupted by the sudden screech of feedback coming over the plaza's hidden speakers, which had been playing upbeat instrumentals throughout the festivities.

Ryan flinched, and many of the Atlanteans around him ducked and covered their ears. A second later, a harsh voice echoed around them.

"Freedom. Must. Fall."

Ryan shot Drew an inquisitive look. Drew simply shrugged, frowning. This clearly wasn't part of the festival.

"Atlantis," the rough voice continued, *"has been at the top far too long. So self-assured in your ways and good intentions. Tell me—where has it gotten society? Look at the state of the world! War ravages the poorest of countries, ensuring that they will never rise to their full potential. Weapons designed for combat are used to slay innocent people in the streets. Inequality runs rampant in so-called 'developed' nations, to the point that people of all classes, of all creeds, are willing to tear each other limb from limb."*

Across the plaza, Ryan saw Amerrest jog up to a small crowd of Atlanteans and begin shouting orders. The Atlanteans proceeded to run off toward the Military District. Were they preparing for something?

"Atlantis had its turn, and it has failed. We are done waiting for you to deliver on your unfulfilled promises. It is time for the Order to rise. We will lead society into a new age. We will show the world the path to enlightenment, and the world will follow us to an age of peace. We are the way. We are the Order. It is time for Atlantis to fall. Make no mistake: this is war."

Then the world exploded.

A monstrous blast rocked the city as the speech cut off. People dropped to their knees as the sky darkened with smoke and the ground shook. Ryan heard shards of stone flying over his head at deadly speed, crashing against the cobblestone. The noise was unbearable. He clamped his hands over his ears. Through the cloud that engulfed the plaza, he could barely see Drew and Zach on either side of him.

"Zach! Are you alright?" Ryan shouted, unable to hear his own words over the ringing in his ears. On his left, his friend was bleeding profusely from a small gash over his left eye; but if he felt the wound, he gave no sign.

"I'm fine!" Zach mouthed, nodding.

Ryan looked to the right and saw Drew peering through the dust toward the source of the explosion. He was wearing an intense look that Ryan had never seen on him before.

"Are you okay?" Drew's muffled voice barely cut through the ringing. Ryan nodded, relieved that he could hear again.

Drew turned back toward epicenter of the blast, where the smoke was thickest. Ryan could barely see the outline of the fountain through the dust.

"The Temple," Drew mouthed, and ran off into the smoke. Ryan looked at Zach, who nodded, and quickly took off after Drew.

Ryan tripped over chunks of rubble as he followed Drew's hazy outline into the slowly clearing dust. Huge shards of marble cratered the cobblestone plaza, and he had to weave around them as he rushed forward to the Temple steps. As soon as he reached them, the dust seemed to clear like a wave, and Ryan stopped, horrified at what he saw.

The area in front of him resembled a war zone. There was a gaping hole in the Temple's façade, and one of the heavy doors had been blown completely off its hinges. Bits and pieces of the building lay strewn over the steps—but the debris was nothing compared to the dozens of injured Atlanteans that littered the ground. People were screaming, some in pain, some for their loved ones. It was like nothing Ryan had ever seen before.

One of the injured, lying nearby, was an Alpha initiate Ryan knew by sight, but not by name. He was white-faced from shock, and struggling to move.

"Ryan! Ryan, over here!"

Drew's voice brought Ryan back to the situation, and he rushed over to where Drew was crouched over an injured man. Blood was spurting from a gash in his thigh, and dribbling steadily from a smaller cut on his forehead.

"How can I help?" Ryan asked immediately.

"Put pressure on the thigh wound while I find something to bandage it," Drew said.

Ryan replaced Drew's hand over the man's thigh, and his fingers were immediately soaked with warm blood. It took everything in him not to stare at the wound or recoil when he felt the arterial pulse. Ryan offered the man a small smile, wishing he knew what to say. The man's eyes darted wildly from side to side, and his breaths came in short, uneven gasps; he was clearly trying not to panic.

"We're going to take good care of you," Drew said calmly as he tore strips from his jacket and started to dress the wound. Ryan dimly remembered that Drew had mentioned he'd been a doctor before he started scouting. "Ryan," he said once the thigh wound was adequately bandaged. "Can you please take care of the abrasion on his head? I'm going to check on Katie over there. It looks like a shard of marble hit her in the chest, and I need to make sure her breathing isn't compromised."

Ryan nodded and proceeded to take care of the man's head wound as Drew ran off again. Once he got the bleeding to stop, Ryan made sure the man was alright before checking on another injured person only a few yards away.

Ryan continued to rush from victim to victim, doing whatever he could to help. Some injuries were simple cuts and scrapes, but whenever he found someone with a serious injury, he shouted for Drew.

After what felt like forever, all of the injured were stabilized. Along with a few medics from the Military sect who had arrived on the scene, Ryan and Drew started doubling back to help with more minor injuries. The medics moved from patient to patient with the kind of speed and grace that only came with experience. They seemed happy to take directions from Drew, given his medical background.

Ryan did his best to help the medics whenever they needed something. It wasn't until he knelt on the hard stone to help one medic splint a woman's forearm that he noticed a dull, burning pain in his legs. He rolled up his pants to find his knees covered in large scrapes—likely caused by his repeated kneeling on the jagged, broken stones covering the plaza. Still, others needed his help, and he wouldn't have dreamed of stopping over such a minor injury. He was thankful for the basic first aid training he'd received during one of the Military sessions.

Ryan was watching Drew set a dislocated shoulder back into

its socket when he heard an odd beeping noise. As Ryan tried to fashion a sling for the injured Atlantean, Drew tapped the band on his forearm.

A holographic map appeared above Drew's watch, with certain areas highlighted in red. Drew tapped the floating image a few times before clearing it with a grim look.

"What's up?" Ryan asked as he finished the sling.

"It looks like there were a few different bombs. One here, a couple in the park, one at the greenhouses, and another at one of the water treatment plants," Drew said in a low voice. "Three people were killed at the plant. Thankfully, no one was hanging around in the greenhouses."

"What do we need to do next?" Ryan asked.

Drew shook his head.

"Keep treating people . . . if you can," he said. He glanced at Ryan's knees. "You sure you're alright?"

Ryan nodded.

"Good. Just keep helping. I've got to go—they just called an emergency meeting of the Intel Council, and they want me there. It doesn't look good. Things are about to change."

Ryan nodded and assured Drew that he was fine before the older man ran off to his meeting.

As he watched Drew dash off, Ryan spotted Carrie making her way toward him from across the plaza. He smiled to reassure her that he was alright, and she returned his smile with obvious relief.

Even with the most life-threatening injuries dealt with, the plaza was chaotic. Slabs of stone from the once pristine Temple lay scattered about, turning the plaza into a hazardous maze slick with a fine layer of dust and occasional puddles of coagulating blood. Ryan recognized one shard of marble from the pediment above the Temple's doors. Despite the numerous cracks and chips, he could still see the fractured Ancient Greek engraving in the stone. For the first time, Ryan was grateful for the impromptu and frankly horrible Greek lesson Sam had given the Betas during their first Technology rotation; but what he read made his heart sink: Light Exposes Shad—

Looking up at the Temple, Ryan was relieved to see the remaining syllable still in place above the damaged doors. Still, the stone's survival provided little solace. It would undoubtedly take a while for Atlantis to return the Temple to its original glory—but that was a problem for another day.

Ryan tried his best to focus on helping his fellow Atlanteans, but one thought kept running through his head: if the message really was from the Order, and if they were telling the truth, then there was about to be a war.

And he had just been drafted into the Atlantean military.

CHAPTER ELEVEN
LIFE OF A SOLDIER

"**G**o ahead and take a seat, Kendrick. Lean forward so that your chest is against the cushion and your head is in the hole."

Ryan crossed the small room and straddled the seat as directed. He was in something akin to a doctor's office, along with the rest of the new Military Atlanteans. They had been instructed to report to a building in the medical sector to get their beacons, and he'd spent the last hour standing in line with a bunch of other newly minted citizens, wondering how badly the procedure was going to hurt. Unfortunately, none of the soldiers who had already had their beacons inserted had come out through the same door, so they were unable to reassure those still waiting.

"Are you familiar with what a beacon is?" asked the doctor who had ushered Ryan into the examination room. The tall man had an impressive blond mustache that wiggled slightly when he talked.

"A little," Ryan said. "It's a chip, right?"

The doctor didn't respond. Ryan assumed the man must have nodded, but he couldn't see anything with his head in the chair's face port.

"The beacon is a small chip inserted at the base of the neck," the doctor said. "It allows us to communicate with others through brainwave projection. It also stimulates the brain by emitting low-frequency omega waves, which will allow you to produce your own omega waves and move objects with your mind. I should warn you, though: not everyone is exceptionally good at using their beacon. Are you ready?"

"Uh . . . yes?" Ryan said. Was the guy really not going to say anything about how the beacon was inserted?

"Then let's go."

Ryan felt something on the back of his neck, and jerked slightly before he realized that the doctor was just applying antiseptic.

"You'll feel a slight pinch. Small bee sting," the doctor warned.

He was wrong.

A sudden, searing pain in the back of Ryan's neck made his vision darken for a second. He couldn't even make himself scream. He just barely managed to keep from arching his back in agony.

And then, just as suddenly, the pain was gone. Ryan took a couple of deep breaths before he spoke again.

"You've . . . never been stung by a bee before, have you?" he asked breathlessly.

"Well . . . no," the doctor admitted. "There aren't any bees on Atlantis. Anyway, you can exit through the door right in front of you. Oh—and your commanding officer wanted me to remind you that you have class in about two hours."

◊◊◊

"How's my scar?" Carrie asked Ryan as soon as he entered the classroom, which was tucked away in a building in the northernmost block of the Military District.

Ryan took a seat next to her and looked at the incision in the back of her neck as she held up her hair.

"It . . . it barely looks like anything," he said. "I mean, it's a little red, and there's a small line, but it already looks like it's healing."

"Nice! Turn around real quick." Carrie checked the back of Ryan's neck. "Yeah, yours too! We're official now! It's so exciting!"

Carrie was speaking rapidly again. In retrospect, the slowest Ryan had ever heard her talk was during the mock battles, and before the final exams.

"Alright, settle down, settle down," called a woman with Korean features as she made her way to the front of the classroom. The room full of soldiers quickly stopped talking and stared at their new leader, eager to start their training. "My name is Jessica Hye. In formal settings, you should refer to me as Sergeant Hye. Otherwise, Jessica is fine.

"This is the only planned classroom time for new soldiers. As of now, you are considered a squad, a group of unassigned new soldiers. Once we determine which of you will become aerosoldiers, you will split into different companies, each consisting of twenty-five soldiers, which allows us to rotate days off for volunteering and leisure. Yes?" she said, apparently surprised, as Rebecca's hand shot into the air.

"How do you become a sergeant?" Rebecca asked keenly.

The corner of Sergeant Hye's mouth twitched. She seemed to be trying not to smile.

"If you do well, you can advance quickly here," Sergeant Hye said. "Promotions are based on merit, not time served. All of you will start as soldiers. Your first potential promotion is to company leader. In ascending order, the next ranks are sergeant, lieutenant, captain, major, general, and finally, commander. As the Head of Military on the Northeast American City, Amerrest is our commander."

"Do all the cities have generals and commanders?" asked James.

"Yes. Each city has a single commander and three generals. One general stays in their home city, while the other two act as ambassadors to neighboring Atlantean cities. Even the best soldiers find that it takes some time to advan—"

"*Wow, I'm bored again,*" came Carrie's voice from right behind Ryan's head.

Ryan jumped slightly in his chair and turned to stare at Carrie, who was snickering next to him. Sergeant Hye loudly cleared her throat, and Ryan looked up to find her staring at him with disapproval. Thankfully, she didn't comment further.

"*Smooth, Ryan,*" came Carrie's voice again. It sounded like she was talking from somewhere directly behind him—but she was sitting just to his right, and her mouth wasn't moving at all. "*Next time, try to be a little more subtle.*"

Ryan gaped at her, perplexed.

"*It's the beacons,*" said Carrie telepathically. "*I've been trying to reach you since Hye walked in. It took a few minutes. Just concentrate on thinking at me. It sounds crazy, but it works! Try!*"

Ryan nodded slightly. He continued to look ahead at Sergeant Hye, but failed to absorb a word she said as he silently called Carrie's name over and over in his head. Carrie didn't respond. Ryan kept calling, louder and louder, until his eyebrows knitted and he broke out in a sweat.

"*You look constipated,*" Carrie thought to him, her tone making it obvious that she was trying not to laugh. Clearly, he wasn't succeeding. "*Come on! You can do—*"

"*CARRIE!*"

Carrie jumped even more violently than Ryan had, her feet leaving the ground for a second.

"Sorry, Sergeant Hye!" she said hastily.

"As I was saying . . ." Hye continued.

"*Okay, I think you got it now,*" came Carrie's voice again. "*This is awesome! It's going to make class so much better.*"

"*You actually sound like you,*" Ryan thought to her. "*I mean . . . I can hear your voice . . . in my head. It's not a computerized voice. How is that possible?*"

"*Here. Read this.*"

Carrie tapped the surface of their shared desk a few times to input a command on the built-in computer. A link popped up on the sleek surface in front of Ryan, and he opened it to find an article that explained how the beacons simulated a person's voice. He only understood about half of it, but it was absolutely amazing technology.

"So remember, if all hell breaks loose, just know these numbers and you'll be fine," Sergeant Hye said to the class. "And don't worry—they'll be preprogrammed into your armor in case of emergency."

Ryan looked up at the board and saw Sergeant Hye writing what looked like complete gibberish. The software automatically transformed her scribbled handwriting into neat letters and numbers, but Ryan was still lost.

REGIONAL: 35.636 – 83.749

INTERNATIONAL: 49.411 08.715

"*Carrie, what do those numbers mean? I missed that.*"

"*Huh?*" came Carrie's voice as she looked up from the desk. Evidently she had been equally distracted.

Ryan was positive he had missed something important, and vowed to pay closer attention. He was part of an army now, and anything a superior officer said might just save his life later.

Thankfully, the rest of the classroom session was actually very interesting, and Ryan was sure that the information imparted to the new recruits would be useful in the long run. By the end of the day, Sergeant Hye had shown them several different schematics of weapons, armor, and technologies that the Order might use on the battlefield. The recruits' desks were equipped with personal hologram projectors, so they could follow along with the Sergeant and find the weak spots in the Demon armor. They learned that most of the Demons wore horned helmets and preferred using flamethrowers as weapons, rather than the light technology used in the Atlantean BEAMs. Ryan had to give the Demons some credit: they seemed to have embraced their rather unfavorable nickname as much as the people of Atlantis embraced their angelic one.

Sergeant Hye spent the last two or three hours of their time together recounting all the global war crimes that could be traced back to the Order.

"The Order's ruthless leader is the worst of all the Demons," Sergeant Hye said. "No one actually knows his true name. The Demons simply refer to him as their 'King.' You see, being true to their name, the Order follows a very strict hierarchy. We've linked this 'King' to several awful events throughout recent history, including a number of famines and pandemics over the past century. He's also fanned the flames of several nationalist fringe movements, and assisted in the suppression of climate change evidence since the 1970s. Despite our best efforts, however, we've never been able to locate him. For the most part, Demon bases are difficult to find, although there is intel that our friends to the north are on to something."

At the end of the day, as the recruits all headed back to their apartments, Ryan asked Carrie what she'd though of the class.

"All the Demon stuff was really interesting!" Carrie said as they hiked up a flight of stairs to their apartment door. "But I'm so happy we're done with classrooms."

"Same," Ryan said. He faced the peephole in the door of the apartment and waited for the biometric scanner to recognize his face. After a few seconds, the word 'Unlocked' flashed on the door, and they heard the click of locks disengaging.

Ryan opened the door and was greeted with a blast of cool air as he and Carrie walked inside. The pair had decided to move in together after finding out they were both going to be in Military, and had found the apartment a few days ago. Neither really wanted to live alone as a new citizen of Atlantis, and since they would have similar schedules, it made sense for them to live together. They'd found the apartment a few days ago, and even though Ryan had never lived alone with a girl before, it had seemed a natural transition after the dorms. So far, there hadn't been any awkwardness.

"Are Amanda and Patrick close by?" Ryan asked as he collapsed onto one of the apartment's comfy sofas. Carrie handed him a glass of water stamped with a stylized *M*, and flopped down next to him.

"Well, not really," she said, propping up her feet. "They live on the east side of the Residential District, closer to Tech, since that's where they work. I think they're actually kinda close to Zach."

"We need to see his place soon," Ryan said. He turned to the television. "Television, video call Zach Lauder."

"*You know you can think the command to it, right?*" Carrie thought to him. The television flared to life, displaying a holding screen that pulsed like phone ringing. "*We can communicate directly with devices now. You don't have to say 'television' or 'mirror' to activate them. You just activate the system you're talking to.*"

"*It's still kinda weird that all the mirrors are computers,*" Ryan thought to her. "*One day, you gotta show me all the different things that act as a . . .* Zach! How was your first day?" Ryan finished out loud as the television screen brought up an image of Zach lounging on a chair in his living room.

"Hey, guys! Dude, I'm exhausted. They had us running around the entire Tech District," Zach said with a huge smile. "They wanted us to see all the different projects going on. Carrie, your brother is awesome. He was showing me around, and we actually had lunch together. Super helpful."

"That's great, Zach," Carrie said. "Your place looks nice!"

"It's amazing!" Zach said as he reached for a small device on the table next to him. The image on the screen flashed for a second before it was replaced by a close-up of Zach's face. The image was shaking, and Ryan could tell that Zach had switched the video feed to a tablet. "Take a look!"

Zach's camera panned over his apartment. Ryan was slightly taken aback at how nice Zach's place was. To be fair, he and Carrie had a great apartment by anyone's standards, but Zach's living quarters outdid theirs in almost every way, albeit subtly. Ryan privately suspected that all the apartments in and around the Technology District were of slightly better quality than the living quarters for the Military sect.

"It looks pretty similar to Patrick's place," Carrie said.

"It's really nice!" Ryan said.

"*What's Zach's roommate's name again?*" came Carrie's voice in his head.

"How's Jonathan?" Ryan asked Zach. Carrie nodded in thanks.

"He's good," Zach said without much enthusiasm. "He's studying right now at one of the libraries. He's always studying. I'm actually not sure *what* he's studying, since we haven't done anything yet, but he's studying. He's pretty chill. But I miss you guys."

"We miss you too!" Carrie and Ryan said at the same time. "But I'm starving," Carrie continued. "Be right back. Need some food," she said as she stood up and left for the kitchen.

"So how have things been, man?" Zach asked Ryan.

"Today was actually kinda cool!" Ryan said. *"Transfer to my tablet,"* Ryan thought to the television. The television's screen immediately went blank, and a transparent tablet on an end table flickered to life, Zach's image filling the screen. Ryan picked up the tablet. "We got our beacons today, and learned all about the Demons. Today was our only day in the classroom."

"Lucky," Zach said. "I think we're going to be mostly stuck indoors. You guys have training?"

"Tomorrow, I think," Ryan said. "They warned us that our training may be a little more intense than normal—you know, because of the bombings."

"Yeah, but you're going to kill it," Zach said confidently. "Just remember that I can still knock you out anytime I want to."

"Uh-huh," Ryan said, smiling. "Is that why I beat you in the mock battle?"

"I let you win."

"Sure you did."

They chatted for a while about their respective supervisors (Apparently Zach's supervisor, Elena Bulfin, was compulsively organized, and had spent the day picking bits of lint off Zach's shirt.), until they grew tired and Ryan had to call it a night. As he hung up, Zach wished him and Carrie good luck with their training.

Ryan had a feeling they would need it.

◊◊◊

Ryan's suspicion was quickly confirmed. Over the course of the next few weeks, pain became a familiar friend to Ryan, Carrie, and the rest of the training squad. When Sergeant Hye had told them they would be participating in physical training, Ryan had envisioned a lot of running, push-ups, and the occasional obstacle course, like the ones they'd encountered in their Military sessions during initiation. But Hye worked them to the point of nausea. Ryan vomited on two separate occasions—and he was managing far better than some of the others.

Hye also enjoyed shouting random exercises for the soldiers to complete in the middle of long runs, just to make sure they could follow orders. After running the equivalent of a marathon every other day for a week, many of the soldiers in Ryan's squad, himself included, could barely move. A personal low for Ryan came when he and Carrie opted to make spaghetti one night after a grueling workout. The two of them sat down to eat their pasta only to realize that, in their exhausted haze, they had both forgotten utensils. Far too drained to get back up to fetch silverware, he and Carrie simply ate their spaghetti with their hands and agreed to never speak of the incident again. Ryan just hoped that the others in his squad were struggling as much as the two of them.

"Everything hurts," Carrie said after a particularly hard day.

She was lying flat on one of the sofas in their apartment. Ryan hadn't even felt up to walking to the chair, so he'd settled for the floor instead.

"I want to get up to get water," Ryan began, "but my abs catch fire whenever I try to move. I think that barbed wire got my leg really good, too. I've got a huge scratch." They'd run a difficult obstacle course earlier that day, one that had involved a good deal of climbing and crawling. Ryan, whose muscle fibers always seemed to be just a small hop away from tearing, had started to feel sore almost immediately after they'd begun.

"You only have one?" Carrie said. Groaning loudly, she sat up on the sofa. "Ow. Ow. Ow. I have at least two cuts on this leg, and another couple scrapes on the other. And I think I hit my head on a rock when we had to crawl."

"You think?"

"Yeah. I'm not sure. . . . I saw stars," Carrie said. "Lord, I'm hungry."

"I think we have chips."

"Can you get them?"

"Seriously?"

"Please?"

Ryan groaned as he struggled to his feet. The pain in his hips made him want to collapse, and he was fairly certain his thighs were about to fall off.

"How does Sergeant Hell expect us to fight tomorrow?" Carrie asked weakly. Hye had announced that the squad would be starting formal combat training the next day.

"You mean Hye?"

"Nope," Carrie said as she flopped back down on the couch.

Once they started combat training, Ryan found he had to agree with the moniker. Hye made the entire squad run laps before they even got started, because one of the soldiers, a timid guy named Sully Pennington, was late. Apparently the poor guy had tripped on the way to the session, and had had difficulty finding the energy to get back up. Ryan sympathized.

Sparring with the other soldiers over the next few days proved to be one of the most difficult things Ryan had ever done. Not only did they continue to run and exercise, but now they also had to beat each other senseless. In the mornings, Sergeant Hye drilled them in new hand-to-hand combat techniques, and she expected all of them to replicate her moves perfectly within the hour. In the afternoons, the soldiers practiced using the same blunted, electrically charged swords and spears they had used during the examinations.

After a few days of sparring, Ryan was one of the few soldiers who had not yet been shocked—but James Green was determined to change that.

Sergeant Hye allowed the recruits to choose their own weapons. Today, Ryan and James were facing off with spears. James was arguably one of the best fighters Ryan had come up against, and neither recruit was able to shock the other with his weapons. Instead, they traded easy hits with fists and the blunt ends of their spears.

"Alright, everyone, CIRCLE UP!" called Sergeant Hye.

Ryan and James finally broke apart and headed toward their leader. Both of them were breathing heavily, and Ryan leaned on his spear for support as Sergeant Hye addressed the recruits.

"I'll be honest with you," she said as she paced in the center of the circle. "It's not looking good. In fact, it looks awful." She glared at Sully for a few seconds before continuing. "The only two of you that even have a chance—a *chance*—against the Demons are Green and Kendrick. You two, front and center."

James shot Ryan a look, and the two of them joined their sergeant in the middle of the circle.

"I want you two to demonstrate how it's done for the rest of them," Sergeant Hye said. "Go until one of you can't." And with that, she joined the rest of the soldiers and motioned for the pair to begin.

Ryan glanced at James and shrugged. The two recruits moved to stand at separate ends of the circle, then turned to face each other, holding their spears at the ready.

"*Good luck!*" came Carrie's voice in Ryan's head. He didn't find her sentiment particularly reassuring, however. In fact, it distracted him.

Before Ryan could steady himself, James charged. Ryan used

his elbow to knock away James's spear, causing his opponent to run right by him, and then turned to attack while James struggled to regain his composure. But James must have predicted the counterattack, because he quickly blocked Ryan's strike from behind his back with his own weapon.

It quickly became apparent that Ryan and James had been sparring partners for too long. Both of them were able to predict the other's moves almost perfectly, and neither could land any particularly hard hits. They alternated between offense and defense, exchanging only minor blows every few seconds. It wasn't for a lack of effort—Ryan and James were both dripping with sweat—but neither was able to gain the upper hand.

Ryan knew that if he wanted to have any chance of winning this fight, he needed to do something unexpected. No sooner had the thought crossed his mind, however, than James's spear struck the top of Ryan's foot. Searing electrical pain traveled up Ryan's leg as his ankle struggled to hold his weight.

Ryan dropped to a knee and glared at James in frustration. His opponent smiled triumphantly, and raised his spear.

Ryan was furious with himself. He could have beaten James. He had been so focused on trying to see things from a new angle, he'd allowed James to overpower him and . . .

A new angle. Ryan looked up at James again. He still had a chance. James had never caught Ryan off guard before—this was completely new territory.

Ryan dropped his spear on the ground next to him. He laid both hands on the ground, palms up. Over James's shoulder, Ryan saw the sergeant shaking her head in disappointment at his surrender.

James's smile widened, and he thrust down with his spear.

Ryan pushed with his one good foot and rolled to the side just as James's spear struck the ground with a resounding metallic *crack*.

Grabbing the spear he'd dropped, Ryan struck, running the point of the weapon up the side of James's leg. With so little force behind it, even a real weapon would never have pierced James's armor, but Ryan didn't care.

James fell to the ground, his electrocuted leg giving out beneath him, and Ryan wasted no time. He swung his spear around and struck James in the stomach.

James convulsed as the shock ran through his core. The training weapons would never kill someone, but a well-placed strike over the heart was definitely powerful enough to give a good shock to the torso, and James was rendered completely incapacitated. The battle was over, and Ryan knelt over his friend.

"Hey, man. You okay?"

Once he was certain that James was nodding in affirmation and not just twitching from the residual voltage, Ryan stood at attention and faced his commanding officer. He could tell Sergeant Hye was trying not to grin.

◊◊◊

No matter how much he tried or how hard he pulled on the joystick, Ryan couldn't get the stupid drone to go where he wanted.

It was the day after his spar with James, and he and Carrie had decided to spend their first volunteer session at one of the city's water facilities. They figured doing something a little more technologically oriented would serve as a nice break from all their intense workouts—but instead, Ryan found the water collection system shockingly infuriating to operate.

He was piloting one of the collection drones, and it was proving to be quite a challenge. In order to pull off some of the more complicated maneuvers, he needed to operate a joystick with his hands while simultaneously working two pedals with his feet.

Unfortunately, Ryan's foot kept randomly twitching from the recent electric shock, making the drone take a sudden, steep dive every time.

"You know, the drone tends to work better when you actually keep it in the cloud," said a friendly voice behind him.

Ryan turned to see Drew leaning over his chair, clearly trying not to laugh. "You've been training for a few weeks now, right? Any body parts fall off yet?" Drew asked with a smile.

"Not yet, but if Hye has her way, it won't be much longer," Ryan said. "What are you doing here?"

"Routine check," Drew said casually. "Since it's a little early in the year to start scouting, they asked me to do a round in some of the water plants and greenhouses to make sure there isn't anything . . . suspicious. The attack really got the Elder's attention, and Amerrest isn't taking any chances. They asked a bunch of scouters to do random patrols. It's not too bad. Just really boring. How's Military?" His voice didn't change at all, but Ryan suspected that Drew had been building up to that question since the conversation began.

"It's actually been pretty good so far!" Ryan said honestly. "I mean . . . it's hard, but I think I'm really going to like it."

Drew looked relieved. Ryan had a hunch as to why his friend was concerned. He had heard some of the new soldiers badmouthing their scouters, as if it was the scouters' fault that their Atlantean career wasn't off to quite the start they had hoped for. Ryan bore no ill will toward Drew at all. Even if there was some bias against the initiates from the Surface, he was in Military for a reason. Maybe the reason was that he should have studied harder or prepared more, but nevertheless, Ryan knew that his failure was not on Drew.

"I think we start telekinesis tomorrow," he told Drew.

"*Have you figured out how to use your beacon yet?*" Ryan heard Drew's voice right behind his head.

"*For the most part,*" Ryan thought back to Drew. "*Carrie says I still drop out halfway through a sentence every once in a while, but I think I got it.*"

"Good!" Drew said out loud. "Getting used to projecting thoughts like that is the first step. You'll have a leg up on people who haven't practiced with their beacons yet. Telekinesis is a lot of fun, but it takes practice, so don't get too discouraged the first day. One of my friends is scary good at it though."

"Is he willing to teach me?" Ryan asked. He had been looking forward to trying telekinesis since Drew had first showed it to him by the fountain in front of the Temple.

"See how you do on your own first. You may be a natural."

◇◇◇

"I have very low aspirations for this session," Sergeant Hye started the next day, as the squad gathered eagerly in the same building in which they had been sparring. Beside her was a crate full of plain off-white balls, each barely larger than a tennis ball.

"*Well, isn't that encouraging?*" Carrie thought to Ryan.

"*Yeah. Drew kinda said the same thing, but at least he was more uplifting about it,*" Ryan told her.

"*You saw Drew?*" Carrie said.

"I know tomorrow is your day off, but using your beacons to manipulate objects requires intense concentration, so I need you all to remain focused," Sergeant Hye continued. "You can picture an object moving all you want, but nothing's going to happen unless you actually force it to move.

"You need to think of your mind like a new muscle. If you want to pick up a rock, you have to physically support it in the palm of your hand. And before you do that, you need to grab it. Levitating an object works the same way. If you want to move an object, you actually have to push it with your mind. You need to project your thoughts, in the form of omega waves, onto the object. At first, you will be weak. Moving an object with your mind is hard work. The heavier the object, the more force it takes to move it. It takes a lot of practice to be proficient with omega waves, so we'd better get started. Frankly, I'd be impressed if anyone can do more than roll a ball across the floor today. Any questions?"

Ryan looked around at his fellow soldiers. Most of them wore blank expressions. Ryan had no idea where to begin, and he suspected most of his friends felt the same way.

"Wonderful!" Sergeant Hye said, as if she knew they were all too confused (and exhausted) to speak. "I want each of you to take a ball. Then spread out so you have plenty of room. Once you find a spot—" She had to raise her voice slightly to be heard over the scuffle of everyone fighting their way forward to grab a ball. "—try to move the ball in a circle around you using omega waves. If you think you've got that down, you can try levitating your ball. I'll be walking around, observing. Get going."

Ryan set down his ball and looked around. Some of his squad mates were staring intensely at the stationary balls at their feet. Others kept stealing furtive glances around the room to see if anyone else was having better luck.

Ryan looked at the ball in front of him. He stared hard, willing it to move with all his might. The only indication of passing time was a gradually worsening crick in his neck. At one point, he saw the ball wiggle and thought he was actually making some progress, but then Sergeant Hye walked by, and he realized it was the vibration of her steps that had moved the ball.

A loud thud suddenly echoed across the room. Ryan looked

up with everyone else to find Sully several yards away, lying un-conscious atop his ball. Sergeant Hye took her time walking over to the fallen man and checked to make sure he was still breathing.

"Don't lock your knees," Sergeant Hye said to the group as Sully started to regain consciousness. "And don't forget to breathe."

And with that, the squad went back to work.

Only a few minutes later, Ryan heard someone utter a hushed "Yes!" He looked up and saw a soldier named Janet smiling widely. The ball at her feet rolled back and forth on the ground as if it were being pulled by invisible strings. She was tapping her thumb and ring finger against her thigh, the way Zach sometimes did when he was excited.

"Everyone, look over here at Janet," Sergeant Hye said loudly. Janet did not acknowledge the sergeant. Her eyes never wavered from the ball. "She figured out a trick that helps a lot of people when they're first starting out. Pretend you're pushing the ball with your hand. If you concentrate on moving the object and go through the physical motions, your brains will fill in the gaps. The trick makes it a lot easier to use your telekinesis. Give it a try."

Ryan looked down at his ball, sighed, and shook his head slightly. He glanced around once more at the others to see whether any of them were having any luck using Sergeant Hye's advice. Most of them were now holding a hand outstretched and staring intensely at their ball with their heads slightly tilted to the side. Still, only Janet's ball was moving.

Ryan watched Janet a little longer, hoping to pick up some type of clue from her, some further insight. But apart from tapping her leg, she was standing perfectly still. He looked a little closer. After staring for what felt like entirely too long, he finally noticed that her tapping wasn't random. In fact, each tap seemed to coincide perfectly with the ball changing direction.

Ryan turned his attention back to his own ball. Instead of just trying to make the ball move, he focused on poking the ball in just one spot. He started tapping his finger on the side of his pants. After a full minute of intense concentration, the ball rocked ever so slightly in place.

Ryan stopped just short of cheering aloud, and focused harder. For a little while, he could make the ball wiggle and shift slightly, but nothing more.

Other soldiers started making some progress and rolling their balls across the floor. The others' success only made Ryan more determined. Sweat beading on his temples from the effort of concentrating, Ryan gave the ball a hard mental poke, and tapped his finger against his leg at the same time.

The ball moved.

Ryan was so shocked that he straightened up for a second. He smiled and tried his luck again. After a few more meager pushes, Ryan was finally able to roll his ball reliably back and forth, like Janet.

"*How are you doing that?*" Carrie asked.

"*It's all about repetitive motion,*" Ryan thought back, not taking his eyes off the ball. "*Try actually pushing your hand back and forth. Don't keep it still.*"

Ryan watched as Carrie slowly moved her outstretched hand forward and back. After about a minute, she developed her own rhythm, and the ball in front of her started to roll back and forth. Ryan gave her an encouraging nod and returned to his own ball, eager to try more intricate maneuvers.

In no time, he was able to move the ball around him in loops. Granted, its path was more of a crooked square than a circle, but he could more or less reliably move it in the direction he wanted.

An hour later, Ryan was satisfied that he was finally able to move the ball in a path that at least somewhat resembled a circle, and was dying to try something else. He looked around and saw Sergeant Hye helping some of the others who were still struggling.

Ryan squatted in front of his ball. He knew the sergeant had said it would be difficult, but now that he had the hang of it, he was bored with just rolling the ball on the ground.

Ryan made a gripping gesture with his hand and focused as he slowly lifted his arm. He tried to concentrate with all his might, but his attention kept wavering as it occurred to him how ridiculous he must look, squatting in front of his ball with his hand gripping air and his face contorted with effort.

Finally, the ball started to rise off the ground. At first, the movement was nearly nothing—just a small hop. After a few more tries, Ryan was able to levitate the ball and hold it in the air for a few seconds before it fell back to the ground. Holding the ball aloft was both exhilarating and draining, but each subsequent attempt displayed improvement, and after a while, Ryan started to enjoy the exercise.

Maybe this Military stuff wasn't so bad after all.

CHAPTER TWELVE
STEPHEN HILLNER

"**O**kay, you guys are actually getting to do some really cool stuff," Zach said to Ryan and Carrie. It was a beautiful day outside, and the three of them were having lunch in the amphitheater, enjoying the chance to catch up and just hang out. They would be volunteering together the next day and had the following day off, so they were in good spirits. Ryan was having fun making his apple do cartwheels in midair for practice while they ate.

Ryan and Carrie had just finished telling Zach all about the training session with their beacons. Zach shook his head. "They just put ours in our necks and pretty much said, 'Have fun!' We've had to figure out how to work them ourselves. Also, the whole thing was a lot worse than a bee sting!"

"Thank you!" Ryan said, glad that he wasn't the only one who thought so.

"How was volunteering with Water?" Zach asked.

"Don't do it," Ryan said simply, letting the apple drop and bounce off the ground. "You said you liked Infrastructure, right? Why don't we all volunteer there tomorrow?"

"Works for me," Carrie said. She tried using her beacon to wipe her face with a napkin, but missed, sending the napkin flopping over her shoulder. She shrugged and left it where it was. "Wow, this food's amazing. Maybe I'm just super hungry? Oooh, don't look! Hye's passing by. If she sees us, she may make us run again."

"Actually," Ryan said slowly, debating whether or not he wanted to risk talking to his demanding sergeant. "I'll be right back. I want to ask her something." He got up and jogged after his superior before Carrie could change his mind.

"Sergeant Hye!" he called out as she made her way toward the back of the Temple.

"Kendrick," she said when he caught up with her. "Everything okay?"

"Yes, ma'am," Ryan said, slightly taken aback. To his knowledge, she had never asked any of her soldiers how they were doing before. Maybe she was a little nicer one-on-one, and this wouldn't be too awkward after all. "I just wanted you to know that I'm willing to do anything."

The sergeant raised an eyebrow in confusion.

"Wait—not like that," Ryan said hastily. "I mean . . . I'm willing to do any odd Military jobs around the city. I want to prove myself, and I'm willing to put in the work."

Sergeant Hye gave him a considering look before speaking. "Thanks for taking initiative. If you're sincere, I may actually have something for you. They're down a man on one of the overnight shifts tonight, if you're willing to fill in."

"Absolutely," Ryan said immediately. "What exactly would I be doing?"

"Well . . . " She hesitated. "I'll let Lieutenant Addams fill you in. He was the one requesting help, and he's the go-to person for this . . . assignment. You'll do fine. Report to the westernmost building in the Military District by nine o'clock tonight. I'll make sure your beacon has the security clearance for it."

◊◊◊

Ryan looked at the dingy shed slumped in front of him. He could have sworn this was where Sergeant Hye had told him to report, but the building was rather decrepit, especially by Atlantean standards, and he couldn't help but feel a little underwhelmed.

As he approached the door, he saw a small red beacon receiver in place of a doorbell. All the buildings in the Military District had similar receivers, but Ryan had never tried to open one before.

"Ryan Kendrick," he thought to the receiver, hoping that the sergeant was true to her word. Sure enough, the beacon receiver turned green and the door swung open. Ryan stepped inside and found himself in a small steel-plated room with nothing but a descending spiral staircase in one corner, which was clanging with footsteps as someone made their way up. A blond man emerged from below, carrying what looked like a thick baton, and extended his hand. Ryan spotted the native Atlantean nail pattern.

"Kendrick?" the man said as Ryan took his hand. Ryan nodded. "I'm Lieutenant Christopher Addams. Feel free to call me Chris when it's just the two of us. How are you?"

"Fine, thank you," Ryan said. "Although I'm slightly confused. What am I doing here? Sergeant Hye wasn't exactly clear."

"Jessica? Figures," Chris said. "She didn't tell you anything? No? Well, long story short, you're going to be on guard duty for the night. Our last guard . . . didn't work out, so we're a little short-staffed, and tonight we're really hurting. I appreciate your help."

"No problem," Ryan said. "Happy to help. Am I allowed to ask what I'm guarding?"

"Not 'what,' but 'who,'" said the lieutenant as they made their way down the spiral staircase. "You'll be one of four guards for a man named Stephen Hillner."

"Four guards?" Ryan said. "He must be important."

"More like dangerous," Chris said, surprising Ryan. They finally reached the end of the staircase, and started down a well-lit but narrow hallway that smelled of antiseptic. "Hillner was—is—an Atlantean from the Surface. I'll try to give you a brief history of the man so you won't be too surprised if anything comes up.

"Atlantis found Hillner near the end of World War II, after he graduated from Columbia University. At the time, he was considering moving to Canada to avoid being drafted, but we picked him up instead. I think he was working as an assistant in a physics lab at the time? It's not important. Anyway, not much is known about Hillner before his college years. He actually doesn't talk about it much, which is impressive considering he never shuts up. Years after he joined Atlantis, we were finally able to dig up reports that noted some adverse childhood experiences and . . . disturbing patterns in his youth. Reports of animal abuse, suspected arson, and even a misdemeanor assault charge that was eventually dropped, but it was harder to get that information back then, since the Surface had no digital recordkeeping yet. One second."

They had reached an impressive steel door at the end of the hallway. The lieutenant stood still for a moment and stared at a beacon receiver until it turned green and the doors opened with a metallic screech.

"Anyway," Chris said as the doors screeched shut behind them, "Hillner excelled on Atlantis. He was at the top of his class that year. There was actually a lot of debate as to whether to put Hillner in Tech or Military. He's brilliant, no doubt about it; but he had an uncanny ability to make cold, calculated decisions under pressure that was hard for our Head of Military at the time to pass up. The problem was, he was a little *too* cold. During one of the battle simulations, he sacrificed his entire army just to trick the computer.

He even shot one of his own teammates with an arrow as part of a strategy during one of the mock battles. In the end, they opted to put him in Tech.

"He did really well in Tech for a while. He used his background in physics and chemistry to work on scientific alchemy."

"Alchemy?" said Ryan.

Chris nodded.

"He was convinced he could get it to work," Chris said. "He kept trying different fusion and fission reactions. He was never quite able to turn lead into gold, which is what he was striving for, but he did make some amazing contributions in the field.

"No one really thought anything would go wrong. At least, not until he was about eight years into his project," Chris continued. His voice started to pick up a little. "At first, it was just small things. He had two people working in the lab under his supervision, and they were the first ones to report anything . . . odd. Apparently, he started having these intense mood swings, and would start yelling at them for no reason. Every now and then, he'd fly into a rage and tear the whole lab apart, smashing glass instruments and throwing caustic materials around. Some people reported random, inappropriate bursts of laughter. Others said he was always muttering to himself, and he started complaining of constant headaches. The Head of Tech at the time found out and instructed him to start seeing a neuropsychologist.

"Apparently it didn't take," Chris added, "because in '55, Hillner had a complete psychotic break and absolutely lost it."

Chris led them through yet another door. Ryan was starting to wonder whether this hallway would ever end. "He was in the lab early one morning with one of his assistants, and he grabbed a flask and smashed it over her head. No one knew anything was wrong for hours—not until the other assistant showed up and found his lab partner on the ground. By that time, Hillner was gone. He hid in the city for two weeks, causing all sorts of chaos. They say it was two weeks of absolute hell. Catching him was supposedly really difficult. He's insane, but he was still wicked smart."

"And he's been locked up since then?" Ryan asked incredulously.

"More or less," the lieutenant said vaguely. "I know how it sounds, but we ran out of options. He never responded to any therapy or medication. We can't send him back to the Surface—he's way too dangerous, and he knows too much about Atlantis. And obviously we can't kill the man. So for now, he's here. We're still trying to work with him. He has weekly therapy sessions, and we're still trying to find out what caused the psychotic break, to make sure it doesn't happen to anyone else."

"Now, when you say he's dangerous . . ." Ryan started.

"Ah, right," Chris said. "Well, there's a reason we have four guards for one man. He's . . . tricky. And smart. And dangerously persuasive. We had to put his most recent neuropsychologist on suicide watch, and he actually killed a guard in '56."

"What?"

"Yeah—something about slamming the guy's head in a desk drawer over and over. But it was a one-time thing, and he hasn't killed anyone since. In fact, I don't think anyone in this city has been murdered since then. And we took out the desk, so you don't have to worry about that.

"Ah, Max—there you are!" Chris said as a man a couple inches taller than Ryan appeared from around a corner. "I want you to meet your other guard for tonight. This is Ryan Kendrick."

"Nice to meet you, Ryan," Max said as they shook hands. With his brown hair and normal nailbeds, Ryan guessed that he was from the Surface. "Has Lieutenant Addams filled you in?"

"I think so," Ryan said. "Please don't tell me there's more . . ."

"Well . . . none that you need to know for tonight," Chris said. Ryan did not feel particularly reassured. "Max, can you grab Ryan a baton? Thanks." Max disappeared through a doorway that must have led to some kind of gear storage. "Now, Ryan, let me give you a couple of pointers. Stephen Hillner will have moments when he seems one hundred percent sane. Don't fall for it. He's going to talk to you. A lot. It's just what he does, and he'll probably be a little worse than normal, because you're new. Honestly, you should just let him talk. Otherwise you'd need to knock him out every ten minutes or so just to get some peace and quiet. It's not worth it. But the important thing is that you should never respond. Ever. It's just a rabbit hole from there. That's how he tends to get to people. That's what happened with the guard that just didn't work out. She started talking with Hillner and then—before she knew it—she started to feel bad for him. We had to let her go."

"Here," Max said, reappearing with a black baton for Ryan. "It's just precautionary; I've never had to use mine. But if Hillner gets too bad, or if he tries to escape, one good shock with the baton will knock him out for sure."

"O-okay," Ryan said slowly, taking the baton. It was a lot of information to process in the span of a few minutes. He felt the weapon buzzing slightly in his hand. "Shock him if he tries to escape. He won't escape, right?"

"No," Chris and Matt said at the same time.

"You'll be fine," the lieutenant added. "And it's about time for a shift change, right?" Max nodded. "Alright. So, Ryan—stand there, and make sure the bastard doesn't do anything weird. Well . . . too weird. Got it?"

"Got it," Ryan said, with a lot more confidence than he actually felt.

Chris nodded and led Ryan and Max around the corner to

another imposing door. A pair of guards stood to either side of it.

"I'm going to leave you guys here," Chris said. "These two will let you in. Good luck, Ryan." And with that, the lieutenant turned on his heel and walked away.

Ryan looked at Max, who offered him a small smile before nodding to the two guards. They must have used their beacons, because the doors opened without either guard doing or saying anything. Max stepped in, and Ryan followed.

The two of them entered a small, cool room. No sooner had they crossed the threshold than two female guards exited the room without saying a word. Max took his place on one side of the door, and Ryan mirrored him on the opposite side, taking in the small room as he did so. Half of the room was taken up by a short cell, and the man inside was trying to get his attention.

At first glance, Stephen Hillner looked like any other man in his late twenties: average height, thin but not unhealthy. His black hair lay in a mess, but it was still apparent that the man tried to take care of himself, even in confinement. If he hadn't been in a cell, Ryan would hardly have given him a second glance. Yet despite his plain, dull-white jumpsuit, the prisoner's demeanor demanded attention. His bright blue eyes stared at Ryan, unblinking.

Ryan tried desperately to avoid making any eye contact, but he could only fake it for so long before he eventually had to look at Hillner. The man's smile was unnerving. It never wavered. Something about it suggested that he alone knew your dirtiest secret, and that he could have some real fun with it if he wanted to.

"Hey there, Young Blood," Hillner said to Ryan. His voice was odd, almost quirky. Ryan could not help but wonder if it was his real voice. "What's your name?"

Ryan remained silent.

"Oooh, strong and silent, huh?" Hillner said, his grin widening.

"Just my type. Alright, then. Young Blood it is!" He took a seat on a plastic chair in the cell and put his arms behind his head. He stared and smiled at Ryan for a few minutes before he broke his silence. "So, Young Blood! What have they told you about me? Did they tell you about how my alcoholic daddy used to beat me and my mother? No, they always leave that part out. I bet they told you that I was crazy, right? That I'm insane?" He started laughing. It came out as some strange mix of a bark and chirp. "Well, I think they're half right. I maaay be insane, but I promise you I'm not crazy.

"What's the difference? I'm glad you asked, Young Blood!" Hillner said as he jumped to his feet again. "You see, people who are insane—like me—just don't think 'right.' They have thoughts that noooo one else has. They make connections that are impossible to make. But *crazy people*—oh, crazy people, they're the ones you have to be careful of. See, crazy people are delusional. They hallucinate; they hear things; they think they're God. That's not me. I'm just Stephen. I'm just an Atlantean. Nothing special. But see, they think I'm crazy, because I discovered the truth."

Hillner looked away for a few seconds for dramatic effect before turning back around. "Oh, I'm not going to tell you—not yet, at least," he said. "Spoilers and all that. You and I have all night together, Young Blood. And of course, Max here can jump in if he wants some of the action. Right, Max?"

Ryan glanced over at Max. The other soldier remained stoic. Hillner started laughing again.

"Relax, Young Blood—you're doing fine. Much better than that last girl. She kept talking to me. Kinda annoying, really." Hillner licked his lips. "Wanna see my tattoos?"

Hillner grabbed two of the bars of the cell, and both of his arms started shaking. "Of course you do!" He took off his shirt and licked his lips again. Maybe it was some type of compulsion. "I have tiger stripes all over this shoulder, and on my back. They're gr-r-reat! And I got this mouth with the tongue sticking out on my ribs over here. Not sure why. It just made me laugh." As if on cue, Hillner started laughing again.

For hours, the man in the cage repeated the same cycle. He would haggle with the two guards—more often Ryan than Max—laugh maniacally, call Ryan "Young Blood," and make sudden, random movements that Ryan suspected were purely theatrical. Given the way Hillner talked and moved, Ryan was convinced he had some type of attention deficit issue in addition to whatever had caused his psychotic break. His comments became progressively lewder and more surprising with each passing hour. It was almost impossible to tune out the erratic outbursts. Ryan did his best to follow Max's lead and keep a straight face, but every once in a while, Hillner would let slip something particularly violent, throwing him off.

"I bet they told you about all the fun I had on Atlantis, right?" Hillner asked Ryan. "Back when I finally realized the truth about this place? Well, I'm going to tell you about it anyway. I'm getting bored, and those were the best two weeks of my life! Let's see . . . let's see . . . what did I do for fun?" He started laughing again. "Oh yeah! I snipped most of the wires in the greenhouses. I don't think anyone was on them at the time, though . . . probably could have planned that one a little better. Oh! Oh! Oh! I poured this stuff into the pipes at the water 'temple'"—Hillner physically made air quotes—"that made everyone throw up." The man started laughing so hard, he had to gasp for air. "There was vomit—*ha*—vomit everywhere! *Ha*—you—*ha*—you couldn't—*ha ha*—you just stepped in it all over the place. Oh, god, *that* one was great."

Hillner continued to tick off his accomplishments. "I turned the fountain water red. It looked like blood. Moses ain't got nothing on me. I think I actually wrote that on a note I pinned to the fountain. I . . . trapped a bunch of people on the subway and made them listen to me singing Elvis karaoke on the train monitors for a few hours. I set the park on fire, but to be fair, that was just to give me time alone in the Temple so I could spray-paint a . . . uh . . . pornographic sketch of Stamaris on all the walls. You should've—*ha*—seen the look on his face when he walked in. He was so red!

"Then, one of my proudest accomplishments: I sneaked into the armory where they store the wings and screwed with a bunch of their wiring. People were kamikazeing all over the place! They'd shoot up in the air a couple feet before they spiraled off and crashed. One person actually died! It was the first murder on Atlantis in eighty-six years, if I remember correctly.

"After that, I had to get away from the city. Took one of the ships and crash-landed in one of the Great Lakes. The Chicago papers said it was a UFO! Atlantis tried to follow me, but I maaaay have tampered with some of the ships before I left. I know one blew up in midair. I think three people died in that one."

Ryan stared at the prisoner. He was starting to wonder whether Hillner ever grew tired of talking, and his face felt like it was about to crack down the middle with the effort of not showing any emotion as Hillner spoke. The man was talking about killing people so flippantly, it blew Ryan's mind.

"You wanna know how they finally got me?" Hillner asked Ryan. He didn't wait for an answer. "It was those Canadians. Why do they have to be so nice? I fled over the border, and the Canadian Atlanteans caught me and shipped me back here. They made a special prison cell just for me—put little emitters in each corner to send out low-level omega waves that interfere with my beacon. Makes it nearly impossible to use telekinesis. It's the same technology they use on the ball and pegs in Toss to make sure none of the players use their beacons to cheat. Anyway, I thought using the omega-wave emitters was so completely unfair. That's why I made sure to send a stray pen on the desk they gave me straight through one of my escorts' necks right before they locked me up. She died instantly.

"Anyway, after that, it was kinda boring for a bit," Stephen said, rocking his chair precariously on its back legs. "I started playing with the omega-wave emitters, and after a while I was able to figure out a pattern to them! That's how I figured out how to beat them, and suddenly, I could use omega waves again. The guards had no idea! Eventually, they got careless, and I got to slam a guard's head into my desk drawer, oh, a couple dozen times. That's when they took out my desk. Between the whole pen thing and the drawer, they don't want me to have any toys.

"And obviously they didn't want me using omega waves again, so they inserted a chip over my beacon. Permanently deactivated me. No beacon, no omega wave stimulation; so no omega waves. Kinda ridiculous, if you ask me. At that point, I just wished they'd take the beacon out of my neck, but *no*. Apparently, it's too 'dangerous' to take stupid thing all the way out—something about damaging the spinal cord. How lame. What's life without a little risk?"

Hillner paused wistfully.

"Anyway, I had to get creative after that," he sighed with a mischievous smile. "At one point, I bit my tongue so hard I started coughing up blood, and they ran to get a medic. They actually fell for it! Unfortunately, they got me in the hallway before I could fully escape. The guards started getting smarter after that. Well, most of them did. There was this one guy who was—well, to put it nicely—he was just dumb. Him and I would chat. I would tell him my secrets, and he would tell me his. That was in . . . 1980? No, '79.

He got comfortable with me. One day, the big softie stood a little too close to the cell, so I grabbed him, banged his head against the bars, took his keys and belt, unlocked the door, and escaped.

"It took them forever to finally catch me again," Hillner said with a huge smile. "I had a blast! Do you have any idea how fun Pennsylvania is? Totally underrated as a tourist destination. That's where you're from, right, Maxxy? The City of Brotherly Love? Anyway, I went to this nuclear power plant. Maybe you've heard of it? Three Mile Island. That place is awesome."

"You caused Three Mile Island?" Ryan said before he could stop himself. Max whipped his head around and stared at Ryan, but said nothing. Ryan felt his face heat up, but Hillner was smiling at him.

"As a matter of fact, I did!" Hillner said. Ryan was surprised the man didn't tease him for speaking. "Atlantis got a whiff of what I was doing pretty quickly, too; otherwise it would have been much worse. By the time they were done cleaning up that mess, I was already in Washington, DC. That's when I got these tats!

"It took Atlantis a few weeks before they finally caught up with me. I was so, so, so close to replicating the Soviet Union anthrax leak. One more week and it would have been perfect! But I guess it wasn't meant to be.

"After that," Hillner said, "they started keeping two guards in here at all times. As if that wasn't enough—I mean, I *am* just one small guy—the entire cell is coursing with electricity. I get a good jolt if I touch the bars. Although, sometimes, I lick them just for fun. I like the tingle."

Hillner carried on talking, but Ryan no longer paid him any attention. Chris had been right: the man in front of him was truly insane. Hillner seemed to be the sort of person who could casually commit mass murder and then go out for a light brunch like nothing had happened. And Hillner only confirmed his insanity with each sentence.

Eventually, Hillner grew bored of reliving his glory days and moved on to discussing sadistic torture techniques, most of which were aimed at Lieutenant Addams. By the end of the night, the one-sided conversation had evolved into musings of unleashing biochemical warfare on Atlantis from within the cell. Just to keep the conversation interesting, Hillner slipped in the occasional inuendo. These were aimed mostly at Ryan, but every once in a while, he would spread the love and include Max, too.

"You know, Young Blood," Hillner said as morning neared, his head tilted to one side, "I see a lot of myself in you."

Despite his best efforts, Ryan was sure his face betrayed his shock at those words. His shift was so close to being over, and he was fighting a constant battle against exhaustion. On top of that, Ryan knew that he had signed up to volunteer with Zach and Carrie the next morning, and after a night of this, he was confident that construction work would be the death of him.

"Absolutely," the lunatic said. "You and I—not so different. See, I think you, like me, see through all the crap. You're not fooled by the façade, are you? The . . . the *mask* that is the face of Atlantis. I can see it in your eyes. Eyes don't lie. Can I tell you a secret? Something I haven't told anyone yet? Maxxy, plug your ears."

The other soldier didn't move. Hillner kept going anyway.

"Those clueless neuropsychologists are always asking *why*," Hillner said. "Why did I do all those things? Why did I finally snap? Well, let me tell you." He paused for a second and leaned forward, so close to the edge of the cage that the electrical current from the bars made his hair stand on end. "Because none of this matters. That's it. That's the big secret. None of this matters. *It's all pointless!* Atlanteans pretend to care about other people, but *that— is—a—lie.* They want you to work and work and work until one day, the pressure makes you EXPLODE! Everyone here is full of shit! Do you think this place is some utopia? That it will save mankind? What kind of utopia has a freakin' army? Sure, they may cure the occasional epidemic, make someone's life somewhere a little better, but this place is a special kind of hell. One where you think you're making a difference and doing something good—but you're not." Hillner started to laugh again, and spoke his next words in a sing-song voice. "You're *no-o-o-ot.* It doesn't matter what you do— every empire falls sooner or later. And one day, so will Atlantis. It will come crashing down, and you're gonna be on it when it does.

"And when I realized all this, I made a vow. The best vow I've ever made," Hillner said. "I vowed to have fun. None of this matters—so why not? Why not have a little fun here and there? Now, I do whatever I want. I'm not burdened by the rules of society. I'm a free man! Uh, figuratively speaking, of course. You'll see. You will. I can tell. It's in your eyes."

Hillner's monologue was interrupted by a sharp knock on the door behind them before the doors whooshed open. Ryan mirrored Max and turned to leave the room as two new guards came in.

"Bye, Young Blood!" Hillner called as Ryan stepped through the door. He could hear the man's grin in his voice. "Hope to see you again soon! I like him," Ryan heard Hillner say to one of the new guards as the door slid shut behind them.

Ryan and Max only made it a few steps down the hall before Lieutenant Addams met them.

"How did he do?" Chris asked Max.

"Ryan did great," Max said immediately. "He didn't let Hillner get to him. But Hillner let something slip about his childhood. I'll write it in the report."

"Great!" Addams said. "Go ahead and send a copy of it to your brother too—he asked to be kept in the loop. Ryan, can we call you if we need someone to fill in again?"

"Absolutely," said Ryan, though he hoped they wouldn't.

"Glad to hear it," the lieutenant said.

The three of them heard a small beep, and Chris quickly checked his watch, which was comprised of a series of attachments that spanned his entire forearm like a greave. Ryan had seen similar watches on several officers, and he wondered whether the length of the watch was related to an officer's rank.

Chris tapped on the screen a few times before speaking again. "I gotta go. Get some sleep, guys."

"Why did you cover for me?" Ryan asked Max as they climbed the spiral staircase together. His feet felt unreasonably heavy after standing still all night.

"Cover for you?" Max asked. He looked confused. "Oh, with whole Three Mile Island thing? That was nothing! On my first night, I talked to Stephen for a few minutes before the other guard finally stopped me. I ended up telling him a bit about my life on the Surface—that's how he knows I'm from Philadelphia—which I thought was pretty harmless. But he's made sure to bring it up somehow every time he sees me, to remind me of my slip-up. Trust me: you did great."

◊◊◊

"So he's real?" Carrie said.

Ryan leaned against the giant slab of granite that he, Carrie, and Zach were working on moving. They had been at their as-signed construction site for only an hour or two, and Ryan was already exhausted. He'd been able to squeeze in just a couple hours of sleep before he had to get up to volunteer. Thankfully, working with no sleep was part of their military training, and he'd gotten used to it. Still, moving huge blocks of stone in the sun was hard work, and the rock was way too heavy to lift with omega waves.

"Oh, he's definitely real," Ryan said. Max had confirmed that it was fine to tell other citizens of Atlantis what guard duty was all about, as long as he didn't give away where they were keeping Hillner or any details of the guards' rotation schedules. Carrie was particularly intrigued, having grown up on rumors of Stephen Hillner. "The man's insane. He kept talking about how Atlantis is a lie and . . . honestly, I don't even know what he was saying half the time."

"How is it a lie?" Carrie asked.

"I'm not sure," Ryan said. "It sounded like he hates this place. And for some reason, he thought I would agree with him. I mean . . . I dunno. Of course I wanted to be in Tech, but Military really isn't that bad."

"Not at all," Carrie agreed. She leaned against the same block as Ryan and took a bite out of an apple. "It's actually oddly chill. I feel like nothing's really changed."

"At least you guys get to be outside a lot," Zach said. He followed his friends' lead and decided to take a break. "I'm going crazy being in a lab all day. And maybe you guys can't see it, but you both have definitely changed some."

"What do you mean?" Ryan asked.

"Well, it's mostly small stuff," Zach said casually. "I mean, you're out here working like you weren't up all night; and Carrie, your appetite's insane. You're eating anything you can get your hands on." Carrie paused long enough to look at her apple, shrugged, and resumed eating. "I don't know; you guys are just . . . more confident. Maybe it's a Military thing. It's actually really cool to see."

"Hey, Ryan," came a new voice, surprising all three of them.

Ryan turned and saw Grayson strolling through the construction site like it was a park. Considering this was the first time Ryan had seen Grayson in the daylight, he could finally rule out his theory that the man was a vampire. "How was meeting Stephen? You should feel honored. Not many people are trusted with guard duty."

"It was . . . odd," Ryan said slowly, slightly taken aback. "Did Lieutenant Addams tell you I was there?"

"Chris? No, he didn't say anything," Grayson said. "And that's a pretty normal reaction. The first time I had to meet with him, he even shook *me*."

"Guard duty?"

"Nah," Grayson said vaguely, "I'd be a horrible guard. Anyway, I have to run. It was good seeing you, Ryan. Carrie, Zach—nice to meet you both."

"Nice to . . . meet . . . yo—who was that?" Zach asked Ryan as Grayson walked away.

"Grayson Morte," Ryan said.

"He seems . . . weird," Zach said. "What's he do here?"

Ryan shook his head and looked at Carrie.

"Never even heard of him," Carrie said. "Apparently he knows us, though."

They both looked at Ryan for answers. He stared back at them for a second, unable to offer any information.

"I really don't care," Ryan said with a hint of exhaustion. "I'm just tired, guys. Come on. We're supposed to be moving granite."

CHAPTER THIRTEEN
INTO THE AIR

"**I**'m sweating my body weight," Ryan said to Carrie.

"You're going to want all the padding," she said.

The two of them were jogging toward the park in the center of the city along with the rest of their squad. Despite the cool early October air, Ryan was burning up. Back in the Military district, Sergeant Hye had instructed the squad to don sets of full-body padding that weighed an extra thirty pounds. Even after all his training, the extra weight and thick fabric made the run much more demanding than usual.

The group followed the serpentine walkways through the park and finally found themselves at the center of a grassy field. Waiting for them were two dark-haired Atlanteans: a man and a woman. On the right shoulder of their uniforms, both of them wore rank markers that Ryan didn't recognize. Sergeant Hye's rank marker consisted of a star with wings on either side, whereas these markers depicted only wings.

"Let's go! Line up," shouted the woman.

"*She seems fun,*" Ryan thought to Carrie.

"*Is it weird that I miss Sam?*" she responded.

"Quit screwing around!" the woman barked as the squad made a crooked line. "I'm Felicia Williams, and this is Oliver Reiner. Over the next few days, we will be evaluating each of you to see if you have what it takes to be aerosoldiers."

"As you may know, Atlantis long ago mastered flight and created the innovation that we know simply as 'wings,'" said Oliver in a flat voice. He spoke as if he was reading from a script. "It is our great honor to have the opportunity to evaluate each of you to determine your aptitude for aerial combat."

"He sounds like he's delivering a eulogy," Carrie thought to Ryan. Ryan tried not to laugh. He felt like he was going to overheat in all the padding, and he hoped these two would hurry up with the speeches.

"Right now, each of you is classified as a terrasoldier," said Felicia. "In a battle, you would be organized into terracompanies. Each company is directed by a terracompany leader. Terracompany leaders respond to sergeants, and the chain of command continues on up. If you do well in flight training, however, you will be transferred into an aerocompany, which consists of twenty-five aerosoldiers led by an aerocompany leader. As an aerosoldier, you will fight the Demons both on the ground and in the air with a set of wings on your back. The wings will greatly enhance your mobility, which is what makes our aerosoldiers some of the most crucial components of our military."

"If you are chosen to don the wings of an aerosoldier," Oliver droned, making Ryan instantly drowsy again, "you will be at an advantage for the rest of your military career. Every ranked officer, from sergeant to commander, is assigned a set of wings, and being proficient at flying will improve your odds of promotion."

"Behind me are a bunch of wing packs," Felicia said, pointing to a heap of what looked like square knapsacks lying some twenty feet away. "I want each of you to put on a pack so that the strap crosses your chest. Once you have it in position, hit the emblem on the strap and await our instructions."

Felicia stopped talking, and the squad exchanged looks before accepting her silence as permission to proceed. Ryan and Carrie walked over and inspected the compressed sets of wings at their feet. Each pack was no larger than a football, and lined with deep blue solar panels. Ryan grabbed one and threw the single strap over his head and across his chest like a sash. At the center of the strap, which was also lined with blue panels, was a large golden emblem depicting the Insignia of Atlantis. Ryan hit the emblem with his palm and immediately felt the strap tighten. Another strap shot around his waist, and a third wrapped around his other shoulder, making a large X. The straps automatically adjusted until the insignia was centered on his chest, and the pack was cinched against his back.

Ryan looked over at Carrie, who was smiling excitedly as her pack centered itself. He returned her smile before tilting his head slightly to get a better look behind her.

On the far side of the field, a number of civilians had set up lawn chairs that hovered a couple feet off the ground, with kids running and playing around their parents' feet. Some had even brought picnics. They were all watching Ryan's squad put on their packs, in obvious anticipation.

"Uh, Carrie, what's going on over there?" Ryan asked.

"They're here to watch," she said, as if that was obvious.

"Watch?"

"Watch us try to fly," Carrie said. "My family used to come every year. It's always hysterical."

"Nice."

"*Ryan, can you help me, please?*" came Will's voice just behind his head.

Ryan turned around to find Will hopelessly contorted. Apparently he'd forgotten that the strap was supposed to go across the chest, and had only slung the pack over one shoulder before slapping the emblem. The result was a complete mess. The original strap pressed down on his shoulder, while the waist strap pinned his arm against his side. The other chest strap had looped itself around his neck, forcing his head into an awkward angle.

"*Uhh . . . let me try pressing the symbol again,*" Ryan thought to Will as he stepped forward to help.

"*No, don't!*" Will replied frantically. "*Already tried that. Just makes it tighter! Hurry! Before Felicia sees—*"

"Natares!" Felicia shouted. "Didn't I tell you how to put it on? This is what happens when you don't listen." She paused for a moment, eyes sharp, and Will's wing pack abruptly popped off and fell to the ground. "You have to use your beacon to unlock it. The command is 'release.' We don't want your wings accidentally falling off if a stray arrow hits the emblem while you're hundreds of feet in the air. Normally, the wings only respond to the person wearing them, but these are training sets that are programmed to respond to Oliver and myself.

"Now that all of you have your wings on *correctly,*" Felicia said pointedly once Will got himself together, "it's time to learn how they work. Oliver?"

"You may be wondering why you were not asked to use wings during initiation," Oliver delivered dutifully. "Interestingly, it's because the wings can only be activated via your beacons. You must direct your thoughts specifically to the wings. To go up, simply think 'up.' To go down, think 'down.' To go left, think . . ."

Ryan could have sworn that he blacked out for a bit while Oliver was going through every possible command iteration. He was also pretty sure Oliver didn't know the definition of the word 'interestingly.' As Oliver began explaining in excruciating detail how to control their speed, Ryan found his thoughts straying to Christmas tunes for some odd reason. It wasn't until he was halfway through

The Little Drummer Boy that he realized the music was actually coming from Carrie, who was just messing with him telepathically. He turned to glare at her, and she chuckled behind her hand.

"Skilled fliers can give less specific orders to their wings," Felicia said, cutting through the music. "They can simply *will* their wings to take them in the directions they want to go. It becomes more natural with practice. For now, I want all of you to spread out. You'll need a lot of room." She waited for the squad to follow her orders. "Now tell your wings to 'Open.'"

"*Open!*" Ryan thought to the pack. His entire body shifted as massive, intricate wings sprouted from the impossibly small pack, throwing him momentarily off-balance. A few yards in front of him, Carrie stood with her wings open and a humongous grin on her face. Her wingspan was almost eight feet, and the wings themselves were absolutely beautiful, made of interlocking solar panels perfectly layered to look like feathers. Looking at Carrie, Ryan could easily imagine how someone on the Surface would mistake an aerosoldier for one of God's messengers.

"Now, I want each of you to hover two feet off the ground," Felicia said, opening the wings on her own back, but remaining on the ground. She turned in a circle as she spoke, addressing everyone. "Keep the 'Up' command short, or you'll skyrocket. Give it a try."

Ryan and several other initiates exchanged anxious looks. Nearby, Will had gone slightly green.

"*Up?*" Ryan thought weakly. He felt a slight pull from the wings, but nothing more. He tried again, a little more forcefully; and the wings pulled him to the tips of his toes before he dropped back down.

A bead of sweat trickled down Ryan's arm. He was excited to fly, but knowing that even a minor mistake could lead to a serious injury made him hesitate. Hadn't Hillner had killed someone by messing with their wings? This wasn't something to be taken lightly.

Ryan shook his head. He just had to get it over with.

"*Up!*" he thought sharply.

With a gut-wrenching pull, the wings lifted Ryan a few feet off the ground. He waved his arms frantically, trying to regain his balance, but his movements proved unnecessary. The wings naturally stabilized him and countered his spastic movements, allowing Ryan to hover in midair, almost completely still.

The straps across his chest and gut were solid, but not having any support under his feet was extremely unsettling. Still, Ryan was determined to get comfortable with his wings. He tried rotating his shoulders, and felt the wings move naturally with his body. He smiled as he continued to play with the wings, rotating left and right at different speeds until he started to get dizzy.

Having no idea how to stop spinning, Ryan tried thinking "*Stop*" in different tones, until he finally slowed down. No more going in circles until he learned better control, he decided. He wanted to try something else.

"*Forward,*" Ryan thought—and he shot straight ahead, a little too close to Carrie. "*No; back! Back!*"—and he rocketed back to his original spot, overshooting it by a few yards.

Ryan composed himself with a huff of laughter. This was going to be fun.

A shout interrupted his thoughts. Ryan turned in the air and saw Will flying spastically about two dozen feet above the rest of the group, jerking back and forth with frantic movements that suggested he was trying desperately to shout any command he could think of at the wings. As Ryan watched, Will dropped rapidly before shooting back up, panicking.

Felicia shot off from the ground to assist the new flyer—just as Will's wings snapped shut in midair. A shout went up from the other initiates as he dropped—Ryan heard Carrie scream—but before he plummeted too far, Felicia spun onto her back and caught him.

A loud cheer went up from the crowd of Atlantean spectators as Felicia gently lowered Will to the ground. Oliver walked over to check on the visibly shaken soldier as Felicia zoomed above the rest of the squad to issue more instructions.

The rest of day was filled with aerial drills and maneuvers. Felicia directed the squad in exercises that tested how well they could control their new toys, and Ryan learned to dread anything Oliver said that began with the word "interestingly," as it always precluded a long, monotonic lecture.

Despite his initial excitement, the lessons were not going as well as Ryan had hoped. Whenever he tried to give a command to his wings, they responded literally, making jerky, uncoordinated movements. At one point, during a low-altitude speed drill, Ryan lost control of his wings and, in a moment of panic, ordered them to go *"Down"* instead of *"Stop,"* dragging himself across the ground for twenty-odd feet before he managed to regain control. Other than Sully and Will, who suffered a midair collision that the Atlantean crowd found immensely entertaining, most of Ryan's squad did much better than him. When their first day of training was finally over, Ryan looked back at the long skid marks his earlier blunder had carved into the grassy field, and sincerely hoped that the rest of the week would be better.

Unfortunately, the next day, Felicia and Oliver started running more and more complicated drills; and while Carrie and some of the other soldiers were able to complete barrel rolls and loops, Ryan frequently needed to break formation just to keep up with the instructors. In one memorable incident, he accidentally clipped one of Felicia's wings, sending her spiraling and swearing loudly as she fought to regain control.

"You'll get better, Ryan," Carrie said bracingly as they left the field at the end of the day. "You just gotta practice a bit more. We still have a few days before they test us. You'll get it by then."

"I hope so," Ryan said as the two of them weaved through the crowd of people who had assembled to watch them fail again. Ryan was pretty sure he'd given them something to laugh at on more than one occasion. "I just can't seem to get the hang of it."

"Ryan, hold up a second."

Ryan stopped and searched the crowd. He was certain Drew had just spoken to him through their beacons, but he couldn't spot his former scouter through the mass of people.

"Go on—I'll catch up with you," Ryan told Carrie.

As the spectators slowly dispersed, Ryan finally found Drew leaning against a tree near the edge of the field. "How's it going?" Drew asked as Ryan approached.

"That depends. Have you been here the whole time?"

"I have. And yesterday, too."

"Then not so well," Ryan admitted.

"It's okay, Ryan," Drew said. "For some people, flying is one of those things that eventually just clicks. Once you get it, everything comes together. Sometimes it just takes a while for that to happen."

"I just hate falling behind," Ryan said. He didn't want to say it in front of Drew, but after he'd been assigned to Military, flying was one of the few things he had really looked forward to trying. For his own sanity, he needed to succeed at this.

"Could you teach me?" Ryan asked suddenly, looking up at Drew. "I've seen you play Toss. You're an amazing flier."

"I don't know, Ryan," Drew said hesitantly. "I've never taught anyone to fly before. . . ."

"Oh, come on. I bet you'd be a great teacher!"

"Well . . ." Drew said slowly, looking thoughtful. Finally, his eyes lit up and he smiled. "Tell you what: meet me back here at seven p.m.," he said. "Let's see if we can make a flier out of you."

◊◊◊

"What's in the bag?"

Drew smiled mischievously as Ryan joined him on the field that evening. Ryan was relieved to see that there were no spectators this time.

"That's for later," Drew said, patting the bulging sack next to him like a gym teacher waiting to surprise his class. He reached down, picked up two wing packs, and handed one to Ryan. "For now, I just want to see you fly on your own for a bit."

Ryan nodded apprehensively and threw on his wings. He wobbled slightly on the ascent, but managed to fly a large lap around the field without incident. Even though Drew was the only person watching him, Ryan couldn't help but feel uneasy.

"*Not bad*," came Drew's voice behind his head as Ryan finished the lap. "*Do one more loop, but try going a little faster this time.*"

Determined to do well, Ryan took one more wide lap around the field. Whenever he had the chance to fly straight for a good distance, Ryan urged his wings, "*Faster*," but he found he needed to slow down quite a bit to bank safely around the corners.

"*Good—come on back down.*"

Ryan landed shakily in front of Drew and closed his wings. Frowning thoughtfully, Drew paced for a few seconds before he spoke.

"Okay, I think I know what the problem is," he said. "You're thinking too much."

"I'm . . . thinking too much," Ryan echoed slowly, not sure

exactly how to take the constructive criticism.

"When you're flying, it looks like you're needing to concentrate before you explicitly give a command," Drew explained. "Your movements seem a little jerky and wooden. Flying is less about giving commands and more about reacting. Once you get the hang of it, your wings will start responding to what you want them to do naturally—not to individual commands."

"So how do I get to that point?" Ryan asked.

"With one of these," Drew said. He reached into the sack next to him and pulled out a bright red ball about half the size of a soccer ball.

"Are we playing catch?" Ryan asked hopefully.

"Not exactly," Drew said with a grin. "Go ahead and fly out about ten feet, over there."

Drew overturned the bag and dumped a dozen or so more balls out at his feet as Ryan got into position and turned awkwardly in midair to face Drew—he still had trouble spinning on the spot while hovering. "You ready?" Drew called out.

"Sure!" Ryan said. "What do you want me to do?"

"Dodge!"

Without waiting for Ryan to respond, Drew hummed a ball straight at his head. Ryan desperately thought, "*Left!*" but he wasn't quick enough. The ball missed his head and collided squarely with his right wing, and the momentum whipped his body around.

Ryan swore loudly before commanding his wings to fly higher, which caused him to overcorrect quite a bit.

"*That wasn't . . . awful.*" Even through the beacons, Ryan could tell Drew was trying not to laugh. "*Let's try again. This time, focus more on dodging the balls than on flying.*"

Drew threw another ball, this time at Ryan's gut. Ryan leaned to his right, hoping he could get out of the way this time. To his amazement, his entire body shifted to the right, and the ball flew past him.

"*It worked!*" Ryan thought at Drew excitedly. "*I did it!*"

"*Good job! Let's go again.*"

Drew continued to chuck the dodgeballs until he finally ran out of ammunition. Other than a particularly painful hit to the stomach, and one incident in which he accidently closed his wings in the middle of a midair cartwheel, Ryan was able to avoid most of Drew's throws.

"You're getting better, Ryan," Drew said bracingly as Ryan helped him retrieve the dodgeballs. "You're starting to move more naturally. Do you want to keep going?"

"Definitely!"

"Good. Then let's step it up a notch."

Apparently "stepping it up a notch" meant dodging two balls at once. Ryan was able to dodge Drew's first throw without too much difficulty, but he was completely blindsided when a second rubber ball came from the side and hit him in the head.

"What was that?" Ryan asked Drew, who was levitating a dodgeball in lazy circles around his head.

"What?" Drew said slyly. "You gotta be ready for anything. Again!"

Now that he knew what to expect, Ryan did a lot better bolting back and forth to avoid getting hit. He quickly learned to change directions in midair to avoid Drew's throws. Before long, Drew started using omega waves to shoot a third ball for an extra challenge.

Ryan laughed despite himself. It was just a game now, and he was starting to win.

Drew was also laughing more now that Ryan was dodging almost everything with ease. By now, the city had long since gone dark, but the field's spotlights shone all around them. "*Last one. You ready?*" Drew asked.

"*Ready!*" Ryan thought back, eyeing the four balls around Drew.

Drew threw one ball at Ryan, and simultaneously shot a second one off the ground with omega waves. Ryan was able to dodge them both, but had to change directions quickly to avoid the last two, which followed soon after.

Ryan was about to relax when he saw Drew make a sharp pulling motion with his hand. Ryan whipped around, threw out his hand, and pushed as hard as he could with omega waves.

A fifth ball that Drew had slung at Ryan from behind stopped dead in its path. It hovered for the briefest moment before dropping to the ground.

"Now, that's how you do it, Ryan!" Drew cheered, beaming.

"That was dirty," Ryan said with a laugh as he landed in front of Drew. It was his softest landing yet.

"Yeah, but you got it," Drew said with a huge smile. "How do you feel now?"

"A lot better. Thank you so much, man."

"I'm happy to do it," Drew said earnestly. "Want to run a few follow-the-leader drills before we call it a night?"

"Let's do it."

By the end of the night, Ryan was able to follow Drew through much more intricate maneuvers than the ones Felicia and Oliver had shown the recruits. He started to love every moment his feet were off the ground. The chilling breeze against his skin when he was zooming over the park produced a rush like nothing he had ever felt. Flying was like being on a never-ending rollercoaster full of quick drops and turns.

Over the remainder of the week, Ryan started looking forward to the flying drills. Even though Felicia frequently shouted at them and the aerial formation maneuvers were often tedious, he was amazed at how quickly flying became second nature to him after his training session with Drew. In just a few days, his flight patterns started to become much more fluid, and he was able to direct his wings by instinct instead of giving them explicit directions. The lessons culminated in an intricate obstacle course through the Residential District, and it was some of the most fun Ryan could remember having since he had arrived on Atlantis.

As it turned out, the obstacle course was much-needed practice for those soldiers who wanted to fight with wings. Oliver told the group that the best fliers would soon be selected for transfer into companies of aerosoldiers. He said that the final test was simple—conceptually, at least. They were to fly through a course of hoops, "just like dolphins," Oliver said.

At the end of the week, most of Ryan's squad boarded an Atlantean personnel transport ship to fly to Nova Scotia for evaluation, although some of the recruits—mainly those who were prone to crashing—had opted to keep their feet on the ground and declined joining the group for the final test.

"*You got anything to eat?*"

Ryan looked up at Carrie, who was sitting across from him.

"*Buried in all this padding?*" Ryan thought back incredulously. "*No, I don't have any food. We just had lunch!*"

Carrie shrugged unapologetically, making Ryan smile. He was grateful they were trying out together.

After a while, the ship landed with the slightest bump, and the squad hopped out, each making sure to take a wing pack as they left. Together they jogged through the shockingly soft green grass over to Felicia, who was waiting for them near the lip of a massive cliff. Beside her, with his hands behind his back, stood a blond man Ryan had never met before, looking very upright and professional as he watched the approaching squad with interest.

As they neared the edge of the cliff, Ryan was hit by a strong, salty breeze from the ocean below. The wind could be a problem, and as he looked around, he saw that others in his squad must have identified the risk as well: some of the girls were tying their hair back in preparation.

"Today is going to be fun," Felicia said to the group with a slightly wicked grin. She made no effort to introduce the man standing next to her. "To determine which of you are to become aerosoldiers, we've designed a course to test your capability with the Atlantean wing packs we've been using for the past few weeks. As Oliver told you earlier, the test is very simple: all you have to do is fly through the rings. It'll be obvious where to go. We'll be evaluating your time, smoothness, and overall proficiency. You can all feel the wind, right? Make sure you correct for it. Oliver will be in the air should things get ugly." She tapped a small screen that spanned the gauntlet on her forearm a few times before she spoke again. "Okay. First up, Ryan Kendrick. Kendrick, stand over there on the pad and get your wings ready."

Ryan walked over to a pressure pad that rested not even a foot away from the edge of the cliff, and tapped the emblem on the strap over his shoulder. The familiar restraints wrapped around his torso as he stepped onto the plate, which lit up with a bright green light.

"The pressure plate will act as both your start and your finish line," Felicia informed him. Ryan wanted to face her, but he was hesitant to turn his back to the cliff. "Your time will start as soon as your feet leave the plate, and stop as soon as you land again. The first hoop is near the bottom of the cliff."

Ryan tried to lean far enough over the edge to see the first hoop without leaving the plate, but it was too far below for him to see.

He took a slow, deep breath. He knew what he was supposed to do, but it was still crazy. His squad had never done anything like this in the practice courses they'd flown before. His stomach churned.

"Well, Kendrick? Get going!"

Before he could lose his nerve, Ryan took a quick step and dove headfirst off the cliff.

The moment of sheer panic was quickly blown away as he freefell, the wind rippling across his face. In its place was pure elation. Almost three hundred feet beneath him, a bright green hoop hovered in the air with the help of small thrusters. The hoop was shockingly narrow—barely wider than Ryan's wingspan. He knew he needed to wait until after he cleared the hoop to open his wings, but that would be cutting it close; just a few feet beneath the hoop, the ocean crashed against the base of the cliff, the noise of the waves drowned out by the wind.

Ryan did everything in his power to aim for the dead center of the ring and wait. The ocean was rushing up to meet him, full of jagged rocks. The anticipation was agony. Every nerve in his body was screaming at him to open the wings.

Ryan's head passed through the hoop.

"*OPEN!*"

Ryan felt a violent snap across his chest as the wings burst open and caught the oncoming air. He angled his body to come out of the dive as easily as possible, less than a dozen feet over the churning water. He pulled up harder than intended to avoid an oncoming wave and felt the saltwater spray his face as he soared across the surface of the ocean.

The next ring was only a few yards ahead of him. Ryan sped up to meet the ring and sharply banked to the right toward his next target. He weaved up, down, left, and right, trying to hit all the hoops. Every chance he had, he pushed his speed, constantly trying to improve his time. Despite the constantly changing wind pushing and pulling from every direction, the wings responded perfectly to Ryan's will. After practicing with Drew, flying was like walking. He knew how to move with a pair of wings on his back. He didn't need to give them direct instructions any more than he needed to tell his legs to move.

The course led him back over dry land and through a small wooded area. Ryan swerved desperately to avoid ancient trees while navigating through the hoops. The targets were coming closer together now, making the course tougher. At one point, a set of rings led Ryan into a huge vertical loop, and he had to fly upside down more than once to hit his next mark. Felicia must have wanted to torture her recruits.

After a few more sudden loops and drops, Ryan found himself flying high above the cliff where he had started. He followed the hoops and continued to soar high above the clouds, feeling more alive with every foot he climbed.

Ahead was an odd set of hoops that unambiguously directed him straight down to the pressure pad on the edge of the cliff. Ryan dove faster than he ever had before, with the wings tucked behind his back. He needed to be an aerosoldier. After failing to get into Tech, he needed this win.

Ryan forced his wings to move even faster. It was risky. His timing needed to be perfect. The ground was rapidly approaching. He could make out individual faces on the ground.

Just a few more seconds. He saw Felicia's eyes, widening with fear.

Now!

Ryan flung his wings open. Both his shoulders popped from the sudden change in force, and the strap around his stomach dug in painfully as he pulled up as hard as possible. His feet touched the ground, and his legs buckled as they tried to absorb the impact. He threw out one arm for support as his body came to an abrupt stop.

For a long moment, Ryan held still, crouched over the pressure plate. No one spoke. His adrenaline was pumping madly, his heart thumping in his chest. He breathed heavily.

Slowly, Ryan looked up at Felicia, and couldn't help but smile at the stunned look on his instructor's face.

◊◊◊

"So you got it?" Zach asked as he collapsed onto the couch next to Ryan.

"Yep!" Ryan said with a huge grin. He passed Zach his drink. "Carrie too! We had some of the fastest times."

"That's amazing!" Zach said. "Who else made aero?"

"Uhh, there's a guy in our squad named Sully," Ryan said. "I don't know if you've met him yet."

"No, I don't think so," Zach said.

"He seems really nice. I'll have to introduce you. He actually came up to me the other day to ask if I could help him train a bit."

"In flying?"

"No, combat training," Ryan said. "He says he keeps getting knocked down. I need to remember to reach out and schedule a time to meet up with him."

"That's awesome," Zach said. "I know I'm not a soldier, but I'm always up for sparring too if he wants extra practice. Wait a minute!" Zach sat bolt upright, grinning. "Roy's not in your squad, right? Did you hear? He didn't get it!"

"Seriously?"

"Yeah!" Zach said with glee. "Apparently he hit a couple of the hoops and couldn't recover in time. He's staying on the ground!"

Ryan snickered. "I can't wait to tell Carrie!"

"Where is she?"

"She went out to celebrate with some friends," Ryan said.

"I'm insulted," Zach said, with mock indignation. "I thought *we* were her friends."

"She mentioned something about 'girls' night,'" Ryan said. When Carrie had told him that she was going out with Rebecca, her sister, and a few of her other girlfriends from the Canadian city, Ryan had invited Zach over for the evening. It was the first time Zach had seen Ryan's and Carrie's apartment in person.

"Well, it gives us the chance to hang out a bit!" Zach said happily. "And we need to celebrate, man! That's a huge accomplishment, jumping straight to aerosoldier. Flying sounds amazing. I kinda want to try out for one of the Toss teams, just to try it."

"You're one of those guys who's good at any sport he tries, aren't you?" Ryan said.

"That's not important," Zach said quickly. "Besides, it sounds like you're the one to beat! You're killing it. Next step, aerocompany leader! And you're going to be a sergeant in no time."

"Thanks, man," Ryan said, appreciating his friend's confidence. "I hope so! Do you have to learn all the military ranks in Tech?"

"No, not exactly," Zach said. "But that reminds me: I think I've found a concentration for my research here."

"What is it?" Ryan asked, sitting up. Zach was always saying that nothing interesting happened in his lab, and as a result, he typically didn't tell too many stories about being in Tech.

"Well," Zach said, looking uncharacteristically sheepish, "since both you and Carrie are Military, I thought I'd focus on military R and D. You know, help you guys out. Plus, that way, I'll get to see you guys more often."

"That's amazing, man!" Ryan said immediately.

"Thanks!" Zach said, looking relieved. "And it's actually really cool tech, too. If everything goes well, I should have something for you guys in a few months. The first time a new citizen creates anything, it has to be approved by Anna before it can enter circulation."

"Anna?"

"Valloris. Head of Tech."

"Right! Sorry; first name threw me for a second," Ryan said. "So, wait. You already know what you're going to invent?"

"Oh, yeah! It's actually really exciting. I'm going to make—"

A sharp knock at the apartment door interrupted Zach. Zach looked at Ryan curiously. Ryan shrugged.

"*Show outside,*" Ryan thought to the door.

Immediately, the door shimmered, as the entire interior surface became a large screen. Outside was a short woman with black hair and dark brown eyes whom Ryan did not know. She was staring at the door expectantly, and bouncing on the balls of her feet.

"Ryan? Carrie? Anyone home?" she called, knocking again.

Ryan groaned as he stood up from the couch and limped to the door. When he'd landed on the pressure plate, he'd injured his knee. The second evaluator at the flight trials, whose name Ryan hadn't caught—if he'd been introduced at all—had come up to Ryan after his flight and told him it was probably just a sprain. The pain was improving, but Felicia had instructed Ryan to take it easy for the next few days.

Ryan opened the door with his beacon before he reached it.

"Ryan Kendrick?" the woman asked as soon as he reached the threshold. "Hi! I'm Harper Bunherst. Nice to meet you. Mind if I come in?" Without waiting for an invitation, she walked inside and spotted Zach on the couch.

"You're not Carrie," she said.

"Nope," Zach said with a smile. He got up to shake the woman's hand. "I'm Zach Lauder."

"Are you Military?" Harper asked suspiciously, taking his hand. "I don't recognize your name."

"Nah, Tech."

"Oh," Harper said. Her face fell slightly, and she turned back to Ryan. "Anyway, Ryan, I was hoping I could talk to you about a service group I lead called Angel Corps. Have you heard of us?"

Ryan shook his head. "I'm not surprised," Harper continued. "Angel Corps is a volunteer organization that goes to the Surface to help those in need. We work in disaster relief, environmental protection, anonymous resource distribution—that sort of thing. Everything is one hundred percent voluntary, and we typically have a couple of projects every year. I don't know about you, but most people from the Surface, including me, came to Atlantis because they wanted to help people. That's why you're here, right? To help others?" she asked Ryan pointedly.

"*Dare you to say 'No' to that,*" Zach thought to Ryan. Ryan had to hide his grin as he nodded.

"Exactly!" Harper said excitedly. "That's why Angel Corps was founded—to give those of us in Military, like you and me, a chance to help people directly. And that's what Angel Corps, and really Atlantis, is all about! What do you say? Are you interested?"

"Absolutely," Ryan said, as Zach telepathically dared him to say "no" again. "When do we start?"

"Our next mission isn't happening for another month or so," Harper said. "We're thinking about doing something for the homeless in one of the major New England cities in November or December. We'll contact you once we settle on the actual dates. You'll pass on the invitation to Carrie for me, right?"

"Of course."

"Can I get in on that too?" Zach asked Harper. "I'd love to help out."

Harper grimaced awkwardly.

"Sorry," she said, her tone somewhat cold. "This is for Military Atlanteans only. It's our chance to make a difference and help others. Besides, that's what you guys are supposed to be doing every day, right?"

Zach blinked in polite surprise, but said nothing. Ryan shot him an uncertain look.

"I mean . . . Harper," Ryan said, "Zach just wants to help out. There's gotta be something he can do, right?"

"Sorry," Harper said, rather unapologetically.

"It's totally fine," Zach said. "*Don't worry about it, man,*" he added to Ryan. Harper nodded, as if it was for the best that Zach had given up.

"Well," Harper said, her huge smile returning as she walked out the door. "It was a pleasure meeting you, Ryan. I'm off to try to recruit a couple more newbies. Welcome to the Angel Corps!" she shouted over her shoulder as she jogged down the stairs and disappeared from sight.

"That was . . . interesting," Ryan said as he returned to the couch and closed the door.

Zach nodded slowly. "She does *not* like people from Tech, huh?"

"Doesn't look like it," Ryan agreed. "It sounds like a cool way to help out, though. Plus, I'd get to go to the Surface some."

"Like an angel from above," Zach cooed with a sarcastic grin. "And now you've got the wings to back it up! They were a little on the nose naming the group 'Angel Corps,' don't you think?"

Ryan sent a small push of omega waves at Zach, making him stumble backward and over the arm of the couch.

"Now, now. That wasn't very angelic!"

CHAPTER FOURTEEN
SECRECY FOR SECURITY

As the end of October approached, neither the cooling air nor the darkening sky stopped Ryan's new superior from cracking the whip. Now that he and Carrie were aerosoldiers, Felicia had become their commanding officer, and she worked them harder than ever. Ryan could never have imagined he would miss Sergeant Hye so much. Their exercises were held at all hours, and they weren't always given advance notice. More than once, Ryan's peaceful sleep was rudely interrupted by flashing lights and the sound of trumpets screeching from speakers hidden throughout the apartment. Carrie quickly confirmed that all the apartments in Atlantis had similar systems built in to wake Atlanteans across the city in case of emergencies.

"Or, apparently, when they want to kill us with drills," Carrie grumbled one morning, shoving a morning snack into her mouth as they walked out the door, the screen on which conveniently displayed the location of their next drill.

She wasn't alone in her annoyance. Several of the other aerosoldiers in their company had already been on Atlantis for a year, and they too were grumbling at the sudden increase in the intensity of the workouts. Rumors were that Amerrest had all the commanding officers working overtime. Even though Felicia never said anything, Ryan suspected that Atlantis was starting to feel outside pressure from the Order.

The more he thought about it, the more curious Ryan was as to why the Order had decided to attack Atlantis now, after years of peace. The rest of the soldiers were curious, too. During one of their conversations, Rebecca, who was serving as a terrasoldier in another company, told Ryan that she had asked her commanding officer the same question, but her terracompany leader had proved just as clueless as the soldiers. If anyone on Atlantis could have explained the Demons' timing, they weren't sharing that information with the rank and file. As for the Demons, they hadn't sent Atlantis another message since they'd set off the bombs around the city— but there was plenty of chatter that they were making moves on the Surface, and that Atlantis was planning to act soon.

But if those rumors were true, Felicia certainly knew how to keep a strong poker face. The only hint she gave of any upcoming conflict was the sudden increase in what the older aerosoldiers in their company called "listening drills." Every so often, either verbally or via her beacon, Felicia would randomly shout orders at the soldiers—orders that were often odd, or sometimes just uncomfortable to execute. While he wasn't completely certain of it, Ryan suspected Felicia was trying to condition the company to follow orders without question in the heat of battle. The training did not come easily, however: once, after Felicia instructed him to make a particularly tight midair turn around a building, Ryan felt a small snap of pain in the side of his neck. He spent the rest of that evening nursing the spot with an icepack.

In addition to the listening drills, the company engaged in combat training—which Ryan found to be remarkably more difficult as an aerosoldier. Typically, Felicia and Oliver would have their aerocompanies pair off on the ground, practice standard combat techniques for a little while, and then fly a dozen or so feet off the ground to finish the fight. Ryan quickly discovered that hand-to-hand combat was substantially harder without his feet planted firmly on the ground. Landing a successful hit required that he perfectly synchronize the movements of his arm, torso, and wings. He also learned that although one strong hit from an opponent could easily end a bout, body weight and momentum were much more important than any individual strike. More than once, he found himself nearly upside down while fighting in midair— but instead of wasting time correcting his orientation, he learned to take advantage of the angle, which always seemed to stun his opponent.

With every training session, Ryan became more confident in his abilities as a soldier. His aerial maneuvers became fluid, and the spear felt like a natural extension of his hand. He even started experimenting with using different techniques against some of the stronger, more experienced soldiers in the company, trying to find new ways to beat them. Every once in a while, an unrefined move would get Ryan hit in the head; but more often than not, he was able to surprise his opponent and win. Soon, he was teaching some of the struggling soldiers a few tricks to try to help them out—especially since Felicia and Oliver acted more like observers than teachers.

"Kendrick," Felicia said in a rather curt voice as she stopped him and Carrie after an especially challenging evening drill. "Present to Personnel Review Room Three right away."

"Yes, ma'am," Ryan said immediately. He quickly tried to wipe away the sweat running down his forehead. "Uh, would you be able to direct me to the . . . personnel room?"

"Personnel Review Room Three," Felicia said. "You've been on this city for five months—you should know how to get around." And without a backward glance, she left.

"Have we been there before?" Ryan asked Carrie.

"No," Carrie said. "I have no idea why she's acting like that. Anyway, the personnel review rooms are in the tall building north of here—next to the gym, just before you hit the Residential District. I'll walk with you."

"Thanks," Ryan said gratefully. "Just give me a minute. I need to tell Sully."

Ryan jogged over to his fellow aerosoldier while Carrie waited for him. "Sully, I'm so sorry, man. I know we were supposed to have our one-on-one session tonight, but I just got summoned to one of the personnel rooms. Can we reschedule?"

"Yeah, of course!" Sully said immediately. "I totally understand—it's not your fault. Maybe sometime next week? I mean, I know you're busy. . . ."

"We can absolutely do it next week," Ryan said without hesitation. He felt awful. "No matter what, I'll make it work. We can spend some time sparring on the ground and then practice in the air for a bit. How does that sound?"

"That'd be great," Sully said earnestly. "Thank you!"

"Happy to do it. But I better get going. I have no idea who I'm meeting, but I probably shouldn't keep them waiting."

"Good luck!"

Ryan apologized and thanked Sully again before rejoining Carrie, and together, the two of them weaved through the Military District in the cool night air.

Finally, Carrie dropped Ryan off in front of the building she'd mentioned earlier. As he made his way inside and up an ornate staircase, Ryan became painfully aware of his body odor. Whatever this was, he hoped it wasn't a formal occasion.

After navigating a maze of corridors, Ryan finally found the correct room, and walked in to find a single Atlantean waiting for him on the other side of a large conference table. After a moment,

Ryan suddenly recognized him as the man who had observed the aerial tryouts in Nova Scotia.

"Hi, Ryan," the Atlantean said as he offered Ryan the seat across from him. "I'm Captain Theodore Tanner. Please call me Theo. It's a pleasure to meet you. I believe you've worked with my brother Max on guard duty?"

"Yes!" Ryan said, remembering his fellow guard from his overnight shift with Stephen Hillner. "Lieutenant Addams mentioned you were involved with Hillner somehow. So you and Max were both recruited to Atlantis?" he said. "That's impressive. So you're from Philly then, too?"

"The blond hair fools a lot of people," the captain nodded with a sly smile. Ryan glanced at the captain's nails to confirm the lack of a diamond pattern. "Even some native Atlanteans. Ryan, do you know why you're here?"

"No, Captain."

"Well, Ryan, it's customary for a superior officer to sit down and review a soldier's performance with them when they are being considered for a promotion," Theo said.

"A . . . a promotion?" Ryan gaped. "We haven't even seen any action yet! Not that I'm complaining, sir," he added.

Theo didn't flinch. "Typically, there are one or two individuals each year who show us they have what it takes to be strong military leaders," he continued. "Not only have you taken initiative as a solider, but you've also proven yourself as a more than competent flier and fighter."

"Thank you," Ryan said gratefully, making a mental note to thank Drew a fifth time for the flying lessons. "I had no idea Felicia was giving me such good reviews."

"Well . . . she's not," the captain said. "Honestly, she really doesn't evaluate you all like she's supposed to. But I've been keeping an eye on you, and I'm impressed. We typically tag a handful of those chosen for Military to watch closely after initiation. Your scores on all of the Military tests were outstanding when you were a Beta. We were fairly certain you would excel as a soldier, and so far, you haven't disappointed us. You know how to take charge, you assist your fellow soldiers in training, and you definitely proved your daring during the aerial tryouts."

"Thank you, Captain," Ryan said again. "May I ask a question about something you just said?"

"Of course."

"You said that you were confident I would do well as a soldier, and that all my Military scores were high," Ryan said. "Is that why I was chosen for Military? I've never been the most athletic or in-shape person, so I've been curious."

Theo nodded. "You did well on both the Tech and Military evaluations," he said slowly, as if he was searching for the right words. "You weren't at the top of your initiation group, but you would have done well in Tech, too. Considering how well you performed in the mock battles and simulations, we decided to allocate you to Military. Plus, no matter what shape you're in, we condition you pretty quickly here."

"No kidding," Ryan agreed. "A week ago, I think I felt my abs for the first time in my life."

Theo chuckled before resuming his professional demeanor. "We'll contact you in the next week or two with more details about your promotion to aerocompany leader. You would be in charge of your own company of aerial soldiers. We'll make sure you have all the training you need before we feed you to the lions—but I'm confident you'll make a fine leader."

"Thank you, sir," Ryan said.

He was about to ask for more details about the duties of an air leader when he was interrupted by three loud beeps. Theo looked at his watch—one of the forearm-spanning ones that the officers wore—and swore under his breath. Ryan wondered when he would get a watch like that—but he figured that now wasn't exactly the best time to ask.

Theo tapped the watch a few more times before looking up and sighing heavily.

"Come on," he said to Ryan. "You're coming with me. Lord knows this guy is going to be your problem soon. You might as well meet him now."

Ryan jumped up and followed Theo, who insisted on a pace just shy of a jog as they made their way out of the building and into the Residential District. Theo quickly led him north past the Temple and amphitheater and into an area comprised of nice houses rather than apartments. Other than during his brief tour of the Residential District with the Betas, Ryan hadn't spent any time in this area, and it was nearly impossible to recognize any of the foreign landmarks at night.

"Captain—am I allowed to ask what's happening?" Ryan asked hesitantly. He didn't want to push his luck.

"It'll be easier to show you," Theo said, peering up and down the street. "Ah—there's one."

He walked up to a solitary, eight-foot-tall pillar that stood in the center of an intersection. During his initiation, Ryan had never gotten the chance to ask Sam about the pillars dispersed around the city, and he hoped Theo would finally tell him the purpose of these strange objects.

As the captain approached the pillar, a holographic keyboard appeared before the column. Theo quickly entered an access code, and a tablet emerged from a small slot on the side of the pillar. Theo gestured to the tablet, and the device floated directly to Ryan, who caught it as the screen lit up, presumably on orders from Theo's beacon.

"Joshua Stennon. Mid-forties. Lives in Washington, DC," Theo said briskly as he took off walking again. "In front of you is all the information Atlantis has compiled on the man—which is essentially his entire life story."

"Who is he?" Ryan asked. He used his beacon to pull up a quick summary of the man's life, actively ignoring the issues of ethics and privacy that nagged at him as he did. Still, it was difficult to read, keep up with Theo, and avoid tripping over his own feet at the same time.

"He's a hacker who's hell-bent on exposing Atlantis," Theo explained, in lieu of Ryan reading the text.

"Is he an Atlantean citizen?"

"No, and that's part of the issue," Theo said. "Born and raised in northern Virginia, he was a solid B student throughout high school, but he was able to attend Georgetown University—largely due to his religious affiliations and his parents' generous donations to the school. He was always good with computers, but this was before Georgetown's computer science program really took off, so he would have majored in electrical engineering."

"'Would have'?" Ryan asked.

"He was expelled during his junior year, when he was caught trying to hack into one of the school's computers to change his grades. The genius decided to do it in plain view of a security camera. After that, he moved back in with his parents for the next five years while working customer service for a large IT firm."

As he scrolled through the information on the tablet, a line of text managed to catch Ryan's eye. "It says here that he previously had a girlfriend . . . who is now an Atlantean citizen?"

Theo nodded. "She worked at the IT company too. She showed

a lot of potential, and was recruited by Atlantis," he confirmed. "That's where things went wrong. Stennon became aggravated that he was never able to see his girlfriend, and that she was so vague about her new job. He became paranoid. He thought she was cheating on him, so he started investigating. One day, he followed her while she was visiting her family on the Surface, and saw her take off in one of our ships to return to the city."

"What's this folder here?" Ryan asked, pointing to an icon labeled "EVIDENCE."

"That's all the information Stennon found on Atlantis," Theo said. "After he saw his girlfriend take off in the Atlantean ship, Stennon became obsessed with trying to find us. He started looking into UFO sightings, and pretty much anything else he could get his hands on that could explain where his girlfriend disappeared to. Slowly, he started to put all the pieces together. Apparently there were a lot more conspiracy theories about us than we realized. There's even a reference to one of our ships in some old Renaissance manuscript he found.

"Even though most of the accounts throughout history called us either angels or aliens, Stennon was suspicious."

"There are tons of files in here about Einstein, Da Vinci, and a bunch of other inventors," Ryan said, scrolling through the folder.

"All citizens of Atlantis. If you look carefully, all of them have holes in their life stories that can only be explained if you know they were recruited," Theo said. "Anyway, Stennon got the idea that there was some secret government agency out there. When he was twenty-eight, he found a highly encrypted network—ours—and made it his personal mission to break into it. Our firewall was top-of-the-line—beyond top-of-the-line, actually. No one had ever come close to breaking it before, not even the Order. It took him six months. He had a twenty-two-second window to break in before our automated system kicked him out, and he did it in just fourteen.

"He was in our system for less than a minute before we caught him," Theo continued. "He downloaded all the information he possibly could and read every word of it that night. He woke up the next morning ready to tell the world about us, but everything he'd compiled was mysteriously erased overnight."

"Atlantis?"

"Yep," Theo said. "We weren't going to let him get all that information out to the public. All he had left to show for his hard work was a page or two of handwritten notes. Ah, here we are— Intelligence headquarters."

The two of them had arrived at a semicircular building made of tinted glass, situated along the northernmost rim of the city. Ryan followed Theo through the door, and they immediately started down a wide staircase.

"Anyway," Theo continued as they made their way underground, "even though we erased all the data he had on us, Stennon still tried to tell people about Atlantis. I believe he went to Homeland Security to talk to . . . I don't know . . . some government official."

"Did he tell them?"

"He tried," Theo said with a smile, "but he ended up talking to an Atlantean instead. She was planted as an aide. He had no idea. She sent him away and took his notes as 'evidence,' but after a while, he must have realized she never acted on them. Since then, Stennon has been trying to regather intel on Atlantis. He's actually gotten pretty close to exposing us a couple of times. I can't even tell you how many times we've had to stop him. And it's about to be one more."

Theo stopped in front of an imposing steel door. It slid smoothly open, and the pair stepped into what Ryan assumed was some type of control room. The space was dimly illuminated by large video screens displaying busy city streets. Workstations with multiple built-in computers were regularly spaced throughout the room, each housing at least two Atlanteans who were working feverishly. In the center of the room, a single Atlantean soldier stood in a small open space, watching the screens.

"You are relieved, soldier," Theo said as he led Ryan into the open space. The soldier nodded respectfully and took a seat at a computer.

"Does someone want to quickly fill me in?" Theo asked.

"Yes, sir," a woman said from behind one of the computers. "Stennon hopes to speak to the Secretary of State tonight after a benefit dinner being held in the heart of DC. The dinner was planned following the tremendous success of an online awareness campaign for a rare neurological disease, and the Secretary is personally invested in the campaign, because her grandfather—"

"I said 'quickly,'" Theo said, without turning around.

"Right," said the operator. "Point is, it's a private event, so Stennon aims to intercept the Secretary of State when she leaves around eleven p.m. He hasn't started there yet, but we believe he will in a few minutes."

"Captain, what are Atlantis's protocols when it comes to security threats?" Ryan asked. After seeing how Theo interacted with the other Atlanteans in the room, Ryan was careful to use the commanding officer's rank.

"Typically, we try to stop the threat by tailing the person in question," Theo said. He was watching one of the screens, which showed a large, formal banquet hall where Ryan assumed the benefit dinner was being held. "That's what the Intelligence Division is for: identifying and tracking threats to Atlantis. We use this building, Intelligence headquarters, to help us monitor and intercept especially high-risk persons of interest. If that's not good enough, we have contingencies in place—electroshock therapies designed to target the memory centers of the brain to make anyone who poses a threat forget about Atlantis. But it's extremely rare for anyone to find us, believe we're real, *and* convince anyone else that we actually exist, so we've never actually had to shock anyone. Not yet, at any rate."

"But Stennon is a considerable risk?"

"Absolutely," Theo said without hesitation, before turning to one of the Atlanteans behind him. "Let me see him."

There was a chorus of "Yes, sir," and a flurry of activity at the workstations. A few seconds later, one of the traffic cameras swapped out its feed. The image of an overweight man with dirty blond hair and a considerable neck beard now filled the screen. Joshua Stennon sat at a desk littered with empty energy drink cans, eating a bag of chips with his mouth wide open. Ryan was sure he had no idea Atlantis was watching him.

Something about the man was unsettling to Ryan. It wasn't until he looked around at everyone in the control room that he figured out what was so odd: Stennon was the first person Ryan had seen in months who looked over the age of thirty.

"For some reason, I thought he'd have glasses. . . ." Ryan mused absentmindedly as he watched a few crumbs fall from Stennon's open mouth. He guessed that Atlantis had tapped into the man's webcam.

"He wears contacts," Theo said softly, with a slight smile.

"Has Atlantis ever thought about recruiting him?" Ryan asked, even as he tried to find the answer on the tablet he was still holding. "He must be pretty smart if he was able to hack your system. And if you inducted him, you wouldn't need to monitor him anymore."

"We almost did," came a familiar voice from behind Ryan.

Drew had just walked through the door. He came over to join Ryan and Theo, clapping Ryan's shoulder as he did. "We quickly realized he would never be able to keep our secrets, even if he was a full citizen of Atlantis."

"Drew here was one of the main scouters who evaluated Stennon," Theo said, not otherwise acknowledging Drew's arrival. "Drew leaked some fake 'classified' information, and Stennon lasted all of ten minutes before he posted it on his blog. Since then, we've used Drew as a consult whenever we need to talk to Stennon. Drew knows him better than anyone else here."

"Captain," called an operator near the front of the room. "Stennon will be leaving within the next five to ten minutes."

"You're up, Drew," Theo said.

"Put me through to Stennon," Drew said to the operator.

"You're talking to him?" Ryan asked. "Even though Atlantis is supposed to be a secret?"

"He already knows about us," Drew said, shrugging. "No point in denying it. This way, I may be able to convince him not to go to the Secretary of State, or at the very least, delay him."

One of the Intel officers nodded to Drew. He must have given Drew a signal through their beacons, because Drew nodded back, looked up the screen, and then spoke loudly.

"Josh! Are you there? It's Drew. From Atlantis."

Ryan watched as the man jumped up excitedly, knocking over his half-full energy drink.

"Drew!" Josh said excitedly. Apparently, they knew each other pretty well, considering they were on first-name terms. Ryan wondered how many times something like this had happened. "I can't see you! Can you see me?"

"I can," Drew said. Ryan noticed that he was speaking slower and more deliberately than usual. He sounded remarkably calm.

Ryan even felt his own heart rate slowing at his friend's steady tone. He didn't know whether Drew was speaking like this in an attempt to stall Stennon, or to defuse the tension; but either way, Ryan was sure it was effective. "Listen, Josh, we know what you're trying to do. We know that you want to speak to the Secretary of State. Josh, I'm begging you to reconsider. You know that Atlantis is real, but in order for us to continue helping people and conducting our research, we must remain a secret."

"I get that," Josh said, leaning forward so that his nose was very prominent on the camera. "I do. But people deserve to know the truth. They should know Atlantis exists!"

"Josh, we've been through this before," Drew said patiently. "You know that's not an option, and you know that we'll have to stop you. Come on, buddy, why don't we just forget about it? I'll even stick around a bit so you can ask me some questions."

Ryan smiled as he watched the obvious internal debate flash across Josh's face. Clearly, it was a tempting offer.

"I'm sorry, Drew, but I gotta do this," Josh said suddenly, setting his jaw. "They need to know. And you can't stop me." Without waiting for a reply, Josh reached for the webcam, and the feed went black.

Theo swore. Drew just shook his head.

"Why does he always say that?" Drew asked no one in particular. "We literally stop him every time."

All the operators started working in overdrive. The screens in front of Ryan shifted to different street views, while another showed a large map of the District of Columbia.

"Car-cam on screen eight, Drew," one of the operators shouted.

Drew turned to the rightmost screen, which was now showing a navigation display alongside a live video of the interior of an empty car. A few seconds later, Ryan watched Josh climb into the driver's seat and throw a fraying backpack onto the passenger side.

"What camera is this?" Ryan asked Theo. The interior of the car seemed a little dated; it definitely wasn't a vehicle that would have a built-in dashcam.

"One that we installed in his car," Theo replied, as if it was a trivial matter. "Alright, everyone, you know what to do. Slow Stennon down."

Despite everything Ryan had seen on Atlantis, watching the Intelligence team at work was both amazing and, if he was being honest with himself, a little frightening. For the first time, Ryan realized how much power Atlantis had, even on the Surface. No matter where Stennon drove, Ryan could see him from at least three angles, while following his progress through the city in real time on a large aerial map. As Josh got closer and closer to the banquet hall, they followed his path down every road. At first, it was difficult to see what the Atlanteans were doing to stop the hacker—but Ryan soon realized that the poor man was being forced to stop at every traffic light.

"Holding at the intersection of Elm and Lee," another operator said as the light turned red.

"Remember," Theo said, "hold him for an extra five seconds at each light. Any longer, and other drivers will start getting suspicious."

"Yes, sir."

Ryan watched as Stennon weaved in and out of traffic like the native urban driver he was. Despite all of the Atlanteans' hard work, he seemed to be making good time. Maybe it was experience from being thwarted by Atlantis in the past, or maybe he was just getting lucky, but it looked like the hacker was going to make it to the benefit dinner in time.

"Do you guys have a backup plan if changing the lights isn't enough?"

Ryan asked Drew as Stennon took a sharp turn at an impressive speed.

"*Oh, yeah. Just watch,*" Drew thought back. "*We've had to do this a few times. Sometimes we have to get a little creative.*"

Whatever Atlantis was planning on doing, they needed to do it soon. Stennon was already in the heart of the city, and he only had two or three miles left to drive.

The hacker took another turn. One of the street cameras that was following the driver switched views as Stennon disappeared around the corner. Suddenly, the entire room was lit a dull orange and gold: the new street onto which he'd turned stopped abruptly—at a huge, well-lit construction site that perfectly interrupted Stennon's route, forcing him to slam on his brakes to avoid hitting the car in front of him.

Even without audio surveillance in the car, Ryan clearly saw Stennon's mouth form the words "Damn it" as he dropped his head to rest on the steering wheel. Next to him, Ryan heard Drew chuckle at the hacker's feeble curse.

Stennon tried to follow a detour around the construction site, but he was forced to stop again almost immediately, when a cop on the next street over walked up to his car and knocked on the window.

"Sir, have you been drinking tonight?"

Ryan listened as the police officer at the DUI checkpoint began to interrogate Stennon.

"That was lucky," Ryan said.

"Luck had nothing to do with it," Theo said. "It's all us. Even the cop is an Atlantean. That's why we suddenly have audio—he's mic'd up."

Ryan couldn't help but be a little impressed with Atlantis's ingenuity. Sure enough, the police officer ordered Stennon out of the car for a sobriety test, despite the hacker's loud insistence that he'd only had a few Red Bulls. Ryan had to suppress his laughter at some of the ridiculous things the police officer was forcing Stennon to do, including having him say every other letter in the alphabet backward, then forward.

Finally, the cop had to let Stennon go—but not before he'd successfully wasted a good ten minutes. Josh's face was red by the time he finally got back into his car and resumed his race downtown. Ryan watched as the hacker drove straight through three red lights, weaving wildly through the traffic all around him. He was lucky there weren't any real police officers nearby.

Ryan's head swiveled back and forth, trying to take in every detail across the various screens—one of which showed the Secretary of State still at the benefit dinner. Another showed Stennon only a mile or so away. Atlantis was running out of time to stop him. What if they weren't able to do it? How would the Secretary respond to a claim that there were giant flying cities all over the world? Despite the very idea sounding ridiculous—to anyone who didn't know it to be true, of course—Ryan couldn't help but feel a little anxious as Stennon got closer to his goal. He was so nervous, he didn't realize that he had begun bouncing on the balls of his feet, until Theo shot him a small smile.

"Come on . . ." Drew whispered.

Ryan looked back up at the camera that showed the banquet. The Secretary of State was making her closing statements. Stennon was only six blocks out. The car camera showed him smiling as he pulled to a stop at a busy intersection. He was confident, and Ryan couldn't blame him. He was going to make it.

Suddenly, car horns blared from every direction. Ryan gasped as a car passing through the intersection ahead of Stennon lost control and swerved straight into oncoming traffic, hitting another car with a loud crash. Before Ryan could even blink, two more cars joined the pileup, effectively blocking the entire intersection. The drivers who had been lucky enough to avoid the collision were trapped in the middle of the intersection. None of the cars were going anywhere, and Stennon was no exception. He was trapped at the intersection, and there was no way he was getting off the street anytime soon.

A roar of cheers replaced the sound of horns as the intel officers all burst into applause. Drew and Theo both visibly relaxed, and gave each other a congratulatory handshake.

"I take it that wasn't luck, either?" Ryan asked Drew with a small smile, which Drew returned.

"There were four drivers actually involved in the collision," Drew said, "and they're all Atlanteans. Two of them live here, and the other two live in DC."

"We actually have a big presence in the capital," Theo said to Ryan. "It helps us smooth over any . . . incidents."

"Plus, we modified all the cars to make them insanely safe for our drivers," Drew chimed in. "And those sirens you hear in the background should be our friendly police officer from the DUI checkpoint. We instructed two of the drivers involved in the collision to complain of neck pain too, just to stall a little longer."

"Looks like it won't be necessary," Theo said, gesturing at the screen that was keeping tabs on the Secretary of State. Ryan watched as the woman climbed into a limousine outside the banquet hall. The driver of the limousine closed the vehicle's door behind her, then turned with a huge grin and gave a not-so-subtle thumbs-up to a traffic camera before driving away.

"That should do it," Theo said with satisfaction. "Come on, Ryan."

Without waiting for an answer, the captain turned to leave.

Ryan quickly said goodbye to Drew and jogged a few steps to keep pace with his superior.

"So, what did you think?" Theo asked Ryan vaguely once they were outside. It had gotten noticeably colder during their short time inside Intelligence headquarters, and Ryan could see their breath as they spoke.

"That was impressive," Ryan admitted.

"What would you have done differently if you were in charge?"

Ryan stayed silent for a moment, considering carefully. He knew he was being tested.

"I would have tried to hack into Josh's GPS," he finally said. "We could use his blind faith in the navigation system to our advantage. Have it take him on a slower route through the city. That way, the op is still successful, but you don't inconvenience or endanger any bystanders."

Theo smiled, and nodded slightly at Ryan's response.

"You'd better get home and get some sleep. Good work today," Theo said; and Ryan was dismissed.

The next morning, while Ryan was volunteering with Zach in the greenhouses, he wasted no time telling his friend about everything that had happened.

"That's crazy . . . what they did . . . to stop . . . the hacker," Zach said. As it turned out, pulling potatoes out of a mesh weave wall required more effort than either Zach or Ryan had expected. Nevertheless, after the initial thrill of jumping off the edge of the flying city, they both found that they enjoyed picking the food that grew beneath the metropolis. It was relatively mindless work, but being suspended from the cables kept their adrenaline pumping.

"I wonder how many times I ran into an Atlantean back home without realizing it." Zach finally managed to yank a cluster of tubers free by bracing his feet on either side of the plant for extra leverage. "There we go. Pass me my basket, would ya?"

"No kidding," Ryan said. He slid the wire basket up the cable for Zach to catch, making sure his own basket of tomatoes was secure. "I'm sure they have a few up in Boston, too. It's kinda weird, but seeing DC made me want to visit Boston again."

"Well, maybe you'll get some leave time with that promotion!" Zach said. "I mean, it's amazing that they're already looking at you for aerocompany leader!"

"Thanks," Ryan said distractedly. He was trying his hardest to reach for a stubborn tomato, which was shockingly difficult to do from the zip line. He'd already tried using omega waves to gather the fruit, but he had only succeeded in telepathically crushing one of the tomatoes. The worst part was that he was unsure whether it was safe to just drop the tomato off the edge of the city, so he had to put the flattened one in his basket, too.

"Yeah. Captain Tanner said he didn't know when the promotion would happen, but he made it sound—ah! Got it!" Ryan carefully transferred the tomato to his basket. "He made it sound like it should be soon. Oh—but can you not tell Carrie? I'll tell her soon, once it's final. I just don't want to . . . you know . . . make it seem like I'm gloating or anything."

"I won't say a thing," Zach promised. He pushed his full basket of potatoes down the cable toward one of the standing platforms for another volunteer to unload. "But dude, you know she'll be happy for you."

Ryan smiled at his friend as he scooted his basket of tomatoes a little closer to him with omega waves. He glanced around quickly, made sure that only Zach was watching, and opted to toss out the squished tomato anyway. He just hoped there were no low-flying planes directly beneath them.

CHAPTER FIFTEEN
To Arms

In a flash, Ryan knocked his enemy over and raised his spear high. It was time to deliver the kill strike. He thrust downward—and froze. Suddenly, he couldn't move. He was completely paralyzed.

Panic built in Ryan's chest. He had no control over his body!

Ryan looked down at Sully. The other recruit was lying on his back in front of Ryan, staring at him with a mix of amazement and respect. In that second, Ryan was grateful for his frozen muscles.

A few seconds ago, Ryan and Sully had been sparring with the rest of their aerocompany. Now, with a flash of shame, Ryan realized he had let the exercise get away from him. Even with his blunted spear, he still could have seriously injured Sully if that final blow had actually made contact.

"Everyone, over here!" Felicia called to all the soldiers in the facility where they were practicing. "Take a look at Kendrick. Can you move, soldier?"

Ryan tried to answer his commanding officer, but even his tongue was frozen. He managed a guttural noise of denial.

"I didn't think so," Felicia said shortly. She sounded more tired than she had only a few minutes ago. "Right now, Kendrick can't move because I won't let him. This is why you need to practice your telekinesis. Omega waves are powerful. You need to be ready to use them on the battlefield, and you must be able to resist the omega waves that the Demons will use against you. In this case, Sully here is lucky that I stopped Ryan before he was able to do some serious damage."

Felicia exhaled as if she had been holding a deep breath. Immediately, Ryan felt his muscles relax, and he staggered as he slowly regained control of his body. Then he quickly apologized and helped Sully up.

"Thank you for not killing your fellow soldier," Felicia said dryly. "Now, I want each of you to go with your partner and practice pushing each other with omega waves, while also resisting your opponent's attack. You can try to counter their pushes with your own omega waves, or by physically bracing yourselves against the force. Go on!"

All the aerosoldiers broke off into their pairs again. Ryan was excited. He had been looking forward to using omega waves in combat training for a while now. Just the week before, he had gotten bored and recruited Zach (although it admittedly hadn't taken much to convince him) to practice. By the end of the day, both he and Zach had become quite proficient at pushing each other back and forth across Ryan's apartment. At one point, Ryan had even managed to push Zach backward so hard that he'd fallen over the coffee table—though Zach had quickly gotten revenge by sending a particularly focused beam of omega waves straight to Ryan's stomach, knocking the breath out of him. In the end, he and Zach had agreed to stop before they broke anything—including themselves.

While he was excited to finally use omega waves in sanctioned combat training against a fellow aerosoldier, Ryan worried that poor Sully wouldn't stand much of a chance against him. He did his best to go easy on his partner for a few minutes before he finally fought back, sending a push of omega waves at Sully's shoulder that torqued his partner's entire body and made him fall to his knees. Ryan quickly helped him up again.

"Thanks, Ryan," Sully said sincerely, looking up at Ryan with astonishingly wide eyes. There really wasn't a resentful bone in the soldier's body. "Are we still good to train tonight?"

"Absolutely," Ryan said. "I'm really sorry we had to reschedule last week, and that it's taken so long to finally do this."

"It's totally fine," Sully said earnestly. "I know we mostly talked about doing combat training, but if you don't mind, do you think you could help me out with this stuff too? I want to get good at using the beacon, like you. I'm still having some trouble with the omega waves. . . ."

"Of course, man," Ryan said, slightly embarrassed by the compliment. "I'll do my best. We have another BEAM practice session tomorrow evening. If we can't get to everything tonight, we can meet up tomorrow after that if you want."

Sully nodded excitedly, making his hair bounce slightly. Ryan couldn't help but be reminded of an excited puppy.

"Perfect," Ryan said. "Wanna try this exercise again? This time, I won't fight back at all. Just try to push me as much as you can."

"Got it!"

Sully jogged away and turned to face Ryan. His face contorted with effort as he tried to hit Ryan with omega waves, and for a second, Ryan felt a small, distinct push in his gut before the force cut out.

"Good!" Ryan said. "I could really feel something at the end there. This time, instead of constantly pushing me, try to send one sharp shove instead."

"Got it!"

As Sully's face twisted in concentration, Ryan braced himself;

however, other than a few quick jabs to his stomach—each one about ten seconds apart—he didn't feel much. Sully wasn't making a lot of progress, though not for lack of trying: Ryan saw a bead of sweat running down the side of the other soldier's face.

Ryan tried to think. There had to be some way he could help Sully.

"Try actually throwing a punch when you push," Ryan finally suggested, remembering the trick he'd used when he'd first rolled Sergeant Hye's ball across the floor. "Sometimes the physical movement can help your brain make the connec—"

A sudden burst of omega waves hit Ryan just under the ribs, cutting his sentence short and leaving him breathless. Eager to improve, Sully had immediately followed Ryan's advice and lashed out at the air in front of him, and Ryan had had no time to brace himself against the attack. The impact sent Ryan to his knees. He swallowed mouthfuls of air as he struggled to catch his breath.

"Crap! Ryan, I'm so sorry," Sully said, rushing over to him.

"It's fine," Ryan wheezed with a small cough. "I think we're even for me almost skewering you now. That was a lot better! Want to keep going?"

Sully nodded enthusiastically and opened his mouth to say something—but a shout cut him off before he could speak.

"Aerosoldiers, fall in!" Felicia commanded. She waited until the company formed into an impeccably straight line before continuing. "We're needed at Command right away. Follow me!"

"*Where's Command?*" Ryan asked Carrie as the company took off in a controlled jog. It was nice to be able to talk to each other without trying to sneak in extra breaths while running. "*How many random buildings are there in the Military District?*"

"*Too many,*" Carrie thought back. "*I have no clue where this one is.*"

The company followed Felicia past the track to the center of the district, and then onward a little way to a dark, squat building with ornate columns and moldings along the roof. Felicia quickly led the way inside and down a winding hallway, which Ryan was starting to think was a staple of Atlantean architecture.

Finally, Felicia ushered them all through an open doorway and into a sterile, stark white room. Descending rows of benches filled three sides of the room, while the fourth featured a large floor-to-ceiling window spanning the entire wall. In the middle of the room was a large table covered in what looked like a layer of fine black sand.

Ryan walked around the table to the far side of the room, near the window, and took an open seat next to Carrie. As he sat, he glanced out the window—and nearly missed his chair.

The window overlooked a large vertical space that dropped like a canyon beneath the surface of the city. Its walls were dotted with wide windows that revealed rooms identical to the one they had just entered. Glancing across the gap, Ryan saw Will and the rest of his terracompany trickling into another room on the other side of the space.

Ryan looked down and saw that the floor of the canyon lay about four stories below them. As he perused the windows, he glimpsed Captain Tanner standing at attention in front of another table covered in dark sand. Theo looked far more intense than Ryan had yet seen him—and the man was hardly laid-back to begin with.

"*There are tons of companies meeting. What do you think is going on?*" Ryan asked Carrie.

"*War,*" she thought grimly. Ryan glanced at her, but said nothing. How could he possibly respond to that?

It didn't help that no one was speaking much. Across from Ryan, Sully was looking around the room, obviously trying to read what was happening. He caught Ryan's eye and offered a smile that Ryan quickly returned.

Carrie smacked Ryan on the thigh and nodded toward the center of the room. Ryan looked up, and was taken aback to see a life-sized hologram of Theo standing in the room next to their table. A quick look through the window confirmed that there was now a copy of Theo in every room.

"Soldiers of Atlantis," hologram-Theo said in a commanding tone. "I want to take this opportunity to thank each of you for your service. For those of you who don't know me, I am Captain Tanner, one of your commanding officers.

"As you all know, two months ago, the Order launched an attack on Atlantis during a celebration, killing seven of our citizens and injuring several others. Since then, all the Elders of Atlantis have collaborated, and they have agreed that the time has come for action. As of now, we are at war.

"The Demons have a strong footing somewhere in Canada, and they have already made significant progress on the Surface, marching westward," Theo continued. His hologram started to pace around the table. "We believe they intend to launch an attack against the Californian City of Atlantis soon, but for now, they're bunkering down in the Rocky Mountains. The remainder of their army is moving east. We suspect they have received limited intel about an Atlantean safe haven in the southeastern United States, and that they intend to launch an attack against it. Based on their current trajectory, we do not believe that they know its exact location, but the Demons are bold and unrelenting. If we allow them to continue unopposed, they will find the haven.

"Soldiers of Atlantis: we cannot let this happen. We must stop the Demons before they advance any farther."

Theo nodded toward the table in front of him, and the sandy

surface sprang to life. Millions of tiny black grains levitated off the table, taking the shape of a grassy, contoured plain.

"We will be confronting the Demons in North Dakota, before they get too far east," Theo said. "By the time we reach them, the Order will be positioned here—" A cluster of grains changed from black to bright red. "And we are going to cut them off here." Green beads of sand appeared on the opposite side of the map. "Our aero-companies will be positioned behind our ground units at the start of the battle. Most likely, the Demons will launch the first attack from the air."

Ryan watched as a few green grains of sand rose over the black plain and collided with the red spheres representing the Order's aerial units. His stomach clenched as the pieces struck each other. Most of the red units fell out of the sky during the simulated battle—but so did a few of the green ones. When the grains representing the fallen Atlantean aerosoldiers hit the surface of the table, they immediately reverted to black. It was as if they had never existed at all.

Ryan looked over at Carrie. She was watching the simulation intensely, and seemed to be refusing to meet his gaze.

Absentmindedly, Ryan began fiddling with the Atlantean medallion that hung over his shirt. The cool metal grounded him. He took a deep breath.

"Terrasoldiers and aerosoldiers," Theo said. "You are to meet in the armory along the westernmost point of the Military District near the edge of the city in exactly three hours. For now, you are all dismissed. Officers, stick around for specific instructions." And that was all.

Ryan followed the rest of his company out of the room and into the crisp fall air. The cold breeze was nothing compared to the chilling silence of the soldiers surrounding him. No one was speaking. Had it not been for the steady tramp of boots, Ryan would have thought he'd suddenly gone deaf.

Ryan was willing to bet that the simulation of the aerosoldiers colliding and falling back to earth had bothered the rest of his company as much as it did him, even if no one seemed willing to admit it. He couldn't blame his fellow soldiers, however: he was no better. It was as if by not speaking about the upcoming battle, the thing for which they had been training for months, they could somehow delay the fight.

Although he wasn't sure why, Ryan found himself walking almost automatically back to his apartment. Beside him, Carrie did the same. Neither said a word. When they arrived, Carrie went straight to her room, and Ryan sat on the couch, at a loss what to do for the next two hours and forty minutes.

After a few seconds, Ryan reached for one of the tablets on the coffee table and opened a new window, intending to create a message to send to Zach. He stared at the blank window for a full minute or two, unsure what to say. He knew that if things were the other way around—if Zach had been the one going into battle—Ryan would have wanted to know about it.

Eventually, Ryan settled on a simple summary of what was happening. He composed the message and sent it. Then he lay back on the couch, allowing the cool cushions to cradle his body, and tried to collect his thoughts.

He wasn't going to die. There was no way. He had trained hard. He knew how to fight. He knew how to use omega waves. He was a great flier. He was not going to die.

But he could.

He could die.

Ryan had never seen combat, but he knew that even good soldiers could be unlucky. Even the best. Even the most experienced.

And while Ryan knew he was good, he was certainly neither of those things.

He was not going to die—but every time the thought surfaced, he started to shake. Today could be his last day on Earth. His last day on Atlantis.

In a surreal moment of clarity, Ryan realized how much he cared about this city. Five months ago, he'd had no idea this place even existed; but here he was, ready to die for it.

Of course, he wasn't going to die.

But . . .

Ryan jumped up off the sofa. He was thinking in circles, and he needed to snap out of this vicious cycle before the battle began.

Desperate for something to keep him occupied, Ryan went to his room and started rummaging through his belongings. His eyes fell on a pile of laundry, and he suddenly felt an overwhelming desire to clean.

Before long, Ryan was folding his clean clothes and throwing the dirty ones in a hamper. He wasn't sure why he felt compelled to tidy up now. Maybe he felt the act was an assertion of some semblance of control over his life—or maybe he just remembered how difficult it had been for him to sift through Jack's belongings with his aunt and uncle after the funeral. If he were to die on the battlefield—he wasn't going to die; but he could, *he could*—he didn't want to make Zach or Carrie go through the same grueling process, and he definitely didn't want them to have to pick up his dirty socks.

Ryan had just finished folding an emerald-green shirt that glowed softly wherever he touched the fabric when he saw something that made him freeze. His backpack, the one he brought with him from the Surface, was sitting deep in a corner of his closet, where he'd thrown it on his first day in the apartment. He had forgotten all about the bag. It was hard to believe how much his life had changed since he'd first come to Atlantis.

Ryan grabbed the bag and sat on the edge of his bed. There was only one thing that could calm him now: Jack.

Ryan used his beacon to turn on his bedroom television as he pulled out his cousin's flash drive. He doubted the televisions on Atlantis had USB ports, but if the flash drive was from Atlantis, there might be another way to access it.

"Show compatible devices," Ryan ordered. A list appeared on the TV screen. Sure enough, the flash drive popped up. *"Pair with Jack's Drive."*

Ryan smiled as a new window populated the screen. He knew hearing his cousin's voice would comfort him, even if it was an old message.

Ryan was about to open the video file with his name on it when he paused and looked at the corrupted folder. The folder's name was no longer complete gibberish, as it had been when he first opened the flash drive on the Surface. Instead, it was simply labeled "Atlantis." Its contents must have been protected so that they could only be accessed from an Atlantean computer.

Ryan opened the folder and was surprised to find only three items: an audio file labeled "COMPROMISED," a video file labeled "To Ryan, if Tech," and another video labeled "To Ryan, if Military."

Even though he was dying to know what Jack had left for him, Ryan couldn't help but eye the audio file. What did "COMPROMISED" mean? Was it referring to Jack's Canadian mission—the one that had gotten him killed? At first, Ryan couldn't see how that could be, as Jack had given him the flash drive a month or two before he'd died. Then Ryan looked at the last edit date for the file and felt his stomach drop. It was the day of Jack's car accident. He must have uploaded the file remotely before he'd been killed. After everything Ryan had seen on Atlantis, he wouldn't be surprised to discover that was possible.

"*Open 'COMPROMISED.'*"

Suddenly, Jack's voice came through the television speakers.

"Initiate real-time file upload. New file name: COMPROMISED," Jack said. His cousin's words were rushed, and his voice shook slightly as he spoke over the revving of a car engine.

"Ryan. I don't know how much you know yet, and I'm sorry, but I don't know what to do and I gotta do something and I don't know who else to tell. Look, cous, things are bad. Really bad. I don't even know where to begin.

"I'm in Canada right now for a mission. Laura and I were supposed to infiltrate the Order's Canadian stronghold. We thought it just a weapons stockpile, but our intel was completely off. They're creating something—something big! They just started. I think I heard one of the Demons say it would take a few years, but it . . . it looks bad. I'm not even sure what it is—but we've got to stop it.

"We tried to steal a copy of the blueprints, but we were compromised. I bought Laura some time to escape, but I think the Demons are still following me. I haven't seen anyone in a while, but that doesn't mean anything.

"That's not even the worst part. After Laura left, I overheard two Demons talking, and . . . Ryan, the Order has an inside man. There's a mole. Someone on the Northeast American City is feeding sensitive information to the Order, and it's gonna destroy Atlantis. I don't know who it is, and I don't know who I can trust. You gotta be careful, man. Trust no one—"

A deafening crash of crunching metal and breaking glass blasted through the speakers, making Ryan jump. He waited for his cousin to speak again, but the audio clip abruptly ended and closed.

The silence was overwhelming. Ryan took a deep breath as his eyes started to burn. He didn't know what he'd been expecting, but it hadn't been that. He hadn't been expecting to hear his cousin's last words before his death, and he definitely hadn't expected to hear the car crash.

Ryan had been wrong. Hearing his cousin's voice had made him feel worse. This wasn't how he should be spending his last hours before the battle.

Ryan quickly stood—and paused. He wanted to leave, but he still needed to know what Jack had recorded for him. There was no way it could be as bad as the audio file. Just to make sure, though, Ryan checked to see when the video files had been made, and was relieved to see that both of them had been created about two months prior to Jack's death.

"*Open 'To Ryan, if Military.'*"

An image of Jack appeared on the screen. He was relaxed and smiling. Ryan felt the tension in his shoulders ease slightly. This was how he wanted to remember Jack.

"Hey, cous," Jack said. "Congratulations on joining the Military sect. You have no idea how proud I am of you. Military is absolutely amazing. Don't let anyone tell you differently. I've loved every minute of being a soldier, and I've enjoyed working with Intelligence even more. I wouldn't have it any other way.

"Whether Atlantis is at war with the Order or not, there will eventually come a time when they ask you to do something dangerous. Something that could get you killed. Maybe that's why you're watching this video now—I don't know. But I want you to know that the people on Atlantis have your back. They're there for you. My advice is this: find someone you trust with your life, and stick with them. You're going to need that person if you plan on surviving this with a shred of sanity.

"Ryan, I really wish we had time to explore Atlantis together. I feel like you and I would've been absolutely unstoppable in Intelligence. You're going to make a great soldier, and an even better leader. If you can, try to finish what I started. I want those Demons to fear the Kendrick name. If anyone can do it, you can.

"I love you, Ryan, and I miss you more than you know. Make me proud. I know you will."

Ryan leaned back on his soft bed and smiled. His breathing leveled out as a soft, bittersweet smile formed on his face.

Somehow, even though he was no longer around, Jack knew exactly what Ryan needed to hear. How had he forgotten that his cousin had also been part of the Military sect?

Ryan huffed a quiet laugh and silently berated himself for feeling disappointed and passed over. He was following in Jack's footsteps. That was something to be proud of.

Ryan stared at the last remaining file in the folder: the one Jack had left for him if he was chosen for Tech. Jack had sounded so genuinely proud of Ryan in the last video—like a father watching his son take over the family business. Part of Ryan wanted to know what Jack would have said if his little cousin was assigned to the Tech sect. Another part was simply greedy to see Jack's face again, to hear his voice and pretend for a moment that things had turned out differently for both of them. But there was a third part of him, a part that had grown over the past five months without his noticing, that told him gently that dwelling on what might have been was not the way forward, and was not what Jack would have wanted for him.

"Delete 'To Ryan, if Tech.'"

Ryan watched as the file disappeared from the screen, and

smiled. He was Military, just like his cousin. That was enough for Ryan.

A loud rap on the front door jarred Ryan from his thoughts, bringing him back to the real world. He hopped off his bed and rushed to open the door—only to find Zach waiting on the other side.

"Hey," Zach said between gasps. He was breathing heavily, and Ryan suspected his friend had run all the way from his own apartment. "I just got your message. I . . . I wanted to see you guys before you left."

"Hey, Zach!" Carrie said a little too cheerfully as she emerged from her bedroom, looking pale. Zach crossed the living room in three steps and wrapped her in a giant hug.

"Thank you," she said softly after a moment, hugging him back. "I take it Ryan told you we're about to leave."

"You guys are going to be fine," Zach said, in an oddly soothing tone that Ryan hadn't heard from him before. "I wish I could be down there with you."

"Nah," Ryan said with a smile. "We need you up here, coming up with the latest tech to help us win the war."

Before Zach could reply, he was interrupted by another knock. Carrie looked at the door suspiciously before opening it with her beacon.

Without waiting for an invitation, Patrick and Amanda, Carrie's brother and sister, practically sprinted inside and nearly knocked her over with hugs. After they finally broke apart, Patrick looked over at Ryan, rushed forward, and embraced him too.

"You be careful too," he said to Ryan before letting go. Amanda immediately took his place.

"I'll try," Ryan said to Patrick as Amanda clung to him. "And I'll do my best to look out for Carrie."

Patrick nodded gratefully. Amanda pursed her lips slightly as she pulled away, but didn't comment. Ryan saw her force a bright smile across her face as she turned back to Carrie, who scowled slightly at Ryan over her sister's shoulder.

Ryan had to bite his tongue to keep from laughing. He knew that Carrie was an amazing fighter who could take care of herself, but she was also his friend, and he meant what he'd said.

Patrick quickly explained that Carrie had video chatted with their parents after returning to the apartment, and Kurt and Sheryl had wasted no time in telling Patrick and Amanda to go see Carrie right away. Ryan was extremely grateful for their arrival. Even though the occasion was somber, their combined energy, along with Zach's presence, undeniably lightened the mood. Ryan almost forgot about the upcoming battle—until the television flashed a warning in bright red letters across the screen:

REPORT TO ARMORY.

Below the message was a timer steadily counting down from thirty minutes.

Carrie's siblings immediately swarmed her again. Ryan turned to Zach, unsure what to say. "Goodbye" seemed far too morbid; but in the end, Zach had him covered: he grabbed Ryan in a tight hug that Ryan returned without hesitation. Everything they needed to say was wordlessly communicated in that hug, even without their beacons.

Once everyone broke apart, Ryan and Carrie said their final farewells before heading out to the armory. Together, they made their way to the westernmost point of the city, where a mass of soldiers and commanders were filing into a long, short building surrounded by a high granite wall.

Carrie led the way as she and Ryan fought through the crowd

to find their aerocompany. After navigating what felt like an indoor maze, the pair finally found them near one of the farthest corners of the building. There, Ryan found a small locker with his name on it, containing a full set of navy-blue Atlantean armor.

Even though they had trained in modified armor, Ryan had never worn a complete set of brand-new gear before. Slowly, he donned the pristine armor, finding that every piece fit his body perfectly. But the combined weight of all the heavy metal pieces started to add up. He couldn't imagine fighting weighed down like this.

Ryan waited until his boots were on before giving the command Sergeant Hye had taught them months ago. "*Connect!*"

Immediately, Ryan felt all the armor pieces shift as the sensors imbedded within them sparked to life. Each segment perfectly aligned with the others, like an exoskeleton, and Ryan felt the weight of the armor lift almost completely. He jumped up and down experimentally, and shook his arms and legs, noticing how the plates moved perfectly with him, as if the sensors allowed the armor to aid his movements. It felt like wearing a somewhat bulky athletic suit, snug and well padded, but flexible. If it hadn't been for the *clunk* of his footsteps and the fact that he was surrounded by soldiers, he could easily have forgotten he was even wearing armor.

Ryan lifted his helmet with its tinted visor off the shelf, but stopped just short of putting it on when a small screen over his cubby caught his eye. The screen showed bright green and blue lines moving up and down in a zigzag pattern, while sequences of small numbers scrolled beneath. It took Ryan a moment to realize he was looking at a readout of his own vital signs, including his heart rate and oxygen levels. One line, labeled "carbon dioxide," was completely still.

Ryan threw on his helmet, which immediately aligned with the rest of the armor he wore.

"*Display vitals,*" Ryan tried, unsure whether the command would work—though in retrospect, he should have known better than to doubt Atlantean technology.

A heads-up display of his vital signs appeared on Ryan's visor. With his helmet on, his carbon dioxide output was registering. There must have been additional sensors positioned throughout the armor to keep tabs on his health, and Ryan was fairly certain that at least one person in Intelligence must be monitoring all the soldiers' vitals.

Something in the back of Ryan's mind told him that at one point, he'd learned who had designed this armor. He tried to remember back to orientation and initiation, but he couldn't recall a name.

"*Who designed the medical sensors?*" Ryan asked through his beacon. In answer, a single name scrolled across the heads-up display:

ANDREW TELLAREN

"Ready?" Carrie asked Ryan. She had decked herself out in her own matching deep blue armor, and now she held out his wing pack for him to take.

Ryan nodded, realized it would be difficult for her to see his acknowledgment thanks to the helmet, and took it off before nodding again. He accepted the wings from Carrie, and the two of them moved to follow the rest of their company down the hall to a large spiral staircase.

The rhythmic beat of marching boots echoed through the stairwell, drowning out everything else. After descending several stories beneath the surface of the city, the staircase finally opened up into a large bay lined with Atlantean personnel ships. Each ship had the same black metallic finish, sleek and shiny, making them look more like fighter jets than transport ships.

The milling troops slowly thinned out as soldiers filed into their assigned ships, each of which was able to comfortably fit a whole company. As Ryan and Carrie passed, one of the ships closed its personnel hatch and began to take off. Ryan watched the ship rise a few feet in the air, rotate on the spot, and shoot out of the large bay opening and into the sky.

Ryan and Carrie continued down the bay with the rest of their company until they found Felicia standing in front of one of the ships. She nodded to each of them as they approached, but said nothing.

Without further guidance, Ryan and Carrie climbed aboard their ship and took two seats side by side. Within minutes, the re-mainder of the seats were filled, and Felicia slapped a button on the wall to shut the main door to the ship. She barely made it to her seat at the head of the ship before Ryan felt the slightest vibration under his feet, indicating that they were already on the move.

Ryan and the rest of the aerocompany quickly strapped in as the ship turned. After what felt like several minutes of maneuvering at a creeping pace, the ship hung for a moment in the air, its engines whirring louder and louder, then shot forward like a bullet. Several soldiers gasped as they dropped several feet before leveling off again.

"*We're out,*" Carrie thought grimly to Ryan.

Ryan only nodded. He knew the drop meant that they were outside the bay, and that they had officially left the flying city of Atlantis.

They were off to war.

◊◊◊

After hours of smooth, silent flying, Ryan finally felt the ship touch ground again. He unbuckled his restraints and stood with a slight groan as he felt his knees pop and loosen up.

"Alright everyone, listen up!" Felicia said as they gathered their gear. "Captain Tanner just sent an update. The Demons are a lot closer than we originally expected. Instead of having a few days to prepare, we may only have a couple hours—at most. So once we get off, run to the gear tent to grab what you need and meet me outside to fall in for formation. Go on!"

At her words, the doors to the ship sprang open, and the company filed out. The sky overhead was overcast but pale, and Ryan had to blink several times before his eyes adjusted to the brightness. When he stepped out of the ship, his armored boot touched the plush grass of an endless, rolling landscape of low hills that stretched in every direction. The cool wind rippled over the long grass, making the hills look like shifting waves. Other than a few command and supply tents set up in the middle of the herd of landing Atlantean ships, the place was completely deserted. There was no evidence that anyone had been to this area in months—maybe even years.

Ryan and Carrie jogged against the wind over to the supply tent with the rest of their company. When they arrived, they pushed back the canvas flap and ducked inside to find a wide assortment of Atlantean weaponry arranged neatly in crates. Ryan saw Will testing the tension of a bowstring before taking a quiver full of arrows and a small dagger with him. On his way out, Will offered him a small nod, which Ryan returned. Considering Will had opted to keep his feet firmly on the ground, Ryan had seen a lot less of his friend since he had joined the aerocompany.

Will jogged away with his bow strapped across his back. The weapon was like nothing Ryan had seen before on Atlantis, with a dangerous-looking recurve that gave it a wicked gleam. Even without seeing it in action, Ryan was confident that the bow could generate tremendous force. Of course, it needed to, if the Demons had armor akin to their own.

Carrie stopped at a chest full of swords to pick up her weapon of choice, and Sully joined her to grab a sword of his own. As he gave his sword a few experimental swings, he caught Ryan's eye and gave him a tight, forced smile.

Ryan patted Sully on the back before moving on to a rack of spears. Unlike the spears he had been practicing with for months, these were not charged with electricity. These were sharp weapons, edged with a composite material whose molecular structure and hardness were comparable to diamond. These blades would pierce anything. They were meant to draw blood, and lots of it.

Ryan picked up a spear and checked its balance in his hands. It was perfect. He took it and joined Carrie by a row of BEAMs lined up against the wall of the tent. They both pulled on the gauntlets without speaking, and the BEAMs seamlessly bonded with their armor.

Ryan, along with the rest of his squad, had practiced using BEAMs a few times since having their beacons inserted, but he had no clue what they would do to a Demon. Would the blast kill one? Knock them back? Stun them? Or would it simply leave a gaping hole in its victim?

On their way out of the tent, Ryan and Carrie each grabbed a round shield about two and half feet in diameter. Most of the Atlantean shields resembled the Roman *parma*, large enough to offer significant protection from projectiles, but small enough to use as a third weapon, to bash any Demons that came too close. Since their wings allowed for greater mobility, shields were optional for aerosoldiers. Not taking a shield made it easier for them to use their BEAMs or a second weapon, but the lack of protection could cost an aerosoldier his life. It was up to the individual to decide whether or not they wanted to take the risk of fighting without a shield. It was a simple choice—safety or aggression—and Ryan chose safety.

He exited the tent with Carrie, and was immediately struck by the chilling breeze again. With the entire legion slowly organizing itself into formation, Ryan and Carrie jogged the length of the field until they located their company. For once, Felicia wasn't studying her charges or berating them over the smallest detail. Instead, she was looking westward.

Ryan craned his neck to see over the soldier in front of him. Along a wide hill just short of the horizon was a large gathering of people.

The Order.

A cold bead of sweat ran down Ryan's arm, enclosed in the Atlantean armor. Even from a distance, he could tell that the Demons vastly outnumbered the Atlantean forces. He tried to swallow, but the hard lump that had lodged itself in his throat made it difficult. His stomach churned.

Ryan glanced over at Carrie. Her eyes darted back and forth across the mass of Demons in their black armor as she considered the battlefield—probably creating and revising multiple strategies in her head.

Captain Tanner had told Ryan that his leadership and strategic skills were the reason for his upcoming promotion, but when it came to tactics, Ryan knew that Carrie was far better than he could ever be. The only problem was that when the time came for her to relay her plans to others—to be the one giving the orders—she froze and lost all confidence in herself. It had happened during the mock battles in initiation, and it had remained a problem throughout their military training. But when it came down to it, there was no one Ryan would've rather had watching his back in a fight, no one he would trust more to devise a strategy that would keep them alive. Grimly, he told himself that if they both made it out of this fight, he would do whatever he could to get Carrie promoted too.

"Well, that'll at least help some. . ." Carrie said absently, looking past Ryan. Ryan turned and saw a group of soldiers in deep red Atlantean armor assembling on the other side of the tents.

"*Who are they?*" Ryan asked.

"*Soldiers from the Canadian City of Atlantis.*"

"*They're here too?*"

"*They're the closest Atlantean city.*"

Ryan watched as the other Atlantean legion fell into formation. The addition of the second city's troops nearly doubled their forces, but Ryan was sure the Demons still outnumbered them. He wondered how many of the Atlanteans from Canada were like him, fresh from the Surface and trying to hide their nerves. If any of them were afraid, he hoped he was managing to hide it as well as they were.

As he was sizing up the Canadian forces, Ryan saw a single aerosoldier soar up from the Canadian army, fly toward the front of the assembled Northeast American legion, and land out of sight. Ryan had to resist the temptation to open his own wing pack, which still hung loosely around his shoulder, and fly up to get a better look.

After a few minutes, two Atlantean soldiers, one in red and the other in blue, walked out in front of the army and across the rolling hills, toward the mass of Demons.

"*Identify,*" Ryan commanded his helmet as he put it on quickly, looking at the soldier in blue. The words DANIEL AMERREST scrolled across the visor as the heads-up display zoomed in, outlining the Head of Military's silhouette in bright green.

"*Do you know what's going on?*" Ryan asked Carrie. She too had her helmet in place.

"*Every time we go to war with the Demons, the first battle starts with a meeting of the leaders from each side,*" Carrie said. "*It's basically a way to make sure both sides fully understand that they're going to war, and it gives everyone a chance to back out.*"

"*Does it ever work?*"

"*No,*" Carrie admitted. "*The damn Demons are too stubborn. They never listen to reason. If this is the meeting, the first actual battle of the war is definitely about to start.*"

Ryan watched as Amerrest and the other solider, who he assumed must be the Canadian Head of Military, made their way to the top of another hill about halfway between the two opposing armies, where a single figure in sleek black armor stood waiting for them. As soon as the two Atlanteans approached the soldier from the Order, Ryan heard minor static come across the speakers in his helmet. Amerrest must have activated an audio feed.

As it turned out, the Head of Military could have waited a bit before patching them all in. When Amerrest and his Canadian counterpart finally reached the solitary Demon, they were greeted with silence. A full twenty seconds of solid tension passed before anyone spoke.

"So this is where you want to make your stand?" the Demon finally said with blatant defiance. The soldier's voice was higher than Ryan had expected, but no less strong. "Here? In the middle of . . . nowhere? With that pathetic excuse for an army behind you? What is it—two legions, at most? It would be more dignified if you just turned back now."

"I'm sorry, but since when has the Order been afraid of a fight?"

the Canadian Head of Military asked. Ryan smiled slightly as his accent came through, and suddenly realized, for the first time that Carrie did not have any appreciable accent. Even though Ryan was obviously unable to see the man's fingernails, he guessed he was from the Surface.

"If you want to start a war, the Order will deliver," the Demon said simply.

"You started the war when you bombed our cities," Amerrest said matter-of-factly.

"But that doesn't mean we won't fight for what's right," the Canadian said.

"No one's to blame here but your 'King,'" Amerrest added.

The Demon's head turned back and forth between the two Atlantean leaders as they spoke.

"Finishing each other's sentences," the Demon said. Ryan could hear the smirk in his voice. "How cute. I guess there's nothing more to say. It was a pleasure being the last person to whom you'll speak." Without waiting for a response, the Demon turned on his heel and walked back to his army. The two Heads of Military watched the Demon for a few seconds before moving. Ryan saw Amerrest shake his head slightly, and the two of them made their way back to the Atlantean army.

The closer Amerrest got, the worse Ryan's stomach felt. He tasted a splash of acid in the back of his mouth, and swallowed thickly to avoid vomiting in his helmet, suddenly conscious of the angle of his legs and the weight of his head on his neck. For the first time in his life, he felt he understood what it was to have an out-of-body experience.

Everything was moving so slowly—except Amerrest. He was walking fast. Too fast. He would reach them in no time, and then the war would start.

Ryan swallowed again, fighting back his nausea with everything he had. He closed his eyes for a second and took slow, deliberate breaths. When he opened them again, Amerrest was moving much more slowly, at a normal pace again.

"*Ryan . . .*"

Ryan turned to see Sully standing behind him, helmet and sword in hand. His sword was vibrating as his hand trembled. He looked pale and sickly, and Ryan could see sweat trickling down his face.

"*Hey, easy there,*" Ryan thought to Sully as he turned to face him, his own fears evaporating. He flipped up the visor on his helmet so his friend could see his face, and put one hand on Sully's shoulder and the other on his arm, so that no one could see Sully shaking. "*Look at me, man. Stay with me. You're going to get through this. You're going to be okay. It'll be over before you know it. Tomorrow, you're coming over to my place. We'll relax, have a drink, and laugh about how insane all of this is.*"

Sully nodded, but looked no calmer.

"*Take a few deep breaths,*" Ryan said. "*You're going to be fine. You've trained for this. I'll be there too. If you need me, just shout.*"

"I'm going to be okay," Sully said, nodding slightly. The color was slowly returning to his face. "That drink sounds nice."

Ryan chuckled. Looking significantly better than he had a minute ago, Sully threw on his helmet, tightened his grip on his sword, and offered Ryan a soft nod in gratitude before Ryan returned to his spot next to Carrie.

"You okay?" Carrie asked Ryan softly once he joined her again.

"I think so," Ryan said honestly. "You?"

"Uh-huh," she said unconvincingly.

Ryan held out his hand, unsure how his friend would take the gesture. Carrie was strong—probably the strongest person Ryan knew. For a single, absurd instant, he wondered why he had never felt anything more for her than he did. Carrie was smart, and funny, and kind, and pretty; but even after training and living together for so long, it had simply never occurred to him to think of her in that way. But as Carrie took his hand in hers and gave a single, firm squeeze, Ryan knew it didn't matter. There was nothing romantic between them, but the comfort Ryan felt just holding her hand was profound. The gesture, while short-lived, was meaningful, and it helped them both. Carrie was a friend, a sister, and a comrade-in-arms.

"Helmets on! Wings up!" Felicia shouted to the company.

Ryan reached up to hit the Insignia of Atlantis on his wing pack, and paused. He traced the emblem with his finger and thought about the matching necklace under his armor, a light weight against his chest.

Ryan took a deep breath and slapped the emblem, straightening his back as the straps tightened across his torso. The straps felt tighter than usual, though Ryan was sure the feeling was due to more than just the restraints.

"Weapons ready!" Felicia called.

Ryan's stomach resumed its violent churning.

"On my signal!"

He tasted acid again.

Felicia turned to Amerrest, who stood at the head of the army. He raised his hand in the air and kept it there, completely still. Everyone waited silently, in grim anticipation.

Ryan was going to be sick.

The arm dropped.

"NOW!"

CHAPTER SIXTEEN
THE BATTLE

Ryan's feet left the ground before Felicia's war cry ended. He soared high, wings open wide, in formation with the rest of his aerocompany.

Felicia ordered them to bank left to hit the Demons from the side. Ryan felt like he was flying on autopilot, even though he was in full control of his wings, soaring as if he had been doing it for years. All his fear and nerves had been left on the ground. He was in the air, back in his element. For now, he was safe.

Unfortunately, the feeling of security was short-lived. Within a few seconds, columns of fire rose from the rapidly approaching Demon army as their own aerial soldiers activated their jetpacks, rising to meet the Atlantean aggressors. Ryan remembered what Sergeant Hye had taught them, and made a mental note to avoid the Order's BEAM-like flamethrowers.

"Confront the enemy flanking to the left."

Felicia's command came through the speakers in Ryan's helmet as her words scrolled across the bottom of his heads-up display. He followed the company as they locked onto their targets—only for his focus to break when a sudden force nearly pushed him out of the sky.

Even though he could see the harsh wind flattening the tall grass below him, Ryan knew the force was actually a Demon trying to knock him off-balance with omega waves. Ryan did the only thing he could think of to stop the Demon: he pushed back.

The neutral space between the Atlantean aerosoldiers and the Order was shrinking at an alarming rate. Before Ryan knew it, the harsh sound of metal on metal surrounded him as the Atlantean aerosoldiers collided with the Demons. Formations shattered as small skirmishes broke out all around him.

Up ahead, one Demon flew unopposed, heading straight toward Ryan. Ryan urged his wings faster, determined to meet the attacker head-on. Should he use his spear, or his shield?

The Demon wielded a sword, raised high. He was getting closer. They were about to collide.

Something bright red flashed across the heads-up display. Ryan raised his shield.

The Demon's sword struck Ryan's shield an instant before their bodies collided. Ryan felt as if he'd flown into a brick wall—but his armor absorbed the force. He dropped a few feet before regaining control of his wings, and the Demon followed, slashing and hacking at him incessantly. He was well trained, and Ryan had to alternate using his shield and spear to repel the attacks.

Ryan knew he needed to get aggressive if he wanted any chance of coming out of this battle alive. With a shout, he surged forward as if he was going in for a tackle, and bashed his opponent with his shield. Caught off guard, the Demon staggered in midair and tried to regain his composure. Ryan took advantage of the split-second opening and jabbed his spear forward at a weak point in the soldier's armor plating, where the chest and abdominal plates met.

The Demon froze in midair. An odd gurgling noise came from under his visor, followed by a wet cough. A second later, blood dribbled down from beneath the visor.

Through the shaft of the spear, Ryan felt the Demon's body

twitch and jerk slightly. With a sickening *slurch*, he pulled the weapon back, leaving a hole in the soldier's chest that quickly filled with dark blood.

Ryan watched as his opponent's jetpack sputtered and died. Slowly, the other soldier tipped backward and plummeted to the earth, picking up speed as he fell.

Ryan had just begun to turn away from the falling body when he was suddenly hit from behind. The vibration of the impact traveled up his shield arm, causing him to lose his grip. The shield slipped from his arm as Ryan whipped around to find a spear-wielding soldier from the Order backing up to prepare for another attack. If Ryan hadn't turned just as the Demon was attacking, the spear would have impaled him.

The Demon charged again, spear in one hand and flamethrower in the other. Ryan had no time to think. He parried the attack with his spear, causing the Demon to zoom by him—then twisted around, held out his free hand, and thought, *"FIRE!"*

A blinding blast of light shot from his BEAM and hit the Demon's jetpack. The Demon went careening to the ground.

Ryan quickly looked around to make sure he wouldn't be caught off guard again. His heart pounded in his chest. Soldiers were swarming all around him, some in blue or red Atlantean armor, others sporting the black armor of the Order. For the first time, Ryan realized how loud the battle was. The sounds of weapons discharging and blades clashing echoed in the tornado of skirmishes all around him as the bodies of both friends and foes dropped from the sky.

Ryan's breath was heavy in his ears. Despite the fighting all around him, none of the Demons seemed to have marked him. He was hovering alone in the midst of the chaos.

Not wanting to become an easy target, Ryan flew in a large arc around the fight until he saw a pair of Demons on the edge of the battle. He flew wide around the unsuspecting Demons until he was behind them. Once he had a clear path, he shot forward, urging his wings faster and faster against the drag from the wind.

The gap between Ryan and the Demons was closing rapidly. His heads-up display flashed red again, and this time he was able to make out the words written across the visor:

IMPACT IMMINENT

He pushed his wings even harder. He could feel his heartbeat in his ears. Faster still.

Ryan raised his spear. One of the Demons started to turn.

At Ryan's speed, the Demon didn't stand a chance. Ryan pushed his spear through the Demon's back as if jousting, then swiftly raised his free hand to the back of the other Demon's helmet, which was adorned with small spikes. Using his momentum to flip over the first Demon's head, he ordered his BEAM to fire at the horned Demon. His target dropped from the air as the burst of light hit him in the head, and Ryan quickly retrieved his spear from the first Demon's body before sending him to join his fallen ally on the ground.

A sharp scream caught Ryan's attention. About fifteen feet directly below him, Felicia was desperately trying to fend off an aggressive Demon.

Ryan dove to help his commanding officer—but it was too late. With a weapon in each hand, the Demon raised a sword and slashed at the gap just under Felicia's helmet. Ryan watched in horror as his company leader's head bent at an impossible angle before she fell out of the sky.

She never came back up.

Ryan tucked his wings in and dropped. A cool fury spread

through his body. Felicia was dead, and this horrible, jeering Demon was to blame.

Ryan angled his spear and landed on top of the victorious Demon. His spear met its mark flawlessly. The Demon's body jerked once, and then it was nothing but dead weight on the end of Ryan's spear.

Ryan shook the body loose with a single jerk and watched it plummet to the ground. He hoped that the Demon's corpse wouldn't land on top of Felicia.

There was no time to mourn. Ryan zoomed off to help another ally fend off a Demon, who opted to flee rather than fight two Atlanteans at once. It wasn't until after the solider from the Order fled that Ryan recognized Carrie in her armor.

"*Thanks,*" she said with her beacon. Ryan nodded.

"*Felicia's . . . she didn't make it,*" Ryan told her.

Even through telepathy, Ryan sensed Carrie's shock. "*What? What . . . what do we do now?*"

"*I don't know,*" Ryan admitted. He saw another Atlantean in Canadian red struggling against two Demons. "*Come on. They need help over there. No one else dies.*"

Ryan and Carrie swiftly flew to their fellow Atlantean, and together the three of them were able to overpower their opponents. Ryan encouraged Carrie and the rescued Atlantean to team up and help others, and he did the same. Within minutes, the Atlanteans had regained a semblance of a formation, despite being paired off in twos and threes with complete strangers rather than their original companies. Even though the Order had the larger army, the Atlantean aerosoldiers slowly began to chip away at the Demon forces.

Just as the tide of the battle seemed to be turning, the Demons pulled away from the aerial fight and joined their ground forces.

Ryan hated to admit it, but it was a smart move on their part. With the assistance of their flying soldiers, the Order's army was able to regroup and successfully fend off the Atlantean terrasoldiers, who had been making progress while the aerial battle raged overhead.

"Ryan!" came Captain Tanner's voice through his helmet's speakers. "We need backup on the ground right away! We're losing ground. Get your aerocompany down here ASAP!"

"*Call company*," Ryan instructed his beacon, hoping it was the correct command. A small blinking light appeared in the corner of his visor, and Ryan took that to mean he'd guessed correctly. "Captain Tanner has called us to the ground for immediate assistance. Flank the Demon army and attack them from the rear!"

Ryan watched as his entire company fell into graceful dives, aiming toward the rear of the Order's army. He quickly moved to join them, careful to avoid looking at the bodies that littered the trampled grass.

The moment his feet touched the ground, a Demon charged.

No time to think. Ryan pushed the Demon to the side with omega waves. The Demon blew right by him, giving him enough time to regain his balance and steady himself for a fight. After a few swift jabs and parries, Ryan managed to dispose of the Demon with a well-placed blow to the foot followed by a quick jab to the neck.

As the Demon slumped over, Ryan turned in a full circle to get his bearings. Atlantean aerosoldiers were fighting all around him, but for every contest an Atlantean won, the Order won one as well. Ryan watched as Sully slashed away at an opponent, dropping the Demon with a quick series of strikes. Before Ryan could celebrate his friend's success, however, a wave of horror hit him. Another Demon was creeping up behind Sully to finish what the first could not, and Sully was completely oblivious.

Ryan felt a chill run down his back. He'd meant what he had to said to Carrie—*no one else dies.*

"*Sully!*" he shouted, both out loud and through his beacon, trying desperately to warn his friend—but the Demon was too close. Ryan only had one chance, and he needed to make it count.

Taking careful aim, Ryan cocked his spear as Sully spun around. Sully spotted the Demon, but he'd never get his sword up in time.

Ryan launched his spear with all his might. The weapon whistled through the air and met the small of the Demon's back only a yard away from Sully.

Sully turned in shock as the Demon's lifeless body fell to the ground with a soft thud. He waved in thanks to Ryan before running off to find another opponent.

Relieved, Ryan ran forward to retrieve his spear from the Demon's back, but skidded to a halt before he could reach it. The path to his weapon was blocked by a pair of Demons. Despite their tinted, horned helmets blocking Ryan's view, he was sure they were glaring at him with something like hunger.

The two Demons approached him with cautious steps, trying to box him in, and were soon joined by a third. On a hunch, Ryan glanced behind him and saw two more Demons approaching from the rear.

The Demons circled Ryan like a pack of wolves. None of his allies were around, and his spear was on the other side of his encroaching attackers. Ryan knew it was bad.

One of the Demons charged—then another, and another. They were all coming from different angles. Ryan had no place to go.

The first of the Demons, this one wielding a curved, wicked-looking axe, took a mighty swing that Ryan only narrowly dodged with a quick roll to the side.

Ryan let his instincts take over. He lifted his hand and ordered his BEAM to fire, not waiting to see whether the shot would land. Instead, he used omega waves to shove another enemy to the side as he charged forward before aiming and firing another concentrated burst of light at a third Demon, then spun around in time to dodge an incoming spear just before it would have impaled him.

With a boost from his wings, Ryan launched himself over his opponent and hit him in the back with his BEAM before the Demon could attack again. Ryan felt a wave of heat across the back of his neck and rolled to the side as a rush of fire surged past him.

Before he could turn around to face his attacker, a blinding pain across his left side sent Ryan to the ground. He dropped to his knees and bent over, clutching his side, and looked up to see a Demon with a bloody sword standing over him.

Ryan tried to scoot away from his enemy, but he couldn't move fast enough. The Demon closed the gap in a few quick steps and raised his sword as he savored the moment, his metal boot pinning Ryan's arm against the earth. Ryan tried to lift his arm to aim his BEAM, but it was useless. For the first time since the battle had started, he was truly afraid. The Demon had him trapped, weaponless.

Ryan thought longingly of his spear, still lodged in the body of Sully's would-be attacker several feet away. Then he had an idea. It was a long shot, but it could work.

Ryan concentrated on the spear with every fiber in his body. The tip of the sword hovered above him. The Demon was done playing with his food.

The Demon brought his sword down—and jerked as, with a sickening wet sound and a flash of metal, the point of Ryan's spear burst through his chest.

Ryan breathed a sigh of relief. Against all odds, he had managed to summon his spear with omega waves before it was too late.

The Demon staggered a few steps and fell, and Ryan rolled out of the way to avoid being crushed. For a moment, he lay on the ground next to the man he had just killed, desperately trying to catch his breath. He checked his side. The Demon's sword had caught a gap in his armor, and through it, he could see a red gash over his ribs. It wasn't deep, but it was shockingly wide and long. Despite its size, however, the bleeding was already slowing.

"*Show vitals*," Ryan commanded. A quick scan showed that his body was compensating appropriately. His heart rate was high, but he was sure that was simply due to adrenaline. He made a mental note to keep an eye on his blood pressure, but otherwise, Ryan thought he would be fine.

Standing gingerly, Ryan retrieved his spear and flew a few stories up so he could better see the raging battle below him.

"Ryan, the Order has broken through our formation." Captain Tanner's voice came through the helmet again. "They're headed for our base. Divert your aerocompany to the rear of our forces to stop them. I'll send another aerocompany your way to assist you."

Ryan immediately relayed the captain's message to his company. The rest of his soldiers met him in the air, and Ryan led them to the rear lines of the Atlantean army, where a mass of Demons had penetrated their defenses.

Ryan landed next to an Atlantean soldier from his own city who was currently holding her own against a Demon. She had lost her helmet earlier in the battle, revealing a scar over her eye. Her short blonde hair was speckled with blood, but Ryan suspected it was not her own. Instead of bothering her, Ryan opted to tackle one of the intruding Demons that was trying to make a break for it.

The battle became a blurry collage of bodies, both standing and lifeless. Light from Atlantean BEAMs met fire from the Demons' flamethrowers, turning the grassy plain into a smoldering mess of searing black scars. The Order relentlessly exploited every break in the Atlantean defenses and Ryan continued to stab, sweep, and slash his way through the Demons, never pausing to confirm a kill, and barely able to take the time to distinguish friend from foe. His world had narrowed down to action and reaction.

But no matter how many Demons fell, it seemed that an endless stream of black armored soldiers kept coming at him. Blood coated the shaft of his spear, making the weapon slick and difficult to control. Ryan started resorting to wilder and wilder attacks in the hope of flinging some of the excess blood off so he could get a better grip—but it was no use, and there was no time to stop and clean his weapon.

The Order's unrelenting surge eventually pushed Ryan and his company up the slope of a low hill. Even though the higher ground was advantageous against the endless waves of enemy forces, Ryan struggled to maintain his footing on the uneven turf.

Despite their best efforts, Ryan couldn't help but feel that they were fighting a losing battle. For every Demon they defeated, another leapt forward. To maintain a barrier between the Demons and the Atlantean camp, Ryan and his company had to keep falling back and regrouping. He briefly caught a glimpse of Carrie helping an Atlantean in red, but an attacking Demon drew his focus, and he soon lost track of her. At one point, Will shot an arrow over his shoulder and straight into the eye of an attacking demon, probably saving Ryan's life—but soon after, Ryan lost track of him as well.

Sweat trickled off Ryan's forehead, and his muscles ached. The wound in his side stung with every swing, but he knew he was lucky he had avoided any other major injuries.

No sooner did the thought cross his mind than a strong blast of omega waves sent Ryan stumbling back. Ryan looked up to see a woman in black armor approaching him with unwavering confidence. Another wave of power rushed over Ryan, almost sending him to his knees. He tried to push back with his own omega waves, but other than a small stutter in the soldier's step, his effort did nothing to slow her down. The tension between the two warriors was palpable, each trying to use omega waves to throw the other off-balance.

Ryan tried to back away as the Demon advanced—and felt his ankle buckle as he stepped into a divot in the earth. He tried to regain his balance, but the momentary lapse was enough for the Demon to take control. She sent a powerful burst of omega waves at Ryan, flinging him backward so hard that his feet left the ground.

In midair, Ryan tried to contort his body so he would have a chance of landing on his uninjured side. He succeeded—but the motion forced him to land on top of a dead Demon a few feet up the slope of the hill. His ribs slammed into the Demon's armor, knocking the wind out of him.

Taking no time to assess his own injuries, Ryan rolled off the body and snatched the nearest object he could find—something small and silver—off the ground as he surged up to face his attacker. She clearly hadn't been expecting such a bold move, and Ryan used her split-second hesitation to his advantage. Before the Demon could blink, Ryan grabbed the small of her back with one hand and plunged the silver dagger he'd grabbed into her stomach with the other. The woman's body sagged toward him, and Ryan half caught her and laid her on the ground. Somehow, the kill felt oddly intimate. It wasn't because the Demon was a woman; it was the way her dying body fell onto his, closing what little gap there was between them. He couldn't just let her fall.

Looking up from the dead Demon, Ryan gazed out across the battlefield. His heart dropped. Atlantis was losing. Allies were falling all around him. There was nothing he could do.

An awful thought crossed his mind, one he was not prepared for: he could leave. He could leave the battlefield, leave Atlantis. He didn't have to die here.

An arrow whizzed by his ear. Ryan looked up to see a Demon several yards away, holding a bow. Ryan held up his hand and fired his BEAM, smiling in grim satisfaction as the Demon went flying backward and fell dead.

No, he could not leave. He was a soldier. A citizen of Atlantis. Ryan quickly shook the thought from his head, embarrassed it had even crossed his mind. This was his new family. Even if Atlantis lost, he would stand with them. A new wave of endorphins rushed over him, giving him new life.

"*James! Up here,*" Ryan called to his friend, who had just cut down an attacking Demon at the base of the hill. He looked up, and Ryan motioned his friend up the slope to join him, along with two terrasoldiers from the Canadian army (after they successfully disposed of a Demon who had been recklessly brandishing a flamethrower), and the woman who had lost helmet, who had the scar over her eye.

"Riley," she said, introducing herself as she approached Ryan. Her blonde hair had accumulated more blood since he had last seen her.

"I'm Ryan," he replied. "Any of that blood yours? Do you need a medic?"

"No, I don't think so," Riley said. She looked at the bottom of the hill and frowned. "*You calling us here for a last stand?*" she asked grimly through their beacons.

"*I hope not . . .*"

But as much as Ryan hated to admit it, Riley may have been correct. Below, a new mass of Demons had assembled, and now, they came rushing up the hill.

"Hold your positions!" Ryan ordered the soldiers on the mound with him. He tightened his grip around his spear. Riley lifted her sword menacingly in a ready stance. This was it.

Ryan took a step forward, bracing for the oncoming attack.

But before any of the Demons reached them, blinding flashes of light erupted around the charging army. All around them, Demons were blown off their feet. In the next instant, a storm of arrows replaced the bursts of light, cutting through the Order's numbers. Many of the surviving Demons fell back to regroup, and those who did not were quickly cut down by the Atlanteans on the hill.

Ryan looked up to try to find the source of the arrows, and smiled.

Sweeping down from the sky was a battalion of aerosoldiers in emerald-green Atlantean armor. Ryan had no idea where they had come from, but he was unbelievably grateful to see them. The new arrivals dove and weaved across the battlefield in perfectly choreographed attacks, hitting what remained of the Demon army with powerful blasts from their BEAMs. Catching on to the sudden change in dynamics, some of the Demons fired up their jetpacks to confront the Atlantean reinforcements.

With the threat to the Atlantean camp diminished, Ryan ordered his own company into the air to support their new allies, circling the green-armored Atlanteans and blocking the path of any Demon that moved to intercept them. The entire momentum of the battle had shifted in favor of Atlantis, and Ryan could hardly believe the difference the reinforcements made. The Canadian and Northeast American forces were able to corral the Demons on the ground, while the green aerosoldiers took out the stragglers and strategically used their BEAMs to target the Demons' remaining regiments.

The Order stopped pushing forward and started to fall back. In a matter of minutes, the combined Atlantean armies had all but decimated what remained of the Order's forces. Ryan had just taken out a Demon who was getting dangerously close to a woman armored in green when a message flashed across his visor.

THE ORDER IS RETREATING.
ALL ATLANTEAN UNITS ARE TO RETURN TO
BASE WITHOUT FURTHER ENGAGEMENT.
—AMERREST

Ryan reversed course and headed back to base, along with the woman in green. Once they got there, Ryan touched down not far from their tents and stretched his back as his wings collapsed. It was the first time he had been able to relax in what felt like hours.

Ryan ordered his helmet to release and savored the feeling of the wind running through his sweaty hair. A second later, he choked at the smell that assaulted his nostrils. Despite the refreshing breeze, an overwhelming aroma of seared flesh, nauseatingly similar to ground beef, mingled with the acrid smell of burning grass and the metallic scent of spilled blood to create a suffocating odor.

"Thanks for the help out there," came a kind voice from over his shoulder.

Ryan turned around to find the Atlantean woman in green armor standing behind him. She had removed her headgear and now shook out a head of red hair, obviously happy to be relieved of her helmet in spite of the post-battle stench.

"Any time," Ryan said. "Thanks for swooping in. I'm Ryan Kendrick."

"Rachel Fonns," she said, shaking his hand. "Head of Military for the Californian City of Atlantis."

"Oh," Ryan said, surprised to find himself speaking with such a high-ranking officer. "Nice to meet you. I'm an aerosoldier."

"Really?" Rachel said in surprise. "The rest of your company seemed to follow you. I would've guessed you held a higher rank. You should! You'd be a good leader."

"Thank you, Commander Fonns."

"You said your last name was Kendrick, right?" Rachel said. Ryan nodded. "I knew your cousin, Jack. He spoke highly of you. I can see why."

Before Ryan could respond, a low, familiar voice spoke from behind him. "Glad you were able to make it, Rachel."

It was Amerrest. He and the Canadian Head of Military stepped past Ryan to shake Rachel's hand.

"Me, too," she said with a smile that seemed too soft for a warrior. "Sorry for the delay. There was a huge storm in our path, and we had to find a safe way around it."

"Doesn't matter," the Canadian said. "You're here, and you saved us. Thank you."

◊◊◊

"Really, Ryan, I'm okay."

Ryan smiled at Rebecca. Most of the uninjured Atlantean soldiers were scouring the battlefield, searching for their wounded and fallen. Ryan saw Will helping Roy to his feet and applying pressure to a nasty-looking wound on the latter's head, and he even spotted Grayson walking across the field with a tablet in hand as if he was taking notes. Ryan couldn't remember seeing him during the fight, but Grayson moved through the corpses like he was on a mission. The strange man had offered Ryan a small nod when Ryan had passed Amerrest and him speaking in low tones after the battle, but that was all.

Ignoring his own injury, Ryan leaned over Rebecca, trying to bandage her leg around the dagger sticking out of her thigh. Even though Ryan hadn't seen much of his friend since he had joined the aerocompany, he was pleased to see that being selected for Military had not dampened her spirits.

"Rebecca, you can't walk," Ryan said, biting back a small laugh. "You crawled halfway back to camp. Come on; let me help you."

"So chivalrous," Rebecca said with a playful smirk.

With Rebecca unable to put any weight on one leg, it took Ryan forever to help her walk back to camp, but together, the two of them managed, joking back and forth the entire way. The banter was definitely preferable to the alternative: the last thing Ryan wanted to do was look down. There were bodies everywhere—both Atlantean and Demon. Even though some soldiers were already collecting the deceased to prepare them for transport home for proper burials, it was nearly impossible to cross the battlefield without stepping on someone's limp fingers or tripping over a twisted leg.

But despite his best efforts to keep moving, Ryan found that his eyes were automatically drawn to every corpse in blue armor. He had to know the faces hidden behind the helmets.

After the fighting had stopped, he and Carrie, who had somehow made it through the battle without a scratch, had quickly found each other—but aside from her, Will, and Rebecca, Ryan still didn't know how many of his friends had made it out alive. As awful as it felt to admit it, Ryan was kind of grateful he hadn't gotten to know too many of the soldiers in the other companies. Seeing the bodies of men and women from his own city made his stomach churn, and he couldn't imagine how much worse he would be feeling if he had known their names.

After reaching camp and dropping Rebecca off with a medic, Ryan set out to look for more of the wounded. He was trudging numbly across the middle of the battlefield when he noticed the body of an Atlantean soldier sprawled beside two dead Demons, his blue helmet knocked halfway off.

Ryan froze. What little he could see of the face beneath the helmet was bruised, but agonizingly familiar. He didn't want to do it, but he had to know for sure.

Ryan's stomach turned to lead as he squatted over the body. He reached out with a trembling hand and slowly lifted the helmet to get a better look at the face underneath.

Staring back at him with wide, unseeing eyes was Sully. His open, friendly face was frozen in a look of sickening shock.

Ryan lost all feeling and began to shake. He placed one hand on the ground to stop himself from falling over, covering his face with the other as the sour taste of bile filled his mouth. He swallowed desperately and looked away from his fallen friend, but it wasn't enough to stop the vomit.

He should have gotten to know Sully better. No. He should have trained with Sully like he'd promised. If he had, then maybe, just maybe, Sully would still be alive.

Ryan had never felt so ashamed. He could have made time for his fellow soldier—for his friend. Sully had been so genuinely kind, and Ryan would never be able to talk to him again. They were never going to have that drink. His eyes burned horribly.

Ryan had no idea how long he stayed there, crouched over his friend, but eventually a pair of Atlanteans approached with a hovering stretcher to collect Sully's body. Ryan tried to stand and get out of their way, but he stumbled. One of the Atlanteans grabbed Ryan's arm to steady him.

Ryan blinked rapidly, trying to clear the fog from his mind. He couldn't remember ever feeling this lightheaded before. It took him a moment to realize the soldier was saying something to him.

"Are you Ryan Kendrick?" the soldier asked again, looking at his watch.

Ryan nodded blankly.

"Incoming message for you: you are needed at the medic's tent right away."

Ryan's stomach lurched. Was someone else he knew hurt?

Ryan staggered to the medic's tent alongside the two soldiers who were transporting Sully's body. He was wobbly on his feet, and he couldn't tell whether his unsteadiness was just from seeing Sully, or if there was something physically wrong with him. One of the Atlanteans watched him carefully, as though prepared to grab hold of Ryan if he started to fall over.

After what felt like ages, they finally arrived at the medic's tent and pushed through the flaps covering the opening.

"Bed! Now!"

Feeling slightly dazed, Ryan looked up and saw a woman from his own city, dressed in the snow-white uniform of the medical corps: a cross between an ancient tunic and modern scrubs. She was pointing at an empty bed and glaring at him. He had a hunch that she was not someone to mess with, and he was too exhausted to try.

Ryan collapsed onto the bed, grateful for the opportunity to lie down. The room was spinning. Was he the only one who had noticed?

"What were you thinking?" the medic said angrily. "You are clearly injured, and you've been walking around out there like nothing happened! You're lucky we've been monitoring your blood pressure! It's tanked in the past thirty minutes. You need blood! Now!"

"Who are you?" Ryan asked, feeling significantly better now that he was lying down.

"Christine Jin," she said as she started removing the armor around Ryan's side to get a better look at his wound. "You should have come here right away."

"So . . . is it bad?" Ryan asked hesitantly, his dizziness fading.

"You'll be okay," Christine said in a tone that clearly told him not to push his luck. "I'm going to have to clean this out, put some glue over it, give you some blood . . . but you'll be fine. You're actually pretty lucky. It's not too deep, and you don't seem to have any burns." Ryan tried to relax as the medic continued to talk. "There's a gentleman in the other tent with awful burns over half his face. He'll be fine, of course. It'll take some time and hard work, but he should recover. Do you know why?"

Ryan had a feeling he knew the answer.

"Because *he* came here right away!" she said pointedly, without waiting for Ryan to reply.

Ryan was right. He gave the medic some noncommittal grunts as she continued to vent. Eventually, her voice became a sort of white noise to him. He drifted off to sleep, completely at peace, knowing he was in good hands.

CHAPTER SEVENTEEN
HARD TIMES AHEAD

"**O**kay, quit staring. You're starting to freak me out," Ryan said with a smile.

A few days had passed since the battle, and Zach had invited Ryan and Carrie over to his apartment for dinner, although the phrasing he'd used had made it clear that the invitation had been less a request than an order. Ryan didn't mind. He appreciated the distraction. Jonathan, whose name Carrie had already managed to forget again, was nowhere to be seen, which seemed to suit Zach just fine.

"Sorry, man," Zach said. He returned to the stove to clean up after the large meal he'd prepared for all of them. It was the first time Ryan had really had the chance to experience his friend's cooking, and his stomach felt like it was actively expanding to make room for all the food. Zach was amazingly talented in the kitchen. Ryan was particularly fond of all the extra cheese Zach added to everything, and it seemed Carrie was, too—she was already working on her second helping. "It's just . . . it's great to see both of you guys." Although Zach didn't add the word "alive" to the end of the sentence, it was unmistakably implied by his hesitation.

Ryan was grateful not only for the meal, but also for Zach's restraint. He could tell that Zach was dying to ask him and Carrie all about the battle, but so far, he had kept his questions centered on their recovery and well-being.

Ryan had tried to give Zach as much detail about the battle as he could bear, but there were some things he couldn't share—not even with Carrie. Already, the nightmares were limiting his sleep—Sully was still never more than a thought away. How could he explain Sully's innocent, dead eyes staring at him in his dreams?

"What was it like up here during the battle?" Carrie asked Zach.

"It was pretty tense," Zach admitted. "No one was really joking. I mean . . . even though pretty much everyone left in the city was Tech, it was still really stressful."

"Especially with my family?" Carrie asked.

"Oh, you know about that?" Zach said. "Yeah, they were messaging me all day, asking if I had heard anything."

"Sorry about that," Carrie said.

"I didn't mind at all," Zach said.

Ryan winced as he got up from the table to help Zach clean. Christine had done an amazing job treating the wound across his side, but sudden movements were still painful for him. He put his hand over his side and tried to straighten up before his friends noticed, but he wasn't fast enough. Zach looked at him with concern and opened his mouth as if he was going to say something—then seemed to think better of it, and stayed silent.

"I'm alright," Ryan said anyway. "One of the Demons cut me pretty good, but the medic fixed me up. Wanna see?"

Zach nodded eagerly. Ryan lifted up his shirt to show Zach the scar running down and across his side.

"This happened three days ago?" Zach said, clearly impressed. Ryan nodded. "It looks like it's three weeks old!"

"I don't know how they did it," Ryan admitted. Both he and Zach turned to Carrie expectantly, but it took her a second to realize they were looking at her—her focus was still on her plate.

"Don't look at me!" she said, swallowing hastily. "I have no idea. I don't do medical stuff."

A loud beep, followed by a quick buzz, sounded on Ryan's wrist, causing him to jump slightly and look at his new communication band. He kept forgetting it was there. Apparently most people in Military enjoyed getting up at the crack of dawn, because the band's watch function had an alarm that was automatically set to go off at six thirty in the morning, and Ryan hadn't found a way to disable it yet.

"What's up, Mr. Aerocompany Leader?" Carrie asked with a grin.

"What?" Zach asked excitedly. "You were officially promoted?"

"It was sort of a field promotion," Ryan said sheepishly as he tapped the thin black band. "They made it official once we got back. That's when they gave me this stupid watch, so they can contact me at all hours." He turned to Carrie. "It's a reminder about the Elder's speech. Were you guys planning on going?"

"Of course!" Carrie said.

Zach merely shrugged. "Are you expected to be there?"

"Yep," Ryan said. "I should probably head out now. Don't want to be late for my very first meeting."

"Guess I'll come too, then."

The three of them left Zach's apartment and slowly made their way to the main plaza, talking about nothing in particular. Ryan enjoyed the idle chatter, which was something he had never taken the time to appreciate before the battle. It was crazy to think that just a few days ago, he'd been fighting for his life on the Surface, and now he was walking the streets of Atlantis, enjoying the warm sun and time with his friends as if nothing had happened.

Despite all the horror and fear, and the disturbing images that flashed unbidden through his head in quiet moments, a part of Ryan recalled the battle almost fondly. The casualties on the battlefield still haunted him, but he had to admit that something about the adrenaline, about being so close to dying, had made him feel alive. He would never admit it out loud, but something deep inside of him yearned for another fight.

Ryan glanced over at Carrie as the three of them turned a corner. She was laughing at something Zach had said, but looking at her, he couldn't help but wonder whether she felt the same way.

Ryan's thoughts were cut short as they arrived in front of the Temple. The cobblestone plaza was filled with Atlanteans, all milling about and talking excitedly. Ryan, Carrie, and Zach weaved their way through the crowd. When they got to the fountain, Zach hopped up onto the rim of the pool, and Ryan quickly joined him.

From this height, Ryan had a good view of everyone in the plaza. He spotted Harper, darting through the crowd as though she was trying to talk to everyone in the Military sect. The other day, she had cornered Carrie and Ryan to inform them that Angel Corps would be going to New York City in a couple of weeks to feed and clothe the homeless before the weather turned too cold.

Ryan continued to scan the crowd. His eyes lingered on a Military Atlantean standing several yards away. A large portion of the Atlantean's face and neck was covered with scars from healing burn injuries, making his smile appear slightly warped.

"*How are you holding up?*" came Drew's voice in Ryan's head.

Ryan looked around, trying to find his friend in the mostly blond crowd, without success. "*Turn around. To your right. Keep going. Keep going. There you go!*" Drew was leaning against one of the buildings lining the plaza. "*I've been meaning to reach out to you for the past two days now. Sorry it's taken so long. You hanging in there?"*

"*Don't worry about it,*" Ryan thought back earnestly. "*I know you're busy. I'm doing . . . well. I think.*"

"*Well for just having survived a battle?*"

"*Exactly,*" Ryan admitted, taking a closer look at his friend. "*How have you been?*"

At first glance, Drew looked no different than he had on the day he'd sat down with Ryan for coffee just months ago—but Ryan could tell that his friend was struggling too. His normally pristine clothes were rumpled, and his hair was a mess. Even in telepathy, he sounded less chipper than normal. Drew may not have fought on the battlefield, but he was hurting—and Ryan knew why.

Less than twenty-four hours after the battle, Ryan had run into Drew—literally—outside of Personnel Review Room Three. When Ryan's unit had gotten back to Atlantis, Captain Tanner had called Ryan into the conference room to officially promote him to aerocompany leader and give him his officer's communication band. As he'd left the room, Ryan had been so preoccupied testing all the different buttons that he'd stumbled into Drew, who had been waiting for him just outside.

"Ryan!" Drew had exclaimed as he wrapped Ryan in a tight hug, before Ryan could even apologize for the collision. "You really had me worried there for a bit. Especially near the end of the battle, when your blood pressure started to tank. I'm glad Christine was able to patch you up."

"She did a great job," Ryan said as they broke apart. "And I'm feeling a lot better today. How . . . how did you know about my blood pressure?"

"Umm . . ." Drew said uncertainly; and for the first time since the battle, Ryan laughed.

"What are you doing over here in the Military District?" Ryan asked, giving his friend an easy out.

"I came to congratulate you on your promotion, of course!" Drew said. "You've been a soldier for all of two months, and you're already an aerocompany leader? Clearly, you've impressed the right people. Congratulations."

"Thank you," Ryan said, his voice trailing off. Even though Theo had told him that he was being considered for a promotion before the battle had occurred, Ryan still wasn't sure he deserved his new position. He felt as if they had only awarded him the promotion so quickly because Felicia had been killed. Despite having nothing to do with her death, Ryan couldn't help but feel a little dirty taking over as the company's new aerocompany leader. But how could he possibly explain that to Drew?

"I also wanted to check in and see how you were doing," Drew said, his tone slightly softer.

At that moment, Ryan knew he didn't have to explain anything to Drew—the other man already knew. "I have some friends who have been Military for years," Drew continued. "I understand how intense it can be. If you ever need to talk, I'm here."

"Thanks, Drew," Ryan said. Even though no one could ever replace Jack, Drew had started to fill the void his cousin's death had left, and Ryan trusted him with his life.

Trust.

Ryan slipped his hand into his pocket, palming the flash drive Jack had left him. He had put the hardware in his pocket before his meeting with Theo, fully intending to give it to the captain. As they were wrapping up their meeting, Theo had asked Ryan whether he had any questions, or if there was anything he could do for the new aerocompany leader. Ryan's hand had been halfway in his pocket, about to grab the flash drive, when he'd frozen.

He couldn't do it. Even though he knew that Atlantis needed to know that there was a traitor in this city, Jack's final message kept playing in his head: *Trust no one.*

But now, standing in front of Drew, the Atlantean he had known the longest, Ryan also remembered Jack's other piece of parting advice: *Find someone you trust with your life, and stick with them.*

Ryan knew he was in over his head. Between whatever the Order was building in Canada and whoever the traitor was in Atlantis, he needed help. And there was no one he trusted more than Drew.

"*Actually, Drew, I really could use your help,*" Ryan had said to his friend through their beacons. Even though he didn't think anyone would overhear them, he didn't want to take the chance.

"*Anything,*" Drew thought back immediately. Ryan was grateful that he had responded telepathically.

"*You know the flash drive Jack left me?*" Ryan asked.

"*The one you opened on the Surface?*"

"*Yeah, that one,*" Ryan confirmed. "*Jack left a message for me on the drive right before he died. It's . . . well, it's pretty heavy. There's some sensitive information from Jack's last mission in an audio file. Atlantis needs to know about it, but I . . . I don't know who I can trust. . . .*"

"*What do you mean?*" Drew asked, his brow furrowing.

"*It's hard to explain—it'd make more sense if you heard the recording,*" Ryan said, not sure how to approach the delicate topic of treason. "*I think . . . Jack thought . . . that there's someone in Atlantis—in this city—feeding information to the Order.*"

"What?" Drew said out loud, his eyes widening.

"*I know how it sounds; I really do. But I trust Jack,*" Ryan thought back earnestly, pulling the flash drive out of his pocket. "*Take the flash drive. That way you can listen to the recording for yourself. I don't know what to do, but at least I'll know it's in good hands if you have it. Please, Drew. I don't know who else I can trust."*

"*Of course,*" Drew said, taking the flash drive. Gone was the look of surprise, and in its place was one of determination. "*We'll figure this out—don't worry. Jack worked with Intel, so if he said there's a traitor, then I believe him. I'll take care of it.*"

As Drew walked away, flash drive in hand, Ryan felt an overwhelming sense of gratitude. Drew believed him, and he seemed confident that they would be able to address the issue head-on.

Now, two days later, looking at Drew across the plaza as they waited for the Elder to arrive to begin his speech, Ryan could tell that the truth had chipped away at his former scouter. As grateful as he was that Drew had agreed to shoulder this burden with him, it pained Ryan to know that he had unleashed this unpleasant truth on Drew.

"*I'm okay,*" Drew said, responding to Ryan's question with a small nod. "*Things have been crazy around here since the battle, and our little . . . side project has been taking up what little free time I've had for the past few days.*"

"*Any leads?*" Ryan asked hopefully.

"*None yet,*" Drew said. "*It's going to take longer than I originally thought to find the Order's agent. We'll need to be careful. We should get together so we can discuss things privately.*"

"*Sure. Want to meet up tomorrow night?*"

Before Drew could respond, an overwhelming silence fell over the plaza, interrupting their telepathic conversation. Everyone looked up at the Temple's roof, where Michael Stamaris had just stepped into view.

The Elder's gait was slow but purposeful, and he exuded a sense of calm that washed over the crowd of soldiers and innovators.

When he was perfectly centered in front of the Temple's newly repaired dome, he stopped and addressed the crowd below.

"Atlanteans," the Elder said to the silent plaza. "We are at the precipice of a new era. Just as the night is darkest before the dawn, so shall our future be. We face an enemy that will stop at nothing to defeat us. An enemy that wants to destroy us. To kill us.

"But," the Elder said with a smile, "even in these dark times, we must remember: light exposes shadow. And that is why I know we will prevail. Not only will we survive this war, but we will rise from the ashes of the Order's attack and enter a golden age. Once we defeat the Order, Atlantis will be able to truly fulfill our mission to serve those on the Surface. For millennia, the Order has tried again and again to silence us, to impede our efforts. But we are resilient. We do not give up! Atlantis will not die. We will fight and we will persevere. I will say it again: This is our time!"

A cheer went up across the plaza.

"Make no mistake," the Elder continued, "it will not be easy. We are fighting a war. And as in any war, we must make sacrifices. Helping those on the Surface through technological innovation will always be one of our main priorities. But in order to win this war, we must remain united. We cannot allow our resources to be divided between the Technology and Military sects. I am confident that our Technology sect will continue to work diligently throughout the coming conflict, but our focus must temporarily shift away from the development of new technology and toward defending the great people on the Surface, defending the freedom for which we stand, and defending Atlantis itself. Atlantis is here to stay. Atlantis will win!"

A loud round of applause rose from the crowded plaza as the Elder humbly held up his hands and began to make his way back to the ground. Zach put his arm around Ryan's shoulder, and Ryan held out his hand for Carrie to join them. Together, the three of them stood on the edge of the fountain, shoulder to shoulder.

Despite the bloody war to come, Ryan smiled. The Elder's speech had been full of hope, and now more than ever, Ryan felt that he had finally found a home, high in the sky. Zach and Carrie were by his side. He was surrounded by family. It was a family that had chosen him—and a family he had chosen.

An unseen force, too deliberate to be the wind, tussled through his hair, and he knew Drew was nearby. Ryan reached up for his necklace and grabbed the Insignia of Atlantis.

He was an Atlantean. He was home.

And he was ready for war.

◊◊◊

The King rapped his fingers impatiently against the arm of his chair. His officer was late, and the King did not like to be kept waiting. The officer was already in trouble. Maybe he was trying to delay the inevitable? It did not matter. Once the King gave an order, it was as good as carried out. Stalling would do nothing to save the man.

The King sat back in his throne, his posture impeccable despite the unforgiving harshness of the granite. The long underground hall was lit only by lanterns, which burned with undying flames that threw unpredictable shadows against the ornate columns that lined the walls. The King smiled as he watched the dancing flames. Fission—not solar—was undeniably the future.

A small blue light appeared on one of the throne's armrests. It was about time.

The King accepted the incoming transmission using his

beacon, and watched as a shimmering hologram appeared before his throne. Kneeling reverently before him was the pathetic excuse for an officer who had lost the battle in the United States just three days prior. Scorch marks from a BEAM covered part of his face, and the King noticed a few fingers missing from his right hand. Good. The incompetent fool deserved it.

"You're late," the King said coolly.

"My King," the man said without looking him in the eye. "I was about to start the transmission when I received terrific news from Portugal. All of our systems are fully operational in central Europe. Despite the resistance, we are making progress toward the United Kingdom and, as you know, in just a few months, we will be fully operational here in North America."

"Yes, I am well aware of our progress," the King said in a bored tone. "What I don't know is what happened on that battle-field. How did you lose the first battle of the war? A failure like that will give you a reputation that will stick with you for the rest of your life, no doubt."

"My King, the Atlanteans—"

"Look at me."

There was a moment of silence as the officer turned his frightened face toward his King.

"The . . . the Atlanteans, u-unbeknownst to us, were in contact with the . . . um . . . their sister city in C-California," the officer stuttered. "Their f-forces were made up entirely of aero-soldiers. They were nowhere near us when the battle started, but they made it just in time to . . . well . . . to . . ."

"Humiliate you?" the King offered. The officer swallowed painfully.

"Yes, sir."

"And why were you not prepared for such an obvious

maneuver?" the King asked, in a tone that implied he already knew the answer.

"There was nothing to suggest that the other city would be involved in the battle, my King," the officer answered, sweat beading on his forehead. "And our informant never said . . ."

"No," the King said simply. "No, that is not why. The reason you were not prepared is because you are incompetent. Unable to see any farther than a few feet in front of your nose. Of course you were not informed of their strategy, you idiot. It would have alerted Atlantis to our agent's existence, and could have completely blown their cover. The best part is, you thought giving me an 'update' on our progress was going to save you. Ridiculous. The Order will be better off without you."

A look of realization followed by sheer panic flashed across the officer's face—but it was too late. Before he could say anything else, a woman in full ebony battle armor stepped into the hologram behind the officer and slit his throat with a long knife. The King had been right: the reputation of losing the first battle of the war had plagued the officer for the rest of his short life.

The King nodded his thanks to the assassin and slapped the controls on his throne. There was just enough time for the armored woman to kneel in the growing pool of blood before the hologram feed cut off.

Of course, in reality, the outcome of the first battle did not matter. It had been a minor skirmish, and certainly it wouldn't have any effect on the King's plans. Still, the officer had been an idiot, so his death was no real loss. And the King had needed to make an example of him.

Still, the officer had been right about one thing: the Order was making progress. It was only a matter of time before they took over the United Kingdom, and the cities in North America surely wouldn't give them too much trouble—especially not with his informant in place. That Atlantean was loyal only to him.

No, the King wasn't worried. In a year or two, once all the pieces were in position, he would be unstoppable. And Atlantis would fall.

The King smiled. It was going to be a good war.

ABOUT THE AUTHOR

After obtaining an undergraduate degree in systems engineering from the University of Virginia, Luke Yesbeck returned to Richmond, Virginia, for three years to work as a medical scribe while he applied to medical school. Currently, he is working to complete his final year of medical school in Roanoke, Virginia. Outside of school, Luke enjoys traveling and has hiked Mt. Kilimanjaro, the highest peak in Africa, and the Inca Trail to Machu Picchu.

CPSIA information can be obtained
at www.ICGtesting.com
Printed in the USA
JSHW020207091221
21112JS00001B/3